JAMES D. DOSS

author of *The Shaman's Game*

A SHAMAN MYSTERY

THE NIGHT VISITOR

"A treasure...a hybrid of Tony Hillerman and Carl Hiaasen, but with an overall sensibility that is uniquely Doss."
Denver Post

U.S.$5.99
CAN.$7.99

"FANS OF TONY HILLERMAN'S NAVAJO MYSTERIES WILL FIND A NEW HOME HERE."
Denver Post

THE SHAMAN MYSTERIES BY

JAMES D. DOSS

"Doss has reproduced the land of the Southern Colorado Utes with vivid affection and has written a novel that is both suspenseful and satisfying."
Dallas Morning News

also:

THE SHAMAN'S BONES
THE SHAMAN LAUGHS
THE SHAMAN SINGS

and coming soon in hardcover:
GRANDMOTHER SPIDER

ISBN 0-380-80393-3

JAMES D. DOSS

THE NIGHT VISITOR

"GET READY FOR DOSS' BEST YET . . . Sometimes lyrical and always entertaining . . . *The Night Visitor* features plenty of Doss' trademark suspense, but adds a sense of fun that makes this book a pleasure."

Denver Rocky Mountain News

"WHOLLY SATISFYING . . . *The Night Visitor* is filled with vivid descriptions of the area, and includes elements of mystery, archaeology, shamanism, and humor blended into an entertaining page-turner."

Albuquerque Journal

"DOSS DAZZLES with his trademark blend of Native-American folklore, science, satire, and suspense . . . quirky, satisfying . . . Wry Officer Moon and irascible Daisy continue to charm as the series' lead characters. The dialogue crackles, and the Southern Colorado atmosphere astonishes, especially at night."

Publishers Weekly

"ANOTHER AMUSING, INTELLIGENT, AND SPIRIT-FILLED MYSTERY FROM JAMES DOSS. It's a ghost story for grown-ups . . . Doss brings the new reader into his Shaman series and makes him feel at home."

Los Alamos Monitor

"TONY HILLERMAN BLAZED A TRAIL WITH HIS NAVAJO MYSTERIES . . . JAMES D. DOSS IS GETTING CLOSE."

San Jose Mercury News

Books by James D. Doss

THE SHAMAN SINGS
THE SHAMAN LAUGHS
THE SHAMAN'S BONES
THE SHAMAN'S GAME
THE NIGHT VISITOR
GRANDMOTHER SPIDER

JAMES D. DOSS

THE NIGHT VISITOR

A SHAMAN MYSTERY

AVON BOOKS
An Imprint of HarperCollins*Publishers*

This is a work of fiction. Names, characters, places, and incidents are products of the author's imagination or are used fictitiously and are not to be construed as real. Any resemblance to actual events, locales, organizations, or persons, living or dead, is entirely coincidental.

AVON BOOKS, INC.
An Imprint of HarperCollins*Publishers*
10 East 53rd Street
New York, New York 10022-5299

Cover art by Tsukushi

ISBN: 0-380-80393-3
www.avonbooks.com

First Avon Books paperback printing: December 2000
First Avon Books hardcover printing: September 1999

Printed in the U.S.A.

10 9 8 7 6 5 4 3 2 1

Dedicated to

James L. Smith of Los Alamos

Nancy Jean Smith of Colorado Springs

and to the fond memory of

Rob Newton
Doc Purdy
Harrison York
Cordell Neal

. . . all of South Carrollton, Kentucky.

The words of the Preacher, the son of David, king in Jerusalem . . .

"To every thing there is a season, and a time to every purpose under the heaven:

A time to be born, and a time to die . . ."

Ecclesiastes

"The shaman usually left orders for the patient to follow. These prescriptions were given to the doctor by his power. They might include painting the face in a certain fashion, praying before sunrise, avoiding certain foods, and, if his powers so directed, giving the patient a new name."

Anne M. Smith,
Ethnography of the Northern Utes

THE NIGHT VISITOR

1

THE END

HE HAS SEEN it all before. A thousand thousand times . . . and more. It happens so quickly—within a few beats of his heart.

A thunderous roar; a yellow arc flashes by his face.
Must escape . . . run . . . run . . .
but his feet are rooted in place.
There is a thin whistling sound . . .
a sudden, mind-numbing pain.

Then . . .
Filthy water fills his mouth . . . he struggles . . . gags.
Bones snap like dry twigs.
He sees the yawning mouth of the pit . . .
is swallowed up in darkness.

Then . . .
Someone comes . . . someone merciful.
It is Death. She whispers to him . . . caresses his face.

Pain slips away like melting wax.
It is over.

Then . . .
It begins.

The Beginning

There is—as the sage has rightly said—an appointed time for a soul to come into the world . . . and also a time to leave it. Before the first is an unremembered history; after the last, an eternal mystery. These are subjects best left to philosophers, mystics, and poets—and others so inclined to squander away precious hours pondering the unknowable. For those of a more practical nature, there is a quite interesting period nestled between birth and death—where the most remarkable things are apt to happen.

No one has a more practical nature than Daisy Perika—that sly old soul who lives near the mouth of *Cañon del Espiritu.* It comes from experience. The Ute woman is filled to the brim with bone-dry summers and marrow-chilling winters. Each of these seasons has salted her days with those ingredients that make a life palatable. Hard times. Unexpected blessings. Hunger that gnaws at the soul. Merry dancing and feasting. Solemn burials sanctified in mournful song . . . shrill cries of those newly come into the dawn.

She has known the warm morning of youth, the cool twilight of old age. And now that darkest of dark nights draws near. These should be days for rest and contemplation, the old woman knows. A time to prepare her spirit for the journey into that eternal world . . . where she will be forever young. But this present world—with its multitude of annoyances, problems, and difficulties—is a very great distraction. By way of example . . .

Not having a telephone.

Arthritis in her knee joints.

The fact that her favorite nephew is still a bachelor.

Charlie Moon should be raising himself a family, bringing

his children out to see her. Daisy Perika has made herself a most solemn promise. She will refuse to die until he marries himself a wife—and that is that.

Once Charlie has a wife to worry about, maybe the Ute policeman will stop nagging her about moving into Ignacio. The Ute elder is quite content to spend her days here in the wilderness. Daisy is, in fact, quite snug in her small trailer. Her home, though it may seem modest, is a way station at the entrance to that great canyon where she hears haunting echoes of words yet unspoken. In this special place, she knows that comfortable security of one who *belongs.* And well she should. The shaman has plied her arcane craft here for seven decades. She gathers black-stemmed maidenhair fern from the cool depths of the Canyon of the Spirits; she plucks antelope horns from the arid wastelands—but will not touch the dangerous jimson weed.

When her aching legs would carry her there, the old woman scours the windswept roof of Three Sisters Mesa for the purplish-blue flower of the cachana, which is also called Gayfeather and Rattlesnake Master. This hardy herb is useful for a variety of ailments—and as a talisman to protect Daisy's fearful clients from *mal de ojo.* The Ute elder—though hardly a timid soul—does not journey to the lofty crown of the mesa more often than is absolutely necessary. Apart from the difficulty of the ascent, this is a holy place, and therefore dangerous to mortals. Here, shimmering ghosts of the Old Ones walk even at noonday—and the pine-scented west winds never cease their melancholy moanings. When the sun sets, there is a black elderberry bush that bursts into scarlet flame . . . but is not consumed. Moreover, every living thing waits in rapt expectation for the signal that this world is about to end—that long rumble of thunder preceding the final, cleansing storm. A cluster of gnarled piñons lingers here as a stalwart congregation, patiently awaiting the arrival of One who *will appear as the lightning comes from the east and flashes to the west . . . when all of the trees of the field shall clap their hands.*

And so the Ute shaman climbs the mesa but seldom . . . and makes haste to depart before the bush is touched by fire.

From her store of pulpy roots and succulent leaves, those delicate petals of pearly pink blossoms, Daisy brews concoctions both practical and problematical. There are varied purposes for her prescriptions, ranging from the ordinary to the exalted. This sly old physician treats a whole host of common complaints, from nosebleed and menstrual cramp to bite of snake and sting of wasp. Any day of the week, the shaman can conjure away bumble wart or other unseemly blot of skin. With one hand tied behind her back Daisy Perika can ward off vengeful ghost, malicious water-baby . . . or other such shadowy presence.

The Ute shaman is, of course, not without peers in her chosen field of work.

It is true that there are a few Navajo hand-tremblers and Apache mystics who wield similar powers. There is a very old black man in Pagosa who can mumble away warts from any part of your body. And there is the ninety-pound Cajun woman the locals call Fat Nelda. She plies her dark art in a rusting yellow school bus just south of Mancos, survives on a diet of green tea, pretzels, and Norwegian sardines. This remarkable *bruja* (so it is claimed) can conjure sturdy new teeth into the gums of old crones and fresh crops of hair onto the shiny heads of those unfortunate men who suffer from an excess of testosterone. She does this for a fat price, of course—and thus the skinny woman's name. Fat Nelda also sports a black eye of polished jet in her left socket, and claims to see tomorrow and even next week through this opaque orb. Other than these few eccentricities, she is an altogether uninteresting character.

Daisy Perika's enterprises extend beyond her medical practice. Because of the Ute blood that throbs in her mottled veins, another privilege is hers by birthright. The old shaman has frequent conversations with the *pitukupf*—that mischievous dwarf-spirit whose underground dwelling is not so far away. His home is an abandoned badger hole in the Canyon of the Spirits. Theirs is an uncomplicated arrangement. The first requirement is that the shaman must take the little man a gift. A small cotton sack of fragrant smoking tobacco. A few turquoise beads on a string. A pearl-handled pocketknife.

This is how it works . . .

Leave the offering by the badger hole. Now sit down just over there . . . under the old piñon. Lean your head against its rough bark. Take your rest. Sleep. And dream. The dwarf will slip into your visions . . . and tell you such strange tales. Accounts of great adventures long past . . . and of others yet to be. Of spirits who come disguised as whirlwinds. Of mysterious wanderers who come from unimaginably distant places.

Even the shaman does not understand everything the little man says. The *pitukupf*—like other oracles—tends to speak in sinuous riddles.

Long ago, the elders say—far longer than even the mountains can remember—the little man attached himself to the Utes. They are his adopted tribe; they nurture him in their hearts and in their campfire tales. He is a friend to the People, but he is also somewhat eccentric. Old Utes warn the uninitiated: never, never tether your horse near the dwarf's home. This goes double for your pinto pony. The little man detests horses . . . especially spotted horses. If they are found near his badger-hole dwelling, he will most certainly kill them. If you don't believe it, ask Gorman Sweetwater, who lost a fine horse in *Cañon del Espiritu* just four years ago . . . strangled with vines.

There are rumors that the *pitukupf* is a thief, but this is not so.

It is true that now and then he borrows a little of this and some of that. And always forgets to return it.

Why?

Because he has his needs. And is somewhat forgetful. He is what he is.

Now the Utes know very well that their dwarf has no dealings with Navajo or Shoshone or Cheyenne, much less the pale-skinned *matukach*. Even so, there are persistent reports that the little man has shown himself to some who are not of the People. An elderly Hispanic woman over at Bondad (she has also seen angels) claims she spotted the dwarf standing on the banks of the Animas on All Saints' Day; he bowed impishly and tipped his hat to her! Five years ago, a white policeman told Daisy Perika how he followed tiny footsteps in the snow and had a brief glimpse of a child-sized creature who walked like a very old man. A Navajo follower of the Jesus Way has mentioned regular talks with the dwarf. They have—so the preacher says—smoked the same pipe. And discussed many deep matters. To the traditional Ute, such reports from Hispanic and *matukach* and Navajo are foolishness—silly talk best ignored. The dwarf would certainly have no dealings with those who were not of the People.

Quite aside from her communion with the dwarf—and like all her shadowy ilk the world over—Daisy Perika dreams many strange dreams. She has beheld horrific visions of blackened, frozen corpses floating above groaning skeleton-trees . . . warm blood pelting down like summer rain has stained her wrinkled face.

These dark dreams, these pale visions, these urgent communions with the *pitukupf* . . . have provided warning of every sort of visitation.

Almost.

Not the least premonition had hinted of what would accompany this approach of night. The skin on her neck did not prickle, neither did shadowy sprite flit in the corner of the shaman's dark eye . . . no coiled serpent writhed a cold warning in her gut. On this particular evening, Daisy Perika had not the least inkling that a very peculiar someone was approaching. No, the shaman's usual resources had thus far failed to quicken her pulse.

And the unbidden visitor was already close at hand. Cloaked by the gossamer fabric of twilight was he . . . sheathed by a dry skin of blue-gray clay. With the same timeless patience as the sandstone women who wait eternally on Three Sisters Mesa for the world to end, he also tarried at his lonely post. Caring not for ticking clock . . . nor phase of moon . . . nor falling aspen leaf that signaled summer's end.

The night visitor, moving in an odd, shuffling gait, comes near to the shaman's trailer home. He is weary and wanting rest. But he has important business to conduct here, and a man's work must be done before he can sleep.

* * *

The mouth of flame flickered . . . blue and yellow tongues of fire licked at the bottom of the blackened iron pot. The thick brown broth responded with a cheerful bubbling and popping. Wielding a stained wooden spoon, Daisy Perika stirred the hearty stew. Rich vapors rose from the brew; they curled and writhed seductively. She sniffed. And was pleased. When the old woman was but a child, her mother had taught her how to prepare this meal.

Bittersweet memories of youth passed before her mind's eye; she sighed with deep yearning.

The Ute woman had lived within a mile of this lonely spot since the day of her birth. First in a house of pine logs with a pitched roof of rusted tin. Now, in a small trailer-home crafted of steel ribs and aluminum panels. Though she sometimes longed for the days of her childhood, Daisy grudgingly admitted that hers was a far easier life than her mother's. She has electricity, a propane tank, a deep well with a Sears Roebuck pump that has not faltered for almost fifty years. She owns a good radio and a black-and-white television that works most of the time. Someday, she might even have a telephone. Someday.

But though a thousand summers have faded with the first frost, as many winters have draped the rounded shoulders of the mountains with shawls of woolly white, much about this land is the same as in her youth—and ever will be. Yes, the important things are unchanged. The brown earth is the same . . . and the blue sky. Three Sisters Mesa still looms above her, as if the Pueblo women who were turned to stone watch over their Ute sister in the rugged valley below. The mischievous winds of autumn playfully fling handfuls of sand against the Ute woman's trailer. Swollen November clouds still carry the pregnant promise of heavy snows in the San Juans.

The night visitor cares not whether snows may cover him . . . nor if the sun will ever shine again. He cannot concern himself with such small matters. His whole mind is focused on his consuming obsession.

Daisy Perika often reminds herself of this: though there are certain drawbacks to living in the solitude of the wilderness, there are advantages as well. Loneliness is more than compensated for by not having to put up with too many fools. Except for Cousin Gorman, of course. Gorman Sweetwater still stops by on his way to check his white-faced cattle who forage for bits of grass in the Canyon of the Spirits, but he is often mildly drunk and always thoroughly foolish.

There are a few visitors who are always welcome, Charlie Moon being chief among them. Daisy Perika feels fortunate to have a weekly visit from her nephew and wishes he would come more often. But a tribal policeman's life is a busy one. And he's a healthy young man whose mind is bound to be occupied by other matters. Like young women. Young men and young women, she reminds herself, should enjoy each other. Life's few pleasures pass us by soon enough.

Daisy Perika once enjoyed the company of men. She has endured three husbands. And buried them all. Now she is very old and enjoys few of life's pleasures. Except for food. Lately, she invests much thought into what she will have for her next meal. Lamb stew is good, that is true. Hamburgers are tasty too. And pinto beans cooked with onions. Boiled new potatoes and fried green tomatoes. Fat bacon snapping in the skillet with a heap of scrambled eggs.

But nothing . . . *nothing* is as good as posole.

Especially if the green chiles are from the flat fields down at Hatch. And the pork is fresh from Fidel Sombra's pig farm up by Oxford. Of course, you must know how to fix it just right. A few pinches of salt. A half dozen good shakes of coarsely ground black pepper. And before the brew goes on the burner, two tablespoons of flour to thicken the broth.

She gave the iron pot a final stir, then twisted the knob to lower the flame for a bubbling simmer. A sudden gust of wind strained against the trailer's aluminum skin. The steel bones squeaked and groaned, but did not break. The sturdy little house was much like its occupant.

The winds blow like a fury around the night visitor, who squats under the tossing boughs of a fragrant juniper. But he does not feel the chill in it.

* * *

Satisfied with the fruit of her labors, Daisy ladled out a generous helping into a heavy crockery bowl and seated herself at the kitchen table. She smeared margarine over the last slab of black rye bread. The cupboard was getting a little bare. Her nephew would come by on Monday and drive her into Ignacio to shop for groceries. It was Charlie Moon's day off from his job at the Southern Ute Police Department, so he'd show up in his big pickup truck. She'd have preferred to ride in the SUPD Blazer—the seat was easier on her back and you didn't have to step so high to get in.

Daisy helped herself to a spoonful of posole. Then, a bite of bread and margarine. A long drink of cold milk. The old woman closed her eyes in rapt pleasure. My . . . such a feast.

Moreover, she was entertained as she supped.

The FM radio dial was tuned to KSUT, the tribe's radio station. And because it was Saturday evening, she listened to a program all the way from Minneapolis. Lots of good music . . . and *The Lives of the Cowboys*, with Lefty and Rusty who had themselves a bath maybe once a year and were always chasing after some saloon gal. Like any woman in her right mind would want to snuggle up to a fellow who smelled worse'n his horse. But Daisy's favorite character on the show was the detective. Guy Somebody. She smiled and dipped up another spoonful of steaming posole. That Guy was always in some kinda scrape. Sometimes he got shot full of holes by gangsters, but he must be a fast healer because he was always healthy enough for next week's show. And like them pitiful cowboys, he was always in love—but never got himself a woman. Maybe he didn't bathe neither.

When her meal was finished, Daisy stashed the leftover posole in the refrigerator, washed the bowl and spoon, and took a halfhearted swipe at the blackened iron pot. She glanced at the great sea of darkness rolling against her window, and yawned. Time for sleep. She switched off the kitchen light, and opened the door to the bedroom at the center of her trailer-home.

This day had been as ordinary as a day can be for a weary

old woman who lives practically in the mouth of *Cañon del Espiritu*. This night would—so Daisy thought—be like ten thousand others. As she switched off the lamp by her small bed, the realization came suddenly—much as a crooked finger of lightning illuminates a dark landscape. A chill shudder rattled the shaman's aged bones.

And she knew as only one of her kind can know. She was not alone.

Someone was there . . . outside.

Cloaked in darkness.

Watching.

Daisy moved warily to the window. She pulled the curtain aside, looked toward the dirt lane that led to the rutted gravel road. The stars were like glistening points of white fire. The cusp of half-moon was sailing high, bathing the earth in a creamy light. She squinted. The few piñons and junipers stood there, precisely where they should be, as familiar as old friends.

But something else stood there among the trees.

A man.

The old woman tensed. And regretted the fact that she didn't have a telephone to call for help. What about the double-barreled twelve-gauge in the closet—was it loaded? Well, if it wasn't, there was a box of shotgun shells on the shelf above it. She flipped a switch, turning on the porch light. Maybe that would scare this prowler off.

It did not.

He moved several paces closer to the trailer; now his gaunt body was illuminated by the sixty-watt light bulb. The night visitor had piercing blue eyes, matted locks of straw-colored hair, an untrimmed beard. And he wore something that caught the shaman's eye. It was a pendant of polished wood, suspended on a cord around his neck. The ornament was long as a man's middle finger. Round on the top, pointed on the bottom. And curved . . . like a bear claw.

The pendant was all he wore.

Except for an uneven coating of caked mud, the man was naked as the day he was born.

Well. This was not your run-of-the-mill prowler.

The winds whipped at tufts of rabbit grass, rattled the dry skeletons of Apache plume. But the frigid gusts did not seem to cause the nude man any discomfort. He merely stood there. And stared at the old woman in the window. He was apparently quite unconscious of his nakedness. Or his mud-caked skin.

The effect, though unnerving, was also mildly comical.

Daisy grinned. The old woman—who was no stranger to either drunks or idiots—opened the window. "Hey . . . what're you doing out there?"

He hesitated . . . then raised his fingers. Touched his mouth.

What'd this yahoo want . . . something to eat? A cigarette?

Daisy noticed something on the side of his neck. Looked like a smear of dried blood. "You hurt or something?"

The visitor passed his hand over his head . . . barely touching filthy, matted hair. He muttered something under his breath . . . showed her his hand. It was no longer empty. On his grimy palm was something smooth and white. And spotlessly clean.

"A hen's egg," Daisy muttered. So the naked tramp could turn his hand to a trick or two. "What else you got up your sleeve? You gonna pull a jackrabbit outta your hat?" But, she reminded herself, this pitiful magician had neither sleeve nor hat. Nor britches.

He stretched out his hand.

Did this dirty fellow want to give her the egg? She waved the offer away. "No thanks, Houdini. I buy mine in town. By the dozen."

The Magician gave no indication that he understood. Nor did he offer a word to explain his presence.

But Daisy Perika felt no need for an explanation from this naked, mud-caked half-wit who was blessed with a small conjuring talent. What had happened was clear enough. This white man had wandered onto tribal lands without permission. Probably a college student on a hiking trip. He was either drunk or pumped up on some kind of drug—only a boozer or a dopehead would shed his clothes on such a chilly night. And from the look of him, he'd stumbled into one of them black-mud bogs over in Snake Canyon.

It was a record for Daisy Perika. Never in such a short space of time had the old woman made so many errors.

But just how he'd gotten himself into this fix was of no great interest to her. If this bug-brain didn't get some help, he'd freeze stiff as a board before morning. And she was the only help within a mile. So she had to do something. Daisy Perika—who was a long way from being a fool—was not about to let a crazy naked white man into her home. She pointed to indicate an easterly direction. "Go that way."

The Magician seemed perplexed by this simple instruction.

She shook her head in annoyance. Must be a foreigner. Having the innate good sense to know that if a person couldn't understand English, you had to speak louder, she yelled. "Head east—down the dirt road. Toward the highway." Eventually, a passing motorist would spot this lunatic. And use their cell phone to call the tribal police. Let Charlie Moon and his bunch sort this out.

The stranger stood like he was planted in her yard, rooted to his tracks. His hand remained outstretched, displaying the object that looked like a egg. He stared at her. Expectantly.

She sighed. This jaybird wasn't going away. He seemed determined to test her sense of duty. "What is it? You want some clothes to wear?"

The Magician cocked his head inquisitively, like a puppy trying very hard to understand.

She raised her voice another decibel. "You wait right there. I'll go and get you some of my last husband's old clothes." *He won't mind, seein' as he's been dead for twenty years.*

Daisy opened the closet door and pushed aside wire hangers holding print dresses, woolen shawls, a man's wool overcoat. A faded pair of bib overalls was hanging on a hook above the shotgun. Just the thing for a tramp. She found a scuffed pair of horsehide boots; a heavy pair of woolen socks was stuffed inside. The old woman muttered to herself: "I'll warn him to stay where he is, then pitch this stuff out on the porch. If the knucklehead has enough sense left to put these clothes on, then I'll make him a cheese-and-baloney sandwich and put that on the porch too. And send him on his way. Then I can go to bed with a clear conscience."

When the somewhat reluctant Good Samaritan returned to the window—ready to shout her instructions—the naked stranger was gone. *Well, thank God and all His angels . . . that's the last I'll see of that oddball.* "Well," she said aloud so God would be sure to hear, "too bad he left in such a hurry . . . I'd have liked to help that poor soul." It was with a sense of considerable relief that she closed the window. And stood there. Watching to make sure he was really gone. Daisy realized that she was breathing heavily, as if she'd climbed the long, rocky trail up the talus slope of Three Sisters Mesa.

The Ute shaman—a member (in moderately good standing) of St. Ignatius Catholic Church—sat down on her bed and said her prayers. She would have kneeled, but her knees were sore. Daisy prayed for some rain—but not enough to flood the canyon. For a mild winter. For the health and prosperity of the People. And for other Native Americans. She prayed for Charlie Moon's safety. And—almost as an afterthought—she prayed for Scott Parris, the chief of police up at Granite Creek. The white man was Charlie Moon's best friend. And the broad-shouldered *matukach* was her friend as well. Even though he had once blown a hole through her roof with a twelve-gauge shotgun—a hole big enough to drop a goat through. With men and children, you learned to overlook such foolishness.

Daisy slid her feet under the covers and pulled the thick quilt to her chin; her head fell upon the pillow. This weary woman, imbued with the hardy spirit of her people—and comforted by the sweet presence of Christ—continued to whisper her prayers.

Our Father who is in heaven . . . Great Mysterious One . . . protect your people . . . Hail Mary, full of grace . . . watch over us . . . He who speaks with words of thunder, hear my voice . . . though I walk through the valley of the shadow of death . . . your rod and your staff they comfort me . . . He who makes his home above the mountains, hear me . . . O Lover of my soul . . . my cup runneth over . . . deliver us from evil. Oh yes . . . help that crazy white man who's all splattered with mud.

And she added this observation and advice for the benefit

of the omniscient One: "The way I figure it, he's either crazy or drunk. Or both. So when you send somebody to help him, it'd be best to tell 'em to be careful. At least that's what *I* think."

Finally, the rambling prayer ended.

As the moon drifted over *Cañon del Espiritu*, Daisy's breathing became more regular.

On a windswept ridge above the shaman's trailer stands a desiccated corpse. She is a hideous, frightful thing to behold—this aged dancer balanced awkwardly on a misshapen leg . . . twisted arms raised in mute supplication to darkened heavens.

Depending upon one's perspective, she is

. . . a grotesque, twisted hag—standing where a living thing once stood

. . . a resinous piñon snag—chop her up for kindling wood.

On this night, the carcass has company. Of a sort.

Under the starlight shadow of the dead branches, the naked figure sits easily upon his haunches. He rolls the white "egg" in his hand. The shaman has given him a name, and so he is the Magician. But he does not deal in common tricks and illusions.

He watches the old woman's home. In an unheard voice that harmonizes with the silent choir of night, he sings to himself. It is a lurid serenade. Of lust. Jealousy. Murder. And urgent business unfinished. A lonely soul's ballad oft spins a melancholy tale of what has been—this grim ode also foretells what is yet to be.

When his silent song is ended, the mute singer does not stir. He will by no means depart from this place until the thing is done. And so he waits . . . for someone who will surely come.

A child.

Charlie Moon turned off the paved surface of Route 151 onto Fosset Gulch Road, immediately crossing the narrow bridge over the Piedra. Rain had been scarce, so the river was low.

Ankle-deep in places. Looked like you could walk across it by stepping from stone to stone.

The wisp of a girl in the seat beside him strained against the shoulder strap and pressed her nose against the window. "I bet there are lots of fishes in there."

The driver did not respond, and this irked the child.

Sarah Frank looked to the Ute policeman for confirmation. "*Are* there lots of fishes in the river?"

He nodded.

"What kind?" she pressed.

"Mostly rainbow trout," Moon said, and jerked the steering wheel to miss a shallow pothole in the gravel road.

"Rainbow," she sighed. "I bet they're really pretty." Mr. Zig-Zag purred; Sarah rubbed the black cat's neck. "Are there any catfish in the river?"

"Nope. Piedra's way too cold for 'em."

She shivered. "Aren't there no other fish to keep the rainbow trout company?"

He thought about this. "Well . . . I s'pose there might be some rattlesnake trout about."

"That sounds scary."

"Oh, they're not dangerous. Just another kinda fish." He waited for the inevitable question.

"Charlie, why are they called *rattlesnake* trouts?"

"For one thing, they got a long, skinny neck."

There was an expression of wonder in her brown eyes, which seemed far too large for her face. "A fish with a neck. *Really?*"

"Sure. That old rattlesnake trout can pop his head out real fast and strike!" He flicked his hand to demonstrate. "Last April, Gorman Sweetwater said he saw one snap a woolly worm off a willow branch that was a good two feet above the water."

She shuddered.

He was on a roll. "It's an evolutionary advantage. Gives 'em an edge over the common water-feeders."

"But with such a long neck wouldn't it be awfully hard to swim?"

"Sure. It could get wrapped around a reed or even tied in a

knot. So when they're not using that long neck, they keep it all coiled up on their shoulders. That's why they're called a rattlesnake trout. Although down in New Mexico they call 'em spring-necked trouts."

She made a face. "I think they sound *icky.*"

"I don't much like their looks myself. But some fishermen prefer 'em to rainbows or cutthroats. Last week Gorman Sweetwater caught a small one. Said he stretched the neck out and it wasn't more'n ten inches long. He let it snap back and only counted three coils. But I guess old Gorman must've took a shine to it anyway. He took it home and put it in a big bowl with his Chinese goldfish."

"Would you take me to see it?"

"I'd sure like to, but it's too late."

"Why?"

"Game warden found out about it. Made Gorman throw the thing back in the Piedra."

"Why?"

"Against the law to keep a rattlesnake trout with less than five coils." *She's a good kid, but kind of gullible.*

"Oh." *Charlie's nice, but he makes up such silly stories.* Sarah Frank clutched the black cat against her chest and squinted through the sandblasted windshield at a dusty road that led into the canyon country. "Are we almost there?"

Moon, who had answered this question a dozen times since he'd picked her up at the Colorado Springs airport, nodded. "Almost."

The child looked up at the big policeman. "Are you sure Aunt Daisy'll be glad to see me and Mr. Zig-Zag?"

Sarah was no blood relation to Daisy Perika, but all the kids called her "Aunt Daisy." "She'll be happy to see you. But," he added cautiously, "she don't much care for cats."

"I know. When I was here before, Aunt Daisy never called Mr. Zig-Zag by his real name. She called him Dishrag and Hair Bag and stuff. And sometimes she kicked at him."

"Kicked him?" Sounded just like the grumpy old woman.

"Well, not real hard. If Mr. Zig-Zag bothered her, she'd kinda push at him with her foot."

"When we get there," Moon said, "I'll go in and have a talk

with her. You'd best stay in the pickup with your cat for a while." This would be a delicate operation.

Daisy Perika had finished her breakfast of bacon and scrambled eggs—the last two eggs in the small refrigerator. She washed the dishes hurriedly and twisted a papered wire around the top of a plastic refuse bag. Grocery day was also take-the-garbage-to-the-landfill day. Though it would be a mild autumn day, the elderly woman pulled on the heavy wool coat her last husband had worn every winter for fifteen years. She wrapped her gray head in a blue cotton scarf.

Impatiently, she sat in her kitchen, leather purse slung over her shoulder, grocery list in her coat pocket. She scowled in the general direction from whence he would come, and tapped the door key on the table. By her reckoning, Charlie Moon was almost an hour late. At intervals, she would get up and putter around the kitchen. Wiping spots of grease off the porcelain surface of the propane stove. Cleaning her horn-rimmed spectacles with a tissue. Setting her wristwatch against the electric clock on the wall over the refrigerator.

Presently, though the windows were closed to the chill October morning, she heard the characteristic grumble of the big V-8 engine. Charlie Moon's old pickup was still far over the ridge, maybe a half mile away. Soon, she could hear the chassis groaning and creaking as her nephew negotiated the deep ruts in the unpaved road.

Well, it's about time.

She checked to make sure the burner valves on the gas stove were firmly shut off, that water from the faucets wasn't dripping in the sink.

Daisy watched through the window as Charlie Moon parked the pickup in the lane that led up to her trailer-home. Funny. He usually pulled right up to the porch, so she wouldn't have to walk so far. And what was that . . . a second head in the cab? Somebody was in the truck with him. Daisy groaned. She hoped he hadn't brought that Myra Cornstone along. Myra's little boy—the one she called "Chigger Bug"—was almost three years old now, and the baby's father was a no-account *matukach* cowboy who'd run off to Nevada or someplace after the child was born. After she'd decided her white man wasn't coming back, Myra had started looking around for someone else to share her bed. For some time now, she'd been making the big-eyes at Charlie Moon. Though the Cornstone girl was a Ute—and no close relation to Charlie—Daisy didn't think this particular young woman would make a good wife for her favorite nephew.

But that wasn't Myra in the truck with Charlie. It was someone much smaller. A child . . . ?

Moon climbed the steps on the unpainted pine porch; the planks groaned under his weight. The tall man rapped his knuckles on the trailer wall.

Daisy Perika pushed the door open and peered suspiciously at her nephew. There was no one on the porch with him; she leaned to look past him at the pickup. Yes. He'd left the engine running, most likely to keep the cab warm for his passenger. And there was that little head bobbing around like a cork when a trout nibbled at the worm on the hook. She grunted and stepped aside. This passed for an invitation for her nephew to come inside.

Charlie Moon removed his black Stetson, ducked his head to pass under the six-foot door frame, and made his way into the old woman's warm kitchen. He patted his aunt on the shoulder. "I guess you're about ready to go into town for some groceries."

"I been ready for more'n an hour," she said peevishly. Daisy went to a window and stared at the pickup. "Who's that?"

"Who's what?" he said. As if he'd forgotten about his small passenger. Or small passengers if you counted the cat.

"Who's that in your truck?"

"Oh, just a little girl. You got your grocery list ready?"

Daisy turned to wrinkle her brow at him. "What little girl?"

"Sarah Frank. I picked her up at the Colorado Springs airport this morning."

"That's Sarah?" The old woman jammed her hands into the pockets of the heavy man's overcoat. Now that was interesting. Sarah's mother had been one of them Papago people, but her daddy had been a Ute. "I thought she was staying with her grandparents down in Arizona."

"She was," Moon said. "But her grandmother died last month. And her grandfather's been put in a nursing home. So the *Tohono O'otam* Social Welfare Department had a talk with the Social Services people in our tribe, and they worked out a deal. Sarah will be placed in a foster home on our reservation." So far, no arrangement had been made.

"Our tribal council is working with them Papagos?" Daisy said with a chortle. "Hah. A Ute goes and makes a deal with them sneaky desert Indians, he'd better count his teeth before he comes home. It costs a lot to take care of a child. One of 'em will drink a quart of milk a day. And they're a bother and a nuisance."

Moon continued as if he hadn't heard her. "Because Sarah is *Tohono O'otam* on her mother's side and Ute on her father's, the tribes will go fifty-fifty on her financial support."

At the mention of cash money, Daisy's left eyebrow raised a notch. "Financial support?"

"Yeah. Monthly payment to cover expenses."

"So who's going to take care of the little girl?"

Moon shrugged. Several well-qualified families had already refused. Had too many responsibilities already, they'd said. The few who had shown an interest were, for one reason or another, considered unsuitable. "I expect there'll be several families who'll volunteer."

"Sure," she said with self-righteous indignation. "All they'll be interested in is makin' some money. What that poor child needs is a good home."

Moon turned away to hide a smile. "Roy Severo and his wife Bertha have talked some about Sarah movin' in with them." It wasn't a lie. Not exactly. They had talked about it—and decided they were too old and set in their ways to raise another child.

Daisy snorted. "Roy and Bertha couldn't raise their *own* children up right. Why, one of 'em is working for some fly-by-night telephone outfit. They say she calls people up right at suppertime—tries to talk 'em into changing their telephone service." Enough said. She squinted through the window.

"Why's Sarah stayin' out in the truck? Why don't she come inside?"
"I figured you'd be in a hurry to leave," Moon said innocently. "And I guess Sarah's anxious to get to Ignacio. And find out where she'll be living."
"Well, we're not going to Ignacio for shopping today," Daisy snapped. "I need to go up to the supermarket in Bayfield."
"Bayfield?" She seldom shopped in Bayfield.
"Sure. They got a big sale goin'."
"Sale? On what?"
She hesitated. "On . . . on broccoli. And artichokes."
"Oh." He'd never seen the least sign of either item in Daisy's kitchen. "Well, I guess I could loop around and drop Sarah off in Ignacio on the way back from Bayfield." He glanced at his wristwatch. "Guess we better get going. The Social Services Office will be wanting to start the processing."
"Start what?"
"The paperwork."
"Paperwork for what?"
"The monthly checks to Sarah's foster parents."
"You know," Daisy said as if the thought had just occurred to her, "there's no need to hustle the poor child off to some strange house right away. You could leave her here for a while. Little Sarah stayed with me once before. I expect she'd feel more comfortable bein' with somebody she knows."
"Well," Moon said doubtfully, "I don't know . . . I'd have to get approval from Social Services."
Daisy dismissed this objection with a wave of her hand. "You can leave Sarah with me when we get back from Bayfield. If those fussy old hens in Social Services give you any trouble, you just send 'em out to see me and I'll clip their feathers."
Feigning reluctance, Moon nodded. The lady from SSO had already agreed to Sarah staying with Daisy Perika on a "trial basis." Before it could become a permanent arrangement, Daisy's home would have to be checked out. SSO would determine whether the elderly woman was physically

and mentally fit to provide proper foster-parent care of the child. But the head social worker owed him a favor or two; it was virtually a done deal. "You know . . . Sarah would have to stay here at least a month before you'd get a support payment from the tribe."

Daisy put on a pained, saintly countenance. "If I was to let a poor little orphan child stay in my home for a while, it wouldn't be for *money*." She held her hand near his face, and rubbed finger against thumb. "The trouble with you young people nowadays is that all you think about is money, money, money."

Moon assumed a suitably sheepish expression. He opened the trailer door for her. "Well, it's not a *lot* of money . . ."

She paused on the porch and scowled at him. "Just exactly how much is not a lot . . . ?"

Charlie Moon pitched the plastic garbage bag into the truck bed; he opened the passenger-side door. The elderly woman puffed and grunted as he assisted her climb into the cab. Daisy Perika settled herself beside the child, who had scooted to the middle of the broad seat.

The girl smiled fondly at the newcomer. "Hello, Aunt Daisy." Sarah Frank held up the coal-black cat for the Ute woman's inspection. "Say hello, Mr. Zig-Zag." The sleek feline blinked warily at the woman's small black eyes, sitting like plump raisins in an oatmeal-pudding face.

Daisy beamed upon the pair. "Why, hello, Sarah." She reached out to pat the cat's head; the animal hissed a warning. "And hello to you, Mr. Rag-Bag."

"Mr. *Zig-Zag*," Sarah said.

Charlie Moon backed the truck into the rutted lane that connected *Cañon del Espiritu* with Fosset Gulch Road. The Ute policeman was feeling quite satisfied with this morning's work. True, Daisy's trailer-home was a little ways off the beaten path. But it was neat and clean. And the old woman could still get around well enough to deal with a child. Daisy was a bit peculiar, of course. She still walked up the canyon sometimes to visit that abandoned badger hole where—so she said—the "little man" lived. But she'd hobnobbed with the dwarf since she was a little girl. Said he'd told her lots of things. Important things. It wasn't just Aunt Daisy; several of the older members of the tribe still believed the *pitukupf* was a real person, even claimed they saw him from time to time. Only last week, the manager of the Sky Ute Motel restaurant had made a report to the SUPD. A substantial amount of food was missing. Moon had questioned the kitchen staff. His chief suspect was a Ute woman whose husband had died last April. She had a minimum-wage job and four hungry children to raise. With a perfectly straight face, she claimed that it "wasn't none of us employees who took the food." No, she explained, the *pitukupf* had sneaked in after closing and carried away two sugar-cured hams, three dozen eggs, and twelve pounds of frozen hamburger. How did she know it was the dwarf? Why, she had seen him when she arrived for work just before sunup. Runnin' away, with a big sack over his shoulder. Moon had wondered why such a little fellow would carry away so much food. He must be stockin' up for the winter, she had suggested.

Moon had dutifully entered this material in his official report:

```
Witness reports seeing suspect leaving Sky
Ute Lodge, approx. 6 A.M. Suspect description
follows:
   Height: approx. two feet
   Name: unknown
   Race: said to be non-human
   Age: said to be older than the mountains
   Clothing: green shirt, funny hat, buckskin
trousers, moccasins
   Last known address: unknown, but individual
of similar description has been reported to be
living in badger hole in Cañon del Espiritu
```

The chief of police had not been amused. But you could put all of Roy Severo's sense of humor into a thimble and not fill it up.

Moon's thoughts drifted back to his aunt, and her fitness to care for an orphaned child who didn't seem to have all that many options. It wasn't just Daisy's visits with the *pitukupf.* The "Ute leprechaun" was a tribal tradition that could be overlooked. But more and more, the old woman's thoughts wandered. She had weird dreams and often awoke with a dreadful certainty that these night visions predicted awful things to come. He knew because she would hound him about her worries. *You're a policeman, so go and stop this thing from happening. Do this. Do that. Call Scott Parris, he'll know I'm right.*

And the poor old woman saw ghosts and spirits everywhere. Last June it was a growling bear-spirit sitting on a piñon stump in her yard; she'd thrown it a donut and the "bear" went away, satisfied with the offering. Month before that, it was the ghost of a Ignacio businessman walking along a street, looking into store windows that hadn't changed (for him) in fifty years. Seeing these haunts was bad enough. But Daisy *talked* to them. And they talked back. But it wasn't like she was getting feebleminded. Well, not *very* feebleminded.

Through the mists, Daisy Perika could see the jutting tower of Chimney Rock. She pulled a scrap of paper from her coat pocket and went over her grocery list. Flour. Salt. Ground beef. Pork sausage. Coffee. Milk. Eggs.

Yes . . . eggs.

This reminded the shaman of last evening's peculiar visitor. "Charlie?"

"Yeah?" He didn't take his eyes off the road. There were holes big enough to break a shock absorber. And you never knew when a deer would step out from behind a juniper, right in front of your bumper.

She blinked owlishly through her spectacles. "You oughta be on the lookout for a white man. Probably on drugs. Walks around naked as a plucked chicken."

"Naked?"

"As the day he was born," she said with a weary shake of her head. It was embarrassing the way people carried on nowadays. "He came by my place two nights ago."

The policeman frowned. "He do anything threatening?"

The old woman shook her head. "But he did do something kinda peculiar."

"What?"

"A magic trick."

Moon shot her a sideways glance. "He did *what*?"

She smiled at the memory. "Conjured up a white egg in his hand. Just like one of them magicians on TV."

"Oh." This was beginning to sound like one of her peculiar dreams. "What'd he look like?"

The old woman frowned thoughtfully. "Skinny. Not so tall. Yella hair. Blue eyes. And all muddy—like he'd fell in one of them bogs in Snake Canyon."

"Well," the Ute policeman said amiably, "I've had no citizen complaints about any *matukach* of that description. But if we cross paths, I'll throw a net over him."

Daisy nodded. "That's just what he needs. A net throwed over him."

Moon tapped the brake pedal as a gaunt coyote loped across the lane in front of the Blazer, and disappeared into the brush. Maybe some drunk had wandered by her trailer-home. On the other hand, the old woman had got to the point where she had a hard time telling the difference between dreams and reality. He couldn't resist teasing her. "You remember anything unusual about this fella that'd help me figure out who he is?"

She snorted. "Well, Mr. Policeman—he was stark naked, all covered with black mud, and pulled a white egg outta his hair. I'd say Unusual was his middle name."

The policeman grinned at Sarah, who seemed fascinated by this conversation. "I mean like . . . distinguishing marks or characteristics."

"Like what?"

He shrugged. "Oh, I dunno. Hanging-scar around his neck. Gold ring in his nose. Big red spider tattooed on his knee."

Daisy Perika shot her nephew a warning look. "Nobody likes a smart aleck."

Moon slowed to steer around a fallen pine branch. "There may be more'n one naked white man sneakin' around in the brush. If I'm gonna catch *your* guy, you got to give me something more specific to go on."

"I think he was some kinda foreigner," Daisy said suspiciously. "German, maybe." German tourists visited Mesa Verde in great droves. Some spilled over onto the Ute reservation.

"German," Moon said with a smirk that irritated his aunt. "Well, that'll help."

"Or he coulda been a Albanian or a Bulgarian," she snapped. "Or a Canadian."

Moon wondered whether bringing Sarah Frank to stay with this peculiar old woman had been a sensible notion. But there was no acceptable alternative. Not until Social Services could find a permanent home for the child.

The grocery shopping was finished. They were headed back to Daisy's trailer-home at the mouth of *Cañon del Espiritu.* Charlie Moon had taken notice of two things. First, his aunt had purchased neither broccoli nor artichoke. Second, she had not mentioned the fact that Sarah was looking for a home. Maybe the old woman was trying to think of a gentle way to broach the subject to the child.

Daisy Perika took a sidelong look at the little girl sitting between her and Charlie Moon. The child was clutching the black cat to her chest. "Well, Charlie tells me you've left the Papago reservation."

Sarah Frank nodded.

Moon was pleased that his aunt—who could be brutally direct—was approaching the sensitive subject with some delicacy. This is what he thought.

Daisy squinted through the windshield. "I hear your Papago grandmother went and died on you. And your grandfather's gone feebleminded and's living in an old-folks home. And here you are—without a roof over your head or anything to eat."

With some effort, Moon held his tongue.

Sarah nodded again. "Yes, Aunt Daisy. I thought maybe me and Mr. Zig-Zag could come and stay with you . . . for a little while."

Uh-oh. Moon kept his eyes on the road. *If Aunt Daisy guesses that this was my idea . . .*

Daisy was pleased that she and Sarah Frank had shared the same thought. But it would be a bad tactic to appear too eager. "Well . . . I don't know how I'd manage with a noisy child in my house. I'm too old to put up with any nonsense."

Sarah rubbed the cat's neck. "We wouldn't have to stay very long—just till some *nice* people want me to live with them."

The old woman scowled at the little girl.

To cover a laugh, the policeman quickly faked a cough.

Daisy fumbled in her purse and found a handkerchief; she blew her nose. "And another thing—I think I'm allergic to Mr. Hair-Bag."

"*Zig-Zag*," Sarah muttered hopelessly.

"When you brought that animal into my house before, seemed like I never could stop sneezing and scratching." Daisy Perika sensed that her nephew was about to say something, and continued quickly: "Tell you what, young lady. We'll try it for just a few days. See how it works out."

Sarah shook her finger in the cat's impassive face. "Now don't you make Aunt Daisy sneeze." She reached over to hug the old woman.

"Hmmmf," Daisy said gruffly. The half-Papago child would be a great nuisance. The cat would always be underfoot, whining at her ankles, wanting scraps from the table. But then . . . she certainly wouldn't be lonely. And there was the support money—almost as much as she got in her monthly Social Security check. Not—she quickly reminded herself and the Almighty—that this act of charity had anything whatever to do with money.

Nathan McFain was walking his fence line when he saw Charlie Moon's old pickup—trailed by rolling billows of yellow dust—rumble by on the gravel road two hundred yards to the south. The rancher paused and pulled at his tobacco-stained white beard. Nathan made it his business to know much of his neighbor's business. The Ute policeman came by once every week to take his aged aunt to town so she could buy her provisions. Nathan pulled a fat watch from his pocket and squinted at the thin blue hands. Charlie and Daisy were running a little behind schedule. He found a package of Red Man chewing tobacco in his jacket pocket and bit off a chaw. The rancher stood there for a full minute, chewing thoughtfully. Then, to punctuate the end of this pause, spat on a fence post. He was missing two lower front teeth. A dribble of brown spittle ran down his chin . . . and onto the whiskers where it added to the brown patina that neatly divided the white beard.

The rancher, whose bent posture and slow walk made him seem much older than his sixty-two years, plodded along. He pushed at loose cedar posts, tugged at rusted strands of barbed wire. Made mental notes of which repairs should be completed before the deep snows came, and those that could wait until after the April thaw. He was approaching a sandy basin in his pasture, shaded from the late afternoon sun by the brow of a sandstone bluff that rose steeply a few yards beyond the fence. The land on the west side of the barbed wire belonged to the Southern Ute tribe. In fact, most of the real estate bordering his ninety-acre holdings was a part of the reservation. His great-grandfather had bought this parcel from a Ute sheepman back in the 1890s. There had been boundary disputes ever since. Nathan McFain, who was one-quarter Navajo on his mother's side, liked to say that he mistrusted all the Utes twenty-five percent of the time—and twenty-five percent of the Utes all the time—as was his birthright.

A Ute elder who heard this insult had responded that one-quarter Navajo blood was more than enough to infect the whole man. And on top of that, the other seventy-five percent of Nathan's blood was *matukach.* So Utes were obliged to mistrust Nathan McFain one hundred and ten percent of the time. And not only that, he had added, the bearded, gap-toothed man was ugly as three billy goats.

On an occasion some years ago, the rancher had suspected the Utes of rolling several basalt boulders that served as boundary markers onto his land. By at least a yard. Maybe two. He wasn't absolutely sure, of course. But a man had to take steps to protect his property from illegal encroachment. So now and again he'd roll the marker boulders in the direction of the Ute holdings. Just a yard. Maybe two.

But within a few months, he was certain the boulders had

been rolled back toward him. Damn conniving Utes. So he'd roll 'em westward again.

The rancher had finally tired of that game and put in a barbed-wire fence.

Nathan was a dour, unhappy soul. An unfortunate man who disproved the adage that you got out of life what you put into it. He had attempted to raise a family. His wife had died when the child was born, some twenty-odd years ago. And his daughter—though he loved her—had been a peck of trouble. For decades, he had labored to bring forth a good living from his acres. He had tried sheep. The hateful creatures conspired among themselves to come down with dreadful diseases unknown to veterinary science, and died by the dozens. They did this just to spite him. He'd tried cattle, and they had waxed fat. But beef prices fell through the floor and into the basement. He planted apple orchards. The flesh of the fruit was sweet enough, but the skins were like leather. And there was the great flock of strutting peacocks whose feathers were to be sold to the Chinese. That was a most embarrassing affair, and it was better not to bring the subject up with Nathan McFain.

Determined to make a few dollars out of his land, he moved from one questionable scheme to another. Most recently, Nathan had converted his holdings into a dude ranch with a half dozen overly tame horses and "scenic riding trails." He had sold ten acres of prime Piedra riverbank land and used the cash to build a row of cute little log cabins that would attract the well-heeled city folk.

But alas, the dudes did not come.

One could make a detailed list of his other failed business ventures, but it was altogether too dismal.

And now—buried in an accumulation of failures—Nathan McFain sometimes felt as if he already lay in the grave. Waiting for the somber men with spades to throw the sod o'er him. But he did not give up entirely. Partially because of an inborn stubbornness. And also because Nathan knew that he was smarter than his more prosperous neighbors. And he worked harder than those slackers. So they must be lucky. On dismal nights when he could not sleep, he grudgingly admitted that it was better to be lucky than to be smart.

What he needed, he told himself ten times a day, was a bit of luck.

As the rancher slowly made his way along the fence, he found himself at the edge of the low, sandy area under the bluff. With last spring's winds, this unsightly pockmark on the face of his pasture had earned the title "blow." The gusts had carried away several inches of loose topsoil. Grass was uprooted; even the stability of the fence was threatened. From the corner of his eye, Nathan caught a glimpse of the skinny young fellow who'd wandered onto the ranch just yesterday, half-starved and eager to work. Jimson Beugmann was up by the barn, tinkering with the old bulldozer. Fellow was deaf as a man who'd been dead a year, but he could read your lips. And this new hand seemed to have a knack with machinery. Maybe he should get Beugmann to fire up the 'dozer and push some soil up against the wobbly fence posts. Like beads on a string, one thought touched another. As long as Beugmann had the dozer over here, he could scoop out enough dirt to make a usable pond for the stock. Holding onto a shaky post, Nathan McFain paused at the edge of the shallow basin.

He hadn't seen it coming. But he heard it . . . the low, whispering moaning.

The whirlwind moved across the pasture, leaning to the left, then the right . . . like an intoxicated giant, reeling and stumbling his way home.

The thing was whipping up bucketfuls of bile-yellow dust.

Forty feet high, twisting winds brewed in some witch's stew-pot, and it was coming right at him. Nathan planted his feet, scowled at the thing, and stood his ground. Nothing but some wind and sand, the *matukach* part of his mind said. It'd pass by. But the one-quarter of him that was Navajo knew better. This was a devil-spirit, sent to torment him. Perhaps to bring on a fatal sickness . . .

It continued to move toward the sandy basin.

When the twister's toe touched the sands, all hell broke loose. The solitary moaning became a heavy, communal roar . . . a company of fiends hatched in a hideous nightmare—eager to rip flesh from bone. Sprigs of dry rabbit brush were uprooted and shredded. Pebbles flew like bullets. The whirling winds gained strength.

Nathan threw his forearm in front of his face, like an old pugilist warding off a blow.

Yards from him, the dust devil paused. And churned.

McFain backed against the fence, heedless of the barbed wire. Until a pointed piece of steel pricked the skin over his spine . . . and an electric signal flashed an absurd message to his brain. *Old man, you are impaled.* The sand and grit was driven against one side of his head; he grabbed the brim of his canvas hat.

Still, the whirlwind did not move.

Nathan blinked, felt the grit of sand between his teeth and in his eyes. The Navajo in him prayed for this evil thing to depart.

And then the winds began to subside.

The roar gradually fell to a whisper.

And died.

He spat sand from his mouth. "Damn," he said. The old man attempted to wipe the grit from his watering eyes. He blinked. Beneath the place where the whirlwind had stood was an almost perfectly circular depression.

And in the center of this depression was something else.

Something like a thick brown finger protruding from the matrix of clay and pebbles. In his unhappy state of mind, it was perceived as an obscene, mocking gesture. He'd once cleared a few scraggly trees from this end of the pasture . . . those damn winds must've dug up an old juniper root. Nathan trudged grimly along the gritty bottom of the blow, toward the intruding presence. He paused to stare at the thing.

Nope. Wasn't a dead tree root.

Odd, though . . .

He squatted. And squinted.

Looked like some kind of bone. A cylindrical bone, slightly curved. And pointed on the end. Sort of like a cow's horn . . . but way too big for that. Not an old buffalo horn, neither. Wrong shape. He pulled off a scuffed leather glove and touched the thing. Scratched the surface with a horny fingernail. Funny. It had the look and feel of . . . stone. His heart began to thump under his ribs. This thing was old. Really old.

Nathan McFain squatted there for some minutes, caressing the ancient tusk with his callused fingertips. The gears under his skull were spinning in overdrive. Under this thing, he assured himself, there would be more bones. Most likely a whole skeleton of some great beast. Maybe even more than one . . . a whole herd of 'em. This man was not in the habit of entertaining small thoughts. Nathan McFain's visions were invariably grand. This latest fanciful picture began to form in his mind. He saw a paved driveway leading to an ample parking lot. There were redwood picnic tables nestled in the shade of cottonwoods. A fine steel building erected over the reassembled skeleton of whatever wonderful beast that lay buried beneath his feet. There were rosebushes planted along the paved walk to the door. And a large, tasteful sign on the building.

McFain Museum

Mounted on the entrance door was a brass plaque. Though it was much smaller than the sign, he could see it plainly.

ADMISSION FEES

Adults $5.00

Children $2.50

Senior Citizens $1.50

Let's see, figure a hundred cars a week, average of two adults and two children per car, that would come to . . . my goodness! And there would be soft drinks and candy bars for the tourists. T-shirts and pennants and bumper stickers. Plastic skeletons of dinosaurs and limestone seashell fossils and whatnot. Some Indian pottery, of course. One hundred percent markup would be fair enough for a first-class joint. There would be tax problems with so much income; it would be necessary to hire an accountant. For the first time since he'd broke ground for the McFain Dude Ranch's bunkhouse cabins, Nathan was a happy man. The rancher was so elated that he did a heavy-footed little jig on the floor of the sandy basin. He was very careful not to stomp on the precious thing that protruded from the earth.

Exhausted from his exertions, he sat down on the rim of the blow and thought about what to do. First—to make sure the fossil tusk didn't get broke—he'd shovel some loose dirt over it. Then, tell Beugmann that the new stock tank could be dug somewhere else. Sure. Farther up the pasture, close to the barn. Then, he'd drive up to Granite Creek and visit Rocky Mountain Polytechnic. Tell 'em he wanted to talk with one of them professors. The kind that digs up old bones.

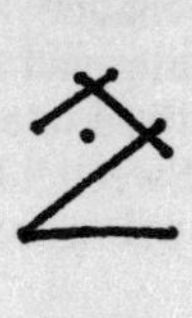

THE SLICKER FROM ARKANSAS

HORACE FLYE FOCUSED pale blue eyes on the rearview mirror. What he saw—over the bed of his aged pickup truck—was the blunt face of the camping trailer. He braked gradually and pulled off the asphalt, easing to a slow stop under a flickering neon sign. Butter, back there in the trailer, was most likely sound asleep. And if he stopped too hard—like he'd done back in Pagosa—she'd likely fall out of the bed again. And yell her head off at him. Butter had a temper, just like her mamma. The bewhiskered man balanced a pair of plastic-rimmed reading glasses on his nose, and squinted at the Colorado road map. *Hmmm. Looks like I'm on some kind of Indian reservation. Close to some little town called Ignacio. Maybe even in it already.* The Arkansas man scratched at his whiskered chin, which itched. A good omen. *Maybe it's about time for my luck to change.*

A sudden gust of wind bent a mountain ash sapling and kicked an empty Coors six-pack carton across the parking lot.

He buttoned up his grease-stained denim jacket, jammed a battered felt hat onto his balding head, then got out and slammed the pickup door. Horace saw the white cloud of his breath; his teeth began to chatter. The weary traveler walked stiff-legged back to the trailer and slammed his palm against the aluminum wall. He grinned uneasily when her pudgy face appeared in the window. "Sweetie, I gotta go in here for a few minutes," he yelled at the pale countenance. "You just watch the TV for a little while."

The face didn't respond. Just stared back sullenly.

Horace Flye nodded—as if Butter was a compliant daughter who would do as her father said. This self-delusion accomplished, Horace turned on his heel.

The small, wiry man walked a few paces to the front of his pickup. He paused in the graveled parking lot, his hands jammed into the hip pockets of his khaki britches. He leaned back onto the heels of his scuffed roper boots and stared up at the scarlet neon sign. It made a sizzling, popping sound—and emitted a pungent electric smell.

Tillie's
Navajo Bar & Grille

There were a half dozen pickups parked out front, and some beat-up old sedans. A big Peterbilt was hitched to a long flatbed loaded with sweet-smelling bales of hay. Horace rubbed at his woolly black beard and pondered the situation. Well, a travelin' man couldn't tell everything just by lookin'. But this was probably as good a place as any. He felt the stare on his back. He glanced back at the camper and saw Butter's round face in the window, her unblinking blue eyes accusing him. He waved halfheartedly and hurried off toward the entrance of the drinking establishment. There was a hand-printed sign stapled to the front door.

NO GUNS ALLOWED ON THE PREMISES
THIS IS A CASH BUSINESS
NO CHECKS NO PLASTIC
NO BULLSHIT

Horace grinned behind his beard. Yep. This was the place sure enough. He pushed on the door. An antique jukebox churned out a mournful cowboy's wail about a wicked woman with a cheatin' heart. The place smelled of beer and cigarette smoke and failed lives. The newcomer paused to give his eyes time to adjust to the cavelike darkness. There was a scattering of tables on a scarred hardwood floor, booths along the wall on each side of the door, a long bar across the far wall. A big heavyset woman was sitting by an old-fashioned mechanical cash register. She wore a tentlike black dress, a dozen silver rings on her stubby fingers, a tight necklace of turquoise beads under her chins, light blue eye shadow to match the beads. As she flipped through the pages of a magazine, piggy little eyes looked up at him. And were not impressed with what they saw.

Whew. This one could stare down a moose with one eyeball. That'd have to be Tillie.

There was a bald-headed man tending the bar; he didn't look like someone who'd give a fellow heartburn. A couple of bearded guys sat at one of the wooden tables, nursing canned Coors and mumbling about reports of black ice at Muleshoe and fifty-mile-an-hour winds up on LaVeta pass. Those would be the hay-haulers. The booths were unoccupied except for a skinny man in a spotless white cowboy hat who listened stoically to whining complaints from a bleary-eyed blonde with a pretty Mexican shawl on her shoulders and a shot glass in her hand. There were several men scattered along the bar, perched on stools that were upholstered in red imitation leather. Horace studied the assortment of bar-side customers with a practiced eye. For the most part, they were a poorly-looking lot. Several hopeless-looking bums with three-day beards and empty eyes. Two pimply-faced youths leering at a copy of *Penthouse*, whispering and snickering. An extremely fat man in greasy coveralls whose butt enveloped the stool. An empty stool separated Chubby from a dark-skinned man with two braids draped down his back and one leg hanging off the stool. The one-legged fellow had a heavy crutch propped against the bar beside him. One-Leg nodded at the bartender, who promptly refilled his mug. He pulled a small roll of greenbacks from his hip pocket and unpeeled a twenty.

Bingo.

Horace approached the bar, and seated himself on the stool between Chubby and One-Leg. He smiled congenially at the bald bartender, who gave the greasy countertop a brisk swipe. "Coors."

He was served efficiently and with no more comment than a barely perceptible nod. He pulled a tobacco sack and papers from his shirt pocket and proceeded to construct a cigarette. Horace licked the paper cylinder to seal the thing, then turned his face toward the man on his right. "So. You a vet'ran?"

The one-legged man turned a dark face toward the stranger and scowled. "Why'd you think that?"

The Arkansas man touched a lighter to the cigarette, and inhaled deeply. "Well . . . I figured maybe you lost your leg in a war."

"Hmmmf," the dark man said, and returned his attention to the almost empty beer mug.

Horace coughed up several puffs of smoke, and waved at the bartender. "Another one for my buddy here."

The Ute, somewhat disarmed by this unexpected favor, watched as the bald man refilled the mug. Then he noticed that the *matukach* visitor was missing the middle finger from his left hand. Though this was not so serious an amputation as his own, the one-legged man felt some small flicker of kinship with the stranger. "So. You lose your finger in the war?"

"Nope," Flye said sadly. "Bear bit it off. And et it right in front of me."

The Indian nodded solemnly. "They'll do that sometimes."

Flye had not been entirely truthful. Three years ago, he had been trading insults with a drunken miner in Bozeman. The man from Arkansas had—unwisely as it turned out—"given the finger" to his adversary. It was such an offer as could not be refused. The miner, who was armed with a razor-sharp Buck knife and a somewhat whimsical nature, had—despite Flye's loud protests—accepted the digit.

The visitor stuck his grubby hand out. The right one, which had all its fingers. "Name's Horace Flye."

The Ute accepted the hand with some reluctance. "Curtis Tavishuts."

"Pleased to meet you, Curtis." And he was. Horace sipped at the beer. "It's a hard thing for a man to lose his leg." He eyed his left hand. "Or even a finger." Horace assumed a faraway, mysterious expression. "But there's lots worser things that can happen to a man." He nodded to agree with himself. "Yessir. Lots worser things."

He waited.

For a long moment, the taciturn drinker did not respond. Finally, as if to get it over with, the Ute regarded the bearded stranger with bleary-eyed boredom. "So what's worse than losing a leg?"

"Well," said Horace in a mildly defensive tone, "there was somethin' awful peculiar that happened to me some years back. But it ain't a easy thing to talk about." He ground out the half-spent cigarette in a dirty glass ashtray.

The Indian shrugged, and took a long drink of beer.

Other conversations in the saloon—if such aimless mutterings could be called conversations—were stilled. Ears were cocked. Problems—especially the other fellow's—were of considerable interest to this motley congregation. Particularly if they were really nasty problems. Like he had an incurable venereal disease or the IRS was after his butt.

Horace exhaled a great sigh of cigarette smoke. "Well, I guess if you really want to know . . . it happened back in Arkansas, when I took a bad fall off'n a ginny mule. And cracked my noggin on a rock. I ain't been the same never since."

The Indian grinned in his beer, but resisted the temptation. Too easy.

Like a pious monk at prayer, Horace clasped his hands and bowed his head. "Some might say it was a gift, I s'pose. But it's not one I asked for. See, after the fall, I had awful headaches for a long time. But worstest of all, it turned out I could *see* things."

Curtis Tavishuts turned to frown at the *matukach*. "*See* things? What kinds of things?"

Horace smiled the beatific smile of one who has accepted

his heavy burden. "Oh . . . this and that. Hants and golliwogs and boogers and such."

The Indian asked for a clarification.

The Arkansas man shrugged. "Ghosts and goblins. Shades of dead folks."

The taste of the free beer went sour in Tavishuts' mouth.

Horace continued his spiel. "Sometimes, I see what's goin' to happen tomorrow. But most of the time, I see *hidden* things."

The Ute barfly was not at all pleased by this revelation. Talk of ghosts and goblins was unhealthy. But what did this bushy-face fellow mean by *hidden* things? "Whaddayou mean, you can see *hidden* things?"

"Well," Horace said with a mild leer at Tillie, "sometimes I can see right through people's clothes."

Tillie blushed. And attempted to hide her ample bosom behind the magazine.

Horace's lewd smirk implied that mere paper was no barrier.

The Ute snorted. "You mean to say you got X-ray vision? Like Superman?"

The bearded stranger seemed to go on the defensive. "Well, it don't work all the time. But *sometimes* I can see through things."

Tavishuts smiled knowingly at the other customers along the bar, who were hanging on every word. "How about right now?"

An expression of unease passed over Horace's face. "Well, it kinda comes and goes. It ain't workin' so well right now, but yesterday I coulda counted all the teeth in your head and the loose change in your pocket."

The Ute turned his attention to his drink. "Bullshit," he said scornfully, "it's all bullshit."

Horace looked hurt. "No it ain't."

"Sure it is. All bullshit. If it wasn't bullshit, you could—"

"I bet I can see what's in your coat pocket."

"Bet?" Tavishuts grinned, exposing a wide gap where four teeth had been expertly removed by his wife—who was no dentist. She had used an ax handle for the operation. "You want to put some cash on the line or is this just more o' your bullshit?"

Horace opened a worn leather wallet. He laid a dollar bill on the sour-smelling pine bar. "This says I can see what's in your jacket pocket."

The Ute cast a doubtful look at the crazy man who had met his challenge. And felt all eyes on himself.

"Put up or shut up," Horace snapped.

"A dollar bet? That's peanuts." Curtis Tavishuts reached into his hip pocket, produced the small roll of greenbacks. And peeled off a twenty. He slapped this beside the white man's dollar bill.

For the first time on this cold day, Horace Flye felt warm inside. And pleased with himself. He withdrew the dollar bill, replaced it with a twenty, and placed a grimy palm over his eyes. There was an excited murmuring among the customers. "I'd 'preciate it if I could have some quiet." While all watched, he concentrated on the issue at hand. Like how fast to leave the bar once he had this sucker's money in his pocket.

Tillie, her modesty forgotten, heaved her great bulk up from the chair by the cash register. She left her *Teen People* magazine behind and waddled toward this odd pair of customers.

His stomach—well aware that it was time for lunch—growled at him. Charlie Moon turned the aging SUPD Blazer south onto Goddard Avenue. It was about twenty seconds to Angel's Cafe. The Ute police officer was anticipating a king-sized blue-corn enchilada. Half a dozen of Angel's featherlight sopapillas, broke open with a spoon-handle and sweetened with red clover honey. A sixteen-ounce root beer in a frosted mug. But he couldn't make his mind up about dessert. Pie, maybe. Raspberry-rhubarb, heated in Angel's microwave. With two or three scoops of vanilla ice cream on the side.

Life was good.

As a rude preamble to bad news, the police radio belched static. Then came the voice from only a mile away. "Officer Moon."

Nancy Beyal was a nice enough young lady, but at this moment the dispatcher's velvet voice had all the charm of a broken fingernail dragged across the blackboard.

"Charlie Moon. Respond, please."

It'd be the usual nonsense. Little Kathi Begay's cat had climbed up a tree and didn't know how to get down. Or Arlin Tall Rain had borrowed another one of his neighbor's pigs. He ignored the summons. Let Nancy bug somebody else.

Another burp of static, followed by: "Charlie Moon, I know *very well* you can hear me, so pick up."

"Shoot." He yanked the microphone off the chrome hook and held it by his chin. "Nancy, I'm goin' off duty. It's time for lunch. Send Elena. Or Daniel Bignight."

"Caller asked for you *personal*, Charlie."

He frowned at the sandblasted windshield. "Who called?"

"A Mr. Clapper."

Didn't ring a bell. "Who's he?"

"A bartender . . . at Tillie's Navajo Bar and Grille."

Must be Gus. "What's the problem?"

"Caller reported a disturbance."

He pressed the microphone button. "Nancy, Tillie's place is not—I repeat *not*—in Southern Ute tribal jurisdiction. Contact the Ignacio town police. They can handle it."

"Caller asked for you yourself, Charlie. Says there's an Indian involved in some kind of fight."

Moon groaned. If a local troublemaker turned out to be a Native American—anything from an Ontario Abitibiwinni to a New Mexico Zuñi—it was SUPD business. "What kind of Indian?"

"Caller didn't say."

He pressed the microphone button. "Weapons involved?" A sensible policeman wanted to know if he was supposed to break up a fight where a couple of drunks had knives or straight razors. Or pistols . . .

"Caller didn't mention any weapons. I'd like to chat with you, Charlie, but I got some other traffic comin' in. Goodbye."

"Shoot." He hung the microphone on the hook, jammed his big boot onto the brake pedal, made a squealing U-turn on

Goddard, and flipped the emergency-lights switch. His stomach growled in protest.

He growled back.

Moon skidded to a stop on the gravel, switched off the ignition, and hit the ground before the V-8 engine had coughed to a stop. The Southern Ute policeman ducked his head under the doorway, and burst into Tillie's Navajo Bar and Grille.

And stood there, and stared.

The tables had been pulled away to make room on the dusty floor for the combatants. A circle of cheerful drinkers stood around the spectacle, shaking fists, waving dusty cowboy hats, stomping heavy boots, laughing raucously, urging the gladiators to even greater efforts. Only a few bothered to glare at the unwelcome lawman.

Moon shoved his way through the ring of spectators.

On the floor were two men, locked in a bitter embrace. One was Curtis Tavishuts. The other was a white man Moon didn't recognize.

They rolled, cursed, groaned, kicked like mustangs, swore like merchant seamen. Moon sized the thing up. Tavishuts had the weight advantage, maybe forty pounds over the skinny *matukach* with the fuzzy beard. But the absence of a left leg was a significant disadvantage to the Ute, so that the lighter man was on top almost as often as the cripple. Aside from a few scratches, neither seemed to be injured. And there was no sign of a knife.

Tillie materialized at Moon's side. "Hiya, Charlie. Whatcha doin' here?"

He didn't take his eyes off the scuffle. "Got a call from Dispatch. Somebody phoned in a report of a disturbance."

"That must've been Gus." Tillie glowered at the bald bartender, who was not to be counted among the spectators. He blushed and turned his attention to a glass that needed washing. "Gus Clapper," she continued with a dreary sigh, "is an old woman when it comes to fights. Any little dispute, he calls in the cops."

Moon pointed at the struggling mass with the tip of his boot. "I'll need to know who . . ."

"Oh, that's Curtis Tavishuts," Tillie said. "He's a regular."

"I recognize *him*," Moon said evenly. "We don't have all that many tribal members missing a leg."

"Oh, you mean the other one." She shrugged. "How'd I know? He looked old enough to buy a drink, so I didn't ask to look at his I.D." She giggled and nudged the policeman with a knobby elbow.

"You never seen him before?"

She shook her head. "Nosiree. He just blew in with the tumbelin' tumblin' weed. And made a bet with the Indian."

"So I guess Tavishuts lost the wager." The one-legged Ute had always been a sore loser.

Tillie frowned thoughtfully at the men writhing on the floor. "As you can see, it ain't quite settled yet. The little skinny guy bet Tavishuts he could see what was in his coat pocket."

Moon sighed. There *was* one born every minute. "And I expect he did."

"Uh-huh." She grinned, showing heavy pink gums lined with tiny, delicate teeth. "A 1996 nickel, made at the Denver mint. Couple of toothpicks. And a piece of peppermint candy."

"And Tavishuts figured out the fellow had dropped the stuff in his pocket before he struck up a conversation?" It was surprising he had that much brains.

She nodded. "Yeah. But only because Tavishuts he don't eat no peppermint nor no other kinda candy—he's got the sugar diabetes. And because there was a fishin' license in his coat pocket the fella never mentioned. So your Indian, he grabbed the little white guy and tried to pull his head off."

Moon nodded. There were one or two fights here every week. "Well," he said wearily, "I'd best put a stop to this."

She hugged him around the waist. "Charlie, honey, my customers is enjoyin' this little scuffle. And those fellas ain't hurtin' each other all that much. So if you could just wait a few minutes, till they're all tuckered out . . ."

Moon pretended to be astonished. "Your clientele are making wagers on the fight?"

She nodded. "First man who's on his feet and stays that way is the winner. And if you break it up, it'll ruin the afternoon for a lot of nice folks. You wanna make a bet? Hank Simms," she nodded toward a grizzled truck driver, "is giving three to two on your one-legged Indian."

"Tillie, I'm a sworn officer of the law."

"The odds is the same for everybody," she said with a righteous sniff. "You bein' a cop don't cut no ice—three to two is the best deal you can get."

"What I meant," he explained patiently, "is that it is considered unseemly for a tribal police officer to indulge in illegal gambling while on duty. Especially when the bet is on who'll come off worse in a bar brawl." He'd have loved to put ten dollars on the skinny white man.

She snorted. "Whatever you say, Charlie. But if you don't like the odds, then at least leave 'em be till they're all give out."

"It's my job to preserve the peace. I can't just stand by while they . . ."

She gave him a motherly look. "You look all out o' sorts. Like you ain't had your lunch. Could I fix you a double cheeseburger?" She batted her huge, false eyelashes at him. "With fries?"

His stomach heard this offer. And was interested. "I don't know . . ."

She grabbed him by the wrist, and used her two hundred and thirty pounds to advantage. Moon felt himself being led away from the spectacle, toward said grille of Tillie's Navajo Bar and Grille. "How about two quarter-pound patties of prime ground sirloin. Not cooked too done. And double cheese. Fresh-brewed coffee. It'll be on the house."

He glanced doubtfully over his shoulder at the combatants. They *did* seem to be tiring . . . "Well . . . if it's not too much trouble."

Tillie headed for the grille, and began to work her culinary wonders on huge patties of ground beef. She peppered and salted and worked in chopped onion. She slapped the pink disks on the griddle, where they popped and sizzled.

Moon's attention was divided. On one hand, there was the

wonderful aroma of burning animal fat. On another, the grunts and curses of the ineffectual wrestlers.

Tillie put on a fresh pot of Big Jim's Java.

Unexpectedly, a shrill shriek pierced the smoke-filled atmosphere of Tillie's Navajo Bar and Grille. "Aiiiieeeeeee!"

It was the white man who protested so loudly.

Curtis Tavishuts had managed to get the smaller man's right ear between his remaining teeth. And was chewing on it with evident relish. Almost immediately, there was a roar of pain from the Indian. The skinny white man had gouged a dirty thumb into the crippled Ute's eye, and popped the orb halfway out of its socket.

Within an instant, Moon was upon them, peeling the weary scufflers apart. It was no easy task. Tavishuts did not wish to loose his yellowed teeth from the chewed ear—he relented only when the Ute policeman twisted his nose. Once the combatants were disentangled, the big policemen lifted them like rag dolls. Because the skinny man was much lighter—and because Tavishuts' missing leg made him much harder to right—the bearded stranger was the first on his feet. Jubilant shouts went up from the apparent winners. There were loud cries of "foul" from those drunks who had backed Tavishuts—and heartfelt complaints that this was not a fair finish. If the cop had not interfered, the Indian would have chewed the man's ear off, and surely come out the winner. Not so, the others cried—a gouged-out eyeball was worth three or four chewed ears any day of the week. All turned to the proprietor to settle the dispute honorably. Tillie, with a Solomon-like solemnity, considered the case. And made her decision: the fight was a draw. All bets were off. There were dark mutterings here and there, but most were satisfied to break even in a fair contest that had been ruined by the meddling lawman.

Moon sat the miscreants in a pair of Tillie's uncomfortable straight-backed chairs, then straddled a similar piece of furniture. He assumed his professional expression of "sorrow at being a witness to this disgraceful conduct" and addressed the Ute first. "Curtis, you're an embarrassment to the People. What's the matter with you?"

The one-legged Indian rubbed at his injured eye and glared at the skinny white man with the one that worked. "This little blue-eyed devil cheated me on a bet—he put some stuff in my pocket when I wasn't lookin' and then he pretended to have X-ray vision—like Superman!" His injured expression appealed mutely to the police officer. Would a real human being do such an unspeakable thing?

"I never did no such thing," Flye lied. "This whiner tried to welch on an honest bet. Where I come from, that's the *worstest* thing a man can do." The stranger, who held a grimy handkerchief over his chewed ear, thrust a daggerlike finger at the one-legged Ute. "Welcher!"

Moon noticed that one digit was missing from the bloody hand. "You lose a finger in the fight?"

Flye shook his head.

"He claims a bear bit it off," Curtis Tavishuts said with a sneer. "That fuzzy-faced bastard can't open his mouth without lyin'."

Moon raised an eyebrow at the skinny, bearded man. "Just where do you come from?"

Chewed Ear puffed out his thin chest. "Arkansas."

"Hah," the Ute said. "Damn hillbilly from Dogpatch."

Moon aimed a warning glance at Tavishuts, then returned his attention to the man from Arkansas. "What's your name?"

The white man spoke without taking his baleful gaze off the surly Ute. "Horace Flye."

"Horsefly," Tavishuts said derisively, and spat on the floor.

"Injun welcher," the man from Arkansas responded, and also spat on the floor.

Tillie bellowed: "Either one of you dummies spits on the premises agin', you'll be cleaning it up with your tongue."

"Blue-eyed devil," the Ute muttered.

"One-legged cannybubble," Horace hissed.

Moon sighed. A lot of children were walking around in men's bodies. "Now both of you keep quiet long enough to listen to what I've got to say." He gave Curtis Tavishuts a hard look. "You know the routine. This disturbance occurred out of tribal jurisdiction but we've got an agreement with the Ignacio town police about arresting Native Americans. So I'll take you over to SUPD and put you in the lockup till we can sort this out."

Tavishuts grunted to show his indifference. The SUPD can was like a second home. And the meals were catered by Angel's Cafe.

The Southern Ute policeman addressed the out-of-towner. "Mr. Flye, as you are not an Indian, you'll be taken into custody by the Ignacio town police who . . . well, speak of the Devil . . ."

The timing was fortuitous. Moon looked out a greasy window to see the freshly waxed Ignacio town police cruiser come to a halt, its tall mast antenna oscillating with a whish-whish sound. A moment later, the bearish form of Sergeant Bill McCullough kicked the door open. He stood there, ten paces from the pair of bar-brawlers. Like an executioner relishing the bloody task before him. The town policeman was shorter than Charlie Moon, barely topping six feet even in his thick-heeled black boots. But he had shoulders a yard wide. A long bullet-shaped head which—because he had no discernible neck—sat directly on the yard-wide shoulders. He peered through nasty little black eyes, set on each side of a long, broken nose. This was a cruel face that might have adorned a recruiting poster for a neo-Nazi organization. But it was all deception. Underneath the fearsome shell was a warm heart, a generous nature. And a wry sense of humor.

Charlie Moon knew this.

Horace Flye, of course, did not.

McCullough's voice was deep, like the rumble of summer thunder. "H'lo, Charlie. You got one for me?"

The Ute policeman nodded. "Looks like we got a bad guy for both of us."

McCullough's massive hand caressed the heavy black baton hanging on his gun belt. His thick lips twisted into a diabolic grin, exposing a row of square teeth such as are rumored to bite through seasoned two-by-fours like they were ripe bananas.

Flye sucked in a deep breath and turned to Moon with a desperate whisper. "Well, I guess you'll have to take *me* to that Injun jail too."

Moon repeated his position with considerable patience. "Like I told you, the Southern Ute police only have jurisdiction over Indians. Everybody else is dealt with by the Ignacio town police."

Horace nodded eagerly. "But I *am* an Injun."

Moon suppressed a smile. The mere sight of Buffalo Bill McCullough had a sobering effect on the criminal element. "Funny . . . you don't *look* Indian."

"Oh, but I am. On my mamma's side, bless her poor soul."

"Oh? Which tribe?"

An unexpected question. There was the barest hesitation as crooked wheels spun in Horace's head. The word seemed to spring from nowhere. "Mugwump."

The Ute policeman cocked a doubtful eyebrow. "Never heard of 'em."

"Oh, that's 'cause they's a little bitty tribe. Almost wiped out a long time ago." The traveler from Arkansas was warming to his task. "You never read that book—*The Last of the Mugwumps?"*

"Can't say I have."

McCullough, wiener-sized thumbs hooked in his gun belt, approached his quarry. Each heavy footstep brought a protesting groan from the oak floor. The buffalo-shouldered town policeman ignored the one-legged Indian. He looked crookedly down the bend of his nose at the hapless Arkansas man. His voice was a deep, resonant bass, seeming to rumble up from some internal volcano. "I s'pose this little pissant belongs to me."

Horace Flye felt like an insect caught in the sticky web of a large, bullet-headed spider. He gazed at the Ute policeman with mute appeal.

"That's what I'd thought," Moon said. "But now he claims to be Indian."

McCullough snorted. "Injun my arse. Looks like a damn shanty Arshman to me."

"Well, he could be *part* Irish." Moon assumed a thoughtful look. "But even if he's only got a drop of Native American blood in his veins, he falls under SUPD jurisdiction."

Relief and gratitude washed over Horace Flye's face.

Bill McCullough tilted his huge head and studied Horace. "What kinda Injun this pissant say he is?"

"Mugwump. On his mother's side."

McCullough was genuinely puzzled. "I never heard a no Mugwumps. They must not be from around here."

"They're from Arkansas," Moon said. "They were almost wiped out a long time ago. There was a book wrote about 'em."

McCullough scratched an ear the size and texture of a worm-eaten cabbage leaf. "Book?"

"Sure," Moon said with feigned pity for the untutored town cop. *"The Last of the Mugwumps."*

"Oh yeah . . . I think I saw the movie." McCullough turned away slowly. "Well, if they're both Injuns, I guess they're all yours, Charlie." His rolling gait took him out the door.

Horace Flye allowed himself a grateful sigh of relief.

Tillie showed up at Moon's side with a grease-stained plastic tray. "Charlie, honey, I got your burger and your fries. And coffee. Been holdin' it for you, whilst you been doin' your poleece work."

He sniffed appreciatively. "The coffee still hot?"

"Should be." She stuck her grubby thumb into the cup, and waited for the thermometric information to reach her brain. "Well, it's warm. I could stick it in the microwave."

"Well, I'd sure like to . . . but I need to get my prisoners over to the clinic. One's got trauma to the ear, the other needs his eyeball popped back into the socket."

Horace rubbed his bleeding ear.

Curtis Tavishuts blinked the bulging eye, which ached like an abscessed tooth.

Tillie shrugged her massive shoulders. "Oh well, I guess I'll just eat it myself." She took a huge bite from the burger.

Moon's mouth watered. His stomach was past growling.

It was late afternoon when Charlie Moon locked the prisoners into adjacent cells. Horace Flye's ear was now cleaned, stitched, and bandaged. The young physician, after a glance at Tavishuts' yellowed teeth, had also given Flye a tetanus shot. Curtis Tavishuts' eye had been inserted back into its socket by a consulting ophthalmologist and pronounced sound enough, though it was watery and extremely bloodshot. And did not look in precisely the same direction as the sound eye.

Tavishuts glowered through the bars at the white man with his good eye. "Goat-faced hillbilly cheat—I bet you married your sister!"

Flye, holding his palm over the bandaged ear, leaned forward on his bunk and returned the one-eyed glare double measure. "Blanket-assed Injun, go stick a feather in it!" The white prisoner had—if only for the moment—forgotten his Native American heritage.

The Ute prisoner raised his heavy crutch like a club. "Soon's I get a chance, fuzz-face, I'll knock your pea-sized brain out."

Flye sneered. "You couldn't hit your ass with a bass fiddle, you cross-eyed hoptoad!" He tapped his temple. "Better men than you has tried, and I still got my brain right here between my ears."

"Between *one* ear," the Ute prisoner shot back. Pleased with what he thought to be admirable eloquence, Tavishuts licked his lips. "That ear I chewed on woulda tasted better with some ketchup."

Flye raised his right hand, which was not missing the offending finger. "Bite *this*, you one-legged cannybubble."

Tavishuts muttered a vulgar curse in the Ute tongue. It had something to do with Flye's ancestors and domesticated animals.

Charlie Moon—weak from hunger and drained of his last ounce of patience—gave them a steely-eyed glare. He did not raise his voice, but it had an edge like a straight razor. "Be quiet."

The prisoners fell silent, but continued to exchange poisonous looks.

Moon proceeded to list the rules. Keep quiet. Do as you are told. Otherwise . . . well, you don't want to know about "otherwise." Though a sullen pair, they seemed to hear him.

Flye, in fact, listened politely.

Tavishuts figured it was mostly bluff. But he had a grudging respect for the big policeman. It was said that one pop on the chin from Moon's fist and a man would forget his name and address for a month or more.

The Ute policeman congratulated himself for handling a bad situation fairly well. He'd hold them for twenty-four hours while his "investigation" of the brawl was completed. Tillie, of course, wouldn't file any charges—she had been grateful for the entertainment value of the brawl. What these fellows needed was a good night's sleep. If they behaved at breakfast, he'd turn them loose tomorrow morning. But now, he was headed for Angel's Cafe and an early supper. Chicken-fried steak. Home-fried potatoes. Lots of brown gravy. He was leaving the cell block when he heard Flye's urgent call.

"Hey there . . . waitaminute . . . Ossifer Moon!"

He turned wearily. "Yeah?"

"I just thoughta somethin'."

"What?"

"Well, what with all the excitement, I'd plumb forgot. I'd appreciate it if you could bring my pickup and trailer over here. And park my rig right outside. And you gotta be careful how you handle that old truck. She's got a manual choke—pull it out just about a inch and a quarter, then pump the gas pedal three times before you try to start 'er up. And when you get the rig over here, don't set the hand-brake on the pickup. Sometimes the shoes stick and I gotta crawl underneath and bang on the brake calipers with a ball-peen hammer before I can get the wheels to roll."

"Half-assed hillbilly truck," Curtis Tavishuts muttered with a sneer. "You ought to get yourself a team o' Arkansas mules to pull it."

Moon silenced the Ute prisoner with a glance. "We're kind of shorthanded, Mr. Flye. When we can get around to it I'll send somebody over and . . ."

Horace was on his feet now, his brow furrowed into a field of wrinkles. His hands were white-knuckled on the door-bars. "You cain't wait that long. She might get cold or hungry or somethin'."

"Who?"

"Why, my daughter. She's in the trailer."

So this fuzzy-faced con artist had a daughter. And she'd

kept herself holed up in the camper while her father was carted off to jail. *If blood tells, she'll be every bit as wacky as her old man.* "Well, I'll take your pickup keys to her. Then she can drive your rig wherever she wants." Maybe all the way back to Arkansas.

"Oh no." Horace Flye shook his head. "She couldn't do that. She's a good cook and housekeeper and such, but I ain't taught her how to drive the truck."

"What's your daughter's name?"

"Butter," Horace Flye said proudly.

Moon was not surprised. It had been that kind of day. Horsefly begat Butterfly. The last—one might hope—of the ill-fated Mugwumps.

Moon was pleased to see Officer Elena Chavez filling out her daily log. He paused by her side and waited.

She signed the log, looked up, and smiled.

Elena had long, black hair. And very pretty eyes set in an oval face—which was also pretty. Moon, temporarily distracted, gathered his thoughts, cleared his throat. "You busy, Officer Chavez?"

"Not if you *need* me, Charlie."

Her eyes seemed to grow into big pools that a man could fall into. Unconsciously, Moon backed away a half-step. "I got to go see a young woman in a camp-trailer. I could use some help."

This piqued her interest. "Oh. You going to make an arrest?"

Moon grinned. "Don't plan on it. But somebody'll need to drive the rig over here. So she can visit her father."

She zipped her leather jacket and made a mock salute. "Let's ride."

They were nearing Tillie's Navajo Bar and Grille. The home of unforgettable cheeseburgers. And fries made with real lard. Moon sighed.

Officer Elena Chavez loosened her seat belt. She scooted across the Blazer seat. An inch closer to the tall man. "Bad day, Charlie?"

He grinned weakly at his fellow officer. "You ever hear of a tribe called the Mugwumps?" Elena was attending the university every other semester, working on her law degree. And she was very proud of her recently acquired knowledge. Liked to show off a bit, in fact.

A thoughtful frown furrowed her brow. "Mugwumps. Hmmm. I think that's what they called Republicans who wouldn't support James Blaine for president."

"Blaine? Never heard of him. Was he from Arkansas?"

"I don't think so." She looked suspiciously at Moon's profile. It was hard to tell when the man was teasing her. "But it all happened a long time ago. Back around 1884."

"But you never heard anything about the Mugwump Indian tribe?"

She shook her head.

"Well, I guess they can't teach you *everything* at the university."

Moon—flanked by Officer Elena Chavez—approached the camp-trailer. He glanced at the Arkansas license plate. The small trailer, like the rusting Dodge pickup truck, had seen better days. Someone—Horace Flye, he assumed—had used duct tape to seal joints along the edges of the gray metal structure. He tapped lightly on the aluminum door. There was no response. So maybe Miss Butter Flye had fluttered off somewhere. Probably inside Tillie's joint, having a burger and a beer.

He tapped on the door again. "Miss Flye . . . are you there? This is Officers Moon and Chavez, of the Southern Ute Police Department. Your father is in custody and . . ."

A face appeared in the square window in the door. A small, roundish face. With stringy yellow hair unaccustomed to a comb, watery blue eyes, and pumpkin-colored freckles. The chubby face pressed itself against the glass. The little nose flattened into an ugly white splotch.

Moon shook his head in astonishment. This was a child. Five years old, maybe. Six tops. They'd have to coax her outside and into the squad car. Then turn her over to a county Social Services representative. He took off his hat and smiled. In what he hoped was a fatherly fashion. "Miss . . . ah . . . could we have a word with you?"

No response.

Elena cooed: "Oh, Charlie—she's just *adorable.*"

There was no accounting for taste. Moon cleared his throat. "I guess you're . . . uh . . . Butter." This grubby little Flye was still in the larval stage.

The cold blue eyes stared up at him.

"Your father sent us over here. So we can take you to see him."

The child's face was deadpan.

Moon tried again. "Would you like to put your coat on and go with us and . . ."

She shook her head.

"Well," he said gently, "your father is real lonesome without you."

The child glared at him. Without blinking.

He turned the doorknob. Locked. He tried all the keys he'd taken from Flye. No luck. The kid had the door latched from the inside.

"Butter," he said gently, "you'll have to unlock the door."

She shook her head again, rubbing her flattened nose along the glass.

A gust of wind, tasting of ice, whipped across the graveled parking lot. A few curious patrons were gathering at the window of Tillie's Navajo Bar and Grille to enjoy this diversion from late afternoon TV. Moon buttoned his jacket. "You see, Butter, it's going to be real cold tonight. You can't stay out here . . ."

With a pudgy hand, she cranked the window open a notch. The little mouth actually spoke. "It's warm *in here*. You're the ones who'll get cold." This said, she laughed in his face.

The policeman—accustomed to dealing with coldhearted felons—realized that some measure of firmness was called for. "Now look, young lady—if you don't open the door, I'll have to force the lock and . . ."

"Wuff!" she snapped.

Moon blinked at his fellow officer. "The kid's barking at me."

To clarify her intent, the child snarled: "You're the Big Bad Wuff."

Moon was mystified. "Big bad what?"

Elena laughed, and the sound was like little bells in his ear. "Honestly, Charlie—you don't know the first thing about dealing with children. The Big Bad Wolf was the heavy in that Three Little Pigs story. Anyway," she said in her lawyer's voice, "you can't break into the camper without a valid warrant. It is—for legal purposes—a private domicile."

"Wolf, huh?" Moon looked down his nose at the little girl's face.

"Big *Bad* Wuff," the child hissed.

A half dozen of Tillie's customers had meandered outside, the better to see and hear what was going on. A merry old drunk waved a long-necked beer bottle and yelled at the Ute policeman: "Don't take no shit off'n that kid, Charlie. Shoot 'er through the winder." He aimed his trembling forefinger at the trailer. Cocked his thumb. Pulled the trigger. "Ka-bam!" His hand jerked backward from the imaginary recoil.

Moon gave this unwelcome advisor a flinty look.

The drunk belched and addressed his words to a sour-looking truck driver. "Cops ever'where 'er all alike. No sensa yoomor."

A truck driver—who had a blue swastika tattooed on his forearm—nodded his agreement in a low growl: "Damn gestapo."

"Charlie," Elena murmured soothingly, "you'd better let me handle this." The man simply did not have a way with children.

Moon stepped aside and made a sweeping gesture with his gloved hand. "Officer Chavez, you are in charge."

She patted his arm in a gesture of consolation. "Let a pro show you how it's done, big man." Elena smiled sweetly at the little face in the window. "Hi there, honey. See, we're here to *help* you. Your daddy is in ja— . . . well, he can't come to you—so you need to go see him. Daddy misses his little Butterpat real bad—and he's so *worried* about you being out here all by yourself."

The pudgy little face had a slit of a mouth. An ugly red tongue stuck out of the slit. "You," the child said, pointing her grubby finger accusingly, "are the Wicked Witch."

Elena gasped.

Moon grinned.

"Wicked Witch," the child screamed, "Wicked Witch. Help, help . . . the Big Bad Wuff and the Wicked Witch are tryin' to get me! Eeeeeeeeeeee!"

The tattooed trucker, determined to involve himself in the commotion, left the cluster of comrades huddled in front of Tillie's Navajo Bar and Grille. Not at all intimidated by Charlie Moon—and disdainful of addressing a police *woman*—he swaggered up and confronted the gigantic Ute. "Hey, whatcha doin', pickin' on a little kid? You got nothin' better to do? Why doncha go somewheres an' arrest a real crim'nal or somethin'?"

Charlie Moon had met such troublemakers a hundred times—filled with righteous indignation and spoiling for a fight. When they regained consciousness, they were always tearfully contrite. Couldn't apologize enough for their rude behavior, blamed it on demon rum. When released, they headed for the nearest tavern. Moon—who was not in the mood to lower the boom—was the soul of politeness. "Oh, you've got me wrong, sir. See, *I'm* not in charge here. I am the Big Bad Wolf."

The trucker blinked. *What'n hell is this cop talkin' about?*

Moon nodded toward Elena. "You will want to address your complaint to my sidekick . . . the Wicked Witch."

Elena shot Moon a venomous look, then gave her full attention to the bewildered intruder. He was wearing a blue cap. On the cap were the words KEEP ON TRUCKIN'. She pointed at the long flatbed hooked to the Peterbilt cab. "That your load of hay?"

He nodded sullenly.

"Then haul it away, buster!"

His voice was annoyingly nasal. "Lissen, you cain't talk like that to me, I got a right to be here . . ."

"One," she said.

"You Injun Smokeys don't scare me none . . ."

"Two."

"I ain't gonna be pushed around. Not by no Judy cop."

"Good for you," Moon said. This would be fun.

"Three," Elena said with an air of finality. The policewoman pulled a cigarette lighter from her jacket pocket, then headed with a purposeful stride toward the Peterbilt.

The trucker looked uncertainly at the tall policeman. "What'n hell's she gonna . . ."

Moon took his hat off, scratched his head thoughtfully. "With Elena, it's hard to say."

"She's bluffin'," the trucker said without conviction.

"Like to place a bet?" Moon said.

"Bet?"

The Ute policeman produced his wallet. "Five'll get you ten she's gonna set your hay on fire."

The truck driver stood for a moment, frozen in stupefied disbelief. He watched the young woman flick the lighter to life . . . and touch the flame to the bristly corner of a bale of alfalfa. "Omigod," he screamed to his backup driver, "Archie, help me stop 'er!" and sprinted toward the truck as fast as his wobbly legs would carry him, slipping and sliding on the gravel. His partner, who had been enjoying this small drama from the relative safety among the motley congregation of Tillie's customers, also scooted off toward the Peterbilt.

The Southern Ute police officers watched the truck depart with a great clashing of gears.

Butter Flye, who had watched the spectacle with some relish, was clapping her tiny hands. When she grew up she wanted to be just like the Wicked Witch.

Moon glanced at Elena, who was grinding her teeth. "You want to drive Mr. Flye's rig back to the station?"

Elena accepted Horace Flye's pickup keys from her fellow officer. Somebody had to convey the trailer containing this hideous child to SUPD headquarters. From there on, the nasty little imp was Charlie Moon's problem. She tried—without success—to start Flye's old pickup truck.

Moon reached over her legs and pulled the choke out. One

and a quarter inches. "It's flooded. Count to fourteen," he said, "then pump the accelerator three times."

She counted to fourteen. Pumped the accelerator three times. Turned the ignition key. The old engine coughed and sputtered. And started. Officer Chavez gave Moon a suspicious look. "How'd you know that?"

Moon patted the rusting hood. "Well, this old baby is a 1973 Dodge. With a four-barrel carburetor. Dodge pickups with four-barrel and manual chokes was kinda touchy that year. But only the ones made for the first five months or so. Then Chrysler changed to Holly carbs."

"Fascinating," she said. *Ultra-boring guy stuff.*

Moon—who had invented the explanation—shrugged modestly. "One other thing—when you get to the station, don't set the parking brake."

Boy, what a nag. "Why not?"

" 'Cause if you do, the shoes'll stick. Then you'll have to crawl underneath and bang on the calipers with a ball-peen hammer. It's a dirty job."

"Oh—yeah. The calipers." Elena did not know what shoes or calipers had to do with brakes. *Maybe Charlie Moon is putting me on . . .*

"You know," he said with open admiration, "that was a pretty convincing show you put on for those truckers."

She frowned at the pitted windshield. "You think so?"

"Sure. You almost had *me* convinced you was gonna set that hay on fire."

"I was," Elena snapped. "It was too wet." She turned to smile prettily at him, then let out the clutch and gunned the engine.

Moon stood in a wake of gritty dust, watching the rear end of the trailer bounce across the graveled parking lot. *Well now. There's more to this woman than a man might have expected.*

Now that the Flyes' battered little craft was safely at anchor in the SUPD parking lot, Charlie Moon was wondering what to do about Butter Flye. It was a tricky problem. The little girl needed looking after, but she wouldn't open the trailer door for anyone but her father. He had choices to make. Like breaking the door and turning the kid over to Social Services. Or he could quietly kick Mr. Flye loose and let him deal with his daughter. That'd work as long as Roy Severo didn't catch wind of it. The chief of police was a stickler for doing things by the book. If he found out Flye wasn't an Indian, Severo would turn the Arkansas man over to the town police in the blink of an eye. Then Buffalo Bill McCullough would have to deal with Butter Flye. Moon smiled to himself. That solution did have a certain appeal. The Ute policeman was helping himself to a cup from the dented SUPD coffeepot when he felt someone staring at his back. He spooned in a half dozen cubes of sugar, then glanced over his shoulder. An accusing expression smoldered in Roy Severo's hard black eyes.

Moon grinned and raised his cup in salute. "H'lo, boss."

The chief of the Southern Ute Police Department said nothing; he nodded toward his office door. Moon followed the little tiger into his den. Severo fitted his compact frame into a padded chair behind his desk and glared at Officer Moon. He did not offer his subordinate a seat.

Moon put his dripping coffee cup on the corner of Severo's immaculate desk, earning himself a scowl from the chief. He sprawled in a hard wooden chair, stretched his long legs, and clasped his hands across his silver belt buckle. He looked innocently around the office, taking in a wall filled with framed photographs of Severo with various politicians and minor celebrities. There was a display board of shooting-match medals. And last year's calendar. He waited for the chief to break the silence.

Severo's glare hardened. "What'n hell you think you're doin', Charlie?"

Moon frowned in pretended bewilderment. "Could you clarify the question?"

The chief of police slammed his fist against the oak desk, jarring a splash of coffee from Moon's cup. "You know damn well what I mean. What're you doin' keepin' a *matukach* in our jail? Or don't you remember that we turn anybody what ain't a Native American over to the town police or the state cops?"

"I assume," Moon said evenly, "that you refer to prisoner Horace Flye."

"You assume right," Severo said through clenched jaws. "That one belongs to Bill McCullough."

The temptation to drop the Flyes in McCullough's soup was a strong one. But the urge to have some fun with the chief proved irresistible. And like so many decisions, drastically altered the future for many souls. "He claims to be Native American."

Severo popped up from his chair like a toy man on a coiled spring. "What? That hairy-faced blue-eyed bastard claims to be . . . one of *us?*" It wasn't all that surprising. Ninety percent of the population claimed to have an Indian great-grandparent.

Moon retrieved his coffee cup and took a sip. "He does. On his mother's side. And it is my understanding that a citizen's claim to Native American ancestry must be accepted as valid unless and until the higher-ups decide otherwise. To turn him over to the non-Indian authorities would be against tribal policy. And," he added slyly, "politically unwise."

Roy Severo sagged into his padded chair with the resignation of a beaten man. "What tribe?"

Moon hesitated. The chief of police, though somewhat gullible, was a long way from being a fool. But it was fun to pull the blanket over his head. "Mr. Flye's ancestors were the remnants of a small group of southern Arkansas mound-builders. The scholarly types know all about 'em—but I doubt *you'd* have ever heard of these people. They're . . ." Moon swallowed hard, ". . . the Mugwumps."

"Oh sure." Severo was stung by Moon's low opinion of his knowledge. "The Arkansas Mugwumps. I met one of 'em when I was in the Marines. A fine bunch of folks. Measles or somethin' almost wiped 'em out, if I remember correctly." Feeling somewhat smug now, he leaned back and put his hands behind his neck. "So what's the charge?"

"Well, I haven't officially filed a charge yet. Mr. Flye got in a fight with Curtis Tavishuts over at Tillie's and . . ."

Severo pointed a finger at Moon. "Lissen to me, Charlie. Curtis Tavishuts ain't nothin but a one-legged mean-assed loudmouthed low-down drunk and a troublemaker to boot who ain't worth his weight in horse manure." This overlong declaration completed, he gasped for breath. "You can hold Curtis for a day or so till he sobers up, but I want that poor ol' Mugwump out of this jail tonight. You hear?"

Moon frowned, as if bridling at the order. "You're the boss." Without waiting to be dismissed, he got up and left the police chief's office.

Roy Severo felt he'd handled the situation pretty damned well.

So did Moon.

Horace Flye was greatly displeased. Here he was in jail, his ear practically chewed off by a drunk who probably had more germs in his mouth than a hydrophobic hound dog. And for what? Just for trying to make an honest dollar. Well, twenty honest dollars. Furthermore, he was highly annoyed at the one-legged Indian in the next cell, who didn't seem to mind being in the jug. The man was sleeping peacefully.

Flye could not rest. For one thing, he had many troubles to ponder. For another, he had drunk seven cups of the establishment's complimentary coffee. It was not a brew meant for those with nervous constitutions. And Flye was a naturally jittery fellow.

He picked up a tattered newspaper off the floor. It was last week's *Southern Ute Drum.* Idly, he began to thumb through the pages. Mostly it was news about the tribe that did not interest him. A front-page story about a water-rights battle. Articles on self-improvement that he certainly did not need to read. Advertisements promoting restaurants and pawnshops and churches. But on page three, he saw something that caught his interest.

EXCAVATION ON MCFAIN LAND

Local rancher Nathan McFain, who has holdings on the eastern boundary of the S.U. reservation, reports finding a large animal bone in his pasture. Mr. McFain has called in Professor Moses Silver and his daughter Dr.

> Delia Silver, experts from Rocky Mountain Polytechnic University. The Silvers are supervising the excavation of the site, believed to contain the fossil bones of an extinct animal, probably a mammoth. This father-daughter team has published several books and a number of scholarly articles on the ice-age animals that once roamed the American West . . .

And the article went on, describing the rancher's temporary plans to cover the excavation site with a large tent. A permanent structure would be erected when the excavation was completed. The scientists would be staying in log cabins on the McFain Dude Ranch. There were two photographs. One of Nathan McFain, pointing triumphantly at sections of bone protruding from the sand.

Horace Flye squinted; looked like Godzilla's ribs.

The second photograph showed the paleontologist from Granite Creek—an aged man with thick spectacles, his arm around a young woman dressed in a plaid shirt and faded jeans. Dr. Delia Silver was an archaeologist. She was smiling, Horace Flye thought, *just like she's looking right outta the picture at me.* He stared at the image of the young woman for some time. Kinda skinny. But still . . . a pretty thing. Delia. Now that was a sweet, old-fashioned name.

Moon stood before the cells, studying a sheaf of papers fastened to a clipboard.

Curtis Tavishuts—perhaps not wishing to be extravagant with his remaining sound eye—did not bother to look up. Also, he was asleep.

Horace Flye—holding the bandage against his chewed ear—eased his aching body off the bunk with a groan. He leaned on the cage door. The Arkansas man had a sly look on his face. "So, did my little Butter give you any trouble?"

"Trouble?" Moon said, with an expression of innocent bewilderment.

"Oh, I just thought that maybe she might've . . . well, you know—kinda gotten sassy with you. She can do that sometimes." *Like when she's awake.*

"No trouble," the Ute policeman said. "She's a little sweetheart."

Flye seemed oddly disappointed. "You sure you got the right trailer?"

"I'm surprised you'd go in a bar and leave such a small child alone. She's kinda young to be taking care of herself."

Horace Flye snorted. "Butter's pretty growed-up for her age. She keeps the trailer clean. She can even cook some, like eggs and pancakes. And she's smart as a whip."

Moon was writing on the clipboard. "Well, that's good. I expect she'll do real well in a foster home."

"What? Foster home? Now waitaminute . . ."

"Oh, I wouldn't worry. It probably won't be more than six or eight weeks till your case comes up."

"You cain't hold me that long . . . not without a charge."

"You evidently don't realize," Moon said, "that the Southern Utes are a sovereign nation. We have our own way of doing things. Like administration of tribal justice," he added darkly.

"But I got a right to call a lawyer and . . ."

"Not here, you don't. We do things the Indian way. Bein' a Mugwump and all," the Ute policeman added in a tone of mild admonishment, "you should know that."

"Well, sure I do . . . but . . . I just cain't afford to stay here that long."

"Don't look like you've got much choice."

"Please . . . there must be somethin' you can do for me."

There was a long pause before Moon muttered under his breath. "Of course, there is paragraph 117-B."

Flye grabbed the bars. "What'd you say?"

"Theoretically, under 117-B, I could arrange for your probationary release. And if you were cut loose it wouldn't be necessary to place your daughter into foster care. But I doubt you'd be interested . . . paragraph 117-B has some tough conditions." He turned to walk away.

Horace felt his pulse racing. "What conditions?" he screeched.

"It's not all that easy." Moon turned to give the prisoner a thoughtful look. "You'd have to find steady work within seven days. And see that the child was properly taken care of."

"I'll do it. I can get a job anytime I want, just like that." He snapped his fingers.

"Well," Moon said doubtfully, "117-B does say I could let you go on probation. But if you don't keep the terms of your parole . . ." He shook his head, as if the consequences were too grim to contemplate.

Flye swallowed; his prominent Adam's apple bobbled. "Like you was sayin'—if I messed up whilst I was out on parole—not that I would, o' course—but if I did, then what?"

The Ute policeman fixed the prisoner with a pitiless gaze. "You break parole under 117-B, we turn your file over to the FBI. Those suits really like to work child-neglect cases that occur on Indian reservations."

"What . . . but I don't neglect little Butter . . . and I thought you said you Utes had your own laws and whatnot . . . so why'd the FBI be interested in me and my child?"

"We got a contract with the Feds. Petty crimes we don't want to deal with, we turn over to them. We pay 'em five hundred dollars a whack—but they only get paid if they win the case and put the criminal in the federal jug. So they have what you'd call . . . motivation. And what with all them Justice Department lawyers just aching to get their teeth in guys like you, they don't lose one case in a hundred."

On this particular day, the thought of teeth in his flesh—though merely a figure of speech—was exceedingly unpleasant. "Okay." Horace rubbed at the bandage over his chewed ear. "Let's go for that B-17 whatchamacallit. I'll do whatever you say."

Moon unlocked the cell door.

Flye waved the folded copy of the *Southern Ute Drum.* "All right if I take this with me?"

"Sure. The tribal newspaper is complimentary. Part of our service."

He gave Flye the clipboard and a ballpoint pen. "This is the binding agreement that defines the terms of your probationary release. Sign here—on the bottom."

The prisoner stared. "But there's nothin' wrote down on it. It's just . . . just a blank piece a paper!"

"No problem," Moon said amiably. "I'll fill it in later."

Horace Flye, holding his coat collar against the chill wind, tapped on the trailer door. "Butter, honey, it's Daddy. Let me in."

Like a misplaced peg, her round face appeared in the square window. "Is the Big Bad Wuff gone . . . an' the Wicked Witch?"

Butter never made no sense. Just like her mamma. Must be somethin' in the blood. "Sure, honey. Now open the door. Daddy's gettin' mighty cold."

The little face frowned at the blood-soaked bandage on his ear. "How do I know you're really my daddy? You could be the Booger-man, dressed up to *look* like my daddy." Her face disappeared from the window.

"Butter!" He banged his fist on the flimsy metal structure. "You open this door right now, you hear? Or I swear I'll take a switch to you an'—"

"Go 'way, Booger-man!" She turned the TV up loud enough to make the trailer walls vibrate.

It was the proverbial last straw. Horace Flye muttered a curse, then sat down on the retractable trailer step. All in all, it had not been a good day. *I got maybe thirty dollars and change in my pockets. Tried to raise a little extra cash, what did it get me? A rasslin' match with a sore loser. It was shameful, too—barely holding my own against a one-legged man with yaller teeth sharp as a possum's who damn near chewed my ear off. Then gettin' hauled off to an Injun jail. Don't even have a wife to come home to no more. And now my own kid won't let me into the trailer. It's sure pure hell raisin' up a young 'un these days. And now the freezin' wind's a-blowin' sand into my face.*

A man can only take so much. Even an Arkansas man who's tough as an old boot. Salty tears made crooked tracks down the channels of his leathery cheeks; his thin body heaved with doleful sobs.

Presently, she turned the TV off. The door opened. The

lower corner gouged him sharply in the ribs. A small head poked out. "I'm sorry, Daddy. But you always tell me to be careful who I open the door for."

Horace Flye was in no mood to be consoled. He turned his head and glared hatefully at the child.

Butter tugged playfully at his ear bandage. "You look funny with only one earmuff." She snickered.

"Damn smart-assed kid," he muttered, and got to his feet. *Shoulda had one of them vasextomee operations years ago.*

GETTING A JOB OF WORK

Fort Lewis College Library, Durango

THE ENGRAVED PLATE on the desk said: RESEARCH LIBRARIAN—MS. PAMELA DRAKE.

Not quite sure how to proceed, Horace Flye waited patiently for the woman to acknowledge his presence.

Finally, she did. The librarian looked up to see a thin man with a bushy beard. And a bandaged ear. He was turning a battered felt hat in his hand. Not a bad-looking man, but he was dressed like a bum. But bums usually didn't come to the desk. They generally used the rest room, then found a quiet corner and snoozed until the library closed. She forced a professional smile. "Yes sir. May I help you?"

He nodded. "Yes ma'am. I need to read up on some things."

Well, he was polite enough. "Such as?"

He looked over her head. Out the mullioned window. Where the pickup and trailer were parked. "Well, mostly about them great big hairy elephants. Mammoths and such."

"Certainly, sir. I can direct you to the section on Pleistocene mammals and . . ."

"And I wondered—you got any books written by this fella—or his daughter?" He unfolded a small section that had been carefully scissored from a newspaper.

The librarian's eyes brightened as she saw the photograph. "Ah. Professor Moses Silver. And his daughter Delia. I know them well—very nice people."

"Are they, now? And you know 'em personal?" He figured it wouldn't take much to get this one talking. And it didn't. Ms. Drake proceeded to tell him all about the Silvers. How the daughter had been married, had a miscarriage. And how her husband had been such a beast—Delia had divorced him last year. How the young archaeologist was an internationally recognized expert in stone-age toolmaking. Such a sweet girl—she was taking care of her aging father whose vision and memory were failing . . . and so on.

Horace Flye was storing all this information away. But she had forgotten his question, so he prodded her gently. "According to the newspaper, they wrote some books."

She tapped the keys on her computer terminal. "We do have a book by Dr. Moses Silver—*Pleistocene Hunters of North America*. And there are several journal articles authored by both the professor and his daughter, who is—as I said—quite a noted scientist in her own right." A small frown furrowed her brow. "In fact, now that I recall, we have a book by his daughter on our reference shelf—it's about how prehistoric people made flint implements, and where they got their materials from. Several beautiful color plates."

He nodded eagerly. "I'd be right pleased to have a look at all of 'em."

Though the answer seemed obvious, she asked the question. "Do you have a library card?"

He shook his head.

"I'll issue you a card if you wish to check out Moses' book. Delia's book and the journal articles can't be removed from the library, but you can read them here." The librarian pointed to the copy room. "If you wish, you can make copies of articles on our coin-machine. It's ten cents a page. Be sure and read the copyright notice."

"Yes, ma'am. Thank you kindly." Ten cents a page was pretty steep. He had a more cost-effective idea.

Horace Flye spent much of the morning in the library. It was downright painful. Reading deadly dry journal articles authored by the Silvers and others of the same ilk written by their colleagues. He was pleased to find an obituary of a famous paleontologist—Dr. Oscar Humboldt—who had spent his life excavating the fossilized bones of mammoths, mastodons, giant ground sloths, saber-toothed tigers, and three-toed horses. Horace used his pocketknife to cut out the obituary and a few articles that seemed relevant to the elephant bones the McFain fellow had found in his pasture. Though Horace Flye was unfamiliar with the tongue-twisting jargons of anthropology, paleontology, and archaeology, much could be understood by context. And—he had learned from long experience—just rolling them big words around in your mouth now and again went a long way toward giving folks the impression that you knew a lot more than you actually did.

•—

Horace Flye steered carefully along the gravel road, watching the trailer in the large mirror mounted on the pickup door. He lifted his foot from the accelerator pedal and shifted down to second gear. There it was. The entrance had a big pine-log structure arching over it, high enough to drive a big truck loaded with hay underneath. A large sign hung upon the structure. The letters were expertly burnt into pine planks.

McFain Dude Ranch

Butter, who had been dozing on the seat beside him, stood up and leaned against her father. "Daddy, where are we?"

The sleet-laden wind swept up gritty sand from the road, mixed these together, and flung them against the windshield. To Horace Flye, this rude greeting was an unsettling premonition. He had, according to his habit, ignored the child's question.

She made a tiny fist and pounded on his shoulder. "Daddy, where *are* we?"

He reached to a knob mounted under the dashboard and turned up the heat. "Feels like the North Pole to me."

"Really?" My, that was interesting. *Maybe I'll see Santy Claus!*

He pulled to the side of the road. "Darlin', you'll need to get back in the trailer now. And don't be peekin' outta the windows. Daddy's got some important business to take care of, so you play hidey-seek till I tell you it's okay."

Used to such admonitions, the child did not object.

Horace Flye was grateful for his daughter's willingness to play the game. When a man was looking for a place to stay for the winter—and a job to boot—well, it was best to keep a kid out of sight. Some people didn't like 'em too much. And come to think of it, they was a whole pile of trouble to take care of. Now that Butter's mamma was gone, what he needed was a good, strong woman. To take care of the little girl. And—he grinned wolfishly—he could do with a little takin' care of himself. Horace remembered the pretty little woman who liked to dig up bones and such, and was warmed by the memory. He'd learned aplenty about Delia Silver's personal life from that talkative old biddy in the library. Delia was a young woman who'd be on the lookout for a good man. So Horace had laid his plans. He'd trimmed his scraggly beard. Taken a bath and used up half a bar of scented soap. Pared his toenails and fingernails. Brushed his teeth with baking soda. Spit-shined his shoes. And put on his cleanest, least tattered shirt and britches.

There was a freshly washed fire-engine-red Dodge pickup parked under a nude cottonwood. Near the corral was a beat-up Jeep Wagoneer, of such age that its last brushed-on paint job was of indeterminate color. Might have once been brown. Or sickly sea-foam green. Or some clever camouflage combination. Closer to the barn was a large flatbed GMC truck, half-loaded with baled hay which gave off a wholesome, pungent odor. Horace parked his pickup-trailer rig, got out, and made sure Butter wasn't peeking from a window. She wasn't. He zipped his jacket, and turned to blink at a solid-looking ranch house. The sprawling one-story structure was constructed of resinous, hand-hewn pine logs that reminded the Arkansas man of railroad ties. The dwelling had recently been crowned with a sparkling blue Propanel roof that clashed with the venerable logs. A fine L-shaped porch looped around the south and east walls; it was provided with an assortment of handsome pine rocking chairs and massive terra-cotta pottery from Mexico. A few potted plants hung from hooks in the porch roof, but the geraniums and less identifiable specimens were wilted gray from the frosts of an early autumn. He knocked tentatively on the door. Twice. Three times. No answer. He gave it up, and wondered what to do next. Must be somebody around here somewhere.

To the north, the land rose gradually to a spiny ridge crowned with a long row of tall, gaunt pines. The trees reminded Horace of something from an old movie. War-painted Indians all lined up on the hill—ready to slaughter the paleface intruders. And he was the paleface intruder. On the gentler portion of the incline and among a sparse assembly of bushy piñon and dark green juniper, an assortment of small cabins was assembled in an unlikely suburb to the ranch headquarters. Horace ambled along a neat graveled path toward the log structures, evidently meant to house the paying guests. The cabins had names instead of numbers; these had been burned into rough pine planks with a rustler's branding iron and nailed over the doors. Horace read them and snorted with a typical tourist's derision at things meant for tourists. Black Bart. Jesse James. Wyatt Earp. Doc Holliday. O-K Corral. Dodge City. Winchester. Colt .45. At one, he stopped and shuddered. Tombstone. For gosh sakes. Who'd sleep easy with *that* plank hangin' over his head? This McFain fella didn't have much of a business sense.

There was an aged Chevy pickup parked beside Winchester. Pretty battered-looking for a tourist who could afford the likes of this place. Most likely, it belonged to somebody who worked here. Like a caretaker. A dusty green Land Rover was parked between Calamity Jane and Geronimo. Horace guessed that would be where those bone-diggin' scientists were bunked. The old goggle-eyed man and his good-looking daughter.

A form seemed to materialize behind the visitor, who didn't notice. To make his presence known, the silent man scuffed his boots.

Horace turned to see a lanky, rawboned man who'd evidently just come around Winchester's stone chimney. His sunburned face was framed in a tangle of yellow hair. A delicate, almost girlish nose was set between pale blue eyes. He was dressed in loose-fitting denim trousers, a ragged-looking gray overcoat that hung to his knees, and scuffed boots encrusted with a mixture of dried mud and manure. He gave the intruder a questioning look, but said nothing.

Horace nodded amiably. "I'm here to see Mr. McFain."

The gaunt man touched his mouth, then his ear.

"What is it," Flye asked, "you cain't talk nor hear?"

The man responded with a nod. He fished a small, spiral-bound notebook from his coat pocket. And penciled in a comment, which he displayed to the visitor.

I CANT TALK BUT I CAN READ
YOUR LIPS IF YOU TALK SLOW

"I'm here on business," Flye said loudly. "You McFain's top hand?"

The deaf man grinned crookedly, exposing an irregular row of yellowed teeth. He scribbled again.

IM HIS ONLY HAND

More hurried scribbling.

NAMES JIMSON BEUGMANN

"I'm Horace Flye." The newcomer offered his hand, which was accepted. Flye indicated the ranch with a sweep of his three-fingered left hand. "Nice place Mr. McFain has here."

Jimson licked chapped lips and grinned. This one had the hungry look if he'd ever seen it. He scribbled on his pad.

BOSS KNOW YOUR COMIN

"No, he don't. But I expect he'll be glad to see me. Could you tell me where to find Mr. McFain?"

The ranch hand hesitated, then wrote on the pad.

ACROST THE PASTURE BEHIND THE BARN
THERES A BIG TENT

Jimson Beugmann nodded to indicate the general direction.

Horace smiled to show his appreciation. "Thank you kindly, sir."

Feeling the ranch hand's eyes on his back, Horace Flye stopped at the corral fence to speak with a natural affection to the half dozen horses who eyed him with uneasy equine curiosity, then turned away to nibble at a bale of alfalfa hay. There was a bulldozer parked behind the barn, next to a small dug-pond that wasn't finished yet. Two hundred yards away, beyond the pasture, Flye saw a rolling clump of woolly-looking hills, like fat sheep gathered close to share warmth. As soon as he passed by the 'dozer, he spotted the peaks of a long, camouflaged tent—U.S. Army surplus, he guessed. It was pitched within a yard of the far fence, and seemed quite out of place below the brow of a crumbling sandstone bluff. Like a circus had got stranded out here in the middle of noplace. As he trudged across the pasture, Horace made it his business to notice small things. Like the fact that the temporary shelter had been rigged for electricity. A heavy black umbilical cord snaked under the skirt of the tent. The outside end was connected to a gray breaker panel mounted on a stout new post. Another black cable arced upward from the panel to a newly set electric pole, where a cylindrical transformer hummed its monotonous dirge.

The canvas shelter had a flap for a door; he pushed this aside and made a quiet entrance.

A half dozen small electric heaters made the place tolerably comfortable, if not actually warm. Horace Flye saw three people in the long tent, which was lighted by a long string of one-hundred-watt bulbs. A tall utility lamp with three powerful floodlights stood at the edge of a rectangular excavation, where a woman was hard at work. Delia Silver—her whole attention focused on the delicate task—was using a dental pick to pry tiny clay-encrusted pebbles away from an arch of fossilized rib bone. The archaeologist was not aware that a stranger had entered the tent. Neither was her father, nor Nathan McFain. The men, sitting on opposite sides of a card table, were engaged in a tense conversation.

Horace Flye—aware that he had not yet been noticed—thought it best to stand by quietly. And watch. And listen. Maybe learn something useful.

The aging paleontologist was sitting at a folding card table across from the rancher, gesticulating with his liver-spotted hands, attempting to explain the facts of life. First, that Mr. McFain shouldn't make any big plans about a permanent display. True, there was a skull, at least one tusk, and a few ribs—but there might not be much more. You could never tell what you'd find—not until the excavation was completed. Because Mr. McFain intended to retain possession of the fossil specimens, the university museum would not provide any funds for the excavation. And there was a very considerable amount of work to do. Mr. McFain would have to hire some workers. And not just any workers, mind you, but skilled technicians—people with experience in paleontological or archeological excavations. The best approach, Moses pointed out, was to bring in a half dozen graduate students from the Department of Anthropology and Archaeology at Rocky Mountain Polytechnic. He could personally recommend several promising candidates. The students would, of course, expect modest stipends. And the rancher must provide them with food and shelter. Furthermore, the university would expect some level of insurance coverage from Mr. McFain. In case of an accident resulting from injury on the job. A portable toilet must be placed near the excavation, and safety was a prime consideration. OSHA rules, and all that.

The rancher was shaking his head in disbelief. How much would all this cost?

Oh, one couldn't say with any certainty. Altogether, probably no more than a hundred thousand. Per year, of course. And the excavation might take three or four years to complete. Depended upon a number of as yet unknown factors.

Nathan McFain—whose pulse was throbbing dangerously in his temples—glared at the scientist through bloodshot eyes and had his say. He was not a wealthy man, not by any means. And even if he was, he damn sure wouldn't want a bunch of college kids living at his ranch. They'd be partying late at night, making all kinds of noise. He had assumed that the Silvers—the daughter was young and strong enough—would be able to handle the excavation by themselves. What was the big deal, moving a few yards of rock and dirt?

Moses Silver—the very picture of a scholar wearied by a fruitless attempt to communicate with a complete nincompoop—leaned back and rolled his eyes in utter dismay.

The practiced gesture had its intended effect on the rancher.

Nathan McFain was a practical man of business, who knew when compromise was called for. "Okay, okay," he said with an air of one defeated, "I'll hire one hand for you. That's it. Just one. And I'll pay minimum wage for eight hours a day. But no benefits." He slammed his palm on the card table to punctuate this final offer. Actually, his backup position was two hired hands. Or . . . if the old egghead was really stubborn, maybe three.

Moses Silver launched into an explanation of the delicacy of such an excavation. One could not just hire some untutored yokel who knew how to swing a pick and fling precious fossil fragments here and there. One must hire careful workers who had relevant experience . . .

It was at this moment that the rancher noticed the intruder. Nathan McFain, without getting to his feet, scanned the newcomer from forehead to boot. "So who're you?"

"Horace Flye's the name." The Arkansas man stepped forward and offered the rancher his hand, which was accepted somewhat grudgingly. "You're Mr. McFain."

"I already knew that," the sullen man mumbled through his tobacco-stained beard.

Flye swallowed a friendly smile. This old fella was a sure-enough hard case.

Delia Silver—pretending to be uninterested in the conversation—had barely glanced over her shoulder at the newcomer. But she pricked her ears for every word.

Flye nodded respectfully at the elderly, bespectacled man. "And I know who you are. You're Professor Moses Silver." Horace was careful to mimic the librarian's pronunciation.

The paleontologist, though mildly displeased with this interruption, was a gentleman. And pleased to be recognized. Moses got to his feet and shook Flye's outstretched hand.

"So what's your business here?" McFain snapped.

Flye darted a look at the rear side of the young woman. She'd looked fine in the newspaper picture. Looked even better in the flesh. "Well, I'm a real admirer of Professor Silver's fine work." *Not to mention his daughter.*

The old man's eyes brightened behind his thick spectacles. "Really? You have an interest then in . . ."

Flye's head bobbed in an eager nod. "Oh yes sir. I know all about them bones you dug up in Wyomin'." It had been painful, but he'd read the scholarly paper three times last night, made laborious penciled notes, and prayed his memory wouldn't fail him. "The Double-Bar-W Ranch. Three mammoths, one of 'em a young 'un. Well sir, that musta really been somethin'. Too bad none of them skeletons showed evidence of butcherin'."

"No," Moses said wistfully. "Though the bones were dated at some eleven thousand years before present. A time when humans walked upon this continent . . . and slew the mammoths. So I had hoped to uncover evidence of a human kill site." The old man sighed as one who had spent years searching for a lost love and not found her. "But it was not to be."

"All the same," Horace said, "I expect it was still a good dig." Good dig. This was an expression he'd picked up in a *New Scientist* magazine article at the library. One about a pygmy mastodon find in Egypt.

"Yes," Moses said, "it was that." He was sure he had this

fellow pegged. A passing tourist. The kind that has a passion for all things ancient. Probably has a collection of flint projectile points, sundry limestone fossils, and whitened Civil War minié balls. "And your interest in paleontology . . . is it of a professional nature?"

Horace Flye—now committed to the game—plunged ahead fearlessly. "Well, I'm kinda what you might call a professional . . . uhh . . . excavator. I've moved a lot of dirt in my time."

The old man's bushy brows raised a millimeter. "Oh. And who have you worked with?"

Horace had memorized everything in the obituary he'd read at the library. "D'you know Oscar Humboldt?"

"Well of course, Oscar was—"

It was necessary to interrupt. "Well, me and old Oscar, why, we're just like this." Flye held two fingers together to demonstrate the intimacy of their relationship. "I worked for him over in Tennessee. Where he dug up all them big masterdon bones in that road cut by the Cumberland River. Hot as blue blazes it was, but I enjoy a good day's work." To demonstrate his fitness, he flexed a small biceps under his shirtsleeve.

Moses was bemused. "So. You worked with Oscar." This fellow didn't seem the type. Oscar Humboldt, like most paleontologists, had generally used grad students in his digs. Back in the days when they were the academic equivalent of slave labor.

"Sure did. Half a dozen times. Why, I could tell you such stories . . ."

"Yes, I'm sure." Moses tilted his head and squinted at the fresh bandage on the man's ear. "You seem to have injured yourself."

Delia had quietly left her work among the fossilized bones. She was at her father's side, listening intently to the conversation. This stranger was at least ten years older than she. Uneducated, certainly. And kind of rough around the edges. But not all that bad-looking. And he was interested in her.

Horace rubbed at the bandage and grimaced. "About a week ago—up by Chilliwack Lake—that's in Canada—I had a little scuffle with a black bear. It was troublin' some little Girl Scouts in their camp."

Nathan McFain grinned at the liar with grudging admiration.

Moses Silver's eyes narrowed with suspicion.

The young woman's eyes grew large. "My goodness—you could have been killed!"

"Shucks, ma'am—it was just a *little* bear." He managed to look embarrassed. " 'Twasn't all that much."

Delia smiled sweetly at him. All men were liars, but this one was such a charming liar.

Encouraged, he held out his left hand so she could see the stub. "I lost that there middle finger in a tussle with a mountain lion. 'Twas down in New Mexico, in the Gila wilderness—four years ago last June. That cougar snuck up on me at night, when I was rolled up in my blanket. I guess it was my own fault. I shouldn't a let my campfire go out."

"Yes," she purred. "A man can't be too careful with big cats."

The effect of this attention from the young woman wafted sweetly over the unrepentant liar, much like the promise of the first warm breath of spring. Horace smiled at the daughter of the pair, but he was careful to direct his next words to her father. "I been up in Alaska and Canada for the last coupla years, doin' some gold-prospecting here and there. Didn't have much luck. Now I'm headin' back toward Arkansas. And I'm kinda lookin' for some work right now. Just to get me through the winter. If you need a top hand here to move some dirt, you just call ol' Oscar. He'll tell you I'm the very man for the job."

"I'm sorry to be the one to break the news," Moses said with downcast eyes, "but Oscar Humboldt passed away about nine months ago."

A wonderful mixture of shock and grief distorted the clean lines of Horace's face. "Old Oscar . . . he's . . . he's dead?"

Moses nodded. "Stroke. We were all shocked—it was very sudden."

Flye turned his back, and walked several paces away. He removed a grimy handkerchief from his hip pocket, and wiped at his eyes. Without turning around, he said: "Poor Old Oscar. I cain't hardly believe he's dead." He waited tensely for a response.

Didn't come.

Time to play the last card. "Well, I guess I'd best be gettin' along now."

Moses and his daughter spoke simultaneously.

"Wait a minute," he said.

"Mr. Flye . . ." she called out.

Father and daughter exchanged pleased glances. It was not the first time they had entertained the same thought.

Horace Flye bit a smile off his lips, then turned to face them.

Nathan McFain—who had been left out of the conversation—was scowling, pulling at his scraggly white beard. This Flye guy sure looked and sounded like a slicker. But he needed a job. And he had a bunged-up ear and was missing a finger . . . so maybe he'd work cheap.

Nathan McFain, who had a nervous habit of pulling at his tobacco-stained beard, walked back to the ranch headquarters with the newcomer. "I can pay you minimum wage for eight hours a day. Any overtime, well, that's between you and the eggheads. If Professor Silver wants to pay you some extra, that's between you and him."

"Well," Horace said, "I guess that might work out all right." *Hot diggity!*

McFain paused by the barn and scowled at the battered trailer hooked to Horace's old pickup. "I don't expect you'd want to winter in that. When the tourist business is slow, my hired help gets bargain rates on the cabins. Jimson Beugmann—he bunks in Winchester. It's got a fireplace and I let him gather deadwood off my property. I could put you up in one of the cabins with a gas furnace . . . O-K Corral goes for . . . say three hundred a month plus utilities. Unless you got somebody with you. Then it's an extra fifty a month per person." McFain eyed the little trailer suspiciously. "You got a wife or anything?"

Horace, avoiding the rancher's piercing gray eyes, shook his head. "No. I useta have me a woman, but I'm alone now." Butter wasn't big as a minute, so he wasn't about to pay an extra fifty bucks a month on account of her. Anyway, this fella looked like he might not be too happy to find out his new employee had a kid. "I guess, at least for a while, I'll just stay in my trailer. Maybe," he added hopefully, "I could plug my electric in somewheres . . ."

McFain, disappointed, nodded. "Yeah. I put in some RV hookups for the tourists. Electric, good well water, sunk a two-thousand-gallon septic tank. Even strung cable TV, but that's been disconnected." The unfortunate entrepreneur shook his head at the remembrance of this folly, then pointed a crooked finger to a long swayback ridge dotted with ponderosa. "They're up there amongst the pines on the east hump of Buffalo Saddle Ridge. Just take the gravel lane around behind the cabins. You can use a hookup for . . . oh, let's say a hundred a month. Long as you don't plug in no electric heaters or hot-plates or stuff like that." He frowned meaningfully at his newest employee. "I got a separate meter on the campsite so I'll know if you do."

"No need to. I got bottled gas for my heat and gas cookstove." Horace used his hand to shade his eyes from the sun, and scanned the piney ridge. It was already looking like home. *Have a mighty nice view from way up there. And privacy to boot. Butter would even be able to go outside and play now and again without being noticed by this ornery old coot.*

For a moment, the rancher forgot about his new hired hand. Nathan stared through slitted lids at the pine ridge. Off to the west—on the yonder hump of the Buffalo Saddle—was the McFain family burial plot. He didn't go out there often; maybe once a year on Memorial Day to clear out the weeds and leave some flowers. It was an awfully lonely place, where the unceasing winds whispered in the dry pines like spirits exchanging secrets. Ghosts gossiping about the living . . . those who would soon be coming to join them. The old man dismissed this dismal image. And returned his attention to the itinerant four-flusher. "So," the rancher said with a merry glint in his eye, "I guess you dug up lots of old bones in your time." Nathan McFain spat tobacco juice on a dry sprig of rabbit bush.

Horace Flye nodded wearily. "Oh yeah. Tons and tons." It

was such a well-crafted lie, he was beginning to believe it himself. "Makes me tired just thinkin' about it."

After the rancher had left with Horace Flye, the scientists attended to their peculiar business. Father and daughter were absorbed in the delicate work of exposing a long arc of mammoth rib. Moses was on his knees, a small pointed trowel in his hand. He spoke without looking at Delia, almost as if he addressed himself. "It is absurd to be conducting this work during the approach of winter."

She sighed—they'd had this conversation a half dozen times. "Then why don't you tell Mr. McFain we'll put it off till May?"

The old man pushed himself erect, and rubbed at the painful knot of muscles in the small of his back. "Because he's too eager to generate a tourist attraction. If we leave, he'll rush in here with a couple of ranch hands to attempt the excavation on his own. And make a terrible mess of it." Or, almost as bad, McFain might call in some of those Young Turks from the Denver Museum of Natural History.

Delia, who was brushing away sticky grit from a fragment of brownish fossil bone, did not respond.

But Moses Silver knew how to get a rise out of his daughter. "So what do you think of our new employee?"

She looked up from her work with the small horsehair brush. "Oh . . . you mean Mr. . . . I can't quite recall his name." It was a transparent lie.

Her father smiled indulgently. "Horace Flye, he called himself. So," he pressed, "what do you think of him?"

The young woman shrugged. "What's to think? One man's pretty much like another."

"On the contrary," Moses wagged his finger at his daughter, "and I quote: *'It is an alluring and enduring lie that all men are born equal.'* "

"And which sage made that pithy observation?" She knew, of course.

"I confess—it was my own modest self." He bowed with a farcical flourish of his hand.

She laughed. "You are such a pompous old poop. And you're politically incorrect to a fault."

He shot back the expected response. "The fault is not mine, child. 'Political correctness' is merely the intellectual McCarthyism that's currently in season."

"And a pernicious poison in the Well of Reason," she reminded him. Just to be helpful.

"That does have a nice ring to it." He brushed gritty dust off his khaki trousers. "I don't think that Arkansas scoundrel would know Oscar Humboldt from Adam's Aunt Minnie. He certainly knows nothing of paleontology. But perhaps . . ." The old man regarded his daughter's upturned face with an impish grin. "Yes, of course—he's more the archaeologist type. It's not a well-kept secret that you're a bunch of grave-robbers skulking around in academic disguise."

The young archaeologist ignored her father's oft-repeated jibe.

He persisted, "I'll wager our Mr. Flye has excavated Anasazi burials with a back-hoe."

Delia smiled at this comic figure who had sired her. "Then why did you agree to hire him?"

Moses chewed thoughtfully on his lower lip. "I do wonder myself. Hmmm. Perhaps because you're so desperate for just such a man and—"

"Daddy!" she screamed in mock anger, and hit his shin with the brush handle.

"Or," he continued, undeterred by the mild attack, "perhaps I agreed to take him on because Mr. Flye has such appalling effrontery. Imagine, daring to insult my intelligence with such a preposterous pack of lies. Anyway," he admitted on a more conciliatory note, "he does look like a man who's used to working with his hands. And," he added with a mischievous wink, "he did fight off a fierce bear to protect those poor little Girl Scouts."

"Shame on you, Daddy, for being such an old cynic."

Moses chuckled, and mimicked Flye's nasal tone. "Shucks, it was just a *little* bear, . . . 'twasn't all that much."

She rapped him again with the brush handle, though more smartly this time. "Maybe he does exaggerate just a little. But he's a nice man. And he needs work."

Moses assumed a more serious tone. "You realize, of course, that Mr. Flye must pass . . . the usual test."

"Yes," Delia said glumly, "I know." And he would flunk it for sure. *Unless he had a little help . . .*

Horace Flye and his tiny daughter were up at dawn.

The head of the family—who appreciated variety in his meals—had a very greasy cheeseburger, canned chili con carne, and a Pepsi-Cola for this morning's breakfast. Butter's first meal consisted of a steaming bowl of canned tomato soup, saltine crackers, and a half-cup of coffee liberally enriched with sugar. Horace swallowed a delicious bite, paused, then burped loudly. One good thing about being a bachelor was that a man could burp and break wind most anytime he pleased.

The six-year-old girl—who had not mastered this art—faked a small burp that sounded more like a hiccup. Then, to enhance the imitation of her father, she wiped her mouth with the back of her hand.

Horace, whose mind was on the day's work, did not notice this small flattery.

The child looked out the long, rectangular window by the small table. Below were a bunch of pretty little cabins with red roofs. And beyond these, a big house with a blue roof. And a great big barn with a fence and horses. Some of the horses were chomping at bales of hay. She could see their breath in the cold morning air. Behind the barn, there was a big bulldozer, like Daddy had drove when he helped them build the forest road in Idaho. Someone had used this one to scrape away the dirt. To make a stock pond, Daddy had told her. Beyond the barn, there was a big field with no trees. And at the far edge of that brown field was the place with the tent, where Daddy had said he had a job of work to do. From up here, the tent didn't look all that big, but Daddy had said it could hold a dozen trailers like they lived in, and then some. From up here, everything looked little. "Are we going to live here, Daddy?"

He nodded over his bowl of chili con carne. "For a while."

"Can I have some more coffee?"

"No you cain't."

"Why?"

"Because it ain't good for you."

She pouted. "Why?"

"Don't you start that. If you want somethin' else to drink, get some orange juice outta the icebox."

"It's all gone."

"Then drink some water."

She rested her chin in her hands. "I don't want no water."

He muttered an oath under his breath, then poured her a small helping of coffee from the enameled blue pot. "Now that's all, y'hear?"

"Yes, Daddy." She took a tentative sip. Soon as he went off to work, she'd wash the dishes. That was one of her chores, along with keeping the place clean. Then she'd boil some water and make herself some instant coffee. With lots and lots of sugar.

"Daddy?"

He didn't look up from his chili. "Yeah?"

"Who's them people I seen down there by the little houses?"

Butter was just like her mamma. Not satisfied till she knew everything about everybody. He recited a list of names, and this seemed to please her.

She repeated them aloud, rolling each syllable along her tongue. "Mr. Mick-Fain. Moses Sil-ver. Deel-yah Sil-ver. Them's pretty names. What was that skinny man's name?"

"Jimson Beugmann," he said. "He works for Mr. McFain. He can't talk a'tall, nor hear a word you say."

"Jim-sum Boog-mun," Butter Flye whispered. "Boog-mun . . . Boog-mun."

He wiped at his plastic chili bowl with a half-slice of white bread, then began to clear the table.

She slid off her bench seat. "Daddy—is Christmas almost here?"

He shook his head.

"You know what I want for Christmas?"

Her father showed no interest in this issue.

The child darted a look at the brown shoe box on her rumpled bed. Two rubber bands held the lid on. A sharp pencil had been used to punch a dozen holes through the cardboard lid. "I want a nice little house for Toe Jam to live in." Her father had named the creature. "He needs a house with doors and windows. And a really nice bathroom." She wrinkled her nose. "One that don't smell bad."

Horace understood that what his daughter really wanted was a house for herself. Butter didn't like the travelin' life no more than her mamma had. He piled his dishes in the sink and turned on the hot-water faucet.

She yanked at his trouser leg. "Daddeeee . . . can Toe Jam have a little house for Christmas?"

Just knee-high and already she was gettin' to be a real nag. "Well, maybe Santy Claus'll bring him one someday." He shot her a fatherly scowl. "When you've learned to mind your daddy." *That'll be the day when a bullfrog learns to play the five-string banjo and sing "Yeller Rosa Texas" all at the same time.*

Though Horace Flye had a certain animal cunning and considerable criminal cleverness, the man had learned not one lesson from his many errors. Like the *pitukupf*, Horace was who he was. But Horace was a practical, simple man. Once things were going his way, he lived each day as if matters would take care of themselves. It was with this positive attitude that he approached his work with the Silvers. And so the first few days were like fine pearls threaded on a silken strand.

On Monday, he was introduced to the site. It was laid out, he thought, like a small version of a miniature housing development. There were wooden stakes joined by strings. The stakes had numbers on them. He asked what the numbers meant. Cartesian coordinates, Moses said, as if this explained anything. But Horace was content to nod sagely at those things he did not understand. By noon, he began to move dirt removed from grids not intimately associated with the fallen mammoth. This was taken to a great pile near the mechanized sifter.

On Tuesday, he was allowed to assist Delia in the photographic work which documented every phase of the excavation. Being close to her was a delight. And he sensed that she was comfortable with him.

On Wednesday, he assisted her father in cataloging specimens. It was bewildering to Horace. These were not even bones. Mostly just little bits of soil selected from carefully recorded places in the gridwork. The old man explained that there would be pollen samples in the dirt. And all sorts of other fascinating things. But to the practical man from Arkansas it was just a lot of trash to put in bottles and label.

On Thursday morning, he was trained to use the mechanized sifter. But only under constant supervision.

On Thursday evening, as he was leaving for his trailer high on the piney spine of Buffalo Saddle Ridge, Delia followed him from the tent. Where her father would not hear their conversation. "Mr. Flye?"

He removed his battered hat. "Yes'm?"

She hugged herself. He was strong. Not bad-looking. Good-hearted. And not overly bright. He lusted after her, of course. Except for the fact that he was not wealthy, this was the description of an ideal man. "I'm having some trouble keeping warm at night."

Horace Flye tried very hard to think of a response. He could not, but it would not have mattered if he had. His throat felt like he'd tried to swallow a dried apple whole.

She watched him with some amusement. "Do you know anything about gas furnaces?"

Though he managed to swallow the apple, his voice was raspy. "Oh . . . maybe a thing 'er two."

Such a modest man. "My cabin is . . . Calamity Jane."

"Yes'm. I know." *Oh my.*

"I thought perhaps you could stop by. And have a look at my . . . heating system. That is . . . if you have time."

He felt his knees wobble. "You just say when, ma'am."

She smiled. "How about . . . this evening. Nine-ish?"

He nodded eagerly.

Horace Flye showed up when the full moon was two hours above the crest of the San Juans. And got to work right away.

He was, Delia Silver observed, good with his hands. He smelled of honest sweat and roll-your-own tobacco that he carried in a sack in his shirt pocket, but it was an agreeable aroma. And he was rather nice.

He fixed her thermostat so it'd By Gosh stay fixed. The cabin temperature went up ten degrees in as many minutes.

She was quite pleased. And aware that furnace work was not a part of his normal assignment. Moreover, Mr. Flye had worked overtime without any pay at all. No, it just wouldn't be right to send him away without some kind of reward. And as it turned out, Delia had something in mind. Something special.

"Mr. Flye?"

"Yes ma'am?"

"You've been very kind." She hesitated. "I want to return the favor."

Horace felt his pulse quicken.

She looked out the window toward her father's cabin, then pulled the shade. "But it'll have to be . . . our little secret."

He tried to speak, but his tongue stuck to the roof of his mouth. So he nodded.

On Friday, Horace was processing loose dirt through the motor-driven sifter. The noisy machine vibrated the soil through a stack of increasingly finer wire screens. All the larger rocks stayed on the top. Intermediate-sized pebbles stopped at various levels, according to size. The stuff that fell all the way through was almost like face powder. It was late in the morning when he found something very pretty on the uppermost mesh, among the rough assortment of stones.

Flye hurried to Moses Silver with his find.

The old man removed his thick trifocals, and held the specimen within six inches of his nose. "Ahhhh," he said, obviously quite pleased. It was a short projectile point, with side notches. Made of a pale reddish-white chalcedony. He slipped the spectacles back onto the bridge of his blunt nose and blinked at Horace Flye. "So . . . you found this in the sifter?" He checked his notebook. "That batch would be quadrant J-22, wouldn't it?"

Horace's head bobbed in agreement.

The paleontologist patted him on the shoulder. "Well, good

for you." He turned to place the specimen in a small plastic box.

"D'you reckon," Horace said, "that this mighta been used to kill the elephant?"

Moses shook his head. "Afraid not. This projectile point was rather far from the remains for us to assume any association with the mammoth." Now a merry twinkle glistened in the old man's eye. "Moreover, the artifact is of much too recent origin to have been associated with an ice-age mammal."

"Oh," Flye said, evidence of his disappointment spreading across his face. "I guess you can just tell by lookin'—how old one of them flint arrow points is."

"Within a thousand years or so." Moses chuckled. "But don't be discouraged . . . just keep up the good work."

Horace returned to his chores.

Delia sidled up to him and whispered. "I see you found the projectile point."

He gave the old man a furtive glance. "Yes ma'am. And I'm much obliged to you." She had showed Horace the pretty little arrowhead only last night. And told him what her father was up to. Moses would plant the artifact where his hired hand would be certain to find it. If the Arkansas man pocketed his find, he'd be marked as a thief and sacked at day's end. Horace Flye—an uncomplicated soul—was not offended that his honor would be put to the test. These folks had a perfect right to find out if a stranger they'd hired would swipe everything he could stuff in his pockets. And it wasn't like he hadn't stolen one or two necessities in his time. Well, maybe a little bit more than one or two. But most of all, he was greatly impressed with such a clever ruse. Old man Silver had a pint or two more brains that he'd given him credit for. *Maybe educated people ain't necessarily dumb. It's somethin' worth keepin' in mind . . .*

Armed with Delia's warning, he had passed the test and was now a trusted member of the excavation team. The Arkansas man rubbed thoughtfully at his whiskered chin. "Your daddy says the arrowhead's not all that old. Looks plenty old to me."

I really shouldn't tell him.

She sure had a funny little grin on her face. "So where'd you find that little flint rock?"

Delia was enjoying her part in this small conspiracy against her father. "I didn't find it. I *made* it."

His mouth fell open. "Made it? But when . . . ?"

"Yesterday evening. Right before you came over to fix my furnace."

Flye stared at her, openmouthed. "No . . . you're teasin' me."

She smiled. He was such an innocent.

And so the day proceeded toward sundown. The odd trio was happily content.

Moses Silver had his ancient bones. And nourished his secret hopes that this dig would be different from all the mediocre ones. And it would.

Delia, who was pleased with Horace Flye, busied herself with a hundred small tasks.

Flye—whose goals were simple—was pleased merely to have a job of work.

It seemed that nothing could be added to such a perfect day. But when heaven's blessings fall like the sweet rains of spring . . .

It was precisely three o'clock in the afternoon. Moses Silver was painstakingly uncovering the lower section of the great beast's pelvis. He looked up at his daughter; Delia was moving lights and reflectors about, preparing to make archival photographs. The old man's voice was tinged with enthusiasm. "I've measured the oblique height of the pelvic aperture. And the width of the illium shaft. By applying Lister's criteria on pelvic measurements, and the work of Vereschagin and Tichonov on the ratio of tusk length to basal diameter—there's no doubt about it. We have ourselves a bull mammoth. A good-sized one, too."

Delia smiled with affection. Even so far from his classroom, Daddy was an incurable academic.

Determination of gender was a boost for morale, though hardly a cause for jubilation. But as Moses worked through the afternoon, he uncovered a great knob of femur. The joint of the thigh bone was neatly articulated to the hollow acetabulum on the pelvis. So it seemed that they might have an intact skeleton.

This brought a shout of joy from the old paleontologist.

Delia hugged her father.

These were good, solid bones. A great sweeping tusk. Another still to be uncovered. Reliable gender determination.

And just perhaps—a mostly articulated skeleton.

It would hardly seem that so many favors could be granted in such a brief span of time. But the hours of this day were not yet exhausted. Nor were its great store of blessings. If blessings they were . . .

Moses, his back aching from his labors, was gently brushing the soil of ages off the upper femur.

The old man paused, holding his breath. Could this be an illusion?

His daughter had also seen it. Delia reached to adjust the flood lamp to better illuminate this discovery.

Along the surface of the bone were shallow, almost parallel incisions. "My God," the paleontologist said, "oh my God . . ."

"Daddy," she said, reaching to touch his trembling hand. All his life, this is what he had most wanted.

Horace Flye, who did not understand what all the commotion was about, kneeled beside the excavation. "Whatcha find?"

The old man looked up, shaking his head in childlike awe. "Mr. Flye . . . we have butcher marks on the bone. This is a human kill site."

Moses had grabbed the gold ring. He had a site where early humans had killed a mammoth! Not the first one to be uncovered, of course—nor probably the most important. *But mine own!*

The mammoth fossils, he realized, would be about eleven thousand years old. Give or take a thousand. It could not have been much earlier. It was a widely accepted maxim—despite scattered hints here and there of more ancient human habitation—that humans had not set foot on the North American continent until about eleven or twelve millennia ago. And the great mammoths had perished within two thousand years of that auspicious arrival of Homo sapiens. Probably from over-hunting, though that hypothesis remained controversial. And now, in the remains of a swampy pond long since dry, man had returned to find evidence of his past.

But things are often not quite as they seem.

A week earlier, Professor Moses Silver had Fed-Ex'ed several samples from the site to a private firm in Cambridge, Massachusetts. At the very moment he had found the marks on the bone, a young woman—surrounded by an array of artifacts of this highly technological society—was working in a laboratory filled with marvelous instruments. The bone fragments had been hydrolyzed to carbon dioxide, which in turn was purified and converted to benzene. Though all the numbers were already stored on a computer disk, and despite the fact that Dr. Weber was a mere thirty-three years old, she had an old-fashioned attitude about recording data. So she took the time to inscribe the information by hand in a bound laboratory notebook.

Prof. Moses Silver, McFain Ranch

Sample b-112/quadrant D-3. (Mammoth bone fragment)
Carbon-14 (apatite): 31,200 YBP +/- 400 Y

Sample fl-119/quadrant D-3. (Plant matter under Sample b-112)
Carbon-14: 31,240 YBP +/- 350 Y

Too bad, Dr. Weber thought. Moses Silver—who was such a nice old fellow—had always wanted a human kill site more than anything in the world. But this particular beast had died far too long ago for that.

Moses Silver was in his cabin, with his laptop computer connected to the single telephone line. He was scanning his day's electronic mail. Two dozen missives; much of it was departmental chaff from his colleagues at Rocky Mountain Polytechnic. Announcements of departmental meetings. A talk by the bright young archaeologist from Stanford. And near the bottom, a note from Dr. Weber. He smiled. She was an efficient young scientist. Already had the bone fragment and the plant material dated. He clicked on the line and opened the mail. And read the brief report.

He shook his head in appalled disbelief. It was one thing to have a mammoth kill site . . . there had, after all, been others. But never one whose age exceeded twelve thousand years. And Weber's analysis of the bone samples yielded an age of thirty-one thousand years. Could he be wrong about the butcher marks? No. Certainly not. He felt his head swimming.

Dr. Silver shut down the computer and unplugged the modem from the telephone line. He dialed his daughter's cabin.

Delia picked up on the second ring. "Yes?"

"It's me."

"Daddy?"

"Delia . . . something astonishing has happened." He proceeded to tell her about the dating.

There was dead silence on the line.

"Delia, are you there?"

"Yes. Daddy, there must be some mistake . . . the fossil remains simply can't be that old in a human kill site." Or maybe the "butcher marks" weren't made by early humans. Perhaps some large carnivore had gnawed on the femur. But she didn't dare raise this possibility. It would break his heart.

He was calm now. "We'll have to submit more samples, of course. And have them dated at different labs. But I know Dr. Weber. She simply does not make mistakes."

"But if it's true . . ."

"If the dates hold—and the marks are indeed butcher marks," he said soberly, "we'll be rewriting the history of early humans in the Americas." He paused to think about his next step. "Delia . . . we'll have to halt all work on the site. And bring in someone to corroborate our findings."

She tapped her fingers nervously on the telephone receiver. "If you're going to do that, you might as well bring in the strongest skeptics in the field. Someone influential."

"Yes," he said. "That's just what we'll do."

"That would be Cordell York. And Professor Newton."

"Bob Newton," he said thoughtfully, "is the best butchermark man in the business. But Cordell York is such an arrogant ass." It was galling to him that his life's profession was merely a delightful hobby to York. But there was more that he would not admit to. That the accursed amateur was a supernova . . . and himself such a minor light. Moses—who was normally a fair-minded man—preferred to believe that York's road to success had been paved with family money and influence. "And he's not really one of us, Delia. The man only *plays* at paleontology."

"That's beside the point," she said. "Cordell York is a world-class expert on ice-age kill sites."

Her father snorted. "He *thinks* he is."

"Daddy, he's very influential. If you can't convince him . . . well . . ." She heard her father's groan quite clearly, and knew what was running through his mind. Cordell York was arrogant. And opinionated. But worst of all—from her father's perspective—York was not a trained paleontologist. He was a graduate of Harvard Medical School; an eminent orthopedic surgeon. York had wormed his way into the community of paleontologists by his brilliant insights. And by generous grants to struggling investigators and several cash-pressed museums. For the past decade, Cordell York had been senior editor of a very influential scientific journal. Primarily because he was an outsider, the surgeon was not well-liked by the older generation of paleontologists. But York was respected. And feared. And that combination could be an enormous advantage to her father. But only if Bob Newton verified that the marks on the bone were made by a flint implement. And if Cordell York decided to support that position. The latter was an especially big if.

He'd been silent for a long time. "Daddy . . . are you there?"

He grunted. "I don't know, Delia. York will treat our dig as a big joke. And I can't imagine Bob Newton coming to an unorthodox conclusion about what clearly appears to be butchering marks on a thirty-one-thousand-year-old mammoth fossil. He'll take the easy way out and conclude that the incisions were made by nonhuman predators."

Delia looked through the darkened window toward her father's cabin, and imagined his anxiety. "I know it's risky. But if we could get both of them on our side . . ."

"Okay," Moses said with weary resignation. "We'll invite York and Newton out to have a gander at what we've found." He said his good night and replaced the telephone in its cradle. Until the dating had been reported, this had been such a fantastic dig. Now Cordell York would be examining every minute detail, criticizing every procedure, questioning every conclusion. *Looking down his nose at me like I was some kind of incompetent amateur.* "Damn," he said. For Moses Silver, this was a heavy oath.

Moses arranged a conference call to Cordell York and Robert Newton. After the usual greetings, his comments were intentionally terse. "Delia and I have been unearthing mammoth remains in southern Colorado. It appears to be a human kill site." He accepted the expected congratulations and took a deep breath. "Thing is, there are some . . . ahhh . . . rather unusual features. All work has been halted, pending consultations with colleagues. We'd certainly appreciate it if you fellows would come out and give us the benefit of your expertise."

This cryptic comment produced the expected questions.

Moses Silver stubbornly refused to elaborate. "These are not matters to be discussed over the telephone. You'll have to see for yourself."

Such a mysterious invitation could hardly be refused. Robert Newton and Cordell York immediately accepted.

It was a mere three days later when the visiting experts were scheduled to arrive. Delia had driven the Land Rover to the busy airport in Colorado Springs. Now, they waited at the appointed gate. She sensed her father's tension and nudged him. "Now remember, Daddy . . . be nice to them. Try not to get excited."

Moses nervously popped his knuckles. "Bob Newton's all

right, except he can't make up his mind about what color socks to put on in the morning. Cordell York is a horse of a different stripe. In fact, he can be a real horse's ass," Moses grumped.

"I know, but he's very important. That's why you invited him," she reminded her father, "not because you like his personality." Delia did not mention Cordell York was also very good-looking. And wealthy. And unmarried.

"York's not really one of us," her father continued.

She knew. "Hush, Daddy—there they are." Delia waved.

And then they were face-to-face with the two Wise Men from the East.

Professor Robert Newton was a small, elderly man, dressed in mismatched clothes that hung on him like cast-off rags on a comic scarecrow. He carried his years as if they were heavy. Newton also carried a brass-headed cane, and not as an ornament. He leaned on it. The scientist's mild expression was one of continual apology, as if to beg excuse for the affront of his existence among more attractive folk.

When the meek inherit the earth, Moses thought, Robert Newton will likely end up with all of Massachusetts. And Rhode Island thrown in.

Dr. Cordell York was, so it seemed, everything that Newton was not. Well over six feet, well under fifty years. Immaculate two-thousand-dollar suit, two-hundred-dollar silk tie, custom-made shoes. This man had never apologized for any wrong done—it simply would not have occurred to him that he could be guilty of any error.

Men considered him outrageously arrogant.

Women thought him outrageously handsome. And dangerous, which is a far greater attraction. The physician's flashing smile exposed rows of perfectly shaped teeth. A fine specimen of the well-bred shark.

It seemed to be going reasonably well. Delia and her father met the visitors with smiles, exchanged vigorous handshakes, and made the usual perfunctory questions about the flight.

"It has been pleasant enough," Newton said thoughtfully. "One is happy to be on the ground, however."

"We're very pleased and gratified that you could both come

on such short notice," Moses Silver said, and meant it. Newton was the scholar-priest who could verify the butcher marks on the mammoth bone. York was the exalted bishop who—if he was so inclined—had the authority to bless Newton's decision.

"Yes," Delia added with a shy look at the tall surgeon. "It's very kind of you to come all the way to Colorado."

Dr. York flashed a half-mocking smile at the young woman. "Well, how could we miss such a remarkable opportunity? Back East, we Philistines understand Moses has parted the waters once more. Claims he's found a human kill site from an age where humans n'er trod." He laughed in genuine amusement. "Now that's quite some miracle. What's next, pray tell?"

Moses and his daughter were not greatly surprised that York had managed to learn about the very early date for the fossils. The laboratory where the workup had been done was not five miles from his home in Cambridge.

Moses—who had prepared himself for this moment—was outwardly quite calm. "Doc . . ." York detested being addressed by this nickname. "I suggest that you wait until you examine the evidence before jumping to conclusions." That was, after all, what good science was about. Not that you'd expect a damned scalpel-wielder to know much of anything about science.

Dr. York, who was actually a gifted scientist, was somewhat taken aback by this mild upbraiding. And surprised by this old man's spirit. Perhaps Moses really *had* unearthed something worth examining.

Professor Newton, embarrassed at his colleague's typical rudeness, attempted to defuse the situation. "Moses, Delia . . . it was very thoughtful of you—driving all the way here to meet our plane. One is quite grateful for such kind attentions."

Moses beamed on the kind little man. "Don't mention it, Robert. I thought it'd be nice to provide you with a ride to the ranch."

Cordell York, who was determined to have some fun with his hosts, remembered Moses' eccentric affection for his old box of bolts. He looked doubtfully down his nose at his elder colleague. "You still driving that dreadful old Land Rover? The one with no springs?"

It was the wrong button to push. Moses felt his face flush. "The Land Rover," he growled, "is the world's finest, most reliable automobile."

Dr. York laughed. "Oh, most certainly. Just the thing for exploring the remote savannas of Africa. Or the Aussie outback. But when I ride on the Interstate, I prefer some modest level of comfort."

Professor Newton attempted to intervene. "Moses has come a long way to meet us. I'm sure we'll be quite comfortable in his automobile, and besides we have much to discuss." He turned to Moses. "One simply can't wait to hear the details of your findings. You must be quite excited to—"

"Nonsense," York said. "I'll rent a car. Bob, can you read a road map?"

"As you wish," Moses Silver said. He turned to the tall, muscular man and made a mocking bow. "We are completely at your service. Would you like for me to carry your luggage?"

Dr. York, who was at his best when crossing swords with angry men, pretended to miss the sarcasm. "Well, if it would please you . . . why not? You may pick them up at the carousel. I'll be at the Avis counter." He offered his luggage tickets to Moses, who could do nothing but accept them. And stomp off in a barely smothered rage.

York winked at Delia. "Your old man's *such* fun." He put his arm around her shoulders. "My dear, you are prettier every time I see you."

He was, she admitted to herself, a bastard who was making sport of her father. But he was a first-class bastard. And Cordell York was funny. It wouldn't do for her furious father to see the smile on her face, but Delia couldn't quite wipe it off. So she walked along between York and Newton. And made small talk with the visiting firemen.

It was the eleventh hour.

Horace Flye, at Delia's request, had returned from his

trailer to set up additional lighting around the critical area of the excavation.

Nathan McFain was there, hugging a heavy red mackinaw around his torso, nervously chewing a jawful of Kentucky Black Leaf tobacco.

The four scientists were sitting around the card table. The visitors had been examining the most recent dating reports. The silence was heavy, pregnant with prospect.

Dr. York, now in his element, had given up his taunts. He had resigned himself—or so it seemed to all present—to be on his best behavior.

This was serious stuff. York pushed aside the dating reports. "It seems quite apparent, Moses, that there can be no question about the age of the fossil bones. Experts from three reputable laboratories agree within a few hundred years. Your mammoth quite definitely expired in excess of thirty thousand years ago."

Moses nodded. He'd not expected anyone to question the age of the bones.

Horace Flye and Nathan McFain watched. And listened.

Delia turned her face to the expert on butchering marks. "Professor Newton, would you like to examine the specimen?"

There was a brief silence. Robert Newton knew that Moses and Delia Silver would want to have their view confirmed: that the marks were made by a hungry human with flint knife. On the other hand, Cordell York would expect to hear that the incisions were made by a predator gnawing on the femur. Either way, he would lose. Disappoint a kindly, hopeful man who wanted a human kill site of unprecedented age. Or irritate a powerful man who would not be willing to accept a finding that challenged orthodox thinking. But, he reminded himself severely, that was not really the issue. In science, truth was the issue. Let the chips fall where they may. But he was so very tired.

"Well," Newton finally said, "it has been quite a long day. One does get rather exhausted . . . Perhaps we should wait until morning. "

Three pairs of eyes glared at him.

"But, if you like, I suppose one could have a . . . umm . . . preliminary look."

Horace—at a nod from Delia—removed a dusty cotton sheet from the pelvis of the beast. And exposed the femur. The fossilized bone was thicker than the heavy end of a softball bat. And just over four feet long.

Moses Silver was deathly pale; he clasped his hands behind his back. To conceal the fact that they trembled.

The young archaeologist patted her father reassuringly on the back.

Horace Flye began to switch on the floodlights over the excavation. Soon, it was brighter than noonday.

Even so, from long habit, Robert Newton removed a small flashlight from his coat pocket. He moved with great delicacy into a position where he could kneel by the specimen of fossilized bone. He focused the flashlight on the longitudinal marks. The specialist in butchering marks cocked his head to one side, and ran a fingertip along the shallow incisions.

He blinked. Muttered to himself. Scowled. Pulled thoughtfully at a pendulous earlobe.

Moses and his daughter waited breathlessly.

Nathan McFain stood with his hands in his coat pockets. Chewing a wad of tobacco.

Horace Flye's sly gaze darted back and forth, between the little man in the excavation and the pretty, anxious face of Delia Silver.

Cordell York smirked. He knew what would happen. Newton would choke.

The expert finally cleared his throat.

All the spectators leaned forward.

"Well," Newton said, "one can be certain that the marks are quite old."

This was an unnecessary observation. It was clear enough that the marks had not been made at a later date than the death of the great beast.

It was almost a minute before he spoke again. He looked up, blinking into the blinding lights to find Moses' familiar profile. "One might say . . . that these incisions could very well be butchering marks."

Moses was pleased, but cautious. One word was worrisome. *Could.*

Cordell York, who had remained aloofly silent, leaped on this. "*Could be*, Robert, or *are*? If you're certain, you surely won't leave us in suspense. You realize," the surgeon added meaningfully, "the import of your conclusions."

Newton most certainly did realize. He was ninety-nine percent certain that these were butchering marks, made by a flint implement. But if he said so, Cordell York would think him an old fool. But if he left a way open that these marks just might possibly have been made by . . . say the teeth of a sabertoothed cat . . . then he'd be off the hook.

Professor Newton, who was too old to be kneeling in drafty tents in cold weather, pushed himself painfully to his feet.

"Well, Bob," York pressed, "let's not equivocate. What do we have here, definitive marks of human butchering activity? Or something . . . more to be expected for remains of such a great age?"

Newton avoided Dr. York's glare. He glanced meekly at Delia, then at Moses. His voice was barely above a whisper. "These . . . ahhh . . . incisions on the left anterior femur . . . One might very well believe them to be evidence of butchering. But more study is required before one can reach a definite conclusion."

There was a heavy silence.

Finally Moses Silver spoke. "Robert, you know damn well that they're butchering marks."

Dr. York, who was enjoying himself immensely, leaned threateningly over the shorter man. "Well—what say you, Robert? Could the incisions on the bone possibly have been made by a scavenging animal? We await the light of your lamp . . . Do illuminate us."

The elderly man was terribly weary from the trip. And didn't like being caught in the middle between two strong personalities. He simply shrugged. Brushed the dust off his trousers. And walked out of the tent.

Cordell York leaned back and laughed. "Old Bob, now he's a real pissant, isn't he?"

For once, Moses Silver found himself in complete agreement with the arrogant ass.

Delia sat down at the card table and put her face in her hands.

The surgeon slipped the scalpel under Moses' skin. "Looks like you'll get no firm support from Bob." And twisted it. "Probably your mammoth died of old age. And wolves chewed on the bones."

Moses faced off with his tormentor. "They're butcher marks, dammit. You heard him say so."

York, who sensed some hostility from Delia, shifted immediately to his amiable persona. "Moses, if this was an eleven-thousand-year-old site, there wouldn't be any doubt about it. I do believe that Robert thinks you might have a thirty-odd-thousand-year-old human kill site here. *Might.* But if he says straight-out that those are butcher-marks, he'll have a dozen experts ripping him apart even before they see the evidence for themselves. He doesn't want to risk his reputation with a definitive statement."

Moses sat down beside his daughter. Doc York was right, of course. As usual. The big horse's ass.

The influential man sat down with his hosts. His face softened. "Look, Moses, I know you think I'm a hardnose."

Without thinking, Moses nodded his agreement with this statement.

This candor amused the eminent surgeon. "But what you're proposing flies in the face of mountains of evidence . . ."

Moses snapped at him. "Doc, the mere fact that no one has found definitive proof of a very early date for human occupation of the Americas does not constitute *mountains of evidence*. It is merely *lack* of evidence." He pointed a shaking finger to indicate the exposed fossil bones. "Now we have it. Butcher marks on a mammoth kill. Twenty millennia before Clovis."

York spread his hands in a conciliatory gesture. "You may very well be right."

Both Silvers looked up in genuine surprise.

"But," York continued quickly, "a few thin lines incised on an ancient fossil bone—though they have the *appearance* of butcher marks—are not sufficient. To turn North American prehistory on its head, your proof must be absolutely indisputable. Otherwise, virtually no one will accept this as a human kill site."

Moses nodded wearily at the wisdom of York's words.

"What you need," the surgeon said reasonably, "is what they found with those bison bones down at Clovis. You need a projectile point. Or a skinning knife. Or a bone awl. Even a simple scraper. An artifact indisputably made by the hand of man."

"Or," Delia added with a sly smile, "by the hand of woman."

This remark broke the tension.

"Doc," Moses said earnestly, "I got a proposition for you."

York, ignoring this impudent use of his nickname, cocked his head. "I'm listening."

"You and Bob Newton join us in the dig. If this proves to be a human kill site—and you can be the final judge of that—then we'll all be co-investigators." He looked to his daughter for her assent; she nodded. "We'll have four authors for the first paper. On the other hand, if you decide it's nothing worth writing home about," he shrugged, "well, me and Delia will slog through it."

"Interesting notion," York said. "Very interesting." His contributions to paleontology had always been of two kinds. Intellectual or cash. He'd never actually taken part in a dig. Might be good fun, at that. He got to his feet. "I'll have to give it some thought. If I should decide to take you up on it, I'll have a talk with the pissant." He bowed to Delia, and turned on his heel.

When he had left the tent, Delia smiled at her father. "Daddy, you're a genius."

"I will not deny it," Moses said affably. Here was the way it all stacked up: Robert Newton was almost certain this was a kill site but was afraid to commit himself for fear of ridicule from his colleagues. Cordell York probably thought so too. And Moses had offered them a tempting proposition. Join up and share the glory if it turns out we've got the find of the century. If it turns out to be nothing, you can disassociate yourself from it. They had little to lose and everything to gain. And Doc York, who loved to needle his less fortunate colleagues in the pages of his influential journal, could certainly not criticize a dig that he'd had a major part in. So if the butcher marks held up to further scrutiny by other experts, York could hardly be a nay-sayer—which was what he enjoyed almost as much as the glory of a stupendous find. No, the smart-assed surgeon had a big decision to make before dawn. The knowledge that Cordell York might have a hard time sleeping tonight pleased Moses immensely.

No one had paid the least attention to Nathan McFain, who owned the site. The rancher-entrepreneur was considerably annoyed to be ignored by this gathering of eggheads. "Well," he grumped, "does this mean I got two more free tenants in my cabins?" The paleontologist and his daughter were paying no rent.

"No," Moses said with a sly grin. "Charge them. And not the off-season rental. Quote them your summer rates. They can afford it."

McFain grinned wolfishly. He was almost beginning to like this old guy. "While you was gone to the airport, I rented a cabin to Ralph Briggs. He has a fancy antique shop up at Granite Creek, and likes all kinda old stuff. Said he wanted to watch the dig."

Moses scowled at the rancher. "This is a delicate piece of science we're doing here, Mr. McFain. We don't need any rubbernecks hanging around in the tent."

McFain shrugged this protest off. "I already told Briggs he could have a look-see. He won't bother you none."

The paleontologist sighed. "Very well. But remember that we have an agreement—I'm in charge of the work under the tent. Don't make any more such arrangements without checking with me first."

"Father's right," Delia added. "We can't be stumbling over tourists while we work."

The rancher nodded amiably. No point in pushing these eggheads too far.

Horace Flye made his way to Delia's side. "Ma'am . . . you

want me to start turning off them lights and kinda puttin' things back in order?"

She patted him on the hand, caring not that her father noticed this small demonstration of endearment. "Yes," she said. "We're done for the night."

DIGGING UP BONES

CHARLIE MOON SAT with his elbows on his desk. Outside his office window, a hook-billed raven landed lightly on the bare branch of a Russian olive. The bird cocked its soot-black head and peered through the window at the Ute policeman. Moon stared back. Wasn't hard to see how—a long time ago—the People had come to believe that such feathered creatures were something more than animals. They were sometimes witches who'd shifted form. Or they carried spirits of the dead to spy on the living. Some of the older people among the Utes still believed this.

Charlie Moon turned away from the raven and dismissed his musings about the exotic myths of his people. The police officer directed his attention to the mundane business at hand. A stack of arrest reports. Patrol schedules. Upcoming vacations. Annual performance reviews. He'd do the work. The chief—if he wasn't busy reading travel brochures—would perform a cursory examination, then scrawl his name at the bottom of the page. Moon's desk work had slowly increased over the past six months. He was gradually becoming more of an office manager than a patrol cop. In fact, he had been given a fancy title that he hadn't asked for. Deputy chief of police. So he wouldn't complain about doing ninety percent of the chief's work for an extra dollar and seventy-five cents an hour to go with the title. The chief of police, who had begun to talk about retirement, was assigning much of his drudge-work to Moon. Roy Severo was barely sixty, but he had dreams of travel with his young wife. To the South Seas, perhaps. Charlie Moon suspected that the council would ask him to take on the chief's job as soon as Severo opted for his golden years.

Moon was the council's first choice for two reasons. First, he was liked and respected by virtually every member of the tribe. More important, he showed no interest in tribal politics, and so would not use a promotion as a stepping stone to higher office. And the odd fact that he had no interest in being chief of police made him irresistibly attractive as the right man for this very sensitive tribal position.

He pushed aside the arrest reports, and checked the day's patrol schedule.

Elena Chavez was covering the west side of the reservation this morning and—according to the dispatcher's notes—had nothing much to report except a broken-down camper from Connecticut. She'd called in a tow truck. Daniel Bignight was working the other end of the reservation. He'd stopped three speeders at the turnoff from Route 60 near Lake Capote, but bighearted Daniel wouldn't give anyone a ticket unless they were drunk. Or got a bit too smart. Or made some dumb excuse like the speedometer hasn't worked right since I hit the deer, Officer. Charlie Moon, who was pleased that nothing untoward was spoiling an almost perfect morning, allowed his mind to drift toward plans for lunch.

Roy Severo appeared behind Moon's chair and cleared his throat. Moon pretended not to hear his boss. Severo pitched the latest issue of the *Southern Ute Drum* onto his subordinate's desk. The *Drum* now ran weekly articles about the progress of the excavation on Nathan McFain's land.

"There's been some talk," Severo said. "About them elephant bones."

Moon, who heard all the tribal gossip, understood that this opaque remark referred to mutterings among members of the tribal council. "What kind of talk?"

"Well," the chief scratched at a thick shock of iron-gray hair, "there's been disputes for a long time about the boundary between the west side of Nathan McFain's pasture and tribal lands. Some of the People claim that Navajo rascal has been moving his boundary markers a yard or two onto our land every time he got a chance."

"McFain," Moon pointed out, "is only one-quarter Navajo."

Severo snorted. "And three-quarters schemer."

Moon thought it useful to inject a bit of relevant history into the conversation. "For at least fifty years, the land on our side of the fence has been leased by Tony Sweetwater's family for sheep grazing. The main markers are a half dozen boulders. McFain claims the Sweetwaters rolled the boundary markers way over onto his land first. When he rolled 'em back, it was just to make things right. He claims he finally had to put up a fence to keep the Sweetwater sheep from grazing out of the flowerpots on his porch."

Severo grunted. "Well, whatever might've happened way back when, there's some talk." The chief of police tapped his finger on the *Drum* article. "Some of the council members figure McFain's elephant diggings may be on Southern Ute land. And they don't feel easy about old bones being dug up. You know, having that Navajo make a profit by disturbing the elephant's spirit's rest and all that."

Sure, Moon thought. But what if it turned out the excavation was on tribal property . . . and there was a chance for a profit. Well, the sleeping mammoth spirit would be in for a pretty loud wake-up call.

As if he could read Moon's thoughts, Severo seemed slightly uneasy. "I just wanted you to know about the talk that's been going around. The council's already talked to a lawyer up in Durango. And hired a surveyor. Since you and McFain seem to get along pretty well, I'd appreciate it if you kinda kept an eye on what he's doin' out there."

The policeman raised an eyebrow. "You mean like spy on him? Check to see if he's moved any fence posts onto Ute land?"

Roy Severo, who missed the sarcasm, pondered this for a moment. "Yeah. That's a damn good idea, Charlie. You think up some excuse to pay our Navajo neighbor a visit. And do it today." And he was gone.

Moon unfolded the newspaper. The follow-up story on the "McFain Mammoth" was on page three. It was mainly more of the same. Except that Nathan McFain was gleefully hinting that there was something "real special" about *this* mammoth. No, he couldn't say exactly what because he had a handshake agreement with Dr. Moses Silver that the scientists would have a chance to publish their findings before the newspapers learned what was afoot here. But it would be big news, he said. Real big. Moon chuckled. The rancher was a born promoter. The policeman's eyes wandered to the photograph over the article. Nathan McFain was standing outside a large tent, flanked by the little bespectacled scientist and his daughter. According to the caption, the tent had been set up to protect the excavation. And provide some warmth for the scientists who expected to work throughout the winter. Dr. Silver, Moon surmised, was evidently quite serious about the publishing agreement or the *Drum* reporter would surely have gotten a shot of the bones that had been uncovered so far. And then something in the background caught Moon's eye. It was a small, wiry-looking man. Dressed in overalls. He had a bandage on his ear. Even with the scraggly beard neatly trimmed, there was no doubt.

This was Horace Flye, in the flesh.

It looked like the Arkansas traveler had conned his way into a job moving dirt. Moon wondered whether the Silvers had any idea they'd hired a slicker. And whether the child was being looked after properly. The McFain ranch—excepting possibly a few pilfered yards of pasture—was outside SUPD jurisdiction. And it wasn't any of the tribe's business who got hired to dig up McFain's mammoth bones. But it wouldn't hurt to pay a social call on Nathan McFain. Maybe find out what Horace Flye was up to. And the chief of police would be pleased if he thought Moon was sneaking around the Navajo's pasture looking for signs of fresh postholes. Well, let Roy Severo think whatever he wanted to think.

Moon parked the big Blazer under the skeletonous limbs of a hundred-year-old cottonwood. And then zipped his sheepskin jacket in anticipation of the gusting November breeze that kicked up dust among the sparse clumps of frost-killed grass in Nathan McFain's front yard. The Ute policeman sat for a moment and looked things over. There was a familiar old yellow Chevy van parked beside Nathan's new pickup. A faded bumper sticker said DON'T DRINK AND DRIVE. So Vanessa was home to see her father. For a normal family, it wouldn't be surprising that a daughter would come home for a visit. But Nathan and Vanessa were just about two notches on the far side of normal. Whenever she dropped in, there would be uneasy hugs exchanged, an unspoken truce. They would manage to behave for maybe a week. Then some small issue would start a chain reaction. She'd do or say something to start a fire in the old man's belly. He'd open his big mouth and light her fuse. She'd explode. There would be a massive flare-up, harsh words exchanged, and Vanessa would roar off in her Chevy van. Sometimes she was away for months. Rumor was, she'd had a drinking problem.

Seemed like everybody had one kind of problem or another.

It looked like Nathan McFain's dude ranch was doing a brisk off-season business. Automobiles were parked in the graveled driveways at several of the log cabins on the pine-studded hillside. Above the cabins, on the long spine of the double-humped hogback called Buffalo Saddle Ridge, Moon could see the edge of the RV campground. And the end of a small, beetle-shaped camp-trailer. Horace Flye's rig, of course. He couldn't see the old Dodge pickup from this angle, but it'd be there. Moon shut down the Blazer's heater, switched off the ignition, and got out.

Far above the small valley where the ranch headquarters was situated, the elfin girl in the camp-trailer was still dressed in her warm flannel pajamas. She raised her father's Navy binoculars to her pale blue eyes. Her small, stubby fingers strained to turn the focus knob. She watched the tall policeman cross the yard toward the ranch house.

For an instant, the big man turned his head and looked directly at her!

She shuddered with the delicious, delightful, fanciful fear that only a child can know.

"The Wuff," Butter Flye murmured, ". . . the Big *Bad* Wuff."

Vanessa McFain opened the front door before the visitor had time to mount the chiseled stone steps. Her bronze hair was done up in a single long braid. She was tall for a woman, and snaky-thin. Her slim hips barely held up her faded jeans, which were stuffed into fancy bull-hide cowboy boots. This one had grown up on a ranch and could sit a frisky horse with the best of them. She had turned into a fine-looking woman.

She gave him a crooked smile. "Hello, big man."

That's what she'd called Moon back when she was a teenager. "Hiya, sleepwalker," he shot back without thinking. When she blushed, Moon wished he could swallow the thoughtless response. It had been almost exactly six years ago—on a chilly September evening. A panicked Nathan McFain had called the county sheriff to report his teenage daughter missing. No, he didn't know how long she'd been gone. He was a heavy sleeper, had just got up around 2 A.M. to relieve his bladder. And noticed Vannie's bedroom door was open—and her bed empty. She wasn't anywhere in the house.

All the local troops had been called out, including volunteers from the Ignacio town police and Southern Ute PD. The Ute policeman had participated in a search that lasted all night. At dawn, Charlie Moon had found her, not a half mile from the western border of her father's ranch. Vanessa had been stumbling about, her nightdress torn, feet bleeding. She'd been cold to the bone, and incoherent. He'd bundled her up in his long coat and hauled her back to the ranch on his horse. Vanessa had been mortified that the big Ute cop had found her wandering around practically naked. The physician's diagnosis had been sleepwalking, complicated by hypothermia and miscellaneous trauma. A dumb reason, she thought, for causing such a big commotion. And it was no secret that Vanessa—even as a teenager—had a drinking problem. One of the state cops had found an empty wine bottle in her room.

Attempting to erase the blunder, Moon reached out to take the hand she offered. "Vanessa . . . I didn't know you'd be here."

She smiled, exposing a dazzling row of perfect teeth, reminding him that she'd once had a mouthful of braces. When Vanessa smiled, she could light up a man's day. "Pleased to see me?"

"Sure." He took off his dusty black Stetson and tapped it on his knee. Moon wondered if she was still drinking. Hoped she wasn't.

"I'm sober," she said as if she'd read his mind.

"So'm I." He nodded toward the Blazer. "That's the only way the chief'll let me drive the squad car."

This brought a tinkling laugh from her lips. She'd had some bad experiences with men. But Charlie Moon had always been so funny. And funny men didn't ever hit you.

He was, though not staring, giving her the once-over. Another twenty pounds would look good on her. She was mostly bones. Nice-looking set of bones, though.

Vanessa knew she was being inspected. And liked it. "So what'd you come out here for? To see the bones?"

If the dark man could have blushed, he would have. "The what?"

"The *old* bones," she said with a knowing smirk. He was squirming. Sort of cute, too. If a man just shy of seven feet tall could be called cute.

"Ahh . . . sort of. I stopped by to say hello to your father."

As if on cue, Nathan McFain's broad, bearded face appeared behind his daughter. "For gosh sakes, Vannie—either ask Charlie in or go outside and do your gabbin'. You're lettin' out all the confounded heat."

Vanessa pretended to be dismayed. "Daddy still insists on calling me 'Vannie.' Like he did when I was a little girl."

"Vannie's still my little girl." Nathan winked at the policeman. "Even if she *is* tall enough to eat leaves off a treetop."

"The real reason he doesn't call me by my right name," she said, "is he *can't.* Daddy gets tongue-tied with words that have more than two syllables."

"Smart-ass kid," the old man muttered under his breath.

She looked up imploringly at the Ute. "I'm not all that tall, am I, Charlie?"

Moon's response was mock-sober. "An experienced police officer learns to steer clear of family disputes."

Nathan chuckled; his belly shook.

"Men," she said to the ceiling, and turned away to lead her guest down a short hallway.

Charlie Moon followed the slender woman and her hulking, round-shouldered father into the warm parlor. It was a large room filled with heavy, dark furniture. Tons of varnished wood and polished leather. The far wall was dominated by a massive speckled-granite fireplace, anchored on a red brick hearth. The mantelpiece was a twelve-foot slab of smoke-stained redwood, a good six inches thick. Over the mantel was the head of a trophy antelope the old man had killed on the New Mexico plains south of Raton. The animal watched Moon through inquisitive eyes of amber glass. The Ute policeman unzipped his jacket and warmed his hands near the snapping yellow flames that were rapidly consuming an armload of split piñon.

Nathan McFain seated himself in a massive Spanish chair. It creaked under his weight. He began to fill his battered brier pipe. When his daughter was at home, he avoided chewing tobacco. She said the smell of it, and the sight of him spitting into a coffee can—well, it made her nauseous. But she knew her father had to have his tobacco one way or another. The pipe was one of those uneasy compromises that neither side was altogether pleased with. "Well, Charlie . . . you come out here to see me," Nathan made a sideways glance at his daughter, "or you come courtin' Vannie?"

Though watching Moon's face for some response to this notion, she shook her head in mock dismay. "You'll have to excuse him, Charlie. They say old men's brains shrink. Dad's evidently started shriveling when he was about forty; must be down to about the size of a walnut."

"If Vannie'd put on some weight," McFain grumped, "I expect I'd be beatin' the young men off with a stick. As it is . . ."

Moon noticed that her eyes were getting that flat reptilian look like a snake about to strike. A warning sign the mouthy old man had missed. "Matter of fact," the Ute interrupted, "the pleasure of Vanessa's company is an unexpected bonus." This earned him a bittersweet smile from the young woman. "Nathan, I been reading in the *Drum* about those old bones you found in your pasture. Thought maybe I'd drop by and have a look . . . if it's all right with you."

Nathan McFain touched a lighted match to the pipe bowl and puffed until the fragrant fuel was cherry-red. "I don't mind. 'Course, you'll have to get past those eggheads who're in charge of the digging. The daughter—that's Delia—she's not such a bad sort. But her old man's a real hardnose."

Vanessa rolled her big eyes. "She has my sympathy. And empathy."

The potbellied rancher studiously ignored his daughter. "See, me and this university professor, we got us a deal. Moses Silver digs up all the bones—and makes sure they're preserved right and all. Soon as we know how much is under the ground—hell, there might be a half dozen of them monsters died in the same place—I'll finish my plans to put up a permanent structure to protect the bones. It'll be a fine museum, where folks can come and see 'em. It'll be real educational."

At a tuition of about five bucks a head, Moon estimated.

"Educational my . . . my foot," Vanessa said. "It's another one of his moneymaking schemes."

Unmoved by this unwarranted attack on entrepreneurial capitalism, McFain continued. "This Moses Silver and his daughter, they'll write up fancy articles for them highbrow scientific journals. But all the bones," the rancher tapped his pipe bowl on the scarred surface of a small table by his chair, "they stay right here. On my property. And these ain't just your everyday mammoth bones, Charlie. These bones is *spe-*

cial." He waited for the Ute to ask what was so special about these particular bones.

Moon didn't take the bait.

"Of course, I'm actually not supposed to tell you *why* these bones is so special. I got this agreement with Professor Silver . . . he's the only one who can make any *public* statements about the bones." If Charlie Moon would just show a little interest, he'd tell him about the great age of the fossils. And butcher marks on the leg bone. Why, this would prove that people had come to America twenty thousand years before all those smart-ass professors had thought!

Charlie Moon had little interest in the paleontologist's scientific papers or Nathan McFain's plans for a museum. The Ute policeman had come to the ranch to see if Nathan's new employee was behaving himself. More likely, Horace Flye was planning some mischief. But the old curmudgeon was in a talking mood. So maybe he could get Nathan to mention hiring the drifter from Arkansas. "All that digging . . . must be a lot of hard work, for just one elderly man and his daughter."

The rancher pointed the pipe stem at Moon. "Lissen, Charlie—I coulda already dug up that whole damn elephant all by myself with just a pick and shovel. But those two are so afraid of scratchin' one of them old bones, they're digging with teensy little dental picks and toothbrushes and stuff like that." He snorted in disgust. "Anyway, I hired a man to help 'em."

Moon turned his back to the fire. "Anybody I know?"

McFain shook his head. "I doubt it. This fella's from Arkansas. Claims he's done a lot of bone-diggin' before this, so I expect the Silvers was happy to get him." He looked through the window toward the long ridge. "I let him park his trailer up at the RV campground. I got everything up there. Electric. Gas. Water. Septic tank. Big investment." And this was the first paying customer in almost six months. The cabins did better. But not by much.

The policeman tried to ignore Vanessa's frank gaze. She seemed amused at something. Him, maybe. "Well," he zipped his jacket, "I guess I'll go over and have a look at the elephant." Best if they didn't think he was concerned about the boundary dispute. Which he wasn't. "Where, exactly, is this hole in the ground?"

Nathan jerked a thumb. "The big tent. Down back o' the barn."

The young woman pulled on a heavy denim jacket—her father's castoff—and jammed a battered cowboy hat onto her head. "I'll take you there. Wouldn't want you to get lost." She took his left arm.

McFain chuckled. "You better look out, Charlie. Nothin' worse'n a woman approaching spinsterhood. I think this chicken's wantin' to find herself a rooster and build a nest."

She stuck her tongue out at her father and maneuvered the tall Ute through the door. Vanessa clung to Moon's arm like a rose vine on a fence post. She leaned slightly against him as they walked around the barn. There was a muttering diesel sound ahead of them. A thin man sat in the bulldozer's steel seat, pushing and pulling on levers with the easy confidence of a worker who knows what he's doing. Almost unconsciously, the policeman's mind made notes. The ranch hand wore a ragged-looking gray overcoat. Faded jeans that were much too large for him. A dirty red sock hat with a little white ball of fluff on the end. Looked like he'd stole his clothes off a scarecrow who'd fallen on hard times.

"New hand?"

Vanessa nodded. "Poor man's deaf. Showed up hungry and desperate for work. And you know Daddy—he can't turn his back on someone who's in need."

Moon nodded. Nathan McFain can't turn his back on a bargain. "What's his name?"

The young woman smiled at the policeman. Charlie Moon was a typical cop. Just couldn't resist the urge to pick up bits of useless information. "Jimson Beugmann."

Moon seemed to be making small talk. "Looks like a city fella." The man's face was very pale, his hands bony. Looked like he'd been sick.

She shrugged as if it hardly mattered. "I imagine he'll work a few weeks to make himself a stake. And then wander off." It was a familiar pattern.

Moon gave the deaf man a friendly wave.

Beugmann, whose gloved hands were occupied with the half dozen levers, nodded in response. He was scooping out a shallow pond behind the barn. It was a satisfying, if simple task, such as children and grown men enjoy. Push away the rocky earth on the slight incline, pile it up on the low end to make a dam. Later on, lay in a four-inch iron pipe for overflow. When the spring snows melted in the pasture, the depression would be half-filled with water. Summer thunderstorms would do the rest.

When they were far enough away from the bulldozer's labored grunting and clanking for conversation, Moon looked down at the top of the woman's head. Her hair was parted very neatly down the middle. Like she'd used a straight-edge with the comb. "So what's so special about these particular mammoth bones?"

She smiled up at him. "Daddy was about to bust because you didn't show the least interest in his big secret. It was mean of you not to ask him—he was *dying* to tell you."

"I'm sorry." He wasn't.

She squeezed his arm. "First of all, these bones are over thirty thousand years old."

"I don't think that's all that unusual," Moon said cautiously. "Few years ago, up in Wyoming, a road crew dug up some mammoths that were over a *hundred* thousand years old."

She nodded. "But that's only the half of it. Daddy's mammoth has butchering marks."

Moon stopped in his tracks. The skin on the back of his neck was prickling. "Are you sure?"

She shrugged. "That's what Professor Silver says."

The Ute took a deep breath. Butchering marks on an animal that was grazing here thirty thousand years ago. That would mean that human beings got here almost three times as long ago as the experts thought. Maybe even some of his own ancestors.

The large tent loomed in front of them. Backed up very close to the western boundary fence, Moon noted. The excavation was right on the edge of Southern Ute holdings. Or—depending on who had moved the boundary markers last—maybe some of it was *on* Ute land. "What's your major up at the university?" he asked. Psychology, he figured. Or sociology.

She broke off a dead stalk of grass and stuck it between her perfect teeth. "Computer science."

"Oh." Moon considered himself a reasonable, open-minded man. He was happy with many of the products of modern technology. Like the Hubble telescope. Fuel injection. Anesthesia. Microwave ovens. Laser gun sights. But computers . . . well, that was another matter. It wasn't so much that he didn't like them. But they were much like porcupines—a sensible man didn't touch one of 'em.

She sensed his disappointment with her chosen profession. "I read lots of stuff in other fields. And go to talks on all kinds of subjects. It's one of the advantages of being in a university town." *Compared to Boulder, things are pretty dull down here on the farm.* She pushed aside the framed door, rigged by Horace Flye to replace the drafty tent flap.

Charlie Moon had expected to encounter a sedate scene inside the sprawling excavation tent. A little old man, scribbling arcane data into a notebook. His prim daughter, picking away at fragments of fossilized bones with a pointed trowel. And Horace Flye, of course. On the lookout for a pocket to pick. It was admittedly an uncharitable thought. But lawmen are not paid to give fellows of Flye's ilk the benefit of any doubt.

The tent door opened onto a scene that was quite different from what the Ute policeman had expected.

It was busy as an anthill on the last day of summer.

A half dozen flood lamps encircled the sandy basin where an assortment of massive fossil bones had been exposed. The excavation was neatly divided into squares by an array of pine stakes. Various colors of cotton twine connected the wooden markers.

An aristocratic-looking fellow was sitting at a folding table, engrossed in a sheaf of papers. Vanessa whispered in Moon's ear. "That's Cordell York. He's actually a medical doctor. The little man in the pit with Professor Silver—that's Robert Newton. York and Newton were called in by the Silvers. Some sort of consultants, I think."

Delia Silver, Moon thought, was prettier than her newspaper picture. The young woman was adjusting an archaic view camera. In the gloomy atmosphere of the tent, the flood lamps were evidently not sufficient for her photographic work. They were augmented by several tripod-mounted aluminum reflector sheets, their surfaces polished to a mirror-like finish.

The two old men were hip-deep in the sandy pit, which was generally rectangular and, Moon estimated, about thirty feet by twenty. Moses Silver was making a measurement on a fossil bone with a pair of calipers. Robert Newton was muttering to himself, pulling at his earlobe.

Horace Flye was working on a motor-driven contraption that the Ute guessed was a sifter. The Arkansas man was on the far side of the floodlit pit and had not yet noticed the newcomers.

The appearance of the intruders was barely noted by the scientists. Moses Silver looked up from his work. He recognized McFain's tall, skinny daughter with a polite nod, but dismissed the tall man in the sheepskin jacket as just one more curious neighbor in a long line of such folk who—despite McFain's promises to keep them away—wandered in and out all day as if the excavation was some kind of dude ranch sideshow. The paleontologist had learned to avoid eye contact with the locals. And so he ignored the very tall man the McFain girl had brought into the tent.

The Ute policeman was content to wait and watch. Vanessa was leaning against his arm. He was surprised to hear the creak of a metal chair from the darkness behind him. And a voice.

"Ahem."

The Ute could not recall ever hearing a person actually use that word—if it was a word. Moon turned. A pale face emerged from the shadows. The head was accompanied by a short, trim-looking body. Astonishingly, he was dressed in an immaculate three-piece suit. Pale yellow silk shirt. Narrow red tie with an opal tack. His small shoes were spit-shined. A pale, immaculate hand was extended to Moon. "I am Ralph

Briggs." He said it as if the name would be instantly recognized.

It was not. Moon accepted the delicate hand. It was cold and limp. Like picking up a dead trout. "Charlie Moon."

"You're a Ute," the suit said. It was not a question.

"Last time I checked my tribal enrollment status," Moon grinned.

"Mr. Briggs," Vanessa said with an amused smile, "owns an antique and fossil shop in Granite Creek." It was fun to needle this little fellow.

"I am," Briggs said to Moon, "an authority of some note on all sorts of ancient things. I have a newsletter . . . The *Briggs Antiquarian Monthly* . . . Most of my subscribers are on the Web. Perhaps you've seen it?"

Moon, who had no intention of getting caught in the Web, shook his head apologetically. "Afraid not."

"I should not be surprised, I suppose." This was evidently a mild rebuke. Briggs' expression softened. "The academic intelligentsia," he nodded toward the gaggle of scientists, "do not welcome the presence of what they consider . . . outsiders. Especially well-informed outsiders like myself. I have found it best to withdraw into the shadows and observe silently. They tolerate my presence," he added bitterly, "on the condition that I shall not publish anything about the excavation in my newsletter. Not until Professor Silver and his cohorts have presented their findings in appropriate scientific periodicals."

"I see," Moon said. Unless a man enjoyed the company of eccentrics, this operation looked to be pretty dull. Soon as he could let Horace Flye know that the local law had not lost interest in him, he'd be out of here. Daniel Bignight's cruiser was parked over by Capote Lake. He would pay a call on his fellow officer, see how many speeders he'd ticketed. Then there would be time to drop by and see Aunt Daisy and the little girl she was taking care of. He hoped Sarah Frank and the old woman were getting along.

Horace Flye—who had been working on the motor-driven shaker—noticed the unmistakable form of Charlie Moon. He approached the policeman eagerly, as if the Ute was counted among his oldest and dearest friends. He poked a grimy paw at Moon. "Well, howdy doody!"

Moon accepted the dirty hand and shook it. It was a warm, firm grip.

Vanessa raised an eyebrow. "You two know each other?"

"Yeah," Moon said. "Kinda." One wrong word and Flye could lose his job.

"I gotta make me a cancer stick," Flye said with a conspiratorial air. "Miss Silver," he looked fondly toward the archaeologist, "she don't want me smokin' inside the tent. You want to go outside while I light one up?"

Moon tipped his Stetson at Vanessa. "I'll be back in a couple of minutes."

She sighed and released her grip on his arm. "I'll be here." She looked down her nose at the three-piece suit. "Enjoying the company of Mr. Briggs, I suppose."

The little antiquarian made a wry face at the tall woman. "How fortunate for you." He gestured to indicate the folding chair in a dark corner of the tent. "Shall we retire to a place amongst the shadows. I rarely have the opportunity to converse with a woman of your . . . stature."

The tall woman was openly amused at this dapper little man. "Suits me, Shorty. You want to sit in my lap?"

He raised an eyebrow. "Why Miss McFain—I do hope you're serious."

Flye followed the policeman through the makeshift door, then closed it carefully behind them. There were still two hours of daylight left, but the evening chill was beginning to settle over the empty expanse of the broad meadow. The Arkansas man pulled a bag of tobacco and a package of cigarette papers from his shirt pocket. It required his entire concentration to fill a paper with the crumbled brown leaf and seal it with spit. He fumbled in his jeans until he found a plastic lighter. Flye touched a flame to the tip of the cigarette, inhaled the smoke, and began to cough. "Just what I needed," he said with perfect seriousness.

Moon shoved his hands into his jacket pockets. "Looks like you've found gainful employment."

"Yep," Flye said. "You can tear up them parole papers now. I'm in like Flynn here."

Moon was amused to realize that the man had taken the charade back at the jail so seriously. "How's your daughter getting along?"

Flye glanced toward the profile of the small camp-trailer on the near hump of Buffalo Saddle Ridge. *Looks like a fat tick on a hog's back.* "Oh, Butter's fine. Whilst I do my work, she stays in the trailer—snug as a puppy under a blanket. I go to the trailer for lunch, then I'm home again before dark. We have our supper and watch some TV and then I put her to bed. Little Butter, she's happy as a flathead catfish in muddy water."

"The thing is," Moon said, "I don't want you to get in any trouble. Or cause these folks any grief. So you—"

Flye, who had hardly been listening, interrupted. "Me and the Silvers, we're big chums, you see. It didn't start out that way. The old man—his name's Moses—he set me up for a fall. Hid a little arrow point in the sand I was siftin'. If I'd a kept it—and it was a pretty thing and probably worth a twenty-dollar bill if you know where to sell such stuff—if I'd a kept it he'd a fired me sure as it snows in December. But I turned it in. So now he knows I'm honest as the day is long."

Moon sighed. "Days get kinda short this time of year."

Flye chuckled, then nudged Moon with a sharp elbow. "Yessir, I did the right thing. And now the old man—why, he'd trust me with his false teeth. And me an' Delia is special friends."

Flye must be exaggerating. "She's taken a liking to you?"

"Didn't I tell you?" Flye said through a series of coughs. "We is *chums*."

"You told me, but what I don't understand is," Moon mimicked Flye's nasal drawl, "*why* you is chums."

Flye blinked. "Why? Because she's sweet on me, that's why."

It was clear from the Ute policeman's expression that he believed this claim to be salted with fool's gold.

"Well, I can *prove* she likes me. Miss Silver told me what her daddy was up to. That he was gonna plant that little arrowhead and see if'n I stole it. And it wasn't even a real Indian arrowhead; she made it herself."

"Seems to me," Moon observed, "she must've had you figured for a thief. If she'd thought you were an honest man, why warn you about the plant?"

Flye—who had not considered the matter from this perspective—looked somewhat crestfallen. But only for an instant.

"But," the Ute admitted generously, "I guess the young lady must be a little bit fond of you. Otherwise she wouldn't have gone to the trouble to save your job."

"Women," Flye said smugly, "takes to me like flies to honey."

Moon might have observed that flies took to items far less fragrant than honey. But he'd said enough already. "The Southern Ute Police Department is pleased that you've found honest employment, Mr. Flye. Just see that you don't pull any fast ones. It would make me look bad for cutting you loose. Then I'd have to come and find you. And," he added darkly, "I'd come all the way to Arkansas if I had to." This was an exaggeration. By about a thousand miles.

Horace Flye winked. "Hey . . . you know me." If his aim had been to comfort Moon, the arrow veered somewhat wide of the mark. The wiry man stubbed out the cigarette butt on his brass belt buckle, then ground it under his heel. "We'd best be gettin' back inside. I don't think it'll look too good, me spendin' so much time jawin' with a cop."

"Well," Moon said equably, "I wouldn't want to tarnish your reputation." He followed Flye back into the tent. Moses Silver, his daughter, and Robert Newton were at the card table, examining Polaroid photos. Cordell York was in the sandpit with the fossil bones.

"That long tall drink of water with the bones, he's Dr. York," Flye whispered hoarsely to the policeman. "He's a real high-and-mighty sawbones from somewheres back East, but they say he knows all about a elephant's teeth. You show him a molar, he'll tell you the critter's license number and what he had for breakfast."

A single brownish-yellow tusk curved upward. Like a

beckoning finger. Moon decided to have a closer look. Cordell York was using a short, stiff-bristled brush to clear sand from a long jawbone. The teeth were enormous, and covered with curly ridges. Moon watched for several minutes and was not challenged by York. Neither was his presence acknowledged by the surgeon.

But a man could only look at a pile of old bones for just so long. Moon stole a glance at the young woman at the card table. Pretty thing.

As if on cue, Vanessa reappeared from the shadows. And reclaimed her rights at Moon's arm.

"So. You get along okay with Mr. Briggs?" Moon grinned. "I think he kinda likes you."

"He lusts after me," she said. "I think he's very cute. And awfully smart. Well-dressed, too." Vanessa leaned her head on his shoulder. "Does that make you jealous?"

"Now I think about it, I guess it does. You never said anything that nice about me." He assumed a sad face. "A fella likes to be told he's cute. And smart. And well-dressed."

"Charlie, I'll try to think of something nice to say about you. But only if you'll say something just as nice about me."

He nodded. "Sounds like a square deal."

Vanessa frowned with concentration. "Let me think . . . hmmm."

She seemed, he thought, to take a long time.

"You're taking a long time."

"It's only because I'm trying to think of some way that you're . . . well, really *special*. Something that distinguishes you."

"Then don't let me hurry you."

"Okay, here it is. You're *taller* than most men."

"Thanks," he said. "So are you."

She pinched his arm. Hard.

Well, a man could only stand so much fun. And business was business. He'd had his talk with Horace Flye, which was what he'd come here for. And twenty minutes of watching a grown man brush sand off an old jawbone was sufficient for the day. It was getting close to suppertime. And nothing very interesting was happening here.

The man in the sandpit paused in his brushing. "My God," Cordell York muttered. And he was an agnostic.

At the card table, three scientists' heads turned simultaneously.

Moses smiled at his colleagues. "Cordell rarely gets excited. But give him a few old teeth to examine . . . well, I tell you, his talents are wasted as a surgeon. Dr. York should have taken up dentistry." He chuckled at his joke.

"Come here," York said. He said it softly. But it was a command.

Delia Silver abandoned a pile of photographs she'd been labeling. The young archaeologist was followed by Robert Newton, then by her father.

York was on his knees in the sand, his pale face inches from the jawbone. "Look," he said urgently, "look . . . look . . ." Like the lone shepherd who has seen the Archangel, and called others from their flocks to behold the heavenly vision.

Delia slipped lightly into the excavation. "What is it, Cordell?"

He pointed.

The silence in the tent was perfect.

Moon squatted in an attempt to get a better view.

Horace Flye stood behind him.

Vanessa McFain could see nothing worth causing a commotion about.

Ralph Briggs had emerged from the shadows.

Moses Silver took off his spectacles and polished them with a cotton handkerchief. "Well, Cordell, don't keep us in suspense. What've you found? One of the teeth have a gold filling?"

The tall man shook his head in wonder. "Come and see."

Delia turned to her father, who was leaning forward, blinking through his trifocals. "Daddy," she said. "Oh, Daddy . . ."

Moses grunted as he lowered himself into the excavation.

Delia moved aside to make room for her father.

York pointed with the tip of the brush handle.

Moses lay on his belly, his spectacles almost on the fossilized jawbone. "Oh my . . . oh my."

Lodged under the long slab of bone was the unmistakable edge of a flint implement.

Moses put a finger close to the marvelous find, but touched neither flint nor fossil bone. "Photographs," the old man said hoarsely, "we must have photographs. And soil samples around the artifact."

Delia was already scurrying away for a tripod-mounted camera. Her hands trembled as she loaded a roll of high-resolution black-and-white film.

It was at this moment that Nathan McFain stormed into the tent. "Vannie," he shouted to his daughter, "I've a notion to drive over to Arboles and get a gutful of Mexican grub. You and Charlie Moon want to come along?" He noticed the antiquarian. "Oh . . . hello there, Mr. Briggs. You can come along too, if you're hungry."

Briggs, if he heard the halfhearted invitation, ignored it.

Vanessa looked over her shoulder at her father. "Daddy. They've found something."

McFain surged forward toward the excavation, almost toppling one of the flood lamps. "Found what?"

Moses blinked up at the landowner, and raised a palm up to keep him at bay. "Our colleague, Dr. York, has discovered what appears to be a flint implement lodged under the left mandible. This will be a very delicate operation. The removal process will take some time to complete. We must have complete silence. All those not involved in the work must stand well clear of the excavation."

Nathan McFain—annoyed at being ordered about on his own property—nevertheless yielded. He backed away muttering something about eggheads and interlopers and who'n-hell-do-they-think-owns-this-land.

Moon and the McFains waited with the antiquarian while flash lamps popped.

Horace Flye was busy with many small errands. The dental pick and horsehair brush were used with great delicacy by Professor York. He had made the discovery; it was his singular honor to begin the delicate process of exposing the artifact.

Minutes stretched into hours. As the tedious work proceeded, dozens of photos were made of the stone implement *in situ.* Delia made standard shots with the 35-mm film camera and close-ups with a high-resolution digital camera, whose output was immediately fed by Robert Newton into a laptop computer and displayed on a dazzling color screen. Each grain of sand near the flint implement was removed with enormous care and placed into small plastic bottles which were duly capped, labeled, and recorded in Moses' excavation logbook.

It seemed to the scientists that the work was moving far too quickly. Something might be missed.

The lay observers thought the work was taking an interminable time.

Finally—it was well past midnight—the artifact was removed from its niche under the mammoth's jawbone. Cordell York held the astonishing thing in his hand. He cradled the few grams of chipped flint like he was protecting the Hope diamond, and posed with a toothy grin as still more photographs were made. Then he offered the artifact to Moses Silver. This was appropriate protocol; Moses was chief scientist on the dig. The old man sat on the edge of the excavation, staring with childlike wonder at this marvelous find that would change his life.

But not quite in ways that he imagined.

Finally, Moses offered the treasure to Robert Newton, who had hardly said a word since the thing had been discovered.

Newton frowned thoughtfully, and murmured, "One is simply astonished . . ." He passed the implement on to Delia Silver—the expert on lithic artifacts. She gingerly placed the flint blade on a paper napkin on the card table, then instructed Horace Flye to bring a floodlight to illuminate her work. She made careful measurements with a plastic caliper. This was a long (thirteen point two centimeters) flake of material that had been struck from a large core. She weighed the blade on a balance scale, and dutifully entered the data into the logbook. This done, Delia began to study the artifact with a large magnifying glass.

Looks like Sherlock Holmes, Charlie Moon thought.

The implement had been pressure-flaked on both faces. And the pink flint was absolutely beautiful. Workmanship was adequate, but hardly brilliant. Even so, the slightly crescent shape of the blade was striking. Like nothing anyone had ever seen from the Paleolithic. Unlike Clovis or Folsom, it would be impossible to classify this artifact into a neat niche. She spent some minutes examining the carefully flaked surface.

Delia's father was fidgeting at her shoulder. "Well?" Moses said.

She barely heard his voice. This was absolutely incredible.

"Well?" her father pressed.

"It's a complex pink flint," she said in a monotone. "With several quartz inclusions."

"We should be able to identify the origin of the material," Moses said hopefully. "There are several quarries of pink flint in Nebraska. And some in Wyoming."

"It's not from those quarries," Delia said with an air of finality.

Her father smiled. She was irritated that he would venture to make observations about an area where she was the expert. "But it's clearly a skinning knife," Moses said.

"Yes," she said. "A skinning knife."

The rancher, who was watching over Delia's shoulder, mumbled to himself. "Well, I guess it's a pretty important find." A magnet to draw busloads of well-heeled tourists to the future McFain Museum.

Ralph Briggs whispered in Nathan's ear. "That is rather an understatement, my dear fellow. This artifact will set North American archaeology completely on its head. An implement of undeniable human manufacture in close association with thirty-one-thousand-year-old mammoth bones is proof positive that human occupation of the Americas occurred far earlier than the Clovis culture."

"So this flint is . . . valuable," McFain said. And licked his lips.

The antiquarian nodded. "Indeed. One could hardly put a value on it."

Cordell York—the discoverer of this treasure—cleared his throat. "I suggest that we present this artifact to the lithic research laboratory at the Smithsonian. They are among the best in the business, and will be able to analyze it for . . ."

"I'll hand-carry it to them," Delia said quickly. "I'd like to be there when they perform their analysis."

Heads nodded sagely in agreement. All were pleased that Delia Silver did not exert her clear prerogative to perform the definitive analysis of the most important flint artifact ever found in the Americas. She was not only a very competent archaeologist; Delia was an internationally recognized expert in the manufacture of lithic implements. And knew more about flint quarries than all of your Smithsonian experts put together. But the scientists understood that it was a political necessity to bring in independent investigators to analyze such an important find. When the word got out, the McFain mammoth site was going to be a very controversial subject. It would help clinch their case if other recognized experts (and potential critics) were involved at the earliest possible time. This was, after all, why the Silvers had invited York and Newton to inspect the excavation.

She rubbed the surface of the glistening flint with the tip of her finger. "I'll book a flight to Washington tonight. I imagine they'll want to keep the artifact for at least a few weeks."

It seemed that the issue was settled. It was not.

Like a striking rattlesnake, Nathan McFain scooped the flint blade off the table.

The scientists were wide-eyed in astonishment at this impertinence.

The rancher was unrepentant in the heat of their harsh gazes. "You people seem to have forgot something," he said. "Everything you dig up on my land is *mine*. This thing ain't goin' *no*place without my say-so." He thrust a thumb at his chest. "I'll decide what's to be done with this here flint rock," he made a sweeping gesture to indicate the excavation, "and with every damn piece of bone you dig up."

There was a dead silence around the card table.

Nathan McFain turned and stalked out of the tent, leaving the makeshift door flapping behind him. Vanessa gave the scientists an apologetic look, then followed her father. She evidently hoped to talk some reason into the cantankerous old man.

Robert Newton, the quiet one, was first to find his voice.

"One is simply astonished at such uncivilized behavior. We have been intimidated by a fat old cowboy with tobacco stains on his beard!"

Cordell York, though greatly annoyed that his singular discovery had been whisked away in such an unseemly fashion, appeared somewhat bemused by the incident. And he never missed an opportunity to needle a colleague. "Well now, Moses . . . I had thought *you* were managing this excavation. But it seems that Mr. McFain is pulling the strings in this little puppet show."

Moses Silver was choking with rage. "That loony old bastard . . . he's a fool. A menace. A cad. A blackguard . . . a villain . . ." The old man was fairly gasping for additional epithets.

Delia Silver's complexion was gray.

Knowing it would annoy Moses Silver, Cordell York pointed out the bright side. "Well, we do have our data."

Moses slammed his clenched fist onto the flimsy folding table, which almost collapsed under the heavy blow. The paleontologist spat his words out like bullets. "Data? Need I remind you that we don't have even a single photograph of the isolated artifact." The scientists exchanged uneasy glances. It was true. There were dozens of shots of the blade *in situ*. All in various states of exposure, half-hidden under the mammoth's mandible. But not one close-up photograph had been made after it had been removed. There had seemed time enough for the technical shots. And then Nathan McFain had rudely asserted his privilege. If the rancher managed to lose the precious flint blade . . . but of course that was absurd. How could even a moron lose such a thing?

Delia patted her father's hand in a motherly fashion. "I'll talk to Mr. McFain after he's had time to consider the implications of what he's done. It'll all work out." She smiled reassuringly. "You'll see."

Moses sighed, but he knew his daughter. One way or another, Delia would damn well get the flint blade back.

Moon watched the scene with more than a little interest. When word of tonight's discovery got out, the tribal council's concerns about the precise location of the land boundary would be escalated to an all-out crisis. There would be shouting and fist-shaking at the council meetings. Lawyers would be sent to do battle. The policeman melded into the shadows beside Ralph Briggs and Horace Flye, who were whispering excitedly. An unlikely pair to have a conversation, he thought.

"Well," Flye murmured, "I never thought I'd see such a big rhubarb over a little piece a flint."

"The rhubarb," Briggs observed dryly, "has barely begun."

He was right.

Three days had passed since the late-night show under the big tent. It was for no small reason that Charlie Moon was in high spirits—he had an invitation for supper. From the lady of the house. And Nathan McFain's pickup was nowhere to be seen. The Ute policeman parked his SUPD Blazer by Vanessa McFain's van. His early arrival had gone unnoticed, so instead of knocking on the ranch house door the Ute policeman made a detour around the barn. He stood, hands in his jacket pockets, and looked across the pasture toward the hulking tent over the excavation. It was possible that Nathan had made his peace with the academics by now. But not likely. The old rancher was mule-stubborn. And Moses Silver was struck from the same mold.

Shadows were growing long and indistinct; the twilight sky was a hard gunmetal blue. To the west, a long blade-shaped cloud was tinged with scarlet. A red-tailed hawk circled majestically over the bluff, alert for the unwary rodent.

Moon turned his attention to the pond, where some progress had been made. The curved blade of the 'dozer was pushed up against the loose dirt of the unfinished dam, which was now knee-high. Beugmann, Nathan's hired hand, had evidently finished his day's work; he'd be having supper in his cabin. This thought reminded Moon of the reason for his visit. Like her mother before her, Vanessa was a good hand with a black iron skillet. Maybe she'd whipped up some fried chicken. Or fried catfish. Or fried something else. His mouth watered at these savory prospects. He turned and retraced his steps around the barn.

The Ute policeman was heading toward the ranch house's

long front porch when a pair of headlights illuminated the barren yard. He waited while a small white Buick pulled up near his dusty Blazer. A trim-looking young woman got out. She wore a conservative dark skirt. Matching dark jacket. White blouse. With a neatly looped string tie. Dark, sensible shoes. In her right hand, she toted a leather briefcase cunningly designed to pass as a large, flat purse. She was trying very hard to look like a prosperous Avon lady. But this one wasn't peddling perfume. Might as well hang a sign around her neck advertising GUN FOR HIRE.

But as soon as she spoke, he began to have second thoughts. Her voice was . . . well . . . sweet. And very feminine. Just like the rest of her.

"Officer Moon, I presume?" She extended a small hand. "I'm Claudia Cleaver. Law clerk. With Barnes, Barnes, and Pettinger. Of Durango."

He accepted the hand and tipped his hat. "I'm Moon. Lawman. With Severo, Chavez, and Bignight. Of Ignacio."

She laughed. "I was told you'd be here."

"And who told you that?"

"Your boss. Roy Severo thought I might want a police escort, said you'd headed out to the McFain ranch."

"You need a police escort to pay a visit to Nathan McFain?" He could guess why.

She jutted her round, dimpled chin toward the ranch house, now comfortably shrouded in twilight. "I am told Mr. McFain can be . . . somewhat ill-tempered."

"Ill-tempered," Moon said with a wide grin. "I think that's the nicest thing I've ever heard said about him. But why've you come all the way out here to see Nathan?"

"The court has responded affirmatively to our request for an injunction on the land boundary question. The official decision will be mailed to Mr. McFain tomorrow, but my firm thought it in the Southern Ute tribe's best interests to deliver a copy immediately."

"Won't his lawyer call him about the outcome?"

She smiled as if mildly amused. "Mr. McFain refused to be represented by an attorney at the hearing. And he didn't even show up himself, which didn't help his case any."

Moon wasn't surprised. Lawyers cost money that the tight-fisted old rancher wasn't about to part with—and Nathan was stubborn enough to snub the court's proceedings. He tapped on the door and heard the light click of Vanessa's boot heels on the pine floor. She opened the door wide, her smile at Moon quickly shifting into an expression of mild surprise when she noticed the small woman in the dark suit. *Has he brought a girlfriend?*

"This is Ms. Claudia Cleaver. She has some business with your father." Now this should be fun to watch.

The woman gave the tall policeman an appraising look. He didn't look quite so scary in the light. "Actually, it's *Miss* Cleaver."

Vanessa stood to one side and motioned with a jerk of her head. "Dad's in the parlor."

Miss Cleaver stepped inside quickly—as if fearing the door might be shut on her—and exchanged strained smiles with Vanessa. Like a black moth, she headed directly toward the light at the end of the hallway.

Moon watched her trajectory. *Smack toward the bull's-eye.*

Vanessa gave Moon a raised-eyebrow look and whispered: "Where'd you find *her*?"

He shrugged innocently. "She just followed me home."

Nathan McFain was standing in front of the wide fireplace, admiring the object he'd placed dead-center on the mantel-piece. In a plain wooden frame—which had a fluffy cotton backing—was the flint skinning knife that had been found under the jaw of his mammoth.

"Excuse me."

He turned slowly, gave her the once-over. And frowned. A woman wearing a man's tie. And a purse that didn't look like a purse. This sure looked like bad news on wheels.

She smiled sweetly. "Mr. Nathan McFain, I presume."

He nodded. "An' who're you?"

"Claudia Cleaver."

Nathan, who was no fool, narrowed his eyes suspiciously at the visitor. "You a lawyer?"

She laughed as if this assumption was terribly funny. "Dear me, no." *Not for another year or so, Pops.* The law clerk did a complete turn, hugging the purse-briefcase to her chest. "Oh, I just love what you've done with this room. It's so . . . so inviting. It makes a person feel so *welcome.*"

"Uh, well," Nathan said as he sat down in one of the massive chairs, "why don't you have a seat." He was sure he had this one figured. Claudia was a city gal who wanted herself a cabin for a few days of rest and relaxation. Probably came down to see the mammoth bones.

Ignoring this offer, she leaned on his chair. "Have you lived here all your life, Mr. McFain?"

Somewhat befuddled by her closeness, he nodded. "Sure have. It was my father's land, and his father's before him." He sniffed. She smelled pretty good. Like she'd just had a bath.

Miss Cleaver gave him a full dose of the big-eye. "I'd love to live in such a charming old house."

The old man's mouth curled into a silly grin. "I might be willin' to take in a boarder. If she was a good cook."

She laughed, as if he were the funniest man alive. And sat lightly on the arm of his chair.

"Charlie," Vanessa whispered, "I think she's going to get in his lap!"

Moon nodded. "Maybe they'd like some privacy."

Vanessa elbowed him in the ribs.

Claudia Cleaver leaned an inch closer to the old man. "I understand you rent cabins?"

"I sure do. By the day or the week. Gas heat in every one of 'em. But I only got a few left, what with all the excitement about the excavation." He was about to add that he could rent her a room in the main house if she liked, but noticed the accusing look his daughter was aiming at him. Damn.

"An excavation," Claudia said, "how exciting. What, exactly, are you excavating?"

Moon was filled with admiration. Miss Cleaver was *good.*

Nathan tried to sound nonchalant. "Oh . . . a great big mammoth. Died ages ago."

She put her hand to her mouth. "Oh my—isn't that like an elephant?"

McFain nodded affably. "Sure is. Lotsa folks want to see

them old bones. Would you like to see 'em? I could take you over to the tent right now . . ." He made a motion to get up.

To restrain him, Claudia reached out to touch his arm. "No, not just this minute."

"Then maybe I . . . maybe Vannie could fix you a cuppa coffee."

She leaned closer to him. "Nathan . . . may I call you Nathan?"

"Why, sure." He blushed. "Hell, it's my name."

"Nathan," she whispered, "you're very sweet. I'd really just like to sit here for a moment. And talk with you."

He swallowed hard, and nodded. He peered at his daughter and the tall Ute policeman. "Uh . . . Vannie, maybe you and Charlie could . . . uh . . . go into the kitchen and whip us up some coffee and cookies and whatnot." *And take your time.*

Vanessa hesitated. Moon put his hand on her waist and guided her into the large kitchen. She leaned against a heavy table and folded her arms. "Charlie, what's going on?"

He glanced toward the parlor door. "I do think your dad's found himself a girlfriend."

Her eyes narrowed. "He's old enough to be her—"

"Boyfriend." He lifted the lid on a steaming pot. "What's for supper?"

She shrugged. "Oh . . . tossed salad. Corn on the cob. Garden peas. New potatoes. Cornbread."

He gave the oven a longing look. "What else?"

She seemed amused. "With all those vegetables, what else do you need?"

"Meat."

"You could do quite well without so much animal flesh in your diet, Charlie."

Animal flesh? He frowned at the back of her head. A woman shouldn't kid around about stuff like that. Especially a woman raised on a beef ranch.

Vanessa was peeking around the parlor door. "It's positively embarrassing to see Daddy drooling over that woman. And at his age . . ."

"I wouldn't worry about it." It was likely to be a very short romance.

* * *

Miss Cleaver whispered. Her breath was warm on his ear. "Nathan?"

"Yeah?"

"I want to give you something."

"Eh?"

Claudia leaned forward. "Here it is," she said. And kissed his forehead.

The old man blushed; he felt his breath coming in short gasps.

Her duty done, Claudia got up. And walked briskly down the short hallway to the door. And let herself out.

Nathan McFain sat there for a full minute, staring dumbly at the door. And then noticed the manila envelope in his hand. It was long. Legal size . . .

He opened it. Inside were three stapled pages. The first sheet had a fancy seal on it.

Moon was about to take a sip at the steaming cup of coffee when the old man's roar shook the house. He spilled the black liquid on his new shirt.

Vanessa, who had been pouring a cup for herself, almost dropped the blue enamel pot. She rolled her eyes. "What now?"

"I imagine," Moon said, "they've had a lovers' spat."

She gave him a look that said, Shut up you are becoming tiresome.

The policeman grinned. "Nowadays, romances don't last all that long."

"It's a damn court order," Nathan McFain bellowed. "That sneaky woman was a damn process-server or somethin'!"

Vanessa was attempting—without success—to grab the papers he was waving about. "What is it, Daddy?"

Nathan's wrath was directed at Charlie Moon, the Southern Ute who happened to be at hand. "It's all on account of that damn land-boundary dispute—with *your* people," he said, shaking the legal document under the policeman's nose. "And you brought her here—to my house!"

Vanessa looked to Moon for an explanation.

He shrugged, as if it was a trifling matter. "I've heard that some of the tribal leaders wondered whether the mammoth excavation—or at least part of it—might be on Southern Ute land. I guess they must've been talking to the lawyers." He smiled weakly. "And you know the sorta things that happen when you start talkin' to lawyers. The tribe asked for an injunction and Nathan didn't hire a lawyer or show up in court to defend himself and . . ."

"Oh my," she said, and turned to her father. "What does the court order say?"

Nathan ground his teeth and squinted at the legal writ. "It says that . . . *'no fossil bones or artifacts or specimens of any kind can be removed from the excavation site.'* Not 'til a court-appointed surveyor comes out here and determines where the property line is. Damn sneaky Utes," he muttered.

What was needed was a change of subject. Charlie Moon rubbed his belly. "Well, Nathan—I'm hungry as a bear who just woke up from an all-winter sleep." He managed a grin. "Vanessa won't tell me what we're havin' for supper . . . except for some corn and peas and stuff. But I figure she's got some beefsteaks broilin' in the oven."

The old man's lips curled away to expose yellowed canines; he licked his lips and snarled: "*I'm* gonna have me some liver. Fresh liver. And I like it bleedin' rare." The rancher's bleary eyes focused on a spot just above Moon's belt buckle. McFain's hand moved toward the sheath knife on his belt.

The Ute policeman—who was quick to pick up on subtle nuances—got the hint.

Vanessa had followed Moon outside. "Daddy's really upset."

"That crack about fresh liver was in bad taste," the Ute grumbled. *Damned old cannibal.*

She gave him a suspicious look. "Charlie, did you know what that woman was here for?"

He kicked at a pebble.

"Charlie?"

He nodded.

Vanessa was stunned at this admission. "But why didn't you warn Daddy?"

"Well, shoot—I didn't know he'd take it so serious." He smiled and put his hand lightly on her arm. "I thought it'd be kinda funny . . . you know . . . to see old Nathan hornswoggled by that slick little law clerk."

"Oh, Charlie . . . you're such a . . . a big doofus!" Vanessa turned on her heel and headed for the porch.

He watched her tall, slender form retreat into the darkness with some regret. Well, so much for honesty being the best policy. *But none of it's my fault. Neither that grumpy old man or his skinny daughter are able to appreciate the humor in things.*

A vast ocean of blackness moves in rolling waves, washing against a towering shore of variegated sandstone. Silver-haired bats and violet-green swallows swim in its cool depths, feeding on swarms of insects that dart about like shadowy minnows. A thousand dark waterfalls spill off mesas, flooding the depths of sinuous canyons, drowning the last breath of day. This relentless tide flows out of the mouth of *Cañon del Espiritu* and ripples along the warm sands toward Daisy Perika's small home . . . which will soon be engulfed. It is by any measure an awesome event. A marvelous drama covering the world from horizon to horizon.

But hardly anyone notices.

Most particularly, Charlie Moon. As far as the Ute policeman is concerned, it is almost dark. Merely this and nothing more.

Moon turned the SUPD Blazer into the narrow dirt lane that snaked off the rutted gravel road toward Daisy's front porch. The lights in the trailer were on. But it was still the Moon of Dead Leaves Falling—when the long winter nights came, the old woman would follow the sun to bed. Especially now that her television set wasn't working. Which reminded him—he was supposed to take the thing into Ignacio for repairs. She'd be better off buying a new set, but Aunt Daisy would rather spend forty or fifty dollars every year patching up that old black-and-white relic from the '60s. Now there was a notion for a Christmas gift. A little color television that would fit neatly on the small shelf in her kitchen. With Sarah Frank living here, that would be just the ticket. Pleased with himself for this insight, Moon switched off the ignition.

Daisy had watched her nephew pull up to the edge of the fan of light from the sixty-watt bulb hanging over the porch. She recognized the wide grille of the SUPD Blazer, but didn't open the door until he knocked.

Moon took off his dusty black Stetson and looked around the kitchen. "Hi," he said to his aunt. And glanced hopefully at the cookstove.

"Hmmmf," Daisy said. "I guess you want something to eat."

Denied his supper by Nathan McFain's wrath, Moon was starving. "If you got something handy."

Sarah was at the kitchen table, drawing pictures on a yellow pad with crayons. Yellow birds and purple flowers. The little girl scrambled out of the chair, scooped up her cat, and came to greet him. "Hello, Charlie."

"H'lo, Sarah."

"Mr. Zig-Zag says hello too." She held the black cat up for his inspection.

Does she expect me to kiss him? He backed away, but nodded cordially. "Good evening, cat." Moon retreated to the stove where his aunt was stirring a thick brown broth that had bits of meat in it. He whispered in Daisy's ear, "So tell me the truth—this little girl too much for an old woman to handle?"

"Not this old woman," she muttered. Daisy gave him a sly look and raised her voice. "Tomorrow's Saturday. Sarah wants Uncle Charlie to take her somewhere, don't you, Sarah?"

Uncle?

"Yes, Uncle Charlie. Aunt Daisy said you'd take me to see the elephant."

Some fast footwork was called for. A distraction. "If she's your Aunt Daisy, I'm way too young to be your uncle. By about a hundred years."

When you wanted something, grown-ups always tried to change the subject. "But about the elephant . . ."

So much for distractions—but maybe she could be discouraged. "It's not a real live elephant like in a zoo. Just a pile of old bones."

"I know," she said brightly, "I read all about it in the newspaper. The bones are from a mammoth. They looked a lot like regular elephants. The ones that lived way up north had long red hair to keep them warm."

"Yeah," he said. "I guess long hair would keep you warm. 'Specially if it was red."

Sarah gave him a puzzled look. Sometimes Charlie didn't make sense.

Daisy's lips twisted into something that resembled a smile. "So is nice Uncle Charlie gonna take this sweet little child to see the elephant?"

This is a hard-hearted old woman. But Moon had not yet surrendered. A delaying action was called for. "Well, I'll have to think about it." Moon thought about it. He had lots of things to do tomorrow. Interesting, useful stuff that didn't have anything to do with crumbly old bones or grumpy old aunts. Or talkative little girls. So he thought.

The old woman tapped the lid of the steaming pot with a stained wooden spoon, "Sarah wants to see the elephant." She aimed a threatening scowl at her nephew. "Does Uncle Charlie want his supper?"

His stomach rumbled an affirmative reply. One last shot. "I've got lots of other things to do tomorrow, so we'd have to get a real early start." He glanced at his wristwatch. "I'd have to get here before the first crack of dawn." That should discourage both of 'em.

Sarah smiled blissfully at the tall man. "I always get up before it's light outside, Uncle Charlie."

Daisy smirked.

Uncle Charlie—who knew when he was whipped—yielded the game. But it wasn't fair. He'd been double-teamed.

Nathan sat very still, staring hard at the legal document. He tried—like Vannie was always urging him—to see the positive aspect of this calamity. He cogitated about it for some time.

Well, maybe there was a bright side to this court order. For one thing, those damn tightfisted Utes would be out a bundle in legal fees. And on top of that, they'd have to pay for the land survey. Could be he was maybe a foot or two onto their land. So let 'em put up a new fence—to keep his stock from eating their grass! Ha. Serve 'em right. Greedy, land-grabbing redskins!

Under the dark circumstances, Nathan was blinded to the rich cultural heritage from his Navajo grandmother's branch of the family. But he was already sorry about giving Charlie Moon a hard time. Wasn't good manners to threaten to cut out a fella's liver and have it for supper. Not when the man was an invited guest in your home. And Charlie was a good man—for a Ute. Moreover, Vannie seemed to like him.

Nathan's daughter was gazing blankly into the fireplace, at a heap of dying embers. A charred husk of piñon log—also consigned to death—was having a last smoke. Vanessa was thinking about Charlie Moon. Such a big, dumb clown. She wondered whether he'd ever come back to the ranch. And whether he liked her. She was tall enough to intimidate most men. On dates, she wore flat heels and slouched in an effort to appear shorter. But Charlie Moon was practically a giant. Surely he felt comfortable with a tall woman. She pricked her ears as the humming sound of an automobile engine disturbed the quiet. But it wasn't Charlie Moon's SUPD Blazer.

Nathan McFain also heard the sound. "We got s'more company." With any luck, it would be somebody to rent a cabin.

Vanessa stretched like a lazy lioness, yawned, and headed upstairs to her bedroom. "Well, I've had about all the excitement I can stand for one day. You can deal with it, Daddy."

The rancher didn't get up from his chair until he heard the sound of footsteps on his front porch. A man's heavy boots. And the lighter step of a woman. He pitched the offensive manila envelope onto a heavy pine table and headed for the door. The old man saw the woman first. After that, he hardly wasted a glance at the broad-shouldered man who stood protectively beside her. *She looks like one of them gals whose pictures are in the magazines showing how pretty the lipsticks looked on their lips. Or the ones that do the shampoo com-*

mercials on the TV. Lovely, ivory skin. Huge blue eyes. And hair the color of ripe strawberries. It fell over her shoulders in great waves.

"Hello," the vision said in a velvety voice. "I'm Anne Foster. This is my friend, Scott Parris."

The friend, who was the Granite Creek chief of police, nodded. He wasn't surprised that the old fart didn't even look at him. Anne had this effect on all of his gender. From puberty to senility, it didn't much matter.

The aging owner of the dude ranch found his voice. "I'm Nathan McFain. You're not a lawyer or somethin' like that, are you?"

Anne glanced uncertainly at her escort, and shook her head.

McFain allowed himself a sigh of genuine relief. "Good. I couldn't take another one o' them right now. Unless she was workin' for *my* side."

The beautiful woman lit up the darkness with a smile. "I understand you have rental cabins."

"Sure do. Every one of 'em has a bathroom, telephone, satellite TV, and a kitchenette. And they come stocked with some food, but you pay the replacement cost if you use it." At triple the retail price. He backed away from the door and made a hospitable gesture to indicate that they should come inside.

They followed him into the pine-scented warmth of the enormous parlor.

Scott Parris liked the room. Especially the massive fireplace. "We'd like to stay for a night or two."

Nathan looked directly at the woman's escort for the first time. Young fella had a sort of hungry, wistful expression when he glanced at the pretty redhead. Not like a husband. And neither of 'em wore wedding bands. "I don't rent a single cabin to couples unless they're man and wife. I'm kinda old-fashioned that way."

"So's she," Parris said glumly.

Anne patted her boyfriend on the arm. "We're not exactly tourists, though, Mr. McFain. I'm a journalist. I might want to do a story on your mammoth excavation."

He showed them to an uncomfortable leather-upholstered

couch, then pitched a pine log on the fire which responded with a flurry of sparks. "Them scientists is awful touchy about newspaper stories. They won't give you the time of day about what they're doin'."

"I don't need much. Just a few facts. And some photographs, of course."

"Well, you got yourself another big problem there. Since the *Drum* published that picture of the bones, old man Moses has had a strict rule: no cameras inside the tent. The tent *I* put up," he added by way of explanation, "that's where they're digging up the bones."

Anne's lovely face mirrored her disappointment. "If I ask nicely, perhaps they would allow me to take just one or two photos."

Nathan McFain shook his grizzled head. "I wouldn't bet my last dollar on it."

Parris smiled. The old man would be missing a good wager.

She removed a small notepad from her purse. Tomorrow—after he'd had time to think about what he shouldn't say—might be too late. "Perhaps you could tell me just a few things about the excavation. For my outline."

"Well, I'm not really supposed to say anything about—"

"Please." Anne hit him with the man-melting smile.

McFain knew full well that he should say nothing whatever about the age of the bones. Or the butchering marks. And most important of all, he must not breathe a word about the flint skinning knife that'd been found under the beast's jawbone. He understood all of these things perfectly well. But this woman's eyes were so large. And so blue. And Nathan—though well past middle age—was not yet dead.

So he spilled his guts.

While he was talking, Anne noticed the framed artifact on the mantelpiece. When he finished his account, she said: "The skinning knife . . . I'd give anything to have a look at it."

McFain hesitated; his gaze left the beautiful woman long enough to fix itself on the framed flint blade. "There it is," he said. Boy, Moses Silver would be fit to be tied.

She approached the massive fireplace for a closer look at the artifact. "May I take it down?"

"Sure. Help yourself." Some fine pair of legs she had. Nope, there wasn't nothing at all wrong with this woman. He wondered whether her young man knew how lucky he was.

Parris knew he was lucky. But he wasn't feeling so young.

Anne brought the wooden frame to Nathan McFain. She leaned on his chair. Her long, wavy locks hung close to his ear.

The old man felt his pulse racing. Well, now. Maybe she'd sit down on the arm of his chair, just like that other woman who'd brought the court order.

But alas, she did not.

Anne stared intently at the blade fashioned of delicate pink stone. "It's quite impressive." But she was wary of such an unlikely tale. The journalist remembered what she'd learned in North American Archaeology 101. The "first Americans" had arrived about twelve thousand years ago. It didn't take a math whiz to deduce that a thirty-one-thousand-year-old fossil mammoth skeleton in Colorado was far too ancient to have been butchered by humans. Something was wrong here. "Mr. McFain . . . you're absolutely certain this artifact was found with the mammoth bones? I mean in close proximity?"

"Sure," the rancher said with just a trace of indignation. "I was there when it happened. Watched 'em dig it out from under his jawbone."

"So the mammoth is a 'he'?"

"That's what those eggheads say. A full-sized bull mammoth. They could tell from his . . . uh . . . pelvis."

She shifted her weight slightly.

McFain felt his throat go dry. Great day in the morning! She had some kinda pelvis herself. The old man—who had been openly gawking—felt the chill of a cold stare from Scott Parris.

Anne sat down beside her boyfriend. Quite close. Scotty was so *cute*. Imagine him being jealous of such an old duffer. But men could be so insecure. She considered asking permission to take a photograph, then thought better of it. The old man might say no. Better not to ask. She found a 35-mm camera in her purse. "Scotty, if you'll remove the skinning knife from the frame, I'll take a photo before Mr. McFain shows us our cabins."

Nathan McFain started to protest. But didn't. She was such a sweet, pretty, innocent thing. And shoot fire, what could it hurt if she took a picture of an old flint rock? Of course, if Moses Silver found out, he'd be spitting up blood. The thought warmed him.

Anne took a dozen shots in little more than a minute. She would also need photographs of the mammoth bones, and Professor Silver would certainly object. But that should be no serious problem.

The rancher chewed thoughtfully on his pipe stem. Despite Scott Parris' annoyance, McFain was brazenly staring at her legs. *If you don't like it, young man, then lump it. Me looking won't hurt nothing.*

Butter Flye, from her lofty perch on the spine of the hogback, entertained her imagination by staring out the small window. Much more interesting things were going on outside the trailer than inside the little television that Daddy liked to watch after his supper. For one thing, all the people who lived in the TV were very small, so they could fit inside the little plastic box. She wondered where they all went when the light in the box was turned off. They must have little beds they went to sleep in. Probably the beds were inside pretty little houses, though. Not in ugly trailers with dirty rubber wheels.

But the people she saw outside the trailer—even though they looked small when they were far away—were very large. Like the Big Bad Wuff who'd come to the ranch house. She'd watched him through Daddy's binoculars when he walked around the barn and looked across the pasture at the big tent where Daddy worked. Then the lady in the white car had come. Wuff went inside the big house with the lady. Nothing happened for a while, until the lady had come back to the white car. Then Wuff had come outside with the skinny lady who lived in the big house. The skinny lady had said something, waved her arms like she was mad, and stomped back to the big house. Wuff stood there looking at the house for a while, then he'd left in his black car.

Butter had stopped spying when Daddy came home. She

made herself a Velveeta cheese sandwich with gobs and gobs of mayonnaise. It was good with an orange pop. After she was through with her sandwich, Daddy had switched off the lights and turned on the TV but it was only a rerun of Wheel of Fortune. So she had taken up the binoculars again. It was dark, but you could still see stuff with the binoculars, even at night. Another car came. A man got out, and opened the door for a pretty lady. The lady had kissed the man when they got out of the car, so she must like him. From the porch light on the big house, Butter could see the lady's long red hair. Then they went inside the big ranch house. When they came out, the old man who lived in the big house had come with them. The pretty woman walked up to the cabins with the old man with the white whiskers, the younger man drove the car along behind them. When the old man left, the lady and the younger man had stood by one of the cabins and kissed again. For a looonnng time. Eeech! Kissing spreads germs that make people sick—that's what Mommy had taught her. So why do grown-ups want to spread germs and get sick? It was a mystery.

"Butter," her father growled, "it's late. Time for you to go to sleep."

Butter put her bunny pajamas on, and took the binoculars as she climbed into her small bed in the end of trailer. Daddy would sleep in a longer bed on the side, which had a center section that went up to make a dining table during the day. She pulled a small, lumpy pillow under her head and lay on her side, staring at her father. There was a small window above her bed and she could see out by just raising up on her elbows. But she couldn't do that now because Daddy would say, Butter what did I tell you to do now lay down and go to sleep or I'll have to whop you one. So she pulled the cotton blanket up to her chin. And stared at him. And waited. It wouldn't be long till he said it.

"Butter, close your eyes."

"But I'm not sleepy, Horace."

"I keep tellin' you, don't call me Horace. It's disrespectful. I'm your daddy."

This nightly ritual done, they both relaxed. He got a beer

out of the small refrigerator and popped the cap. And gave his full attention to the brew and the TV.

"Mommy says you drink too much likker."

"Your mamma ain't here and this ain't likker," he shot back. "It's medicine."

"Are you sick?"

"No. I don't never get sick, 'cause I always take my medicine. Now put a sock in it."

Horace Flye watched the small television screen until well past the late news. He waited for his daughter to go to sleep, but her eyes were wide open. He'd learned long ago that it was no use to insist that she go to sleep. That just made it worse—she'd lay awake all night if you told her she had to sleep. So he sat there. And watched the weather report. And a talk show where people were complaining about the government. And an old John Wayne movie. Still, her eyes were wide open, like two fried eggs.

Shoot. Only female I know who's as exasperatin' as her mamma. He faked a yawn, turned the TV off, and undressed. Horace Flye climbed into the larger bed. He counted to thirty, then faked a snore.

Within minutes, he heard regular breathing from the child. Taking care to make less noise than a two-pound tomcat walking on a wet log, he slipped into shirt and trousers. And buttoned his heavy winter coat. He switched on a tiny nightlight, and stood quite still, watching his daughter. Her lips were barely parted, her breathing even. Yep, Butter'd sleep like a sack o' beans all night now. Not that there was all that much night left. But he had an invitation. A very special invitation.

Horace Flye slowly turned the latch. The hinges on the aluminum door were well-oiled, so he hardly made a sound as he left.

A moment after the door was closed, the child was fumbling frantically for the binoculars. Daddy was *so* easy to fool. She propped the heavy instrument on the narrow aluminum windowsill and watched him make his way down the winding path that led to the cabins. He stopped once to look back, and she caught her breath. But Daddy must've not seen her in the window, because he turned and started down the side of the ridge again, walking real careful. Like a man afraid he might step into a hole.

The child watched her father pause by a cabin. She lost sight of him as he turned the corner toward where the front door was. She focused the binoculars on the side window, and got a glimpse of him being let inside. He had a big smile on his face. Then someone pulled a red curtain, and she couldn't see anything at all.

But she wasn't sleepy. Not at all. Butter Flye felt like something was going to happen on this night. Something important. So she'd just wait and see what it was. But in spite of premonitions, little children must have their rest.

So she did eventually drift away.

Daisy Perika has been sleeping quite soundly for hours. And—heaven be praised—almost without troublesome dreams. But now, not long before the sun will float up like a yellow balloon over the San Juans, the shaman begins to be troubled in her slumbers.

It is so peculiar. I'm not me. I'm someone else. And my head hurts like thunder. And I'm laying here flat on my back. It's dark, and wet and awfully cold. And now somebody's throwing dirt in my face! Stop that . . . stop . . .

The dreamer tries to move her arms . . . but is paralyzed. She opens her mouth to call out. No sound will come.

God . . . please send someone to help me!

Sarah Frank, hearing the awful groans and moans, slipped out of her bed and scooped up the sleeping cat from his box. The child hurried to the old woman's bedroom, and held the creature close to Daisy's face. "Wake her up, Mister Zig-Zag."

Whether the sleek black feline understood the child's command is a matter for conjecture. But the animal did lick the old woman's lips with his corrugated tongue, which had the texture of gritty sandpaper. Moreover, he did this with some gusto.

Daisy Perika awoke with a terrible start, to feel something loathsome scratching against her mouth—and a pair of bright yellow eyes staring into her own. She raised herself on one elbow and swatted viciously at the animal. "Aaaaaa . . . get away from me!"

Mr. Zig-Zag, who attached not the least importance to the unpredictable emotions of human beings, was not at all bothered by this abrupt rejection of his ministrations.

Sarah, on the other hand, was hurt by this inexcusable rudeness. She drooped her lower lip. "He was only trying to help, Aunt Daisy. You were having a bad dream and we wanted to wake you up."

Daisy collapsed back onto her bed, gasping for air. Compared to being smooched on the mouth by a filthy black cat, being buried alive didn't seem half-bad . . . but what had brought on such an awful dream?

Something I ate, most likely.

Butter Flye had awakened to find herself still alone in the small trailer. She lay on her back, listening to the wind moan in the big pine trees. It was calling to her—saying something scary she didn't want to hear. The child clamped her hands over her ears. Butter wondered where Mommy was. And wished Daddy would come home. She felt terribly alone.

But she was not alone.

Just outside the trailer, there was a ripple in the darkness.

The mud-caked figure made not the least sound as he placed his hand close to the window . . . within inches of where the child's head rested on a lumpy pillow. His grimy fingertips almost touched the glass . . . but not quite. The Magician did not see her. But he was acutely aware of her warm presence, and it pleased him.

This was the one he had been waiting for.

The child was startled by familiar sounds. First, the door of Daddy's truck opening with a whining squeak. Then it closed with a solid thunk. She heard the starting motor grind for the longest time. Finally, the engine sputtered to life. She got up on her elbows and watched while the truck moved away slowly . . . leaving her and the trailer behind. Along the long dirt road that followed the knobby spine of the ridge, then down into the valley where the headlights illuminated trees and bushes. It kept on going. Past the cluster of cabins among the trees. Right by the big house where Daddy's boss lived. Along the driveway and under the big sign at the main road. And then it was gone, like a firefly swallowed by an owl.

The child was not alarmed. From time to time, Daddy would leave in the middle of the night. Usually, he'd come back home just before dawn. "Cattin' around," Mommy had called it. That was one of the reasons Mommy had left them, Butter thought. Because Daddy went out a lot at night. That and he never had no money and he drank like a fish. But she wondered what "cattin' around" meant. Maybe he was out looking for cats. The ways of grown-ups were mysterious and not much worth thinking about. So she laid down on her small cot and pulled the cover up to her nose. And closed her eyes to the darkness.

"Now I lay me down to sleep . . ."

DISAPPEARING ACT

FOR ALL HER big talk about getting up early, Sarah Frank had not been pleased to roll out of her warm bed while it was still pitch-dark outside. Now securely belted into the front seat between Charlie Moon and Daisy Perika, the dark-haired girl rubbed her eyes and yawned.

Daisy Perika, to her nephew's surprise, was in rare good spirits. Disgustingly cheerful, in fact. The old woman was always ready for an outing.

Moon, who had expected to have a hearty breakfast at his aunt's trailer-home, had been fed a hurry-up snack. A single fried-egg sandwich on white bread; a lukewarm cup of coffee. *Instant* coffee. This did not do much to improve his outlook.

They were heading away from Daisy's trailer-home, almost directly east. The greater of the heavenly lights was just rising over the crisp profile of the San Juans. A long crack snaked like a thin rainbow across the laminated glass. This fault—combined with a variety of pits from gravel and a decade of sandblasting—made the Blazer windshield worse than useless when the sun was looking the driver right in the face. The Ute policeman pulled down the brim of his black Stetson to shade his eyes from the blinding beams that illuminated every pit and crack in the glass. When he turned north at Fosset Gulch Road, the sun wouldn't be so bad. But in the meantime, there was nothing to do but squint. It was not, he assured himself, like he was completely blinded. But if anything much smaller than an elk stepped in front of the Blazer he was dead meat.

What this old bucket of bolts needed, Moon decided, was some new glass. Also a rebuilt V-8. Fresh coat of paint would be nice. Wouldn't hurt to jack it up and install a new transmission, exhaust system, and some new snow tires.

Best solution was to jack it up real high. And drive a brand-new automobile underneath.

Sarah Frank spoke her first words since a hurried breakfast. "I gotta pee."

Moon pretended not to hear.

"You might as well stop," Daisy said.

He pulled onto the edge of the rutted lane and set the parking brake.

Sarah unbuckled her seat belt, craned her neck, and made a wary inspection of the barren landscape. "Where's the bathroom?"

Daisy was fumbling with the door handle. "Out there's the world's biggest bathroom," she chuckled. "All the animals use it, whenever they please."

"Animals?" Sounded icky.

"Sure. Deer and raccoon and mice."

Sarah frowned. *And woolly bears and cobra snakes and red-eyed lizards.*

Daisy pushed the door open and pointed. "Hurry now—right over there's a nice little bush you can hide behind."

A chill gust of wind blew dust into the patrol car.

Sarah shivered and glanced up at Moon. "It's all right, Charlie. I don't have to go now."

He rolled his eyes, put the Blazer into gear, and eased back into the most prominent set of ruts. And for a few moments things were peaceful.

Nothing lasts.

With no warning, a very loud disembodied Voice called out: "Charlie Moon. You there?"

The little girl, startled by this sudden query from nowhere, screamed. "Ieeeeeee . . ." This outburst emptied all the lobes of both her lungs. She inhaled. "Who . . . who was that?"

"Who was what?" Moon responded innocently.

Daisy patted the child's hand. "Don't fret, Sarah. It was just the police radio." She shot her nephew a scowl. "Charlie shouldn't have it turned up so loud."

"Oh," Moon said, "the radio." He twisted the volume knob, then reached for the microphone. "Moon here. What is it, Nancy?"

The dispatcher's voice was crisp and clear. "Charlie . . . or can I be so informal? You want me to call you Deputy Chief of Police now?"

" 'Your Excellency' will do," Moon said dryly.

"Okay by me. Soon's you have time, Your Excellency—check with Daniel Bignight. He's waitin' on three."

"Understand. G'bye." He turned the channel selector button on the obsolete Motorola radio. All the other SUPD patrol cars had fancy computer-control consoles. Moon was determined to keep his life simple. "Daniel—this is Charlie."

The response was almost immediate. "Mornin', Charlie. I'm here at Capote Lake."

"Good for you. What's up?"

"Abandoned vehicle. On tribal land."

Moon frowned. Why was Daniel Bignight bothering him with an AV report? Probably it was listed as stolen and the young officer was eager to tell his supervisor about the coup he'd counted. Or maybe there was a body in the vehicle. Or maybe Daniel was lonely and wanted someone to chat with. One way to find out. Moon pressed the mike button. "Tell me about it."

"I got a 1973 Dodge pickup. Arkansas plates. Some empty Coors cans in the cab." He read off the license number. "And it's registered to a Horace Milchester Flye."

Moon smiled. Milchester? Mr. Flye had not listed a middle name for the arrest report. "Is there a camping trailer hooked to this truck? Or parked nearby?"

"Nope." There was a pause. "No trailer I can see."

"And no sign of the owner?"

"Nope. But the pickup's unlocked, key's in the ignition. Hood feels cold, so I guess it's been here for at least a coupla hours."

"Sit on it, Daniel. I've got a delivery to make. If Flye shows up, give him a breath test, and notify me. If I don't hear from you, I'll come by and have a look. So just relax. Take a coffee break."

There was a smile in the amiable Pueblo man's voice. "Ten-four, Charlie. I'm already breakin' out the thermos and the donuts." *It'd be nice if those rumors about Roy Severo's retirement plans were on the up and up. Charlie Moon would make a good chief of police. And he'd sure be an easier guy to work for.*

Moon hung the microphone onto the dashboard mount.

Daisy frowned over the child's head at her nephew. "What's that all about?"

He shrugged under his sheepskin jacket. "The abandoned pickup belongs to a guy who works for Nathan McFain. At the mammoth excavation. Sounds like he parked by the lake, had a few beers, then wandered off to relieve himself. I expect he saw Bignight's police cruiser show up and decided to stay outta sight till Daniel leaves. But it's pretty chilly weather, so Flye'll probably show up before Daniel finishes his sack of donuts." The Arkansas man had left his truck on Southern Ute property, but the trailer was probably still at the McFain ranch. Which was not in Moon's jurisdiction. Might be a good time to notify the state police. Something had to be done. A child deserved more parental attention than the little girl was getting . . .

"Now I *really* gotta pee," Sarah said.

Moon could see the humpy silhouette of the Flye trailer as soon as he turned into Nathan's driveway and passed under the long sign which advised the hopeful dude that he (or she) had arrived at McFain's haven for city folk who craved to experience the thrill of the wild West with the added benefit of microwave ovens and satellite television (149 CHANNELS, the sign said in small print).

Nathan McFain's pickup was parked by the long front porch. There was a thin coating of frost on the windows. Vanessa's Chevy van was in its customary spot under a bushy willow. So Nathan's skinny daughter had managed to stay with her father for more than a week. Moon smiled. Must be a strain on the both of 'em.

The Ute policeman had intended to drive directly up to the ridgetop RV camp and check to see whether the Flye trailer was occupied. And if the child was there, make sure she was okay. But parked beside a cabin called O-K Corral was the familiar red Volvo. And exiting from the Corral was his best friend. Moon slowed the Blazer; he pushed a button to lower the window.

"Hey, Mr. Chief of Police," he called, "ain't you a little ways outta your jurisdiction?"

Scott Parris, who had been about to open the Volvo trunk, turned and smiled. "Hiya, Charlie." He saw Daisy Perika hunched up in the Blazer. The old woman had a shawl wrapped around her shoulders. Parris nodded respectfully at the tribal elder.

She nodded back. This *matukach* was a pretty nice fellow. For a crazy white man who'd once shot a big hole through her roof.

Moon got out to shake his friend's hand. "What brings you here?"

"Anne. She's writing an article about the mammoth bones."

"Oh," Moon said with a raised eyebrow. Well, this was cozy.

"I'm in the O-K Corral," Parris said with a rueful grin. "She's next door."

"Oh," Moon said again. "You two really ought to get married."

"We have an . . . arrangement."

"Yeah?"

"We'll get hitched soon as she pops the question. Unless I'm too old by then."

Moon regretted raising the subject. Scott Parris had proposed to the beautiful woman last year. She'd turned him down flat. Something about a former marriage. A macho husband who liked to use his fists on women. She'd gone down for the count and wasn't quite ready for another round. "So you came along to keep her company."

"It's my day off." Parris noticed the child in the SUPD Blazer. "Is that who I think it is?"

"Yeah. Sarah Frank. She's staying with Aunt Daisy for a while."

Parris smiled at the little girl. "I bet she wants to see the bones."

"You got it."

"Why don't you guys come inside. We'll fix you some breakfast."

Now this sounded interesting. Especially after what little Aunt Daisy had provided. He looked up the ridge toward the RV park. "What's on the menu?"

Parris, who was familiar with his buddy's preference for deep-fried food, glanced toward his girlfriend's cabin to hide a grin. "Anne brought some cereal. Skim milk. Strawberry yogurt. Texas-Red grapefruit."

"Uh . . . thanks anyway, pardner. Matter of fact, I already had something to eat this morning. At Aunt Daisy's."

"Then at least come and say good morning to my main squeeze."

"That'll be a pleasure."

Charlie Moon left his aunt and the little girl in the company of Scott Parris and Anne Foster. Someone had to check on Horace Flye's small daughter. There was a sinuous but inviting path leading up the hill through the piñon grove, so he parked the SUPD Blazer in a graveled lane that wound around behind Anne's cabin. And began the long walk.

Butter Flye, who had watched the arrival of the black police car with considerable interest, put the binoculars aside when she saw Wuff coming up the path. Being lonesome for company, she was quite pleased that the tall man was headed for the trailer. He must be coming to visit her—there was nobody else up here. But the others in the party were of more interest to the child. She wondered who the little black-haired girl was. Was Wuff her daddy? And the old lady who walked with a stick and was all bent over. Maybe she was Wuff's mamma. Whoever they were, they must be friends of the other man and the pretty red-haired lady because the old bent-over woman and the red-haired lady had hugged and then the red-haired lady hugged the little black-haired girl. Like a big, happy family. Probably all of them lived in nice little white houses with lots of grass and trees.

The policeman was halfway up the hill when he heard the sound of an engine. It was Nathan McFain's pickup. The old man wasn't leaving the ranch, though. He was making his way up the long graveled road that ascended the hogback. So maybe Nathan was paying a call on Horace Flye. Or thought he was.

Even with the tall man's long stride, the pickup got to the RV park well ahead of him. When Moon topped the ridge, Nathan—oblivious to the policeman's approach—was eyeing the camp-trailer. Moon slowed his pace. Nathan evidently realized that if the pickup was gone, Flye was gone with it. The rancher muttered something Moon couldn't hear, then reached for the doorknob.

Moon was two yards behind him when he spoke. "Good morning."

Nathan jumped like he'd been stung by a wasp. He whirled to face the voice. "What?"

Moon grinned. "Sorry I spooked you, Nathan. I guess Flye didn't show up for work, huh?"

"Well . . . no. And they need him at the tent. Thought I'd come up here and see what's keepin' him."

The policeman pointed out the obvious. "Looks like his pickup's gone."

"Yeah. Maybe it broke down somewheres. Flye's old Dodge is a real pile of junk. Not worth runnin' off a cliff."

Nathan was in a nasty mood. Maybe he was still unhappy about the process server. And the court-ordered land survey that might give the Utes a few yards of his pasture. And a piece of the mammoth excavation. "Daniel Bignight found Flye's pickup parked over at Capote Lake. But maybe his daughter's at home."

McFain's jaw dropped. "Daughter? But . . . but he lives by himself."

"That what he told you?"

"Well, he never exactly said but . . ." The realization gradually grew in the old man's eyes. "That sneaky little son of a bitch. I told him up front I'd have to charge him extra for the RV hookup if he had anybody with him. I was square with him, and the little bastard played me for a sucker."

Moon saw a small face appear in a window. When he made eye contact, the face was quickly withdrawn. Butter had evidently been told that she must not be seen by the landlord. "She's not big enough to make much of a difference. Let's see if I can arrange an introduction. You and her may get along just fine."

McFain turned on his heel and waved off the suggestion. "I don't want to meet no kin of Horace Flye's. When he gets back here, his ass is fired. And he'll have an hour to clear out. You see him before I do, you tell him that." The rancher cranked up his shiny pickup and roared away.

Moon, who remembered his last experience with this child all too well, tapped somewhat tentatively on the sloping roof of the beetle-shaped trailer.

As before, the little round face appeared in the small window in the door. Pug nose flattened against the glass. Cold little blue eyes staring at him like he was peddling encyclopedias. Pumpkin-colored freckles splattered all over her face. What was it Yogi B had said? Ah yes. *Déjà vu all over again.*

"Hi there," he said with the most congenial smile he could muster.

No response.

"I bet you remember me, Butter, I'm—"

"You're the Big Bad—"

"Yeah. That's me."

She tried to see behind him. "Where's the Wicked Witch?"

"That's Wicked Witch *Elena.*" He waved his hand to indicate the western end of the reservation. "She's out there somewhere. Doing something despicable, I guess."

"She have a big black car like yours?"

This kid don't miss much. The SUPD Blazer was parked almost out of sight in the piñon grove at the foot of the ridge. "Nope. When she's on patrol by herself, Elena rides a big black broom. Goes about the countryside makin' cows go dry and mean little kids break out in freckles."

Butter didn't smile.

This kid was a tough audience. "I need to talk to your father."

"He's gone in the truck."

"When did he leave?"

"Last night. When it was real dark."

"Did he tell you where he was going?"

She shook her head. "I was sleepin'."

He leaned on the trailer roof. "You have any idea what time it was?" Dumb question. Poor little kid probably can't tie her own shoes, much less tell time.

"I didn't look at the clock, but it was way after John Wayne went off."

So maybe she could tell time. "Ah. And which John Wayne movie was that?"

She shrugged. "The one with all the fightin' and shootin' and Indians."

"Oh yeah. I remember that one. D'you have any idea where your father may have gone?"

The child thought about this for a moment. "I expect he's been cattin' around. And by now he's laid out somewheres, piss-eyed drunk."

Moon winced. "Now where did you ever hear language like that?"

"That's what Mommy always said about Daddy when he didn't come home."

"Oh." The by-the-book routine would be to report the situation to the Archuleta County Child Welfare officer. She'd contact the judge, the judge would notify the sheriff's office, and somebody would come out and take Miss Butter Flye into custody. They'd most likely have to rip the door off the hinges first. But that would be their problem. In the meantime he had to make sure she was okay. "It's kinda cold out here. You warm enough inside?"

She nodded.

"You got plenty to eat?"

"I'm fixing to make me a fried egg with cheese on top. And a sausage patty. And biscuits."

His stomach growled. She must be kidding. "You're kidding."

She gave him a puzzled look.

"No . . . I mean . . . you actually cook your own breakfast? Even biscuits?" Maybe Butter Flye is an Arkansas midget.

"I'm not a *baby.* I just turned six last month." She held up four fingers and both thumbs. In case Wuff didn't know what a big number six was.

"Well, you be real careful. Don't burn your fingers or nothing. Hot grease is dangerous stuff."

This man was funny. She liked that.

"I'll be back to check on . . . I mean I'll want to talk to your father. When he shows up." He turned to leave.

Butter watched him make a half dozen paces down the path. With every step, she got lonesomer and lonesomer. "Mr. Wuff!"

The policeman stopped and looked over his shoulder.

"You want to have some breakfast with me?"

Moon seemed doubtful. "Well, I don't know . . . Do I have to eat outside?"

She unlatched the door.

It was with some difficulty that he folded his tall frame into the cramped camping trailer. He crouched to make his way through the painfully small door. At its apex, the arched steel ceiling was barely six feet from the plywood floor, so it was impossible to stand upright. The policeman was mildly surprised to discover that the Lilliputian home of the Flye family was—for the den of a scroungy-looking bachelor and his tiny daughter—rather neatly kept. The little girl wore a sacklike dress she had pulled on over flannel pajamas. She flapped around in blue cloth house slippers that were much too large. Her mother's, Moon guessed.

He assisted the child, who deftly converted her father's bed into a breakfast nook. With a bit of twisting and grunting, he slid into the bench seat which gave him the best view of her domestic activities.

She stood on a wooden box in front of the stove and began to prepare a breakfast. The oven had been preheated. All of the required ingredients were on a scarred Formica counter at her elbow. A half-carton of eggs. A partially used package of pork sausage. Grated cheddar cheese in a plastic sandwich bag. A canister of refrigerated biscuits. Salt and pepper shakers. Various instruments for cutting, stirring, spooning, flipping. A stainless steel skillet sat on the tiny two-burner gas stove, a ring of blue flame flickering underneath its blackened bottom. Moon watched with quiet admiration as Butter made the pork sausage into patties. She plopped them into the skillet, which responded with a delicious crackling sound. When this greasy task was completed, she wiped her tiny hands on a paper towel.

This was, he decided, a remarkable child.

Expertly, she cracked an egg on the edge of a coffee mug. "How many you want?"

There was only one sensible response. "How many you got?"

She glanced at the carton. "Five."

"Five is a nice round number." In normal circumstances, Moon would not have thought of eating this little family's last egg. Or even their first. But by lunchtime this child would be well provided for. And when the law caught up with the scoundrel Horace Flye, he would be charged with child abandonment and jailed. The Flyes' camp-trailer would not be needed for quite a long time, so it was only sensible to clean out the small refrigerator now. Moreover, the delectable aroma made him ravenously hungry.

Butter, having disposed of the eggshells in a plastic garbage bag, smacked a long cardboard cylinder firmly against the edge of the counter. Whitish-gray dough began to ooze out. She peeled off the plump disks one by one and plopped them onto a cookie sheet. "I'll have to make alla these biscuits." She slipped them into the oven. "They don't keep very long after you open the can."

"Well . . . we'll just have to put our heads together," the big

Ute said with a thoughtful frown, "and work out some clever way to get rid of 'em."

She shot him a sideways glance and almost smiled. "There's a jar of blackberry jam in the cupboard."

"There, you see? The excess biscuit problem is practically solved already."

There was a long silence while she tended the skillet.

"Remember . . . watch out for the grease."

She scowled at the skillet. "I been doin' this ever since Mamma left us."

Another long silence.

"Maybe Daddy ain't coming back this time," she said with a little sigh. "Mommy went away and never did come back." She turned the piercing blue eyes on him. "Do you want cheese on top of your eggs?"

He shook his head dumbly.

She spoke without taking her watchful eye off the skillet. "D'you live in a house?"

"Yeah."

"Daddy and Mommy and me, we always lived in this trailer. Someday I want to live in a real house." She salted and peppered the eggs. Whenever policemen came to see Daddy, they always took him away. Now a policeman had come to see *her.* "What are you gonna do with me?"

Charlie Moon tried to speak but could not. And his appetite had said *adios*.

Scott Parris held the tent door open for Daisy Perika and Sarah Frank, then followed Anne into the shelter. The visitors were pointedly ignored by the scientists, who were busy with many tasks.

Daisy—who felt as one treading on graves—remained at a respectful distance from the mammoth's partially exposed remains. Something was wrong here.

Anne Foster, noting that the child was shy, took Sarah Frank's hand and led her toward the excavation pit. Sarah paused by one of the tripod-mounted sheets of polished aluminum. And stared at her reflection in the mirrored surface. "What's this for?"

Anne explained that the reflectors were used by photographers to direct light where it was needed.

The Ute-Papago girl was satisfied with this explanation; she glanced at the clutter of large bones, then looked up uncertainly at Anne.

"It's okay. Go ask the man what he's doing."

Robert Newton was busy in the excavation pit. He was making close-up photographs of the femur when he became aware of the little girl. He greeted the child with a grandfatherly smile. "Good morning, young lady."

This was a nice man. She looked him right in the eye. "I've come to see the bones."

"Ahhh . . . one is always pleased to see young folk who are interested in the past. Would you like to know more about the mammoth?"

She nodded shyly that she would.

The paleontologist put his work aside. He provided Daisy's youthful ward with a rather thorough explanation of the excavation. Gradually, Sarah began to ask the sad-looking little man about certain issues that were important to her. ("Did he ever have toothaches?" "Did lions and tigers kill him?" "What happened to all his skin?") The scientist did not talk down to the child, but dealt with her queries as worthy of thoughtful, accurate answers. This made Sarah feel important. And very grown-up.

When Robert Newton had completed his conversation with Sarah, Anne Foster steeled herself. It was time to reveal her profession—and her intent to write a detailed article about their work. She headed for Moses Silver.

Scott Parris waited in a dim corner of the tent with Daisy Perika. The lawman was wondering how his darling would handle this delicate negotiation. The Ute elder thought about more fundamental issues. Birth. Life. Death. And the presence of evil. The shaman muttered urgent prayers in the Ute tongue. And wondered what might be required of her.

Polite introductions were exchanged between the journalist and Moses Silver. At Moses' invitation, Anne Foster seated herself at the card table. Robert Newton, sensing that something was afoot, had left his place in the pit to join Delia and

Cordell York. The three academics, exhibiting various levels of tension and expectation, stood—literally and figuratively—behind the chief of the excavation.

Anne took a deep breath. "Dr. Silver," she looked up politely to acknowledge the presence of the other scientists, "none of us has time to waste. Let's get right down to business."

York was pleased at her directness. *Poor old Moses . . . I'll wager he's underestimated this one.*

Moses Silver nodded curtly. "Tell me how I may be of service." You'll get nothing, his stern expression said.

"It's simple, really. I have a story to write. And I'd like to ask a few questions about what you've found so far." *And get straight answers.* "I'll also need to take a few photographs of the excavation." She offered him the gift of a soft smile.

Moses returned the smile. His manner, if slightly condescending, was not unfriendly. "Miss Foster, I regret to inform you that at this early stage of our work, photographs of the fossils are absolutely out of the question. Once we have published our findings in an appropriate peer-reviewed scientific journal, then—if our results should warrant it—photographs will be made available to the press."

She tapped a ball-point pen on the card table. And stared at him with the large, blue eyes. For some seconds. Which seemed like minutes. Small beads of perspiration appeared just above Moses' upper lip.

Daisy Perika chuckled; she nudged Scott Parris with her elbow. "I'll bet you two dollars she gets to take her pictures."

Parris, who knew his woman, politely refused the wager.

"I do understand your position, Dr. Silver," Anne said finally, "and I respect it. No reputable scientist wishes to have his," she glanced up at Delia, ". . . or her work reported first in the popular press."

Moses smiled warily. "I'm pleased that you understand our position."

"So," Anne continued, "I'll simply have to go with what I have. It should be enough . . . though confirmation of some of the facts would have been preferable." She reached out to shake his hand. "Thank you so much for giving me a hearing."

Moses shook her hand like an automaton. He swallowed; his Adam's apple bobbled. "Excuse me, Miss Foster . . . but I hardly see how you could have sufficient information even for a story in one of your . . ." He'd almost said "tabloids."

"Well, I appreciate your concern. I have enough for a terrific story."

It was Delia who dared ask the question. "What could you possibly know?"

"The mammoth bones are well over thirty thousand years old . . . and there are the butchering marks."

Moses felt his stomach churn. It had to be Nathan McFain who'd talked. The bloody idiot!

"Without your verification, I won't be able to sell my story to *Time*," Anne said serenely, "but there are . . . other markets."

Moses felt the beginnings of a migraine. "Such as, perhaps, the *National Enquirer*?"

Anne smiled sweetly. He expected an immediate denial that she would submit her story to a tabloid. Let him sweat!

The implications of her non-reaction brought a chill to the ranks of the academics.

Robert Newton fairly shuddered at the thought. It would be bad enough to have a speculative story about the excavation in a respected newspaper. That, they could survive. But a supermarket tabloid that specialized in impregnations by aliens and sightings of Elvis Presley in the White House? One's reputation would be forever soiled.

She got up and pushed her chair aside. Time to drop a small grenade. "Additional photographs would have been very helpful. But I do understand your position."

As she had intended, Moses had keyed in on the critical word. "Excuse me, Miss Foster . . . did you say *additional* photographs? From this, one must assume that you have already obtained unauthorized . . ."

The waters had been troubled. Now she rolled the depth charge overboard. "Mr. McFain was very kind. Last evening, he allowed me to take several photos of the skinning knife that was discovered . . . under the jawbone of the mammoth, if I understand correctly. Of course, if you wish to deny it, I'd certainly accept your word." *Gotcha.*

Moses paled into a wooden silence. Even Cordell York was hushed. It was Robert Newton who surprised everyone by speaking, though he was merely muttering to himself. "This is simply unforgivable. This rude fellow confiscates the artifact, and now we learn that he has allowed this journalist to . . . Well, it is just astonishing."

"I'll take that as a confirmation that the flint blade was found as reported," Anne said evenly. She scribbled meaningless scrawls on her notepad as she muttered: "Confirmed: age of fossil bones . . . butcher marks . . . flint artifact found in association with bones." She looked innocently up at Moses. "Unless you wish to deny that these are the facts."

"McFain!" Moses yelled, and banged his fist down on the card table, which utterly collapsed at his feet. "That confounded idiot told her everything!"

Anne, though startled, was unperturbed. "I'd really like to take a few photographs of the mammoth bones . . ."

"Certainly not," Moses said sullenly. "Whatever you publish, it will be without authorization."

Delia's hands were on Moses' shoulders, her strong fingers gently massaging the old man's tight muscles. Her dark eyes appealed to Anne Foster. *Please don't give my father a hard time.*

Robert Newton's face wore a mask of serenity, but he was nervously pulling at a pendulous earlobe.

Cordell York sighed. The old man was foundering. Clearly needed a bit of help. "Excuse me," he said.

The other scientists were surprised to hear such a polite phrase pass the arrogant man's lips.

"I believe I have a solution." York directed his remarks to Anne. "It happens that I am senior editor of a distinguished quarterly journal that deals primarily with North American vertebrate paleontology. Our winter issue is almost ready to go to press, but I am prepared to e-mail a short technical note this evening, presenting the Silvers' preliminary findings. The article would carry today's date. By this means, the initial scientific paper will precede any publication in the popular press that may result from your efforts. This will help deflect criticism from our straightlaced colleagues and thereby enable the

Silvers to provide you with an accurate summary of their findings to date. In the spirit of such mutual cooperation, we would expect you to publish nothing more than a . . . uhh . . . sober and factual account of what you learn here."

Anne swallowed a sarcastic response. "It's a deal."

Moses looked up at the vain man with grudging respect. "It seems a workable solution. Not," he added bitterly, "that we have much choice."

Delia Silver beamed on Cordell York, who accepted this adulation as his just due. "I think it's a simply wonderful idea."

"I would rather describe my contribution," he said brightly, "as a wonderfully simple idea. But all praise is gratefully accepted."

Anne Foster was completing her photography of the mammoth bones when Nathan McFain, accompanied by the dapper antiquarian, barged into the tent. "So," he boomed, "I see you got to take your pictures."

She nodded. "Everyone has been very kind. And cooperative."

The rancher thought Moses Silver looked ten years older. McFain was inordinately pleased by Silver's unexpected capitulation to the pretty journalist. "Hah," he said, "well, I'm glad to hear it."

Moses shot Nathan McFain a look that would have shaken a lesser man.

McFain absorbed the impact and lobbed back a wicked grin. The rancher was well aware that he had always been more tolerated than welcomed (on his own property!) by these standoffish eggheads. Now it was apparent that none among the academics intended to acknowledge his presence with so much as a "good morning." So they were still pissed off about him taking *his* flint blade. Well, they'd get over it. Or they wouldn't. All the same to him. As far as he was concerned, they were here to do a job. Much like hired help, except better. They worked without pay.

Ralph Briggs—who might have been a soul mate to Cordell York—watched with delighted amusement as the paleontologists snubbed Nathan McFain. The exception was Delia Silver. Though she kept at her work, she nodded and smiled at Nathan. The young archaeologist, the antiquarian guessed, would be the one to try and talk some sense into the rancher's thick skull. Explain how important it was that all artifacts remain under the control of her father. At least until every bit of data could be gleaned from them. *Well, lots of luck, kiddo.*

Butter was perched on Charlie Moon's shoulders, her tiny hands clasped around his forehead. She was enjoying the ride. It was funny, she thought, how people smelled different. Mamma always smelled like her perfume. Daddy smelled like tobacco. This big policeman smelled like soap. "Giddup, Wuff," she said.

Moon had his broad-brimmed Stetson in one hand, the other was occupied with a pillowcase stuffed with a few belongings the child had insisted on bringing. "Don't forget," the Ute policeman said, "if anybody asks you—you're a Mugwump."

"Okay." She frowned. "What's a Mugwump?"

Moon grinned. "An Indian tribe. Some of your daddy's relatives."

"Oh." These were new kinfolk to the child. But all additions to her small family were welcome. "Giddup *faster,*" the little Mugwump said, and dug her heels into his chest.

Moon and his small burden were entering the tent just as Anne Foster took her final photograph of the excavation.

The antiquarian was the first to notice the appearance of the gigantic man carrying a chubby blond tot. "My soul," Ralph Briggs said in mock horror, "what have we here, poor fellow—a horrible growth on your neck?" He made a funny face at the girl.

She made a face back. More particularly, she pulled her lower lids down with her fingers, to expose a nauseating roll of pink flesh under her pale blue eyes. And stuck her tongue out at him. It looked like a raw sausage.

The antiquarian was—in his own words—chagrined. Not to say nonplused.

Moon lowered her tiny feet to earth.

Except for Daisy Perika—who gave the elfin newcomer a wary look—the child drew the women like iron filings to the poles of a magnet.

"How sweet," Anne Foster cooed.

"Well, well—who is this?" Delia Silver asked.

"Meet Miss Butter Flye," Moon said.

"A butterfly," Anne said as she patted the tousled yellow mop. "My, what a little angel!"

"Little insect," Briggs muttered acidly.

Scott Parris watched Anne's interaction with the child. Maybe someday she'd want one of her own. Or maybe two . . .

Daisy Perika leaned to have a close look at the small creature. "Butterfly, eh?" These white people were apt to have the most peculiar names.

"This is Butter," Moon explained. "Daughter of Mr. Horace Flye."

Delia's hand went to her throat. "Oh my God," she whispered. "I had no idea . . ."

Nathan McFain stared uneasily at the child.

Butter stood very still, one hand clutching the precious pillowcase.

Robert Newton kneeled beside the child. "The usual reason we have young guests is that they want to see the elephant."

The blue-eyed child gave him a blank stare.

Newton persisted. "Do *you* want to see the elephant?"

Butter nodded, and was led off by the hand to hear lurid tales about the huge beast whose bones lay in the sandpit. Sarah Frank, who had been upstaged by the arrival of this rival, followed along pensively. Giving the chubby little white girl the once-over. Then the twice-over.

Daisy sidled up to her nephew, and whispered. "What're you doin' with that little girl?"

"Police business," Moon said dismissively.

"Hmmmf," she responded. Charlie Moon could be downright mean.

Moon caught Scott Parris' eye. At a nod from his friend, Parris followed the Ute policeman outside the tent. Moon noted with some satisfaction that Aunt Daisy was a few paces behind them. He'd counted on her curiosity.

The old woman stood well away from the lawmen, looking this way and that, taking a deep breath of fresh air. My, it was nice to be outside on such a fine morning.

Moon—pretending not to notice her presence—directed his words to Parris. But he spoke loud enough for Aunt Daisy to hear every word. "Little girl's father's left her at home alone." He nodded toward the long, pine-studded hogback. "They have a camp-trailer up there on the ridge. Looks like he's off on a drunk somewhere."

Daisy's expression made it clear that she had no interest in what her nephew might have to say. She hung on every word.

Parris frowned at the tent door. "So what're you gonna do with her?"

Moon seemed to think about it for a long moment. "Well, I sure can't leave her up there on the ridge all by herself. The kid needs somebody to look after her until her father comes home." Moon waited for his aunt to take the bait.

Not a nibble.

Parris, who knew his friend very well, guessed what Moon was up to. "Well, you could always turn her over to the tribe's Social Services people," he said helpfully.

"Yeah. But you never know who'll end up with the kid once they're in the system." Moon rubbed his chin thoughtfully. "I think maybe I'll ask Gorman Sweetwater to look after her. He's got a big, empty house." He saw Daisy's back stiffen. "And Gorman's got a nice farm. Dogs and cats. Pigs and chickens. All kids like animals. And I expect he'd like to have a little girl around for a while." Time for the irresistible wiggle of the lure. "And Gorman's a responsible fellow."

She was stomping across the pasture toward him, waving her oak walking staff. He smiled inwardly at the expression of outrage that twisted her face.

"Gorman Sweetwater," Daisy fairly spat the words out, "is an old fool. Not to mention being a drunk. And not only that—he's taken to wearing one o' them Dodger baseball caps. He puts it on backward, like some big goof."

Moon played the innocent. "Oh, I don't know . . ."

"No, you certainly don't," she snapped. "That's no place for a little girl. That old goat'd be feeding her red chili and Mexican beer and takin' her to rooster fights."

He snickered, knowing this would infuriate her.

"Don't you laugh at me, Charlie Moon!" She rapped at his leg with her heavy walking stick.

Ouch. He rubbed at his shin. "You've just assaulted a sworn officer of the law."

"One more star in my crown," she said in a pious tone.

Time to set the hook. "Well, if you can think of a better place than Gorman's . . ."

"What's *wrong* with you?" she said, pointing west with the walking stick. "My place is just a mile over the ridge. She can stay there for the afternoon. All night if she needs to."

"I don't think that'd be a good idea," Moon said with a doubtful shake of his head. "One kid to look after is enough . . . for someone your age."

"My age . . . what am I, one foot in the grave?"

"And I'd have to take that little camp-trailer over by your place. It's got all her stuff in it. No . . . I don't think it'd work. You have *two* girls to look after, you're bound to lose at least one of 'em."

Furious, Daisy turned to Scott Parris. "Can you pull a trailer with that ugly foreign car o' yours?"

Parris, who had gotten a barely perceptible nod from Moon, nodded cautiously. "Sure. I got a ball hitch on the bumper."

"Then," she said to the *matukach* lawman, with a contemptuous glance at Moon, "you hook up that little girl's trailer and haul it over to my place. Me and the children will ride with you and your girlfriend." She waved the heavy oak stick menacingly at Moon. "You got a problem with that, Mr. Policeman?"

Moon held his palms up in mock surrender. "I still think it's a mistake."

"Hmmmf," she said. It was good for him, every once in a while, to see that when her mind was made up she couldn't be pushed around. Imagine, leaving a tiny child with Gorman Sweetwater! Charlie Moon must be keeping his brain in his watch pocket.

When the trio entered the tent, they saw Sarah Frank standing off near the edge of the shadows. All by herself. But Butter Flye had the adults eating from the palm of her grubby little hand. Exulting in all the attention, she searched the pillowcase, and proudly displayed bits of tattered clothing.

Yellow-and-white socks.

Bits of tiny underwear.

A hank of scarlet ribbon . . .

Charlie Moon had just cranked the Blazer's engine when he saw Nathan McFain making determined strides toward him. The rancher threw up his hand in a gesture meant to detain the policeman. Moon lowered the window and waited.

"Charlie," Nathan said, "I'm sorry about poppin' my cap like that about Horace Flye shortchanging me on the RV rental. Look . . . it's okay if the camp-trailer stays on my property for a while. The man was my employee, so I got a responsibility to his daughter."

Moon cut the ignition. "You have any idea why he might've left?"

He shook his head glumly. "No mystery in that, Charlie. The good-for-nothing little bastard just decided to skip and leave his kid behind." The rancher spat tobacco juice onto the curled bark of an old cottonwood. "I expect his pickup broke down over at the lake. He's hitched himself a ride and headed back to Arkansas, most likely."

Moon nodded. "Could be."

"If it's the kid you're worried about, Charlie, I'll make some arrangement to see she's looked after. At least till the . . . uhh . . . authorities can do something with her."

"That's thoughtful of you, Nathan. But it's been taken care of."

"Who's gonna look after her?"

"My Aunt Daisy."

The old man frowned suspiciously. "What happens to that hillbilly or his kid ain't no concern of the Utes."

"Might be," Moon said. "Flye's truck was found on tribal land." But the Ute policeman thought about Nathan's offer. It made some sense. After a few days, Daisy would tire of taking care of two children. And if . . . no, *when* Horace Flye sobered up and remembered he had a daughter, the McFain ranch was where he'd expect to find her. It was hard to imagine the cantankerous Nathan taking care of a little girl. But Vanessa would enjoy Butter's company for a few days.

Jimson Beugmann's intrusion interrupted these thoughts. The deaf ranch hand pulled a dusty Jeep Wagoneer alongside Charlie Moon's Blazer. He nodded respectfully at the Ute lawman; Moon returned the gesture.

The rancher scowled at his employee. "Where'n hell you been?" Nathan snapped. "There's a pile of work to be done."

Beugmann—who had difficulty lip-reading Nathan when the old man talked too fast—was unfazed by this onslaught. He fumbled for the notebook in his coat pocket, then penciled a response.

ILL GO START THE DOZER UP

Nathan spoke more slowly. "The bulldozer? What for?"

More hurried scribbling.

THOUGHT ID MAKE THE POND A COUPLE FEET DEEPER

"The damn pond's deep enough already," Nathan snapped. "And Horace Flye's not at work today. So you head over to the tent and lend them eggheads a hand with the diggin'."

The deaf man—who had understood barely half his employer's words—shrugged, put the Jeep in gear, and chugged past the barn and across the pasture, leaving a trail of silence in his wake.

"The worstest thing about bein' in any kind of bidness," Nathan McFain said with a weary shake of his grizzled head, "is findin' yourself some reliable help."

The small lake, named after the Capote band of Utes who had originally inhabited the lands near the headwaters of the Rio Grande, is situated in the southeast armpit of the T where Route 151 drops off 160 like a taproot. Officer Daniel Bignight was parked just outside the gate across the graveled road that meandered down to the water's edge. The Taos Pueblo man had drunk a quart of sugary coffee and consumed a half dozen jelly-filled donuts before he saw the familiar black Blazer approaching from the south. Pleased to have company, he waved happily at Moon.

Charlie Moon got out of the Blazer; a sudden gust of wind helped him slam the door. "Mornin', Daniel." He frowned at the open gate. "How come that ain't locked?"

Bignight shrugged. "Somebody from the fishery department must've been here in the last coupla days, stocking the lake with rainbows. Deerskunk, probably. You know how he is about gates."

Moon did know. Arthur Deerskunk was conscientious enough when it came to looking after the tribe's fishing interests. But the absentminded man had probably never remembered to lock a gate in his life. He was about to ask where Flye's truck had been found, when he saw it. The police officers walked down the lane toward the lake, whose mirror surface was a shimmering picture of pale blue sky dotted with feathery wisps of cloud. The pickup was in a small grove of willows. It sat precariously on an incline. Almost like Flye had considered driving into the waters, then thought better of it.

"No sign of the owner, I guess."

"Nope," Bignight said. "I don't think he's gonna show." He tended to have hunches about such things. They were rarely off the mark.

Moon paused by the old vehicle and frowned at the marshy bank. "Flye's that Arkansas fella who got into a fight over at Tillie's Navajo Bar and Grille."

Bignight grinned. "Sure, I remember 'im now. They say Curtis Tavishuts just about chewed his ear off."

"He's been working at Nathan McFain's ranch. Keeps a little camp-trailer in McFain's RV park. He left in his pickup last night . . . sometime after two A.M., I guess." He glanced meaningfully at his fellow officer. "You don't suppose he decided to take a . . . uh . . . swim."

Bignight—who understood the euphemism only too well—

shook his head. "Early this morning—I must've got here a good hour before sunup," he pointed a stubby finger at the lake, "there was a thin skim of ice going out about six feet from the bank." It had melted in the late morning sun. "After I found the truck, I walked around the whole lake. The ice wasn't broken nowhere, Charlie. He couldn't of gotten into the water without stompin' through some ice." Bignight grinned. "Not unless he took a helluva big flying leap."

Under the circumstances, Moon didn't think the remark was funny. But then Daniel Bignight didn't know about little Butter Flye. "Anything we can learn from the truck?"

"Nothing much. Except he left the keys in the ignition. And there're a half dozen dead Coors cans in the cab." Both men were silent for some moments.

Moon stared at the lake. Trying to dismiss the absurd image of Horace Flye leaping over the ice like a gazelle.

Bignight kicked a bald tire. "Maybe he came out here, sat around long enough to kill a six-pack. Then his truck wouldn't start."

Moon nodded absently. If that was the case, Flye might have attempted to walk back to the McFain ranch. And got lost in the wilderness. City-bred deer hunters disappeared out here almost every year. Some were never found.

Daniel Bignight eased his fleshy frame into the cab, and scooted behind the wheel. The policeman tapped his right foot on the accelerator pedal, stomped his left onto the clutch. "I always liked these old pickups. Give me a straight shift any day. Better gas mileage. And a man feels like he's driving a honest-to-God truck when he's got a standard transmission."

"Give it a try," Moon said.

Bignight turned the key in the ignition. The engine cranked. And cranked.

Moon recalled Flye's instructions. "It needs some choke."

Bignight pulled the choke button and tried the starter again. The old V-8 coughed, then sputtered to life. Bignight looked at the tall Ute, and stated the obvious. "Nothin' wrong with the truck, Charlie. Maybe he just got too drunk to start it."

Moon nodded absently. He pulled on his gloves. One by one, he picked the empty Coors cans off the floorboard.

Sniffed at them. Odor wasn't all that strong. He turned each container upside down to see if anything was left. Not a drop. Evaporation had had time to do its job. So these cans hadn't been emptied last night. "Arrange to have the truck taken back to Ignacio, Daniel—and bag everything in the cab." He glanced at the rear of the pickup. "And the bed, too. This looks like he just went off and left it, but let's treat it like . . ." His voice trailed off. Like what? Like a little girl's father wasn't ever coming home again? There was no evidence of that. Horace probably had a bottle with him. He was probably curled up somewhere under a willow, sleeping off a drunk.

Maybe not.

Charlie Moon had his share of hunches too.

Scott Parris drove slowly with a wary eye on the rearview mirror—watching the camp-trailer bounce and weave behind the Volvo. Anne was beside him. The old Ute woman was in the middle of the rear seat, with a little girl on each side.

The chubby blond child got up and leaned on the seat behind the driver.

Parris frowned at her image in the mirror. "You oughta sit down."

Ignoring this suggestion, Butter Flye put her grubby hand on his shoulder. "Do you live in a house?"

"Sure."

She ran her finger along his collar. "I allus lived in that little trailer with Daddy and Mommy. But someday I'm gonna live in a nice white house. With green shutters. And a big yard. With lots of grass and trees. And birds."

"Good for you, kid. Now sit down."

Anne Foster had barely heard the conversation between her boyfriend and the waif. The redhead was lost in her own thoughts. She had two dozen photographs of the mammoth excavation, including close-ups of the "butchering marks." And Moses Silver had confirmed what she'd heard from Nathan McFain. This was the most important North American archaeological discovery since the fluted spear points were found in association with fossil bison and mammoth bones near

Clovis, New Mexico. And that was more than sixty years ago. She'd have to move fast, before someone else got wind of this. But she had already telephoned the science editor at *Time*—and Bernie was hot to trot. *Get the manuscript to me by day after tomorrow,* he'd said, *and we'll make next week's issue.* This would be an all-night job at the word processor—and in the darkroom. One way or another, the draft and photographic prints would be going out by Air Express tomorrow morning.

Daisy Perika, settled placidly on the rear seat, had said not a word since they pulled away from the McFain Dude Ranch. Except for Butter Flye's remark to Scott Parris, the girls, one at each of Daisy's elbows, had also remained silent. Sarah Frank was very still. Shy in the presence of the new child, Daisy assumed. Little Mothball . . . no, her name was Butterfly . . . had gathered more of her possessions when they hitched up the trailer. The chubby white child had gotten a small shoe box in her lap. The lid—which was secured with rubber bands—had holes punched in it. Like something inside needed to breathe. The Ute woman frowned warily at the cardboard container. "What've you got in there?"

Butter Flye looked up at the wrinkled face. "Somma my stuff."

"What kind of stuff?"

"Neat stuff. Some sand. Pretty rocks. And my jools."

The old woman cocked an eyebrow. "What's 'jools'?"

Butter was astonished at such ignorance. "Jools is like dimuns and rubies and rhinestones and things like that."

Daisy—who about a thousand years ago had been a little girl herself—nodded with sudden comprehension. Jewels . . . little bits of colored glass.

Butter Flye pulled at the rubber bands. "I used to keep Belly Button Fuzz in here."

"Good place to keep it." *Peculiar child.*

Butter sighed wistfully. The white hamster had died just a day after Daddy named him. "Now I keep Toe Jam in here. You want to see?"

Daisy wrinkled her nose and raised a hand in defense. "No, thank you. Just keep the lid on it." Peculiar wasn't the word. "Where're you from?"

"Black Dog Holler. That's in Arkansas."

"Oh." Well.

"I'm glad to be going home with you."

"Well," Daisy lied shamelessly, "I'm glad too."

"The Wuff said I'd like it there."

"The what?"

"The great big man."

"You must mean Charlie Moon."

Butter nodded.

A little warning bell tinkled inside her skull. Daisy squinted suspiciously at the pale little face. "Exactly *when* did Charlie say you'd like to come and stay with me?"

"When he was ridin' me on his back. Down to the big tent where they got them elephant bones."

Daisy Perika was struck dumb. Why, he'd had it all planned out! *Charlie Moon—with his silly remarks about leaving this child with Gorman Sweetwater—he's snookered me into taking this freckle-face tubby into my home. And he'd probably misled me about how soon the little toad's father would show up. So now I got another mouth to feed.* No doubt about it. Her trusted nephew had pulled a fast one on her. She'd always thought Charlie Moon was not too bright, but oh so nice. But what a slicker and a scoundrel her young relative had turned out to be.

It made her very proud.

But not so proud that she wouldn't find a way to get even.

COVER STORY

ANNE FOSTER'S HAND trembled as her finger touched the numbers on the telephone. She listened. It rang three times . . . four.

Scott Parris picked up. And yawned. "H'lo."

Her voice was electric with excitement. "Scotty—have you seen it?"

He sat up in bed. Looked around. "Seen what?"

She shook the magazine in her hand, in a vain attempt to get his attention. "My story on the mammoth excavation. It got a full page in *Time*. The editor hardly cut a word, Scotty. And they even didn't change my title—'Paleontologists Astonished'—or my subtitle—'Mammoth Hunters in the Americas Thirty Thousand Years Ago.' "

He rubbed his eyes and tried to sound excited. "Wow."

"And that's not all."

"Tell me, babe."

"You remember the flint blade . . ."

He frowned. Blade?

". . . the artifact I photographed in McFain's parlor."

Oh yeah. He closed his eyes and nodded.

"Scotty? Are you there?"

"Sure. I remember. In the frame on the mantelpiece."

"Well, my color photo of the artifact made the cover."

He opened one eye. "No kidding—you got the cover of *Time*?" Now that *was* something.

She shouted into the telephone. "Scotty—do you have any idea how many people—all over the world—will read my story?"

He grinned. "Hundreds and hundreds?"

"Don't be a smarty. And meet me at the Sugar Bowl. Lunch is on me."

FIFTEEN KILOMETERS NORTH OF 'URAY 'IRAH
SAUDI ARABIA

Some twelve thousand miles away, a cool darkness had already slipped across the barren expanse of rolling dunes, whose shimmering waves were but a hint of the underlying sea of viscous hydrocarbons. In the midst of this arid ocean, a magnificent barge lay at anchor . . . tethered to the distant city by a serpentine rope of asphalt. It was the collector's desert home. There were no electric or telephone lines. There were three fifty-kilowatt diesel-powered electric generators in a subbasement. And two microwave antennas cunningly concealed on the flat roof. On this night, the seas were up. A relentless wind blew gritty sand against panes of rose-tinted glass of mullioned windows set like glistening jewels in walls of pink Italian marble.

On the third floor, behind one of these windows, a thin, nervous man sat alone. From the burning dark eyes set in a gaunt, haunted face, a stranger might have guessed him to be an artist. Or a fanatic. He was neither.

The thin man, having had his modest dinner of broiled lamb and mildly seasoned rice, was secluded in the one room in his enormous home that was totally private. No one—not his favorite wife, not even his most trusted body servant—dared enter this sanctum.

Though a minor prince among his people—an aristocrat unaccustomed to any menial labor—he maintained this small museum by his own efforts. Once each month, he cleaned the glass in the display cases with a mixture of ammonia and distilled water. Weekly, he used a red foxtail brush to remove powdery alkali dust from basalt statuary of thick-lipped Aztec potentates, Mimbres pottery embellished with red rabbits and blue lizards, hideous face masks hammered from Inca gold. Every object represented the very finest—and rarest—in its category. The fact that much of it had been stolen—that virtually all had been smuggled across international borders—that blood had sometimes been spilled . . . this only served to sweeten his pride in the collection.

On this particular evening, he sat at an antique rolltop desk with a small cup of aromatic Turkish coffee. An unfiltered American cigarette dangled from his thin lips. The collector stared at the magazine cover, much as an overheated juvenile would drink in a Miss November centerfold. Indeed, the prince was filled with a burning desire . . . an unnatural lust. For this treasure. For the oldest flint implement ever discovered in the Americas.

This unique, beautiful artifact spoke to his soul. Softly. Seductively. Like a faraway lover. *Bring me to you. I will be yours alone . . . forever and forever.*

His lips moved in a silent whisper. "And so you must. And so you shall."

According to the article in *Time,* the priceless artifact was hanging in a frame over the fireplace in some old fool's house. Within a short time, it might not be so available. It would be necessary to act quickly. The wealthy man picked up a blue telephone, and was automatically connected to the EUTELSAT W-Series communications satellite positioned in a stationary orbit far above the eastern Mediterranean. He dialed a number with a British prefix. An unlisted Oxford number.

After three rings, there was an answer. "Yes?"

The Arab chose his words carefully. "We have business to discuss." He allowed a pregnant pause. "Urgent business."

"Certainly. Shall I pop over?" The expense account was more than generous.

"That will not be necessary. I shall arrive at Heathrow tomorrow evening. On Lufthansa—the usual connection through Berlin."

"Very good, sir. My driver will meet you." In the Rolls, of course.

Charlie Moon pulled the big SUPD Blazer off the paved road. He shifted into low and eased along the partially graveled lane that wound down the long incline toward Capote Lake. He stopped on the spot where Horace Flye's old Dodge pickup had been found by Daniel Bignight, and shut off the ignition. And set the parking brake.

Moon stared at the shimmering surface of the cold waters. And thought his thoughts. And then he remembered something. Something so very simple.

Butter Flye had said her father had drove off late that night in his pickup. There was no reason to doubt that she'd heard the truck engine start up sometime past midnight. But like all of us, the child made reasonable assumptions. For example: that it was her father who drove his pickup away in the middle of the night. The Ute policeman didn't know who had driven the truck away from McFain's RV campground on the top of Buffalo Saddle Ridge . . . and to Capote Lake where it was abandoned. But Charlie Moon was dead certain about one point.

Horace Flye had not parked the pickup on this slope at the water's edge.

Moon sat at Daisy's table, sipping his after-lunch coffee. The old woman was running hot water into a sink filled with dirty dishes. The girls had left the table and disappeared somewhere into the far bedroom where Butter Flye now slept with Sarah. Daisy squirted lemon-scented detergent into the water; she looked over her shoulder to make sure the children were out of earshot. "What've you heard about that *matukach* skunk who ran off and left his daughter?"

Moon drained the cup. "Nothing."

"So what are you doing? Waiting for something to happen?"

"SUPD has bulletins out to half a dozen states with Flye's name and description."

"So why don't you call in the FBI?"

"The Feds wouldn't be interested. There's no evidence a major crime was committed on tribal lands."

"Well, how long am I supposed to take care of his little girl?" Daisy whispered hoarsely. "She eats like a starved pig."

Moon was about to respond when Sarah Frank returned to the small kitchen, trailed by Butter Flye. "Uncle Charlie," the Indian girl said, "lookit what Grandma gave me." She offered a miniature treasure for his inspection.

Butter immediately scurried out the kitchen door and down the porch steps. They heard another door slam on the Flyes' camp-trailer.

"She keeps most of her junk out there," the old woman said. "Runs in and out all day."

The object Sarah had produced was about as big as the end of Moon's thumb. He used his fingernail to pry off the little lid. The workmanship was remarkable. "Nice. Very pretty. Your grandma make this herself?"

Sarah nodded proudly.

"Papago horsehair baskets," Daisy Perika muttered under her breath. "What can you do with 'em? Not big enough to stuff a grasshopper in." What foolishness.

Butter, who had returned from her brief errand, pushed her way past the older child. She plopped a shoe box on Moon's knee. "Lookit *this*."

Moon, knowing his duty, pretended to be interested. "What've we got here?"

"It's my box of pretties. You want to see inside?"

"You better watch out," Daisy muttered as she scrubbed a blackened skillet. "The child claims she keeps belly button fuzz and toe jam in there." She grimaced. "Ugh."

"Well," Moon said, "I don't know. That kinda stuff don't appeal to me all that much."

"Silly," Butter said, "Belly Button Fuzz was what Daddy named my hamster."

Daisy, who was banging pots and pans around in the cupboard, lost contact with the conversation that followed. Sarah Frank—annoyed at being upstaged by the upstart—had withdrawn to the far bedroom with her tiny horsehair basket.

Moon tapped his finger on the perforated box lid. "So, you got a real live hamster in there?"

She shook her head. "Belly Button Fuzz died."

"Sorry." But she hadn't said the corpse wasn't in the box. "I hope you gave your pet a decent burial."

Butter Flye nodded. "Daddy put him in a plastic san'wich bag. I dug a little hole in a cornfield. Then we said some prayers."

"I guess Mr. Fuzz was up there in years, so it was his time to go."

"No, he wasn't all that old. Daddy said it was liver trouble. Belly Button Fuzz drank too much beer for his own good."

"Oh." With the Flye family, nothing was a surprise.

"Then Daddy got me Toe Jam."

Moon considered this. "Me, I'd rather have a hamster."

She pulled the lid off the shoe box. "See?"

Moon blinked.

Toe Jam blinked back.

The plump creature was sitting on a hump of sand. The mound was littered with bits and chips of colored glass and stone. All the colors of the rainbow. Toe Jam stared up from his residence at the policeman. One thing was clear. He was unafraid of the law.

"Don't you think he's cute?"

Moon had a long look. "Cute" was not the word to describe this creature.

"And there's jools all around him," Butter said proudly. "That," she pointed at a chip of cherry-red glass, "is a real ruby."

The Ute policeman pointed at a small chip of pink stone. "What's this?"

"Just a pretty rock. But this," she put the tip of her finger on a chunk of transparent quartz, "is a big dimun. I could prob'ly sell it an' buy me and Daddy a real house."

"Uh-huh. Well, you better keep this stuff in a safe place."

She replaced the lid on the box. "Daddy found Toe Jam by a fillin' station where we stopped to get us a bottle of pop."

"What's he eat?"

"Daddy mostly likes eggs and chili and cheeseburgers . . ."

"No, I mean the other . . . I mean Toe Jam."

"Oh, he eats bugs and worms and flies. Stuff like that."

Daisy, her task at the cupboard finished, turned around and glared at her nephew. "What's she got in that box?"

"You don't want to know," he said grimly.

Her dark eyes snapped. "Yes I do."

"Toe Jam," Moon said.

The old woman shuddered and shook her head in dismay.

Moon got up to leave as Sarah returned to the kitchen. The Ute-Papago child said a shy good-bye.

The chubby blond child tugged urgently at his trouser leg. "Wuff?"

"Yeah?"

She offered him a small wad of tissue paper. "This is for you."

Being a prudent man, he was not eager to accept the gift.

But Butter Flye pressed the packet into his hand with an impish grin. "Want to know what it is?"

He shook his head.

She ignored this cowardly reaction. "It's some of my pretties. For you."

Moon pressed his thumb gingerly on the tissue paper and felt the sharp edges. "Well . . . thanks." Now he'd have to bring the kid something in return. And something for Sarah Frank, of course. Candy, maybe. Kids like candy. And sugar gives 'em lots of energy. He started to drop the wad of paper into his coat pocket.

The little girl looked up at him expectantly, her sharp blue eyes peering through bangs of corn-yellow hair, her pumpkin freckles darkening ominously. "Ain't you goin' to look at 'em?"

"Well . . . sure I am." He unfolded the tissue. Tucked inside were a dozen fragments of colored glass, a few chips of stone. A significant portion of this poverty-stricken child's earthly treasures.

She flashed him a gummy smile. "D'you like 'em?"

He nodded.

"Have you found my daddy yet?"

"Not yet."

"You will find him, won't you?"

Charlie Moon closed the trailer door and made his way down the porch steps. Aunt Daisy was right. Butter Flye's father was missing and he'd done nothing much more than go through the usual motions. And hope the man would show up somewhere. Maybe it was time to make something happen. But how?

The Ute policeman paused and stared at the Flyes' little camp-trailer. Might be something inside he'd missed.

The tall man had forgotten what a cramped space this was. A place built for midgets. On one side of the sink, there were two drawers. In addition to a few mismatched eating utensils, there was the usual assortment of odds and ends. A can opener. An unopened pack of cigarettes. A plastic cigarette lighter. A bone-handled pocketknife. A worn whetstone. A small can of gun oil. A scattering of pennies, paper clips, thumbtacks, rubber bands. Under the sink, he found a plastic waste container, two rolls of paper towels, a small box of tools. On a shelf over the table were a few old magazines. And some stapled papers . . . articles by the Silvers about earlier excavations of fossil bones. Looked like Horace had cut them out of a journal. Somewhere, there was a librarian who'd like to strangle the man from Arkansas.

He opened a closet that was not two feet wide.

Not much here. A couple of shirts on wire hangers. A patched pair of khaki work pants. Neither the father or the kid had much to wear. There was a plastic bag on the floor. He removed the tie-wrap and found an assortment of stale-smelling dirty clothes. If Horace had stayed around a few days longer, maybe he'd have made a trip to a Laundromat. And taken his little daughter to town with him . . .

It was a melancholy thought.

The visitor inspected the parlor. The huge fireplace was rather inviting. And the mantel-piece was quite impressive. Her nervous little dog was sniffing at a pile of logs on the hearth.

Nathan McFain put his finger on the guest book page. "You can sign right here."

"Certainly."

The rancher watched the small woman sign the guest register. She was quite fastidious with her script, seeming to draw each letter.

Beatrice Alistair-Lewis

And she talked like a foreigner. "You're not from around here, are you?"

She scooped up the fuzzy terrier in her arms, and managed an amused smile. "How did you guess?"

"You don't talk like us."

"I am obliged to hear you say so."

What'd that mean? "You from back East?"

"Very. I am originally from Aberdeen."

"Oh." Wherever the hell that was. "Well, I hope you like your cabin."

"Though somewhat rustic, it will be adequate. I know we shall like the fresh air." She kissed the dog, who returned the favor by licking her ear. "Shan't we, Sweets?"

Charlie Moon was raising his fist to knock on the door, when it was yanked open. Nathan McFain's bearded face emerged, his brow wrinkled in a surly scowl. "Come on in, Charlie."

Moon followed the rancher into the large parlor.

Nathan waved a hairy paw. "Sit anywhere you want."

Moon lowered his long frame into a heavy chair constructed of thick oak and stretched cowhide. "I guess it's too much to expect you've had any word from Horace Flye."

"Nope. I figure we've seen the last of that bird, Charlie." He rubbed his eyes and groaned.

"You look like you've had a bad night, Nathan."

The old man turned and shook his head like a great bear. "I've been better, Charlie. A damn sight better. Seems like everything around here's goin' to hell in a handbasket."

Ever since he'd known Nathan McFain, the old man had always been complaining about one thing or another. "Anything you want to talk about?"

Nathan plopped onto a massive leather-upholstered couch that was a match to Moon's chair. "Well, for one thing, I been robbed!"

"Robbed? You mean someone held you up?"

"Well, more like burgled, I guess." Nathan looked somewhat sheepish. "Some bastard must've snuck in here last night while I was asleep. And stole it. Practically right from under my nose."

"Stole what?"

Nathan pointed glumly at the fireplace.

Charlie's eyes followed the gesture. He understood immediately. The frame that had been on the mantelpiece wasn't there. Somebody had stolen the flint blade. "Anything else taken?"

Nathan McFain shook his head. "Not that I've noticed."

The old man's house was about two hundred yards from Southern Ute jurisdiction. "Have you reported this to the county sheriff?"

"Nope. Not yet." The old rancher glanced sideways at Charlie Moon. "Hell, Charlie, it's too damn embarrassing to tell the cops. See, I left the doors all unlocked last night, like I always do. And it ain't nothing but an old flint rock anyways, so what'll the cops care if it's gone? It's not like somebody stole a horse or something. But if them bone-diggin' eggheads find out it's gone, they'll be all over me like greenflies on a warm cow pie." He whined to imitate the tone they'd take: " 'If you'd left it with us, we'd still have it. But no, you hadda take charge of it, and now it's gone.' They'll think I'm just a dumb old fart, Charlie. So don't you breathe a word about this."

Moon pushed himself to his feet. "So what are you gonna do?"

The rancher let out a long sigh. "Nothin' much I can do."

"Strictly speaking, this isn't Southern Ute business." Not unless the land survey showed the thing had been found on the People's land. "But if you want, I'll do some checking. In case someone tries to sell it."

Nathan McFain shrugged. "Okay. Just as long as you don't let it slip that the damn thing's gone."

Moon made no promises. It might be necessary to inform the tribal council.

"Thing is, Charlie, I don't need no extra troubles. This has been a bad week. Horace Flye takes a hike. Now I don't have nobody a'tall except Jimson Beugmann to help those scientists dig up them mammoth bones. And they aren't too happy about it, I can tell you."

"He ought to be able to do a good job for 'em."

The rancher made a rude horse-snort. "Beugmann's deaf as a stump and stubborn as a Missouri mule. Never will do what I tell him. If I tell him to mend a fence, he'll be off tinkerin' with the bulldozer. If I've told him to haul in some hay for the stock, then he'll be 'dozin the pond deep enough to drown any tinhorn tourist that slips in. The man has an attitude problem, Charlie. He oughta be grateful to have a job here. It ain't easy for a . . . a man like Beugmann to find work."

Moon said nothing. McFain—who was a tight man with a nickel—probably wasn't even paying the deaf man minimum wage.

McFain had a full head of steam up now, and was rolling downhill. "I let Beugmann use one of my best cabins. Unless I check on him, he lets it get filthy as a hog sty. Tracks mud all over the carpet. It'd cost me a hundred dollars to get the cabin cleaned up. And to think I was too nice to ask him for a deposit."

The policeman listened with an impassive expression. Truth be known, most of Beugmann's pay was probably deducted for his use of a cabin McFain couldn't rent during the off season. No, Beugmann wasn't much more than an indentured servant. Moon looked sideways toward the slope, where the small log structures were perched among piñon and juniper. "How many of your cabins are occupied right now?"

"Aside from Beugmann's, just the four the scientists are staying in. I had a tourist yesterday—little woman with a dog—but she checked out this morning. The pretty redheaded woman and her boyfriend left a couple of days ago—but they're friends of yours, so I guess you already knew that."

He did. Scott Parris and Anne Foster were back in Granite Creek. "What about the guy who runs an antique store up in Granite Creek?"

"You mean that little Ralph Briggs fella? He checked out two or three days ago. Said he liked watchin' the diggin', but he had a business to run."

"When, exactly, did Briggs leave?"

The old man shrugged. "I guess it must've been . . . say . . . Tuesday morning when he checked out."

Moon looked over the old man's head at a decorative cluster of blue corn mounted on the paneled wall. It was probably a small coincidence that—in a manner of speaking—Horace Flye had vanished on the same morning. But very early, and under cover of darkness.

THE NIGHT VISITOR

There was an almost comical aspect to the combination of Daisy Perika's house-trailer and the Flyes' small camper. The latter was pushed up close to the Ute woman's home, its rusty steel hitch sitting on a cinder block. Like a fat calf nuzzling its mother for milk.

The shadowy figure who watched from the windswept ridge had not the least perception of subtle comedy. Indeed, he had no discernible sense of humor. All through the long evening, he had kept himself well away from the shaman's lair. Finally, when the moon had slipped from behind a feathery curtain—and the last light was turned off in the old woman's trailer—the intruder approached the Ute elder's small fortress in the wilderness. The silent figure slipped past still sturdy ranks of piñon and juniper, evaded a column of barbed yucca spears, merged into the moonlight shadow of a lightning-scarred pine that stood like a tireless sentinel near Daisy Perika's home.

After several minutes, he approached the Flyes' small camping trailer. And stood in his customary silence . . . pondering the diminutive home that rolled on black rubber tires. He knew that it was merely an empty shell . . . there was no one inside. But in the larger structure there were three human souls. And an animal. He moved toward the far end of the Ute woman's trailer home.

Where the children slept.

Time was running short. Soon, he must decide which of these it was to be. He felt a peculiar closeness to the smaller child with yellow hair . . . she was so like himself. But it was the dark girl who floated like a witch in his visions . . . she had very special qualities.

It was a difficult decision.

Mr. Zig-Zag, curled up in his cardboard box at the foot of the children's bed, raised his head. He blinked suspicious yellow eyes at the small window. Instinctively, a bristle of black hair stood up on his neck. But the cat made no sound.

Butter Flye opened her eyes and looked toward the window. She saw the pale face floating there. The child pulled the covers over her head, and closed her eyes. "Go 'way," she whispered. "Go 'way, Booger-man."

Sarah Frank—deep in a dreamless sleep—stirred as if aware of an unwelcome presence. But the Ute-Papago girl did not awaken.

Butter trembled under the covers, and wished Daddy or the Wuff was here to help her. A very long time passed. About eleven seconds. When she was unable to stand the suspense, the white child peeked from under the quilt with one blue eye.

There was no face in the window. The Booger-man was gone.

"And don't come back," she snapped.

But he would.

Daisy Perika felt a deep sense of unease. A dark sinuous current, writhing like some great serpentine creature, moved just beneath the surface of her consciousness. Sleep, so greatly desired, had withdrawn like a shy dream lover . . . just out of reach. The old woman got out of bed and hobbled to the window that looked over her rickety porch. The moon was partly obscured by a thin haze of clouds, but her eyes were well-accustomed to this near-darkness. There was nothing much to see outside; just what was always there. Except for the stark profile of the Flyes' little trailer. An ugly thing, she thought. Like a great bug. Daisy closed the curtains and slipped back into the warmth of her bed.

Nerves, that's all it was.

The night visitor melted into the shadows. But he had made his decision.

When Butter Flye awoke that morning, Sarah Frank was already pulling on her pretty blue dress.

The white child sat up in bed and rubbed her eyes. The sun was shining warmly through the window-glass on the multicolored quilt. It was a bright, real world. The Booger-man's visit seemed like a bad dream. Butter had lots of bad dreams and Daddy always said it was best not to talk about the hobgoblins and boogers and such or they'd come back to pay another call. So she did her best to forget the pale face at the window.

At breakfast, Butter dawdled. She had not finished her bowl of Cheerios when Sarah left the table to take Mr. ZigZag his morning dish of milk. The plump child sat and watched the old woman putter about the kitchen. After due consideration, she spoke: "Daisy, I want to ask you something . . ."

The old woman was annoyed. "That's no way to address one of your elders."

This rebuke produced a puzzled expression.

"It's disrespectful. No little runt like you should be callin' me by my first name."

The little runt was not offended. "What should I call you?"

The old woman smiled crookedly. "How about Princess Minneegoochie?"

"Princess *what?*"

"Oh, never mind." She slapped the tot playfully on the head with a potholder. "What was it you wanted?"

"I don't want to sleep in the bed with Sarah no more."

"Why not?"

"She makes funny noises and keeps me awake."

"Noises?"

"Like this." Butter threw her head back, closed her eyes, and opened her mouth. And produced an awful series of snorts.

Daisy grinned. "So she snores. Well, I guess I could fix you up a bed in the bathtub."

Butter banged her spoon on the table. "But I don't *wanna* sleep in no bathtub."

"Well," the old woman said, mimicking the child's nasal whine, "just where do you wanna sleep?"

"In my own place. Where all my stuff is."

The old woman glanced out the kitchen window at the Flyes' battered camping trailer. "You mean out there—in that ugly little contraption?"

Butter Flye nodded eagerly. "Mosta my stuff is out there."

Daisy considered the request. Home—be it ever so homely—was where your stuff was. And your own bed was always the best place to sleep. Surely no harm would come of letting the little girl sleep in the camp-trailer. But like a bluefly trapped in a bottle, an urgent warning buzzed around in the old shaman's skull. "No," she finally said with a resolute shake of her head. "During the daytime, you and Sarah can play out there. But before the sun goes down, you got to come inside."

Butter Flye saw that Daisy's face was set like flint and knew it would be pointless to protest. The little girl's blue eyes narrowed with outrage; her pumpkin-colored freckles took on an angry tinge of crimson. She would not be pushed around by this mean old woman.

Charlie Moon was asleep.

The telephone rang.

He groaned, rolled over, fumbled in the dark for the receiver and pressed it to his ear. "Yeah?"

"Charles? Is that you?"

"I think so."

"I've been trying to find you."

"You did. Have you had a chance to—"

"The task has been completed."

He sat up on the edge of his bed, dreading either kind of news. "You have any luck?"

"Luck, my dear boy, has nothing to do with it."

"Then you found—"

"Of course. Though—as you know—the credit is none of mine."

"Tell me." He listened to the terse report and experienced an odd, mixed reaction. The police officer was elated with this apparent victory. The man felt a dull coldness settle in his groin.

". . . and that, Charles, about sums it up."

"What're the chances it's a mistake?"

There was a thoughtful pause on the other end of the line. "There is, of course, always some small probability of an error. I'd estimate . . . perhaps one in a hundred."

"Thanks," Moon said grimly. "I owe you one."

"That you do." There was a distinct click, followed by a dial tone.

The Ute policeman stared at the telephone. And wondered what to do next. One option was out of the question.

Sleep.

So he sat at the kitchen table for a long time. Staring with an unfocused stare at the cover of *Time* magazine. Imagining a complex jigsaw puzzle—with one very significant piece lost. The weary lawman was convinced that no part of his brain was actually working. But somewhere in the darkness, something clicked. It was much like an electric shock. Had the missing piece been presented to him as a gift? Moon found his coat, removed the small parcel from a pocket. He dumped its contents onto the colorful magazine cover. For almost an hour, he used the gleaming tip of a Buck sheath knife to maneuver the small bits into various positions. But it just didn't work. No, it was an interesting little game, but the pieces simply didn't fit. He yawned. Might as well give it up. Get some sack time before the sun came up.

And then . . . he moved the right piece into the right place.

* * *

The children sat in the tiny camp-trailer, applying stubby crayons to a Denny Dinosaur coloring book.

"I guess I better go," Sarah said. "Aunt Daisy will need me to help her clean up the supper dishes." When speaking to the child who was two years her junior, the eight-year-old assumed a superior attitude befitting her seniority. "You better come with me."

Butter looked out the window at the gathering hints of twilight. "So the Booger-man won't come in here and get me?"

"There ain't no such thing as a Booger-man," Sarah said in an uncertain tone.

Butter expertly applied Lemon Yellow to the hooked teeth of a *Tyrannosaurus Rex.* "Yes there is. I *seen* him."

Sarah felt a cold shiver tickle her spine. "Where'd you see him?"

The white child fell into one of her sullen silences.

"You know what Aunt Daisy said about you stayin' out here after dark."

Butter frowned at her memory of the obstinate old woman. Big people were always telling you what to do. And most of the time, you had to do what they said. But sometimes there was a chance to get even.

The older girl was getting fidgety. "You better come inside."

Butter decided upon a delaying action. "I ever show you Toe Jam?"

Sarah shook her head.

Butter pulled the shoe box from its hiding place in the tiny closet. She set the enclosure on the table and grinned puckishly at the Ute-Papago child. "You wanna take the lid off?"

Sarah hesitated. "I ain't afraid. But it's *your* old box—*you* open it up."

With all the sense of drama natural to small children, Butter removed the rubber bands. And slowly raised the lid.

Sarah leaned forward and made a horrid face. "Ick. He's ugly."

The white child shook her head. "Not to his mamma, he

ain't." Butter's mamma had always told her how pretty *she* was.

Mr. Zig-Zag, who had been napping in the sink, got up and lazily stretched one leg at a time. Then came to have a look at what was inside the box. The black cat hissed at the beady-eyed creature.

The beady-eyed creature hissed back.

This, Sarah thought, was an odd sort of pet. "What does he do?"

Butter shrugged. "He eats bugs and worms and stuff."

Sarah grimaced at the thought. "That all he does?"

"Well, there's a trick that Daddy taught him."

"What kind of trick?"

Butter told her.

The older child frowned. "I bet that's bad for his lungs."

"His kind," Butter explained patiently, "don't got no lungs." The child did not know a lung from a kidney. But she had learned that if you make a statement with firm conviction, it is likely to be believed.

"I don't know," Sarah said doubtfully. "It sounds kinda dangerous. Children your age shouldn't play with matches. And anyway," she added with increasing confidence, "I don't think he could do that."

"Watch, I'll show you." Butter Flye—who had the necessary props close at hand—demonstrated her pet's remarkable ability.

In her wonder at this miracle, the eight-year-old child forgot the natural superiority of her additional years. "Wow," Sarah said, "that's really cool."

"Yes," Butter agreed. And it raised some very interesting possibilities. She slipped the lid onto the box. "You know what we could do?"

"What?"

The white child explained what. Leaving out not the smallest detail.

"Oh my . . . I don't know—that wouldn't be very nice. And we could get in trouble."

Butter shrugged. And played her ace. "Okay . . . if you're such a big fraidy-cat."

And thus was the gauntlet thrown down—that ageless challenge which had provoked so many ill-advised adventures.

And would again.

It is a quite odd and unexplained phenomena—how an otherwise ordinary dream sometimes weaves a carefully plotted tale that . . . But the thing is best illustrated by an example. The dreamer finds herself in a restaurant, having a cup of green tea. Suddenly, a ski-hooded gunman bursts in. The terrified customers are ordered to keep their hands in sight; a pale clerk empties the cash register. As the bandit leaves, he warns everyone to stay put. And fires a warning shot.

Nothing so unusual about the dream.

Except this: the sound of the pistol shot coincides precisely with the backfire of an automobile passing just outside the dreamer's bedroom window. It is as if the anonymous author of the dream-tale had foreseen the future and carefully arranged the plot to provide the dreamed gunshot at the precise moment of the real-world backfire.

The old shaman who lived near the mouth of *Cañon del Espiritu* had had such peculiar dreams before. And was about to have another.

As the sun is barely over the mountains, Daisy Perika is dreaming a simple dream of a sweet summertime, decades ago. She is a skinny girl on a family outing: a picnic on the banks of the Pinos. Her mother has spread a red-and-white tablecloth over the grass. Daisy, as always, is more interested in fishing than in helping her mother. She has tied a Mormon cricket onto the hook with a long strand of her black hair—and immediately catches a fine cutthroat. She watches as Daddy cleans the fish. Now, her mother is lighting a little fire to cook the trout . . . In her lovely dream the old woman can smell the aromatic smoke curling up from dry juniper twigs. But this didn't smell at all like juniper smoke. It smelled more like . . . the sleeper's nose twitched . . . like tobacco smoke.

Daisy drifted up toward consciousness. And felt the nearness of . . . something.

She opened one eyelid.

And saw *it.*

Perched there, unblinking, on her chest. Inhaling . . . exhaling . . . inhaling . . . smoking a cigarette!

The old woman's first instinct was to scream and fling her old body out of bed onto the floor. But she did not scream. Neither did she move a muscle. Because Daisy Perika is made of very tough old stuff. Like pine knots and elk horn. And ninety pounds of rawhide and oak held together with a glue of pure stubbornness. But there was another reason for her resolve: she had heard the sound of giggling from the kitchen. She smiled a thin smile. It was those mischievous girls, who thought nothing of frightening an old woman halfway into her grave. Just for a bit of fun.

Daisy moved her right hand slowly from under the covers. She snatched the cigarette from the horned toad's mouth. The old woman had expected the fat lizard to be startled, to scuttle off. But Toe Jam had evidently been in the quirky Flye family far too long to be surprised at anything human beings might do. Or maybe the habit of smoking had addled his pea-sized brain. The creature stared blankly at the woman's face, and seemed to belch. A small puff of latent smoke popped from his mouth. It is true that there is not much expression on the face of a horned toad. Even so, the elderly Ute woman was of the opinion that the reptile seemed much relieved to be rid of the cigarette, and grateful for her intervention.

Daisy heard a whisper that sounded like Sarah's voice: "What do you think she'll do, when she wakes up and sees him . . . ?" More giggles.

The old woman smiled. She deftly scooped up Toe Jam. And for the first time since she had been a child, Daisy pulled the quilt over her face . . . and snickered. But this was not a wholesome snicker.

There was, indeed, a certain malicious quality about it.

As she prepared breakfast, Daisy Perika remembered her own youthful pranks.

Like the time she'd put a gopher in Daddy's coat pocket. A pocket gopher, of course. When Daddy had reached for his twist of Bull Durham tobacco, the sudden appearance of his fingers had startled the sharp-toothed rodent. Daddy, judging from his high-stepping and heartfelt curses, had also been more than a little surprised. The stern man—who had not appreciated the subtle humor in the thing—had tanned little Daisy's backside with a willow switch. Old grump. Served him right that his finger had taken six weeks to heal.

So Daisy Perika understood that children will do such things. But one must deal with youthful shenanigans in the proper spirit. There were several appropriate ways for an adult to react—and every response used the opportunity to strengthen a child's education. Daisy Perika's favorite method was this: show the nasty little buggers just who they are messing with!

The old woman pretended to be unaware of the growing alarm shared by her small guests. The girls thought themselves unnoticed by a woman whose senses they assumed to be dulled by age. They were darting about Daisy's bedroom. Searching in her bed. Under her bed. In her closet. Clattering about the tiny bathroom. Finally, they wandered around the kitchen, glancing surreptitiously into corners. Sneaking sly looks under the table. Exchanging puzzled shrugs. Well, Toe Jam would turn up sooner or later.

When the old woman called them to breakfast, the girls dutifully took their appointed places at table. Daisy smiled sweetly at them. My, such worried little faces. She parceled out hot biscuits, then brought a heavy iron skillet from the stove. She sliced a puffy omelet into halves, then divided one of the halves into equal parts. Each child duly received her quarter-share.

Daisy poured each a small glass of milk, then sat down and sniffed contentedly. "I hope you two slept good last night."

Two little heads nodded. Two small hands reached for forks.

"I slept pretty good, myself," Daisy said. "But this morning, I woke up kinda sudden-like. Bad dream, I guess." She managed a shudder.

As if she were blind, the children glanced at each other and grinned knowingly.

The old woman spoke with an unusual gentleness. "Eat your eggs now. Before they get cold."

The children did as bidden, munching little bits of omelet. And discovered that it was very good. Had lots of cheese. And little bits of meat. So their appetites improved.

Sarah Frank held up a biscuit. "Aunt Daisy, may I please have some jelly on my bread?"

"Sure," Daisy said. Such nice manners. She smiled at Butter Flye. "You want some jelly too?" This plump one never said no to food.

The white child nodded; her ponytail bobbed.

The old woman got up, put one hand on a painful hip joint, and hobbled over to the cupboard. She headed back with a small jar. "You girls enjoy your omelet?"

Two heads nodded.

"It's a new recipe I just thought up this morning."

"I know," Sarah Frank said. "You put chicken in it."

The old woman turned and shook her head. "Oh no. Something with lots more zing than chicken."

Sarah was puzzled. "Tuna?"

"Nope." Daisy chuckled as she slammed a jar of grape jelly onto the table. "I'll give you a hint: 'Breakfast is where you find it.' "

This produced only puzzled expressions.

She leaned close to the children's bewildered faces. "I found part of our breakfast just as I woke up this morning. It was *looking* at me!" She paused to allow time for this revelation to sink in.

The children's eyes grew large. It was Sarah who spoke. "D'you mean . . ."

Daisy sat down. The old woman looked across the table at her victims. "That was my very first horned-toad omelet."

These innocents could barely comprehend such a horrid thing. They stared in horror at the barbarous old woman, who was calmly picking her teeth with a sliver of wood. They eyed the remnants of the omelet in their plates.

The bits of food seemed to look back. To accuse them. *Cannibals!*

The girls looked at each other. Butter Flye began to wail. Sarah Frank put her hand over her mouth and gagged. They ran onto the porch and made valiant attempts to spit out any bits of poor Toe Jam's carcass.

Daisy rocked back and forth, laughing until salty tears streamed down her leathery cheeks. Served the little criminals right. *That'll teach them to put a smoke-belching lizard on me when I'm asleep.*

But there was an empty chicken tin in the plastic garbage bag under the sink. The horned toad was tucked away in her kitchen cupboard. In a red coffee can with holes punched through the plastic lid. When the time was right, she'd slip the ugly creature back into his shoe box.

But not right away.

7

A COLD WALK IN MOONLIGHT

IT WAS WELL past midnight. An egg-shaped moon with the patina of dry bone hung over the shaman's trailer-home. Near the mouth of *Cañon del Espiritu*, a famished red fox sniffed along a fresh rabbit trail. On this night, the hungry fox was not the only predator prowling the darkness. Looking for something young . . . and tender.

The children were in the guest bedroom at the far end of Daisy Perika's trailer. One was in a deep sleep. One was not.

Sarah Frank flopped an arm awry, swatting the smaller child across the face.

Butter Flye pushed the offending limb away.

Sarah rolled on her side, pulling away the covers.

Butter moved closer to her bedmate, tugging ineffectively at a corner of the wool blanket. It barely covered her legs. The smaller child shivered and whimpered. "I'm cold," she said pitifully.

Sarah responded with a croaking snore.

Butter sat up in bed, her tiny hands doubled into fists. She kicked viciously at the larger girl's leg.

Sarah offered another snore in response.

Well, that did it. Butter slid out of bed and pushed her small feet into tattered bunny slippers. She wrapped herself in a thin cotton coat and stood staring at the bed she'd left. Wondering what to do. She could wake the old woman up and complain. But Daisy had threatened to make her a bed in the bathtub! That sounded awfully cold and hard. And what if the water came on when she was asleep and started filling the tub? Would she float to the top like a cork and bob around till someone fished her out? Or sink like a stone to the bottom . . . and drown?

Butter Flye shook her head in defiance. No, she wasn't going to sleep in no stupid bathtub. But the child knew just what she would do. Where she'd sleep just fine. Real warm and snug. She pulled on a long coat over her pajamas. The child unsnapped her change purse and pocketed the trailer keys. She slipped down the short hall. Past the bed where the old woman was sleeping. Into the kitchen. She reached for the doorknob. Turned it. Made a little squeak. In a moment she was on the porch, gently closing the door behind her.

Ooooo . . . it was so cold out here! She hurried down the porch steps and ran to the small camping trailer. She pressed the key in the lock and turned it. In a moment, she was inside, tumbling into her bed.

Forgetting to latch the trailer door.

She pulled the covers up to her nose. How sweet it was to be in her own bed. Soon, she began to get warm. All except her nose. She closed her eyes. And soon drifted away into a bright, happy world of singing birds . . . meadows . . . a stream filled with large goldfish. Before her was a small white house; its yard was surrounded by a picket fence. Miniature rose-bushes with pink and white and yellow blossoms lined a red-brick walkway.

On the porch was her father. He was whittling a piece of red cedar into the shape of a little dog. A plump blond woman was sitting in a rocking chair. Crocheting pretty red and blue flowers onto a white cloth.

"Mamma," she called out.

The woman leaned forward. "Well, now—it's about time you showed up. I been real worried about you."

"Mamma . . ." she said again, and tried to run. But her feet were so heavy . . . No matter how hard she tried, Butter could not get to the porch.

The woman rocked back and forth in the chair. "Child," she said, "you need to be careful. Don't be talkin' to no strangers. You hear me?"

"Yes, Mamma . . . I hear you . . . but . . ."

The scene faded away.

The child found herself alone. In a dark woodland. The trees were big and ugly . . . they had twisted, wrinkly arms for branches . . . awful hands with bony fingers that reached out for her. Again she tried to run . . .

The singular figure stood over the small bed, his head cocked curiously. This child with yellow hair seemed oddly familiar. As if she was someone he had known. One of his people . . . even one of his own kin. But he could find no place for her in his memory. Worse still, he could not quite remember precisely who *he* was. Only that he had been terribly wronged. And that he had something important to do. Something that must be done soon.

This was a pretty child. So plump.

He reached out to touch the golden locks of her hair.

Butter Flye stirred in her sleep. She blinked her eyes. Saw the pale, bewhiskered face.

The man was standing by her bed. Staring at her. He was awfully dirty. Like he'd been wallowing with the hogs. And he was rolling something in his hand. Something white . . . looked like an egg.

The child sat up, rubbing at her eyes. This must be part of the dream. "I remember you," she said. "You peeked in my winder when it was dark outside."

The intruder leaned forward; now his face was very close to hers. He stared. His pale blue eyes did not blink.

"Go 'way," she said, "or I'll tell Daddy."

He seemed unimpressed.

And then she remembered that Daddy had gone away. "I'll tell the *Wuff*." That ought to scare him.

It did not. Truly, he did not fear the Wuff. Nor have reason to.

"I know who you are."

At this, he cocked his head.

She pulled the covers to the bridge of her tiny nose. "You're the Booger-man."

Daisy Perika felt a small hand on her arm. The hand was shaking her.

"Aunt Daisy . . . wake up!"

She groaned. Children were such an awful nuisance. Especially when you needed a good night's sleep. "What is it?"

Sarah was shivering in her thin nightgown. "I just woke up—I had to go to the bathroom."

"You don't need my permission." Daisy rolled over on her side and waved her hand. "Now go away."

She stamped a bare foot on the cold floor. "Aunt Daisy—it's Butter."

The Ute woman groaned. "What's she done now?"

"She's not in the bed."

Daisy pushed herself up to a sitting position. "What . . ."

Sarah was wringing her hands. "I just woke up and she was gone."

The old woman got up and pulled a robe around her body. "Well, she's probably sleepin' under the bed or somethin'."

The girl shook her head, snapping the short braids about her shoulders. "I think she's gone outside to—"

"Why'd she go outside? It's cold as a brass apple out there."

" 'Cause she's been wanting to sleep out there in that little trailer. In her own bed. She told me so, two or three times. Said you wouldn't let her."

"Oh." The old woman was terribly tired. "Well, if she is, maybe we should just let her be."

Sarah yanked at Daisy's robe. "No. I think something's wrong."

"Why?"

"I just do."

"Hmmmf," Daisy said. She found a flashlight and waddled toward the kitchen door, yawning.

Sarah followed the old Ute woman outside and down the porch steps. Daisy tried the door on the Flyes' camp-trailer. It was unlocked. Daisy stepped inside the small trailer; the plywood floor squeaked. She moved the flashlight beam around. There was the little girl's bed. It had been slept in. Daisy put her hand under the covers. Still a little warm. The child had been here . . . and now she was gone.

But where?

As Butter hurried along beside the night visitor, she could see her breath make a cloud in the moonlight. There were sharp-edged rocks in the deer path; the child felt them through the thin soles of her bunny house slippers.

She looked up at him. "Where're we goin'?"

No answer.

"I'm really cold."

He kept up his steady pace, so that her little legs were fairly running.

"Hey—you!" she shouted.

He did not look at her.

She stumbled over a juniper root, and took a hard tumble.

He stopped, and squatted. Stared at the small child in a most curious fashion.

"My knee's skinned," she sobbed. "And my feets hurt."

Daisy Perika carried a stout oak staff; she hurried along without speaking. The night was piercingly cold; her hands and feet were already numb. But she hardly noticed this discomfort. Inside, she was paralyzed with an icy fear. Trying not to imagine all the awful things that could happen to a six-year-old child wandering around alone in this dark wilderness. A child who was supposed to be under her protection.

Sarah Frank, close by her side, carried the flashlight.

"Aunt Daisy?"

The old woman did not answer.

"Where are we going?"

"To the closest neighbor."

"Who's the closest—"

"Nathan McFain." She pointed with the staff. "His ranch is just over that ridge."

"Why are we going there?"

"Nathan has a telephone."

"Who're you gonna call?"

"Police."

"Oh." Then Aunt Daisy thought something bad had happened to Butter.

Yes. The police. And what would Charlie Moon say when he heard that the little *matukach* child had just wandered off? Worse still, what would her nephew think? Well, she knew the answer to that. He'd think she was a foolish old woman . . . who should never have been trusted to look after children.

Now, the Magician was leading the child into a very dark place.

Butter could see nothing at all. But she could smell a familiar, earthy scent. It was like a freshly plowed field. Or a newly dug grave.

The Ute elder and her youthful companion approached the McFain ranch from the west. Daisy and Sarah stood for just a moment, at a place below the crest of the bluff, looking over the pasture. The barn . . . the ranch house . . . the scattering of log cabins on the far ridge—all had an unreal appearance. Like hollow toys. The dark tent that covered the mammoth excavation was like an enormous black bird, huddled over a dreadful nest filled with bones. And other dead things.

The old woman and the child helped each other through the boundary fence, which was topped with two strands of rusty barbed wire.

Daisy Perika was already heading across the pasture when Sarah called to her. "Wait."

"Wait for what? I got to wake Nathan up and use his telephone to call . . ."

Sarah, flashlight in hand, was headed toward the darkened tent.

The old woman had to hurry to catch up with the child. "What're you doing?"

Sarah painted a smear of light on the tent door. "She's in there."

"How do you know that?"

"I just know." The girl's thin body was suddenly wracked with shudders. Her teeth chattered.

The shaman had sensed nothing. But Daisy Perika did understand this sort of intuition. And she knew from past experience that Sarah Frank was a most remarkable little girl. She took the flashlight from the child's trembling hand. "I'll have a look. You wait out here." If the little white girl was really inside that dark tent . . . The old woman patted Sarah's shoulder. "Anything funny happens, you run for the big house and wake everybody up."

Sarah seemed not to hear.

Daisy Perika cradled her walking staff under one arm, and pulled the tent door open. She flashed the beam of light around the excavation site and saw what she'd seen before. Sturdy tent poles. Spindly-looking card table. Tripod-mounted aluminum reflectors and camera lights. And, of course, the mazelike array of excavations in the earth. Some of the smaller slots had been filled with dirt already sifted for artifacts. But the larger trenches were empty. Very deep they seemed in the half-darkness. Dank pits, cluttered with the bones of an ancient beast. And perhaps there was more . . .

She took a few faltering steps inside. Toward the excavation.

And looked in.

A great, sweeping tusk beckoned at her like a giant's curled finger.

Step into my grave.

Her foot slipped; dirt spilled into the pit.

Daisy backed away, gasping hard for breath. As she

turned, the beam from the flashlight swept across a pile of sifted earth. Laying face-up on the mound of dirt was . . . the child.

The Magician stood on the bluff, rolling the "egg" in his hand. Watching the black-haired little girl who waited outside the tent. Wondering when his work here would be finished.

Daisy approached the tiny figure slowly, as in a dream. It was as if someone had tossed a broken doll onto a rubbish heap. Butter Flye's blue eyes were open, her yellow hair askew. She was very still.

The old woman sensed a presence behind her. She whirled, raising the heavy staff like a club.

It was Sarah.

Daisy's voice was little more than a croak. "I told you to wait outside."

Sarah did not speak; she ignored Daisy's futile attempt to urge her away. She approached the still figure of Butter Flye and kneeled. Sarah reached out, and touched the smaller child's pale hand.

The still figure did not stir.

"Wake up," Sarah whispered.

Butter's lips parted . . . and moved.

The older girl leaned close. And listened. Then turned to Daisy. "She'll be all right."

"Thank God," the old woman said gratefully. "Oh, thank God." Now she must get them home. And quickly.

Though she had to stop and rest a dozen times, Daisy Perika found sufficient strength to carry the small child back to her trailer-home. Butter Flye's arms and legs were limp and clammy-cold. Once in her kitchen, the Ute woman warmed a coarse woolen blanket in the oven and wrapped the child in it. She sat by the bedside to keep a close watch over her.

Sarah Frank was close by Daisy's side, also watching the pale face of the child who now slept with an almost unnatural soundness.

Daisy did not look away from Butter's face as she spoke. "Sarah—what'd she tell you . . . back there in that tent?"

Sarah had already decided that she wouldn't reveal everything Butter had said. Not just yet. But there was one thing Aunt Daisy should know. "She said . . . 'He's here. Down under the dirt.' "

The old woman felt a chill shudder ripple along her spine. She swallowed hard. "Under the dirt? Who did she mean?"

Sarah shrugged.

Daisy rubbed at her chin. All the way back from the excavation tent—and without any reason that she could explain—the old shaman had nursed a growing suspicion. Suspicion had matured into certainty. It had to be that naked white man who'd showed up in her yard that night—the one who'd pulled the egg out of his hair. One way or another, the Magician had a grimy hand in this night's dirty work. Her mouth made a grim line. Somebody needed to hunt that mud-caked fellow down.

And put him out of business. Permanently.

Charlie Moon, of course, was just the man who could do it.

But her smart-aleck nephew thought she'd dreamed up the Magician, so she wasn't about to ask the big yahoo for any help. More to the point, Daisy didn't want Charlie to find out that she'd let the little girl wander off in the middle of the night. But she would not admit that this had anything to do with her decision, nor was she the least troubled about the course she had chosen. Living for so many years in this lonely place, Daisy Perika was accustomed to solving her own problems. *So here I am, just a feeble old woman on my own . . .* Her mouth twisted into a wicked grin. *A pitiful old woman with a twelve-gauge shotgun. Who's more than willing to use it.* More to be feared than a dozen policemen. *Next time I meet up with that mud-caked white man, he'll wish he'd turned himself in to Charlie Moon!*

But first things first.

Very early that morning, while both children were sleeping, Daisy Perika went to her kitchen. From a high cupboard shelf, she removed a red coffee can. She pulled off the lid, reached in, and got the fat horned toad. And placed him in Butter Flye's shoe box. The one where the *matukach* child kept all her "pretties."

Pretties, indeed!

The Ute woman glowered at the horned toad. "I don't know what that little girl sees in *you,* Ugly-face."

It may have been because the old woman had gone too long without sleep. Or perhaps it was a trick of the light. But the old shaman could have sworn that Toe Jam winked at her.

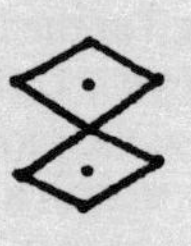

THE BANSHEE

CHARLIE MOON TURNED off the gravel road, and passed under the McFain Dude Ranch sign.

Vanessa McFain was unloading boxes of groceries from her battered Chevy van. The Ute policeman allowed the SUPD Blazer to coast to a stop. The tall young woman—dressed in tight-fitting faded jeans and a loose wool sweater—was pulling a fifty-pound bag of potatoes from the rear of the battered automobile. She turned to give him a look. There was, he imagined, a little bit of welcome in it.

Moon tipped his black Stetson. "Can I carry some of that stuff for you?"

She shrugged. "I can use some help . . . Some of it's pretty heavy."

The Ute policeman had once seen her throw an eighty-pound calf over her shoulder and walk away with it. Moon took a sack of potatoes under his arm, then another of onions.

Vanessa scooped up a cardboard box. "So how's the little girl doing?"

He played dumb. "What little girl?"

"Flye's kid. I hear she's staying with your Aunt Daisy."

"I guess she's doing okay." He followed her to the house.

"I don't suppose you've found her father?"

He grunted, and she took this as a no.

She kicked the ranch house door open. "He's probably in Arkansas by now."

The Ute policeman ignored the jibe. *Finding Horace Flye was no longer the issue.* Moon carried the potatoes and onions into the huge kitchen.

They made another trip to the van. She had bought a small cedar chest, which he carried upstairs to her bedroom. The room was a surprise. Pink satin bedspread. Pink shade on the night-lamp. Pink silk curtains fringed in white lace. Her lair was more feminine than he'd expected.

She noticed his appraisal of her boudoir, blushed a pretty pink to match the satin bedspread, and hurried him away downstairs.

Vanessa leaned against the kitchen door frame, hands on her slim hips. "You want some coffee . . . or something?"

"Oh, I'm all coffeed up." He wondered what *something* was. Tea, most likely.

She smiled. Charlie Moon didn't have much imagination. But he was nice. And good-looking. And just the right size for a woman who was six one in her bare feet. She wished he'd showed up an hour later. *Given me time to get a shower. And slip on a pretty dress.* "Charlie?"

"Yeah?"

"Did you come out here to see me?"

"Sure. That please you?"

"Not for a minute." Vanessa turned aside, tossing her hair at him. "I got guys comin' out here all the time."

He grinned. "Well, I don't blame a one of 'em."

She pouted. "Well, you could act a little bit jealous." She came very close. Fluttered her eyelashes at him.

My goodness. *She has big eyes. And she smells good.* Like a regular woman. He licked his lips. "That offer of coffee . . . or something . . . it still good?"

Vanessa flashed him a wicked smile. "The *coffee,*" she murmured, "is still hot."

"Oh."

They walked around the barn, encountering odors of alfalfa hay, dried manure, and sweaty horses. The passed the stock pond, which was still under construction. When the snows thawed, when the spring thunderstorms came booming over the San Juans, it would fill quickly enough. A light autumn snow had fallen on the previous night, barely enough to cover the dead grasses in the pasture. Moon paused to have a look at the yellow Cat 'dozer, sitting with its broad rusty blade pushed against the earthen dam. "Always wanted to drive one of these," he said wistfully. "Since I was a boy."

You're still a boy, Vanessa thought. Like a possessive mother, she took his hand.

They headed across the pasture, toward the large tent. Their boots crunched in the snowy grasses. He didn't have to slow down for this one. The tall young woman easily matched Moon's long strides.

Nathan McFain, who leaned against the central tent pole, noted the appearance of his daughter and the policeman with a nod.

The excavation tent was a scene of intense activity. Jimson Beugmann—who had been recruited to fill in for the absent Horace Flye—was pushing a wheelbarrow of sifted dirt toward one of the several side trenches that had been partially refilled.

Cordell York was sorting through a stack of black-and-white photographs.

Moses Silver scurried about, giving an order here, a suggestion there. Fussing like an old hen.

His daughter was on her knees, deep within the major trench, on the opposite side of the partially exposed mammoth skull from Robert Newton. They were, under the watchful eye of Nathan McFain, excavating the lower portion of the upswept tusk. "It would be best to remove the tusk," Newton said to the rancher. "Sticking up like this—unsupported—it's likely to get damaged."

Delia nodded her agreement. All it'd take was someone losing their balance and falling against it; the thing would snap like a dry pretzel.

"I want it right where it is," Nathan snapped. "You can put somethin' in to brace it." The paying tourists would appreciate a sweeping mammoth tusk that beckoned like a whore's enticing finger. These eggheads didn't have no sense of style.

Robert Newton sighed helplessly. "It's your show." *Show* being the operative term.

Nathan gave his willowy daughter a hard look. Vanessa was leaning lightly on Moon's arm. "I thought you was busy unpackin' your van."

Vanessa winked at the tall policeman. "It didn't take long to get everything done. Charlie carried the cedar chest up to my bedroom. He's *so* sweet."

Nathan cocked a watery eye at Moon. This big Ute cop sure seemed to be hanging around a lot. Maybe he was taking an interest in Vannie. Well, she could do worse. And it wasn't like she was all that young anymore. She was goin' on twenty-four.

The others in the excavation tent had gradually become aware of the Ute policeman's presence.

Jimson Beugmann dumped his wheelbarrow load into a side trench. The thin young man began to smooth the rubble with a square-blade shovel. He glanced furtively through dirty blond locks at the policeman. Cops were never good news. And he had a bad feeling about this one.

Moses Silver paused in his pacings. "Officer Moon, welcome to our workplace."

Moon accepted the outstretched hand.

Cordell York looked up from his photographs, then returned his attention to his work.

Robert Newton, busy in the pit, blinked up at the tall form. Stiff from his labors, he crawled out of the excavation. The elderly man got to his feet with a chorus of grunts and groans.

Delia Silver also climbed out of the trench; she brushed the dust off her jeans. "Hello," she said.

Moon removed his hat and nodded at the pretty archaeologist. "Good morning."

Delia looked uncertainly from Vanessa's face to Moon's. They made a nice-looking couple, she thought.

Moses' brow furrowed above his round spectacles. "I say, Officer Moon—have you had any word about our missing employee? Mr. Flye, I mean."

The Ute policeman had expected the question; he shook his head. "He hasn't turned up so far."

The absentminded paleontologist had forgotten to shave; he rubbed at a day-old gray stubble on his chin. "Odd. Can't imagine Flye leaving his child behind. Hope he hasn't met with . . . some misfortune."

Moon hesitated. He swept his glance over the upturned faces. Even Cordell York was waiting for his response. "Nothing's been heard of him since one of my men found his pickup over at Capote Lake."

Delia paled. "You don't suppose he's . . ."

"Well," Moon picked his words with care, "I can tell you . . . last week or so, I've been looking for a *body*."

Delia closed her eyes. "Oh, God."

Moon set his face like a stone mask.

Cordell York found all this most interesting. "How, exactly, does one go about finding a corpse, Officer Moon? I mean," he made a sweeping gesture, "there is a great deal of wilderness out there."

Moon fixed the man with a searching gaze. "It's not as hard as you might think." Which was not exactly true.

York grinned. "Really? How so?"

"Dogs," the Ute policeman said simply.

"Dogs?" Nathan McFain echoed.

Moon nodded.

The rancher frowned. "What kinda dogs?"

" 'Specially trained ones. They sniff out dead bodies. We've been searching over at Capote Lake."

"And . . ." Moses Silver prompted him.

"Haven't found any sign of Mr. Flye."

"It would seem," York observed, "that would eliminate your only promising area to search."

Moon maintained the poker face. "Yeah. I can see how you might think that."

York seemed genuinely puzzled. "But if Mr. Flye abandoned his vehicle at the lake and then came to some harm—and his body is not in that vicinity—where would you possibly expect to find his remains? It appears that you are faced with a quite intractable problem."

The Ute spoke in a voice barely above a whisper. "Maybe Horace Flye didn't leave his pickup at the lake."

The academic frowned thoughtfully, as if this was a simple problem in elementary logic—and this Ute was a dull student who must be led by the hand. "But surely, that's where you found the abandoned vehicle. If Mr. Flye did not leave his truck at Lake Capote, how else could it possibly have . . ." York's voice trailed off. He took a deep breath. "Oh yes. I do believe I see what you're getting at." Well now . . . he had underestimated this rural policeman. "But if not near the lake, then where would you expect to find . . . ?"

Moon decided he'd said enough. He murmured a good-bye to Vanessa who looked at him with startled doe-eyes. He turned on his heel and left the tent.

Those left behind exchanged wary glances. What did this all mean . . . ?

The Ute policeman walked briskly across the frozen pasture.

Feeling seven pairs of eyes tickling the back of his neck.

Or maybe eight . . .

THAT NIGHT

The land passed down through three generations of McFains to Nathan was bathed in mottled moonlight. Cloud-shadows moved above the earth like a herd of great, lumbering beasts.

It was a surrealistic picture painted by a gifted madman. The long ranch house under outstretched arms of gaunt cottonwoods. The slightly leaning barn with its steeply pitched roof, a gloomy study in gray. Behind the barn, the gaping wound in the earth that would soon be transformed into a pretty pond where sleek horses would take long drinks. The pasture touched with snow, a thin white shroud spread over the dead grasses. At the end of the sloping field—and under the bluff—the dark sprawl of the tent over a beast's grave that had been opened by curious humanoids. To look upon the stony bones of ages known only by the crumbling residue death had left behind. On the bluff immediately above the dark tent stood another dark form.

A man.

He wore a long dark coat and broad-brimmed black hat. The night breeze played with the skirt of the coat and chilled the man's face. Like a lone watchman in his tower, this silent sentry stood at his post. And waited. On this side of the fence, he had jurisdiction. Charlie Moon had his feet planted on Ute land.

He had been waiting for too many hours to count on one hand. At dusk Moon had watched the last souls—Moses Silver and Robert Newton—depart from the tent below and make their slow way across the pasture. He had heard echoes of their thin voices, the crisp crunching of their shoes in the snow-encrusted grasses. One by one, he had watched the lights go out in the cabins—and in the windows of Nathan McFain's home. The last light to dim was upstairs in the ranch house. Behind pink curtains in Vanessa's room. So she was in bed now, her long legs stretched out between the satin sheets. She was warm, he supposed.

He was not.

This realization made him feel utterly alone . . . and gave the cold breeze teeth of ice.

But he stood there. Until long after all below were asleep. All but one, perhaps.

Sometime after midnight, he heard the slow, rhythmic beat of an owl's wings. The Ute soul that lived deep in his marrow whispered that this was an evil thing. A bad omen. But he knew that it was nothing more than a hungry night creature searching for food.

An hour later, a half-starved coyote trotted across the frozen pasture. Sniffing here and there for the stray mouse.

Later still, three mule deer vaulted Nathan's barbed-wire

fence. They pawed at the thin crust of snow, grazed in his pasture, then disappeared into the night.

The bone-pale moon settled on the long ridge behind him. Then sank into some distant sea. Now there was only starlight. Finally, clouds like thick blankets of frozen wool were pulled over the sleeping earth.

The Voices began to whisper inside his head.

"This is a fool's errand."

"No it's not," he replied silently.

"No one will come."

"Yes they will."

"You should be in bed."

Moon had no sensible answer to this bit of practical wisdom, so he held his tongue.

During the next five minutes, another hour passed.

A mile to the south, the cold, weary policeman saw the yellow glow of headlights. And heard the soft purr of Officer Daniel Bignight's Chevrolet. Good. Daniel was on time; and the amiable fellow was always good company. The Taos Pueblo man would be doubly welcome tonight.

Moon squatted by his companion. He rubbed his numb hands together and sniffed expectantly. "So what've you got in the paper bag?"

Daniel Bignight, who had paid a visit to the all-night gas station/convenience store in Bayfield, sat on the rolled-up blanket and spread the feast before them. "A roasted chicken. Had 'em triple-bag it, so it should still be warm."

Moon nodded his appreciation. "What else?"

"German potato salad. And two cups of hot coffee. He-man size."

"You bring any dessert?"

Bignight was mildly offended by such a question. "Sure. I got us some little chocolate cakes. The kind with cream filling."

"How many?"

"Half dozen."

Moon blew warm breath into his hands. "Sounds like enough for a midnight snack."

As they ate, Bignight eyed the dark form beside him. "Charlie?"

"Yeah?"

"Could I ask a question—about what we're doin' out here in the dark?"

"Sure. A good officer always informs himself about the situation."

"Well?"

"Well what?"

"Well, what'n hell are we doin' out here, Charlie?"

The Ute bit into a greasy drumstick. "Watchin'."

Bignight blinked at the barren landscape. "Watchin' what?"

Moon pointed a chicken bone.

"You mean old Nathan McFain's spread?"

The dark form nodded.

"But Charlie—that ain't Ute land."

Moon was silent.

"What I mean is—it ain't in our jurisdiction."

"Well," Moon said reasonably, "there's been a boundary dispute. For all we know, old Nathan may be squattin' on a little bit of the People's land. And Nathan's not a Ute. Matter of fact, he's one-quarter Navajo. So you see my point."

Bignight didn't. "Neither am I, Charlie. Not a Ute, I mean."

Moon nodded thoughtfully. "Nope, but most of the People figure bein' a Taos Pueblo man is almost as good as bein' a Ute."

Bignight thought about this. Charlie Moon was putting him on again. "So what exactly do we watch for?"

"Whatever." Moon wadded wrappers from several small cakes and stuffed them into the paper bag. "I'm done watching for the night." If anything was going to happen it would've happened already. "But you can keep your eyes peeled over thataway." He nodded in the general direction of the sprawling barn. "You see anything unusual, you wake me up pronto."

"Unusual?" The Taos Pueblo man did not care for the unusual. "Like what?"

"Like somethin' that shouldn't be out in the middle of the night."

"You mean like sensible folks?" Bignight said sullenly.

"Right," Moon said. "But don't you wake me up for any ordinary goings-on." The big Ute rolled up in his blanket.

Bignight squinted into the darkness. "Whatta you mean, ordinary goings-on?"

"Oh," Moon said sleepily, "you know. Things a man'd *expect* to see in the middle of the night. Mountain lions. Ghosts. Stuff like that." That'd keep the Pueblo man awake.

Bignight seated himself on a cold basalt outcropping. Charlie Moon was kidding him again. Hadn't been no mountain lions seen around here for . . . well, for months. But ghosts . . . that wasn't funny. Every civilized man knew that ghosts came out at midnight. And walked the earth till the first hint of dawn.

"Charlie?"

"Yeah?"

"What with old Nathan bein' . . . oh, never mind."

"What's on your mind, Daniel?"

"Well—him bein' part Navajo . . . I was thinkin' of . . . well . . . *skin-walkers*."

"Don't worry yourself about skin-walkers," Moon said. "McFain's three-quarters Irish. Skin-walkers don't hang around with Irishmen. It'd be more likely a banshee came here with the McFain clan."

There was a long, pregnant silence, while Moon waited for Bignight's response.

"Charlie . . . what's a bant-shee?"

"Some kinda spirit. Comes out at night, they say. And screams."

The Taos Pueblo man felt a coldness stir in his belly. "Screams?"

"Real loud. At least that's what they say."

"Why does it scream, Charlie?"

Moon's smile was hidden in the darkness. "Oh, different reasons. Sometimes it calls for somebody. Hollers out their name."

Bignight knew he shouldn't ask. "Why does it do that?"

"Because that's a banshee's main job. To call for the one who's gonna die that night. If you hear one callin' my name,

I guess you'd best wake me up. But if it hollers *Daaannnniell . . . Daaannnniell . . .* why, you can just let me sleep."

"Oh shit," Daniel Bignight muttered.

Nathan McFain—though weary as only old men can be—could find no rest on this night. Sleep eluded him. So he lay awake and listened to the silence. The dark world outside was occasionally disturbed by the nocturnal rustling of hunter or prey—and the wind hummed sonorously under the eaves. But the innards of the ranch house seemed unnaturally quiet. He strained to hear a reassuring sound from his daughter's room. The creak of a spring as Vannie moved in her bed.

The old man turned over on his lumpy mattress for the tenth time in as many minutes. Now he lay on his back, looking toward the ceiling. Toward where a ceiling was. Or should be. Into the blackness.

His bones were ready for rest. But his imagination was working overtime.

Charlie Moon, rolled up in his blanket, had slipped into a deep sleep.

Daniel Bignight was more than a little annoyed. Nothing kept Charlie from getting his rest. The big Ute, he imagined, could lay down on a big pile of sharp rocks and sleep through a howling blizzard.

Nathan McFain had left his bed. The old rancher was downstairs, in the parlor. He had slipped on a warm plaid shirt, a pair of brown canvas overalls, a sock hat. Then, with a nervous glance out the window, he buttoned a lined denim jacket. He thought of pulling on a pair of socks and his comfortable old leather boots, then decided that the wool-lined moccasins would be sufficient. Such a small matter this seemed. Certainly not a decision that would seal a man's fate.

Nathan turned the doorknob. It squeaked. Made enough noise to raise the dead.

Raise the dead.

Not a healthy thought, the Navajo part of his soul whispered.

Vanessa McFain sat on the edge of the bed; she stared out her bedroom window. And saw nothing. She leaned back against the headboard and closed her eyes. And listened to the old clock on the wall.

The tarnished brass pendulum swung.

Back and forth.

Tic.

Clac.

Tic.

Clac.

Like a skeleton's heartbeat.

Ever so gradually . . . running down.

Why had Daddy gone outside? What on earth was he *doing* out there?

Nathan McFain stood by the half-finished pond, and surveyed his earthly realm.

The breeze was still now. No deer grazed in the pasture. There were no foxes slipping about. No distant call of coyote or owl. The quiet was tangible . . . almost oppressive.

The Taos Pueblo man had—despite Charlie Moon's talk about ghosts and "bant-shees"—gradually managed to relax. Moreover, the Ute's rhythmic snoring was making his comrade sleepy. Gradually, Daniel Bignight leaned forward. The SUPD officer blinked. And yawned. And yawned again. Within moments, Bignight's eyes closed. Almost immediately, he began to walk through his dreams. There were many nice things there. Fat beagle-hounds. Candy canes. And Christmas . . .

And then . . . as if at the edge of a nightmare . . . he heard something.

Daniel Bignight sat up with a sudden jerk that popped the bad vertebrae in his neck.

"What'n hell was *that?*" he whispered. Must've been dreaming. *That damn Charlie Moon and his ghost stories . . .*

he's got me hearing things. He squinted. No. It was not his imagination. Something had moved. Down there in Nathan's pasture. Close to the barn. Might just be one of Nathan's horses. Might not . . .

And then Daniel Bignight heard it again. The low, moaning wail . . . calling to him.

The old rancher felt eyes staring at him.

But that was foolishness. Childish foolishness. And he was no child.

And then he felt it . . . a hand. Icy-cold fingers. Grasping his bare ankle.

Vanessa was certain she'd heard something. Something outside.

She pulled a robe over her shoulders and headed downstairs.

Nathan McFain stumbled across the pasture like a wild man. He tripped, fell to his knees. In a moment he was back on his feet, pumping his old legs as fast as limbs and lungs would permit. Every breath was a stab of cold steel in his heaving chest; spittle ran down his chin and froze on his white beard—the sound of his heavy boots echoed across the frozen earth. The rancher had no idea which way he was running . . . until he fell headlong into the canvas wall of the tent. He felt his way along the coarse fabric until he found the door, fumbled desperately with the latch, and fairly threw his body inside this shelter. Like a rabbit evading a hungry coyote.

He sat there in the darkness, quaking like a small child.

Daniel Bignight was on his feet. He'd completely forgotten about Charlie Moon. He was not thinking about his duty as an officer. The policeman was not thinking at all.

He was operating on instinct alone.

The panicked Taos Pueblo man was focused on a single, overriding goal, which occupied his whole mind. Getting far away from here.

* * *

Charlie Moon—who had been enjoying a dreamless slumber—was rudely awakened. Something heavy had fallen across him. He looked up and saw the familiar profile of Bignight's round head. The Ute policeman pushed himself up on one elbow. "Daniel?"

The Taos Pueblo man's eyes were wild white spots in his dark face. He was breathing in short gasps, attempting to get to his feet.

"Daniel, what's got into you?"

This question—with its hint of reproach—calmed Bignight slightly. Enough that he found his voice.

"It's that damn bant-shee, Charlie . . . screamin' at me!"

Nathan McFain had managed to calm himself somewhat. But he was a divided man. The sensible, Irish portion of his soul knew he'd been a fool to let his imagination run away with him like that. Could've fallen and broke a leg. *Then where would I've been? In a damn bad fix, that's where.* But the quarter of Nathan that was Navajo could still feel the cold fingers on his ankle.

He pushed himself to his feet, but was disoriented in the total blackness inside the tent. Wondering where that damn light switch was. He had to get out of here. The rancher stood very still in the darkness. And thought his thoughts. Everything had started going bad when that whirlwind showed up in the pasture. And uncovered that cursed elephant's tusk. He could see it clearly now. Those damn old elephant bones—they'd been the beginning of all his bad luck. The dream of a museum—like all his earlier notions—had been foolishness. There would be no hordes of well-heeled tourists flocking way out here and paying hard cash to see some crumbling old bones. Not with a big-time attraction like Mesa Verde just a couple of hours down the road. Yes, he'd been a fool. But there was a way to fix things. Nathan said it out loud.

"I'll run these damn eggheaded professors offa my land. Tear down this plug-ugly tent. Get the 'dozer over here and cover up these old bones once and for all."

It seemed that a cold presence drifted near to him. Imagination, perhaps.

Nathan clenched his fists . . . didn't dare to breathe. There was no sound. Not a thing to see in the darkness. No whiff of the scent of man or animal.

But he sensed the icy presence. . . just like he'd felt it up by the barn.

His old heart began to thump under his ribs. He could actually hear its ragged beat. But he would not panic again. No sir. He was Nathan McFain, half grizzly bear, half buffalo, and three-quarters rattlesnake. He'd killed three men in his time, two of 'em with his bare hands. "No," he said aloud. "I won't be skeered. Not of any damned spook." He reached into his pocket and found a cigarette lighter. His hand trembled. He had to make enough light to find the confounded electric switch. With light, the thing that wasn't actually there anyhow would go away.

He raised the lighter.

Flicked the wheel.

Tiny sparks flew to the wetted wick.

A small flame burst to life, and illuminated his craggy face.

The fire also illuminated another face . . . not a yard from his own.

The old man tried to call out, but managed only a dry, croaking gasp. One hand went to his chest. Unconsciously, he took a faltering step backward.

The pale, bewhiskered face seemed to float in front of him.

He backed away another step.

Another.

Nathan's heel slipped over a crumbling precipice. He felt himself falling backward. He felt a single, thudding blow to his back . . . a very brief pain.

And then . . . nothing.

Daniel Bignight—though embarrassed by his unseemly panic and clumsy attempt at flight—was also annoyed with Charlie Moon's questions. The Taos Pueblo man became morose and sullen; he refused to say another word about the "bant-shee." He did tell his superior officer that somebody had run hell-for-leather across the pasture. Whoever it was, he thought, had gone into the big tent.

Charlie Moon advised his subordinate that he would go to the tent to check it out. Much to Bignight's relief, he was instructed by Moon to remain on the low bluff.

The Ute policeman made his way down the jumble of basalt boulders and crossed Nathan McFain's barbed-wire fence. But he did not hurry. No telling who might be in the tent. Man'd have to be a fool to go busting right in the door. In a broad path across the pasture, there were dozens of footprints in the snow. Many headed away from the tent, as many toward it. No way—at least in the darkness—to tell whether someone had recently passed this way.

Moon squatted. To make a smaller target in case the somebody in there was armed.

"Hello inside," he called. "This is Officer Moon. Southern Ute Police."

His answer was a dead, unnerving silence.

He moved a dozen paces away, removed a small radio transmitter from a belt holster. He clicked the transmit button three times.

Bignight's voice crackled in the tiny speaker. "Charlie?"

He spoke softly into the microphone. "I'm goin' inside the tent. You hear any commotion, first you call Ignacio for help. Then you get down here and back me up."

"Charlie, I don't think you should—"

Moon switched the transmitter off. He moved to the rear of the tent, which was a scant yard from the barbed-wire fence. He slid—as quietly as possible—under the edge of the canvas structure. With no light from moon or stars, the darkness was complete. It was like being inside a coal mine. The policeman kneeled with his back to the canvas and tried to remember every detail of the layout. The major excavation trench would be directly in front of him. Some smaller exploratory trenches off to his left, mostly refilled with dirt. But still deep enough for a man to hide in. Or for a policeman to fall and break a leg in. He found a small flashlight in his coat pocket and held it in his left hand. He used his right to ease the heavy .357 magnum from its leather holster.

And prayed he wouldn't have to use it.

And that if he did, he could hit what he aimed at.

He reviewed the few facts at hand. Daniel had thought he saw someone run across the pasture, and into the tent. So whoever it was should still be in here. But when Moon had identified himself, there had been no answer. There had to be a reason. Might be that the fellow didn't want to be bothered by an officer of the law. Furthermore, he might be armed . . . and nervous. Not a reassuring thought. There was another possibility. Maybe there was nobody hiding inside the tent. Maybe Daniel Bignight had imagined the whole thing. *My own fault for spooking him with the banshee story.* The policeman got to his feet. He held his left hand as far away from his body as possible, and flicked on the flashlight. The narrow beam stabbed a long white dagger into the belly of the darkness.

Three things happened simultaneously.

Another beam of light stabbed right back at him.

The silhouette of another man appeared directly in front of Moon. The apparition had a flashlight in one hand. A revolver in the other.

Moon's finger tightened on the trigger.

A split second before he fired, the meaning of this apparition became all too apparent. The image of this adversary was a familiar one. He'd seen his own reflection. Ugly brute. Enough to scare a fellow half to death. The Ute policeman grinned sheepishly at the tripod-mounted aluminum reflector and lowered the barrel of his weapon. "Damn near took a potshot at myself," he muttered. That would have given Daniel Bignight something to snicker about.

Moon swept the beam over the paleontologist's musty inner sanctum. He could see three stout tent posts. Jimson Beugmann's wheelbarrow. The card table, one broken leg bandaged with duct tape. The beam glanced at an oblique angle off another of the tripod-mounted reflectors. A dusty camera case. A roll of yellow nylon rope. The motor-driven sifter. Three very neat piles of gray sand.

But no human being.

On the farthest post, closest to the entrance, there was an electric light switch.

He began to move toward the switch. He was passing the deepest part of the excavation when he saw the man. Instinctively, Moon raised the barrel of the .357.

The face was Nathan McFain's. Staring back at the policeman through goggled eyes, one gnarled hand reaching out . . . grasping at nothingness. He looked like . . . What was the old expression? Like somebody who'd seen a ghost. His blue-lipped mouth was gaped open in a silent scream.

But Nathan was deathly quiet now.

Moon holstered the heavy revolver.

Daniel Bignight—as wide awake as he'd been in his entire life—paced nervously on the bluff. When the small radio crackled in his hand, he jumped.

Moon's voice was deadly calm. "Daniel?"

"Yeah, Charlie?"

"Put a call in to the station. Tell the dispatcher to send the state police to the McFain ranch, then contact the Archuleta County sheriff's office." The sheriff wouldn't be overjoyed, being pried out of his warm bed on a cold morning. But police business is often brisk in the small hours. "After you make the calls, come on down here and keep an eye on the tent."

"Charlie—what's going on?"

"It's Nathan McFain. He's . . . had an accident."

"I'll call in an ambulance from Pagosa."

"Don't bother. He won't need the paramedics."

"Oh." That was clear enough. "How'd it happen, Charlie?"

There was a long pause. "Daniel, this thing isn't in Southern Ute jurisdiction. We'll leave it to the state cops. And the county sheriff."

Bignight understood. This wasn't SUPD business. So it wasn't any of *his* business. "But it's an accident?"

"Right." Charlie Moon had studied the rancher's footprints. And he'd found McFain's cigarette lighter near one of the tripod-mounted reflectors. Looked like Nathan had thumbed his lighter, seen his face in the polished aluminum sheet. Must've been startled . . . and took a couple of steps backward.

And tumbled into the excavation pit.

Like a man who had aged decades in one night, Charlie Moon walked ever so slowly across the pasture. Toward the unfinished stock pond . . . the barn . . . the McFain ranch house. It was all uphill. But every painful step must be taken. Someone had to tell Vanessa McFain that her father was dead.

It was understandable that the policeman was in no great hurry to perform this melancholy duty. Indeed, Moon should have been pleased to be delayed . . . to be hailed down by the outstretched hand.

He was not.

Vanessa had made up her mind. She'd go outside and look for him. The young woman was reaching for the doorknob when she was startled by the heavy knock. Daddy must be back from his night wanderings—but why would he knock on his own door? It wasn't locked. She flung the front door open.

The man on the porch was Charlie Moon.

The Ute policeman stood there, twisting the broad-brimmed black hat in his hands. Not looking directly at her.

Vanessa tried to think of something clever to say. "I'm always glad to see you, Charlie. But you could give a girl some warning before you come calling . . ." She noticed that someone else was standing two paces behind Charlie Moon. A woman. It was the archaeologist, Delia Silver.

"It's late," Moon said in a monotone. "I figured you'd be in bed . . ." Vanessa was wearing a long woolen overcoat.

"I woke up when Daddy went outside. I was just going to check on him when I heard your knock."

"Why'd he go outside in the middle of the night?"

She shrugged. "To check the stock, I guess. Last Sunday, he found some cougar tracks by the barn. I've been up waiting for him." She glanced at the clock on the wall. "What brings you by at such an ungodly hour?"

The Ute policeman opened his mouth. Tried to say the words.

"Charlie," she said in an urgent whisper, "what is it?"

"It's . . . your father."

She backed away. "Oh God, Charlie . . . don't just stand there . . . tell me what's happened!"

His throat felt like sandpaper. "I'm sorry, Vanessa. Nathan's had an accident."

Her hand went to her mouth. "Accident . . . Is he hurt bad?"

Moon couldn't find his voice. But his face spoke for him.

"Oh my God. He's . . . he's dead?"

He nodded.

She stood there, staring blankly at this pair of intruders. Absurd thoughts buzzed through her head. *I must be asleep . . . this is an awful nightmare. I'll wake up in a moment. It'll all go away . . .*

Moon took her hand in his.

But Charlie Moon is so warm . . . and solid. So this is real. Daddy is dead. Laying out there somewhere. But how did this Ute policeman know about it so quickly? "Charlie . . . where is he?"

He ground his teeth. No way was he going to tell her. There were some things that weren't fit for a woman to see. Or a man, for that matter.

"Vanessa . . . the state police should be here in a little while. I'll have to . . . ahh . . . help them some. Delia will stay with you."

How strange. Charlie and Delia were moving away so rapidly . . . she saw them receding at the end of a long tunnel. And felt her legs going limp, buckling at the knees.

As Vanessa fell, Moon scooped her up in his arms. And carried her up the stairs to the warm, pink bedroom.

Moses Silver—who occupied the cabin next door to his daughter's—had heard the voices when Charlie Moon came for Delia. He'd gone outside to see what was amiss, and heard enough to understand that Nathan McFain was in the excavation tent. Moses wasn't sure whether the rancher was dead or seriously injured. The Ute policeman had given the elderly paleontologist strict orders to stay away from the excavation, at least until the state cops or the county sheriff showed up.

As soon as Moon had left with Delia, Moses banged on two more cabin doors. Robert Newton and Cordell York must be told. The three scientists conferred upon the issue, and all were agreed. There was only one thing to do. They headed for the excavation site.

Daniel Bignight, who had his orders from Charlie Moon, refused to allow the scientists inside the tent.

Cordell York glared at the amiable policeman. "Officer, there is an injured man in there. And I am a physician."

Bignight glanced toward the tent door. "He ain't just injured. I think he's kinda . . . well . . . dead."

York's tone was acidic. "You *think?* Have you examined the victim for a pulse?"

"No, I ain't even seen him, but Charlie Moon told me . . ."

The physician recalled rumors about the boundary dispute. "Tell me—do you Indian police have jurisdiction on this property?"

"Well, no, but . . ."

"Then stand aside, young man. I must determine whether the victim requires medical intervention. If you prevent us from entering the tent, you may very well have a man's death on your conscience."

Bignight was wavering. Charlie *had* said McFain was dead, hadn't he? Well, in a way he had. In so many words . . .

York played his hole card. "I feel compelled to warn you—should the victim die because you have denied him medical attention, there are legal ramifications. Both criminal and civil."

The police officer felt a cold knot tighten in his gut. "Well, I guess it wouldn't hurt none to have a doctor take a quick look at 'im." Bignight eyed the pair of paleontologists. "But who are these guys?"

York nodded to indicate his companions. "Dr. Silver and Dr. Newton are my . . . uh . . . assistants."

"One does feel honored," Newton whispered sarcastically to Moses Silver, who snorted.

With some misgivings, Bignight finally relented. While the

SUPD officer kept his post, the scientists entered the tent. Turned on the lights. And approached the excavation with all the eager curiosity of children.

There he was, Nathan McFain. That curmudgeonly old man who had given them so much trouble. In the main trench. Spread-eagle on his back. His plaid shirt stained with a great blackish smear of coagulated blood, sightless eyes gaping, bewhiskered mouth wide open. Like a man who had suffered an astonishing, final surprise.

The broken-off mastodon tusk protruded neatly through the center of his chest.

"Rather a lurid scene," Dr. York observed.

"Ghastly," Moses Silver agreed.

Robert Newton nodded grimly. "One is shocked quite beyond words."

Moses shook his head. "This is a terrible, terrible calamity."

Dr. York squatted, and cocked his head thoughtfully. "Looks bad, certainly. But hardly what I'd call a *calamity*."

"How can you be so glib?" Moses shot back. "This is just awful."

The surgeon's tone had a calmness bordering on arrogance. "My esteemed colleague, you are overreacting. The injury is not all that serious. With proper attention, he can be mended good as new."

Professor Newton was speechless.

Moses Silver was wide-eyed with astonishment. "Surely you don't mean . . . not even you could . . ."

"Certainly. I can and shall." The surgeon squatted and pointed. "Look there . . . you see? Repair will be straightforward. We'll have the old fellow back to normal in no time."

His elderly comrades also squatted. And craned their necks to see better.

"Ahh," Moses Silver said with frank admiration, "you're right, by gum." Yes indeed. The mammoth tusk *had* fractured quite cleanly. A little cement, and it'd be right as rain.

Robert Newton breathed a grateful sigh. "Oh yes. Well, then . . . one is quite relieved."

The investigation, headed by the Archuleta County sheriff's office, was thorough and competent. Every soul on the ranch was questioned. Moon and Bignight were significant witnesses, and told what they knew about the rancher's unfortunate demise.

Most of what they knew.

Daniel Bignight didn't see any compelling reason to mention the awful shriek of the "bant-shee" calling his name.

What were they doing in the neighborhood?

Moon's explanation that they just happened to be patrolling the reservation boundary at 3 A.M. didn't sit too well with the Archuleta County sheriff, but the Ute policeman stuck to his story.

The state police provided valuable technical assistance. The verdict was never in doubt. Death by accidental cause.

Three days later, after the coroner was finished with it, McFain's body was released to the family.

Moon pulled the SUPD Blazer in front of the small cabin called Calamity Jane. Moses Silver, dressed in an ill-fitting black suit, was standing near the Land Rover. Waiting for his daughter, the policeman assumed. The paleontologist gave the freshly washed patrol car a brief look, the Ute policeman a polite nod.

Cordell York and Robert Newton were thirty yards away at another cabin, leaning against the physician's rented Lincoln.

Moon turned at the sound of an engine cranking. He watched Vanessa McFain turn the Chevy van and head up the tail of Buffalo Saddle Ridge, trailing twin billows of bone-dry yellow dust.

Delia Silver appeared in the doorway of Calamity Jane. She paused, staring at Moon. Then glanced uncertainly at her father, who was pointedly inspecting an antique pocket watch. She hurried over to Moses. Father and daughter had a tense conversation. The old man shook his head in bewilderment, gave Moon an annoyed look, and got into the Land Rover.

Delia headed across the lawn of pine needles toward the Ute policeman. The young woman looked very fetching in her charcoal dress and pert little black hat. Purse and shoes to match. Yes, this was much better than faded jeans and dusty work shirts.

Moon tipped his black Stetson.

"Good afternoon," she said. As if they were meeting for some ordinary social occasion.

Moses Silver—hunched up in the Land Rover—was watching under bushy eyebrows. Dr. York and Robert Newton were also eyeing this unexpected development with ill-concealed interest. All three men were wondering why Delia Silver had chosen the policeman's company. What was this all about?

She looked up at the tall man with an odd mixture of suppressed anxiety and childlike hope. "I wondered whether you could give me a ride. Up to the cemetery."

Moon nodded amiably, and opened the Blazer door. It was a long step up in her tight skirt; he steadied Delia's elbow with his hand. He was in no hurry to depart, allowing York to take the lead, and Moses Silver to putt along far ahead in the Land Rover.

When they topped the first hump of Buffalo Saddle Ridge—at the RV park where the Flye trailer had been—Moon shifted into low gear and slowed almost to a stop. Delia's gaze followed his. "I didn't know that Horace . . . that Mr. Flye had a daughter. Not until after he . . . he disappeared that night."

"I guess he kept it quiet. So Nathan wouldn't charge him extra rent."

They drove down into the saddle; the lane wound among a scattering of towering red sandstone monoliths. The wind was not so constant here.

"Officer Moon?"

"Yeah?"

"Do you think there's any chance of finding the stolen artifact?"

It seemed that half the county knew about the theft of the flint blade. He shrugged. "You can never tell. May already be too late. Then again . . . maybe we'll get lucky."

Her face was suddenly pale as new snow. "If you should find it . . . please bring it directly to me."

Moon pulled to a stop under a great slab of sandstone that cast a long, cold shadow. He cut the ignition.

Delia looked at him with some alarm. "Why are we stopping?"

He turned to look at her upturned face. "Because you've got something to tell me."

She licked her lips. "Why should I wish to tell you . . . anything at all?"

"Because," he said evenly, "I'm the only one who can help you."

She was silent for a moment. But after she started, the words fairly poured out.

On the previous day, Jimson Beugmann had used a miner's pick and a heavy mattock to grub out the five-foot-deep slot in the half-frozen earth. He would've gone six but he'd hit a shelf of fine-grained sandstone that was, he thought, harder'n a Reno whore's heart.

Today, Beugmann was dressed in spotless black trousers, his best Roper boots, and a heavy mackinaw jacket. The deaf-mute's thin, unreadable face was half-shaded by the broad brim of a gray felt hat. In honor of the solemn occasion, he'd stuck a small raven's feather in the band. A wind-choir hummed dark anthems in the pine branches and whipped his stringy blond hair around his shoulders. Having little status as a mourner, the lately arrived ranch hand had positioned himself well away from his former boss' fresh grave; he leaned against the pink bark of an aged ponderosa and chewed on a dry sprig of skunk grass. Jimson Beugmann was a practical man, who planned ahead. His shovel was artfully concealed behind the pine trunk. When all the preaching and crying was finished, somebody had to stay behind and fill up the hole.

Vanessa McFain stood at the head of the coffin with her Aunt Celeste, who had come all the way from St. Louis. The minister was a wrinkled Navajo elder from Farmington; he held a much-used black Bible in his leathery hands.

Cordell York, Robert Newton, and Moses Silver stood on one side of the grave. Each of these men had, in his own way, a certain presence that added dignity to the small gathering. Delia Silver—who did not acknowledge the curious stares of her father and his colleagues—stood on the opposite side of the yawning hole in the ground. She kept very close to Charlie Moon.

This did not escape Vanessa McFain's notice.

Presently, Delia took Moon's arm. And leaned on him.

The Free Methodist minister raised his arms—and the Book—as if to silence the voices of the winds. The mournful humming in the trees fell to a whisper.

He began. "We are gathered here to say farewell to Nathan McFain, a loving father." He nodded to acknowledge the last member of the McFain clan. Vanessa, who seemed to be deaf, was staring dumbly into the mouth of the grave. Wondering what it all meant. Or perhaps that was the wrong question.

The preacher continued. Speaking of the uncertainties of this life. Of how our days are numbered . . . and not one of us knows the number of them. Of the immeasurable love of God. And of His tender mercies. Of how men must shun the Devil.

And then the whirlwind came.

The furies howled. They slapped faces, tugged at sleeves, sucked up mouthfuls of dust, spat out sticks and stones . . . and uttered vile threats.

It seemed that the small congregation might be swept away.

The men choked and coughed, and attempted to cover their eyes.

Delia clung desperately to Charlie Moon's big frame. The Ute planted his boots in the loose soil and enfolded the small woman in his arm. He gritted sand between his teeth and assured himself that this was a natural phenomena. Nothing but a dust devil . . . hmmm . . . an unfortunate turn of phrase.

Vanessa McFain stood like a lone pine. She leaned, but did not fall.

The little minister was an uncommonly stubborn man. And one who knew his enemies. He raised his Bible, and shouted above the roar:

"Eye has not seen, nor ear heard, nor have entered into the heart of man the things which God has prepared for those who love Him!"

The immediate reply stung his ear. *We have come to dine on a soul. This is our place. Go away.*

Only the Navajo minister perceived these words from the hot mouth of the swirling vortex. Ready to do battle, the old warrior shook his fist in furious defiance. "Go straight to hell," he shouted.

Only the voices perceived these words from the mouth of the prophet. And the whirlwind, thus rebuked, whined. It departed from them, winding its crooked way downhill . . . through a stand of dwarf oak . . . into the dark valley. And was gone.

It was over.

Most of the mourners had departed.

Cordell York and Robert Newton had left in the rented Lincoln.

Moses Silver and his daughter had chugged away in the old Land Rover; Aunt Celeste—at a signal from Vanessa—had ridden with them.

The little Navajo Methodist had gravely shook hands with Vanessa, told her that God would sort all things out, and left in his new Ford pickup.

Now only four remained.

Vanessa McFain, smothered in her grief.

By her side, Charlie Moon.

Jimson Beugmann. At a nod from Vanessa, he began filling the grave with earth.

And Nathan McFain, of course. Whose remains would rest in silence. And whose troubled soul was forever at peace.

Finally, Beugmann tamped the last shovelful down neatly. The silent man nodded respectfully at Vanessa, gave Moon an odd look, and stalked away.

Nathan's spirit also departed.

Now there were only two.

Moon put his arm around the tall woman's shoulders. Vanessa looked up at him through red-rimmed eyes. "God, Charlie . . . it's hard."

He nodded. His mother was buried not five miles from this spot. Over in Snake Canyon. In a cleft in the stone wall. Only last year, he had repaired the masonry wall with blue clay from the Piedra. He had no idea where his father's body was.

She turned, and hugged him. "Charlie?"

"Yeah?"

"What'll I do?"

"Well, you're the boss now, so I expect you'll have to run the ranch."

She sniffled. "I guess so." She didn't feel like running anything. She felt like running.

"Charlie?"

"Yeah?"

"What'll I do first?"

He thought about it. "Well, you could tell those bone-diggers to get on with their work. Your father's plan for a museum ain't such a bad notion."

"I can do that tomorrow. What'll I do tonight?"

"You'll go up to Durango with me. To the Strater Hotel."

She pulled herself away and looked up at him with large eyes. "To the hotel?"

"Sure. I'll buy you supper."

"Oh. Is that all?"

"Nope."

She managed a thin smile. "So what happens after supper?"

"I'll bring you home."

He could've said I'll *take* you home. She pinched his arm. "And after you bring me home, Charlie . . . will you tuck me in?"

Moon seemed not to have heard. He was looking over her head. At something very far away. But it was coming closer. Soon, he'd be able to make it out.

She sighed. Charlie Moon always acted like her big brother. And he'd sure stuck close to that little Silver gal.

Damn! He just didn't have a clue.

Or maybe she didn't have quite what he wanted.

But he did.

And she did.

The dining room at the Strater was quiet, the waiter gracious and most accommodating. Vanessa McFain picked at a meatless lasagna. Charlie Moon would have enjoyed his grilled chops more if she hadn't watched him eat every bite with an accusing eye. Like they'd been hacked right off her pet pig. Dessert, which was more relaxed, was followed by excellent coffee.

In Moon's pickup, she leaned her head on his shoulder. It was a pleasant drive back to the ranch. Her ranch.

They took a long, moonlit walk on the near hump of Buffalo Saddle Ridge. He had little to say, except for a single question. About what had happened that night.

"What night?" she asked.

"The night Horace Flye disappeared."

Vanessa hesitated. Then talked. She told him about waking up. Hearing an argument downstairs. Her father . . . and another man. Yes, it might have been Horace Flye. It must have been; her father's employee was gone the next morning. But she couldn't understand how Flye could have left that darling little girl behind. A man who'd do something like that ought be horsewhipped!

Moon didn't tell her Flye was dead. Mostly to change the subject, the Ute policeman asked her about the stolen flint blade. Did she have any idea where it might be?

She hesitated, then admitted that she did have a notion. Vanessa told him about a peculiar conversation she'd overheard. It was probably too late, she added, to do anything.

He admitted—with some regret—that she was probably right.

Finally, when all was said, he took the sleepy young woman upstairs to her bedroom. And tucked her in. And sat beside her bed, holding her hand. Charlie Moon did not depart until she was lost in dreams.

That night, his own dreams were troubled.

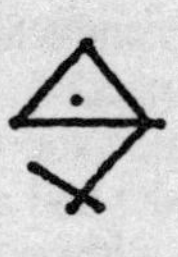

MAKING THE SALE

ANNE FOSTER LIFTED her foot off the accelerator, and slowed. And watched. The journalist pulled her Mercury off the two-lane asphalt road and parked on a wide place in the road that was—according to the neatly lettered green sign—a scenic overlook. She used the telephoto lens on her 35-mm camera to watch the Mercedes. The road dead-ended at a huge bulge of basalt that looked like a gigantic, overturned pot. So he was heading toward the Iron Kettle. And if she had it figured right, the British guy who'd checked into the Cattleman's Hotel would be along before long.

She thought about it. It wouldn't be possible to follow Briggs along the dusty road without being spotted. Maybe even caught between the shady antique dealer and the Brit. She was not particularly afraid of Ralph Briggs; the man was about as threatening as a teddy bear. And Mr. Soames—though he had a reputation for smuggling artifacts across international borders—seemed civilized enough. But the Brit was accompanied by a thug with ball-bearing eyes set in a cinder-block head. Kind of fellow who ate nails with his Wheaties.

No, she certainly couldn't drive her shiny new car to the Iron Kettle. Ralph Briggs and his contact must be under the impression that their business was conducted in complete privacy.

But the truth was, she needed help. She found the cell phone in her purse and dialed the Granite Creek police station. She'd tell Scotty that she had a big story about to break. He'd jump at the chance to witness an illegal exchange.

No, the dispatcher told her, the chief of police was not in his office. No, she did not know where Chief Parris could be reached. Would Miss Foster like to have Mr. Parris' pager number?

No, that would not be necessary.

Like all his vital statistics, from hat size (XL) to shoe (eleven), Anne had the number memorized. She dialed, got the pager tone, and entered her cell-phone number.

She waited anxiously for five minutes. Ten. Fifteen.

No return call.

As usual, he'd turned it off. Damn! What was the use of having your own special cop if he wasn't there when you needed him?

What to do?

She needed to get close enough to take photographs through the telescopic lens. But not so close as to be noticed. And high enough for a good shot. Sure. On the crest of that long, pine-studded ridge, just to the south of the Iron Kettle. A perfect spot to spy on Ralph Briggs. There was a deer trail snaking along under the cover of scrub oak and ponderosa. She had a pair of hiking shoes in the trunk. And a good pair of legs.

That's what Scotty had told her.

Ralph Briggs had arrived at the meeting place when the sun was barely over Salt Mountain. The antiquarian—who was a romantic—surveyed the hump of stone called the Iron Kettle. If he'd seen this pile of basalt first, he'd have given it a grand name. Thunder Stone Fallen from Mars. Something nifty like that.

It was an extraordinarily fine day. The musky aroma of sage was given a keen edge by the sharpness of morning frost. At the foot of the boulder-strewn ridge, Briggs' powder-blue Mercedes sat like a fat, luminescent beetle. Waiting to convey him back to Granite Creek, some eight miles to the southeast. The automobile was parked at the edge of an unpaved road which meandered here and there in aimless fashion, wriggling like a nervous yellow snake anxious to find its way out of the dark cleft between Salt Mountain and Six Mile Mesa. The antiquarian sat comfortably in a folding canvas chair. His eyes were shaded from the sun by the branch of a withered juniper that grew out of the crack in a basalt shelf. Between puffs on a fine Costa Rican cigar, he sipped gratefully from a thermos bottle of steaming hot chocolate. The antiquarian—though by the chemistry of his genes a pessimist—was in excellent spirits on this lovely morning. He congratulated himself on his ability to sense a rare opportunity. And seize it. Moreover, he had selected a quite suitable site for a meeting. Today, Ralph Briggs felt young for his sixty-two years. Gay at heart. Definitely a man on the way up.

But genes are constructed of extremely tough old stuff, and are very determined. They will have their way.

Of course . . . if for some reason this Soames fellow did not show . . . if the Brit thought he could buy the blade for a song . . . if Soames' client lost interest . . . if if if.

He glanced at his pocket watch. Eleven minutes before noon. *High Noon.* In his mind's eye, he saw the gaunt, haunted visage of Gary Cooper—the newly married town marshal with his back to the wall. He saw the outlaws at the depot, loading their six-shooters . . . waiting for the noon train that would bring the killer with the pockmarked face to town. And he saw the sweet, innocent face of a willowy Grace Kelly. The pacifist Quaker bride who—when the chips were down—would shoot a hard case in the back.

She would do it for her man.

The remembrance of this romance brought a tear to his eye, tied a tight knot in his throat.

Now it was ten minutes before noon. Briggs pictured himself riding away in a little buckboard wagon with Grace Kelly, to live happily ever after. He wiped at his eyes. Forgot all about what he was doing here.

But wait.

There was a small trail of dust on the road. Might be only a Forest Service pickup. He lifted a small pair of binoculars to his eyes and followed the dirt road to the approaching smudge. The optical instrument jittered in his trembling hands. One could not expect to recognize a face at this distance, but it was a black Lincoln Town Car. So this would be the British broker.

At precisely one minute before noon, the black barge pulled to a lurching halt behind Ralph Briggs' Mercedes. The driver got out. A square-headed man in a rumpled blue suit, who moved as if he was muscle-bound. Square Head paused to glance at Briggs' German automobile, then toward the summit of the Iron Kettle. This brief inspection completed, he said something to the passenger, nodded, and opened the rear door. A tall, very thin man dressed in an immaculate gray suit emerged.

"It's him," Briggs said aloud.

Loud enough to frighten a horned lark perched on a juniper branch above his head. The creature fluttered away in a startled flapping of wings, landing on a stiff sprig of fringed sagebrush. She blinked beady, accusing eyes at the human who had disturbed her peace.

The antiquarian flashed a smile at the lark. "Hello, cutie." He whistled his best imitation of a warbled birdsong.

The horned lark did not reply.

The dapper little man returned his attention to the visitor from Britain, who—as he had anticipated—had not come alone.

"Okay boys," Briggs said in a remarkably good imitation of Coop's easy drawl, "Come and get it."

He watched with keen anticipation as the pair of men slowly made their way up the winding path among the scattering of black boulders.

Anne Foster had mounted her camera on a lightweight tripod. She focused the telephoto lens on Ralph Briggs' pixie face. "Smile," she said.

He smiled.
Snap.
Snap.
Snap.

Briggs pushed himself up from the canvas chair; he shook the outstretched hand of his British visitor.

"Mr. Soames, I presume?"

"Mr. Briggs?"

Neither man paid the least attention to the square-headed fellow who lugged the oversized briefcase.

"So good of you to come all this way, Mr. Soames."

"I am pleased to make your acquaintance, Mr. Briggs." Dealing with strangers was risky. Only last summer, a weasel-faced fellow in Lima had showed him a dozen gold figurines unearthed by grave-robbers. The figurines were authentic. The "seller" was not. Weasel-face was an agent of the Federal Police. Armed with a 9-mm semiautomatic pistol, a voice-activated tape recorder in his coat pocket. It had been a damn near thing. A slight tic jerked at Soames' lower lip. "You must understand, of course . . . that I deal only in objects which may be legally purchased and transferred across international borders."

Briggs' eyes narrowed. "Relax, Mr. Soames. This is an up-and-up deal. I represent the . . . ahhh . . . owner of the artifact. And you don't have to make any speeches for the record. I am not wired."

"Then," Soames said, "you will not mind if my associate searches . . ."

Briggs held a pale hand up. "Certainly not. But fair is fair . . . you and your associate must also agree to be searched."

Soames glanced at Square Head, who had a bulge under his left armpit. "Well, I suppose there is something to be said for mutual trust."

Square Head retreated several paces behind his master, folded his muscular arms, and played the dummy. See nothing, hear nothing, know nothing. He was, Briggs thought, typecast for the role. The American host gestured toward the picnic basket. "Perhaps you'd care for some refreshments. I have strawberries . . . and champagne."

The European looked suspiciously down his nose at the basket. "From California, I presume?"

Briggs pretended to miss the barb. "The champagne is, of course. Strawberries are from Mexico."

"Thank you kindly, but I'll pass. I'm on rather a tight schedule, Mr. Briggs. Other business presses." It was true. On the morrow, Soames had a clandestine meeting in Many Farms. Chap with a selection of stunning Anasazi pottery that had been—not so long ago—the pride of a museum in Salt Lake. And then it was off to the Yucatan where an enterprising young lady in Kantunilkin had unearthed a fabulous jade statue of Kuklucan, the plumed Serpent-God of the ancient Maya. "Let us get right down to brass tacks, as you Yanks like to say."

"Suits me," Briggs said easily. He removed a pint of perfect strawberries from the picnic basket, and popped a plump specimen into his mouth. He chewed, watching his guest thoughtfully. "I expect you'll want to see the merchandise."

Soames' smile had no hint of mirth. "Indeed."

Again, the antiquarian slipped his hand into the wicker picnic basket; he removed a beautiful box of carved rosewood. He placed the container gingerly on a flat shelf of basalt, flipped a brass latch, and opened the hinged lid to reveal a lining of purple satin. Resting upon the sumptuous bed was a long, slender object. Wrapped in faultless white Taiwanese silk. Proper presentation was an essential part of any sale.

Soames stretched out his hand toward the box. "May I?"

"Certainly. But do be careful, Mr. Soames. Wouldn't want you to drop it."

The Brit sniffed to show his displeasure at the unnecessary caution from this two-bit American merchant. But without moving the object from the box, he carefully unwrapped the silk.

And there it was.

A seven-inch sliver of translucent pink flint, chipped by some ancient artisan into the form of a slightly curved blade.

Tony Soames found himself holding his breath. Aside from its scientific value, this was quite a lovely thing. And—being the sole link to an unexpected epoch in American prehistory—one of extraordinary value to a museum. Or a wealthy collector. He turned to his host. "You do understand that I must be certain of its authenticity."

"I personally guarantee it." Briggs jabbed the smoking cigar stub at his guest. "This is the very same artifact removed from the mammoth bones at the McFain mammoth site. I was present when it was discovered."

"How convenient for both of us. Nevertheless, I must assure myself . . ."

Briggs grinned like a coyote dining on freshly killed rabbit. "What—you don't trust me . . . after all we've meant to each other?"

Soames smiled sadly. A pity that one sometimes had to deal with such vulgar folk. He produced a device from his shirt pocket that had the appearance of an expensive pen. He removed the cap. The device was tipped with a small diamond stylus.

Briggs felt his shoulder muscles stiffen as the Brit scratched at the surface of the flint artifact. But he'd expected as much.

Soames was not surprised to learn that the object was stone. It was much too heavy to be an ordinary epoxy replica. But epoxy could be loaded with heavy minerals to simulate the density of stone. Contented that the material was indeed flint, he snapped his fingers.

Square Head opened the briefcase, and produced a copy of *Time*. The Brit sat on the basalt outcropping for some minutes, using a large magnifying glass to compare the details on the flint blade with the artifact pictured on the magazine cover. There could be no doubt about it; they were one and the same. He turned to the American. "Shall we discuss terms?"

"I trust," Briggs said, "your client is well-heeled."

"I hope," Soames shot back testily, "that *your* client does not intend to be greedy." The lower the purchase price, the higher his fee. But he would not receive less than expenses plus twenty thousand dollars. "Upon my recommendation, of course, my client is prepared to pay . . . I should expect . . . twenty-five thousand American dollars."

Briggs' eyes widened in a shocked expression. "I do hope you're joking. Such a small sum is out of the question. My client would be insulted. In fact, now that I have time to think about it, *I* am insulted."

Soames ignored the diatribe; the little man might be selling cod in a Liverpool fish market. This was only an opening offer. One expected to bargain a bit and all that. But he intended to have the artifact for no more than a hundred thousand. "Twenty-five thousand dollars for a simple flint blade is a rather generous sum."

"I suggest you consider raising your opening bid to at least one hundred thousand," Briggs said, ". . . something to get the auction going."

Tony Soames paled; his voice dropped to a raspy whisper. "Auction? You told me nothing of any auction . . ."

"Since we had our telephone conversation, another potential buyer has turned up. Of course—if your client doesn't participate, there won't be any auction. I'll only have the other collector to deal with." Ralph Briggs glanced anxiously at his wristwatch. "Look, Mr. Soames, it's almost twelve-twenty. I'm scheduled to make an overseas call at half-past the hour. I prefer to conduct my business in private. You'll surely forgive me if I seem inhospitable . . . but it's time we said our good-byes."

Soames ground his teeth. "I have not crossed an ocean to return to my client empty-handed. And I daresay I've made you a fair offer."

Briggs' dark eyes narrowed to thin, lizard slits. His false teeth chomped down on the cigar. Gary Cooper did not backwater. Neither did he. "What's on your mind?"

Square Head, who had been smoking an unfiltered Mexican cigarette, dropped the butt and ground it under his heel.

Soames took a step forward; he pointed a perfectly manicured finger menacingly at Briggs' stubby nose. "I would not have you mistake my meaning. It is this: when I leave this godforsaken place, I *will* have the artifact in my possession."

Briggs glared back. "Don't piss around with me, you

Limey gopher." Not exactly how Coop would've responded, but it'd have to do.

The Brit nodded at his silent companion.

Square Head casually pulled his suit coat apart, to reveal a polished-leather shoulder holster. It was filled with a wicked-looking automatic. He grinned meaningfully at Briggs, displaying an odd assortment of nicotine-stained teeth.

"This hardy fellow," Soames said evenly, "is my assistant. He handles irksome tasks . . . such matters that I would not wish to soil my hands with." He noticed, with some surprise, that Briggs did not appear to be impressed.

The antiquarian responded with a calmness bordering on boredom. "I am going to do you an enormous favor—in the way of sage advice. Stand very still, Mr. Soames . . . smile if you can manage it."

Soames did not smile. He glanced to his right, then his left. Over his shoulder. And saw nothing.

To Square Head, Briggs said: "Now listen very carefully, chimp-face . . . do *not* move your grubby hand toward that automatic pistol. To do so would invite the most unfortunate consequences. Which—in case you do not get my meaning—means that you will likely get your noodle blown off."

Square Head spoke for the first time; his growling accent hinted of South Philly and other points east and equally urban. "It's justa bluff, Mr. Soames. Mr. Fancy Pants is here all by hisself."

Soames smiled uneasily. "I am inclined to agree with you." Actually, he was inclined to think the little man had something up his sleeve. But a gentleman cannot appear uncertain in front of the hired help.

Square Head rolled his hairy hands into knobby fists. "Just gimme the word, Chief, and I'll kick his scrawny little ass up between his shoulders."

Briggs raised his voice. "Dude, please show yourself."

Twenty paces to Briggs' left, from behind a large basalt boulder, a man appeared. He was mounted on a fine chestnut, which tossed its head and whinnied. The newcomers stared in wonder at this most unlikely apparition.

Except for his ostrich-skin cowboy boots, the horseman's

outfit was . . . different. The bareheaded man wore a crisp black tuxedo. Spiffy white boutonniere. Pale yellow silk shirt, with standing collar and French cuffs. Spotless white tie. Dark glasses.

And a very ill-tempered expression.

"Cripes," Square Head said, "looks like he stepped offa a weddin' cake."

Soames—in spite of this surprise—remembered where he was. This was America. A former colony, populated with quite peculiar folk. The Brit's mouth twisted into a bitter smile. "I assume, Mr. Briggs, that this nattily attired fellow is your fashion consultant?"

"Dude," the antiquarian said, "is somewhat eccentric. He insists on dressing formally for any business meeting. I have protested, of course—but he will have his own way." He sighed wearily. "So I make allowances. Really good accountants are hard to find."

The Brit raised a querulous eyebrow. "Accountant . . . you don't say? Keeps your books, does he?"

Briggs shook his head. "Not that kind of accountant. Dude . . . he *settles* accounts for me."

Square Head's hand had slipped under his jacket.

"Don't," Briggs warned.

Too late.

Simultaneously, two things happened.

A short-barreled .38 caliber pistol materialized in Dude's hand. He didn't have time to fire it.

A rifle cracked . . . A 30-30 slug hummed like a bumblebee barely three inches over Square Head's bald head and did a zinging ricochet off a slab of black stone.

Another man had appeared a few yards to Briggs' right. This one wore a broad-brimmed felt hat and scuffed leather jacket. He stood behind a juniper snag, casually resting a Winchester hunting rifle in its crotch.

"That," Briggs said, "was Cowboy's warning shot. He is also my accountant. You may wish to know that he can shoot the hind legs off a grasshopper at two hundred yards. I have seen him do it." This was understood by all to be an exaggeration. But from where Cowboy stood, a quite ordinary marksman could have put a lead slug into the thug's ear.

Square Head, being not nearly as dumb as he looked, allowed his empty gun hand to drop to his side. "Sheesh," he grumbled.

Dude dismounted from the chestnut and holstered the .38. Even through the dark glasses, he was staring holes through Square Head.

Square Head, unable to do much else, stared back.

Tony Soames had not expected such thorough preparations from his American counterpart. He had, he admitted to himself, underestimated the vulgar little man. And the value Briggs placed on the Paleolithic blade.

The antiquarian spoke in a consoling tone. "Sorry about this, Mr. Soames. But I did attempt to warn your associate not to make any threatening move."

The Brit was worse than angry. He was embarrassed. He'd hired the bodyguard from a very reputable family in Philadelphia—mainly as protection for the cash he transported in the briefcase. He had enough—he thought—to buy the McFain blade. And several other artifacts and works of art. But he'd overplayed his hand by bringing along this gun for hire. And threatening Ralph Briggs. So it was the American's party now. "Where do we go from here?"

"Do you wish to take part in the auction?"

Soames hesitated, then nodded.

Briggs adopted a conciliatory tone. "Then I suggest that we forget the recent unpleasantness—call it a communications problem. Seeing that you wish to participate in the auction of this unique and fabulous artifact, you may do so. But I must make a firm condition."

"Which is?"

"To avoid any repetition of this unfortunate misunderstanding, you must dismiss your enthusiastic employee from these proceedings. I suggest that he return to your automobile. It is hard to concentrate with bullets flying—and one can never quite predict the outcome of violent acts. I am a man of some standing in my community; it would be inconvenient for me to explain the violent demise of your associate. Or . . . of yourself."

"I do see your point, Mr. Briggs." At a nod from the Brit, Square Head ground his teeth. And growled. But he departed.

Briggs popped a delicious Mexican strawberry into his mouth. "You will be able to contact your client by telephone?"

Tony Soames nodded. The prince—who knew when the meeting was scheduled—would be on hand for a call. Just in case something came up. Something had. He nodded to indicate the Town Car. "I have a telephone in the automobile."

"You need not trek back to your car; Dude has already made arrangements for communications."

Soames glanced without malice at the rifleman in the cowboy hat, then at the man in the tuxedo. "I was wondering whether you had another armed cowboy . . ." he glanced at Dude's spotless tuxedo, ". . . or perhaps another headwaiter . . . skulking out there somewhere behind a rock."

"Perish the thought, sir. With what I have to pay these very able fellows, a modest entrepreneur like myself can hardly afford a *third* accountant." Briggs glanced worriedly at his pocket watch, then produced a pair of identical cell phones from the picnic basket. He offered one to his guest, which was graciously accepted. The antiquarian smiled sweetly at the Brit. "Now . . . do you wish to make a serious opening bid?"

Soames did not hesitate. "One hundred thousand." Oddly, the figure warmed him. This was the big time.

The antiquarian stubbed out his imported cigar onto a pitted boulder. "That is, at least, a respectful beginning. I will make my call." He pressed a series of buttons on the cellular telephone. There was a delay of perhaps twenty seconds. They seemed like as many minutes to Tony Soames.

Finally, Briggs spoke. "Oh, good day." A pause. "Yes, that's right . . . no, it's not daytime there, is it? Ha Ha." A shorter pause. "Certainly I have it. You've received the photos, I take it? Yes. Very good. Well—the thing is—I do have a competing proposition from another party. One hundred thousand. American dollars, of course." He chuckled, as if embarrassed to report this paltry offer. "I mention this just to get the ball rolling, as we say. A representative of the other buyer is with me. I am awaiting your bid."

There was a pause, while Briggs nodded at the unseen person. "Yes." Another pause. "Yes, certainly." He turned to Soames. "Two hundred thousand dollars."

Soames wiped a clean linen handkerchief across his forehead, and sat down heavily on the basalt outcropping. The Brit dialed a long string of numbers. Within moments, he smiled weakly. "Hello. Yes, it's me." A pause. "Yes sir. I'm here in the States . . . no, I have not yet finalized the transaction . . . well, it's a matter of price. I only learned of it a few minutes ago, but it seems that we must . . . ahhh . . . bid." He listened to the Arab, and swallowed hard. "Two hundred thousand . . . yes sir . . . American dollars. Yes, I understand. Please hold, sir." He turned to Briggs and cleared his throat. "We bid three hundred thousand." *Stick that in your ear, Yank.*

The antiquarian sighed, as if this was such a tedious business. He put his ear to the small telephone. "Hello . . . are you still there? Good. The bid is three hundred thousand. Do you have a response? Very good." Briggs glanced at the Brit. "Three hundred and fifty thousand."

Tony Soames shook his head in dismay. "I rather doubt that my client will . . ."

Briggs smiled a malicious smile. "Three hundred and fifty thousand, Mr. Soames. Going . . . going . . ."

Soames abruptly raised his hand; he spoke into the telephone receiver. "Sir . . . the bid is three hundred and fifty. I believe that four hundred thousand would probably . . . Yes sir. That will, of course, practically deplete the cash reserves I have on hand. It will be necessary for you to wire sufficient funds for our other business . . . yes, of course. Will you please hold the line?" Having recovered much of his dignity, he smirked at Ralph Briggs. "My client will go four hundred thousand. But not one dollar more. This is absolutely his final bid."

Briggs nodded, and spoke into the telephone. "The other party has offered four hundred thousand. Would you wish to go . . . say four hundred and fifty?" He shook his head. "No, I'm also truly sorry. But I do understand. Yes, I agree . . . if the transaction based on the competing bid should not be consummated for any reason—I'll most certainly inform you.

And you'll have the item for your bid of three hundred and fifty. In any case, I'm sure we will do some very interesting business in the future. I have a newly-discovered piece of Mimbres pottery that is absolutely breathtaking. The bowl is sixteen inches across . . . a black lizard with red eyes curled up on the inside. Yes . . . of course I'll send photos along forthwith. Good-bye, old friend." He pressed the OFF button and turned to Soames. "It seems," he said, "you have purchased a most remarkable artifact for your client."

Soames spoke into the telephone receiver. "The transaction is agreed upon. Shall I proceed with the exchange?" A brief pause, a useless nod to the man on the opposite side of the globe. "Very good, sir. Yes sir. I will. Good-bye."

Soames returned the telephone to Briggs. He squatted, turned five discs on a combination lock, then opened the briefcase. He began to place bundles of greenbacks on the folding lid of the picnic basket.

The man in the tuxedo came near, to watch the count. When it was done, and at a nod from Briggs, Dude picked up a bundle. He tore off the paper band, and selected several hundred-dollar bills at random. They looked quite new. He rubbed his thumb across the surface. No ink smudge. That was good. Holding the bills up to the sunlight, he inspected them with considerable care.

Soames—insulted by this precaution—was tight-lipped with rage.

"Nothing personal," Briggs said in a consoling tone, "just normal business practice. My accountant," he said like a proud father, "is an A-number-one expert in funny money. Dude once worked on a fake-twenties dodge in Oak Park. That's in Illinois."

"The bills," Soames said sourly, "are quite genuine."

Dude grunted, and nodded his agreement with this statement.

Ralph Briggs placed the cash in the picnic basket and closed the lid. "That seems to complete our business."

Tony Soames wrapped the beautiful flint blade in the silk cloth and placed it in the rosewood box. He gave Ralph Briggs an oddly suspicious look. "I have a feeling, old boy, that you've gotten the best of me on this transaction."

"Not at all," Briggs said in a consoling tone, "this is a win-win deal, Mr. Soames. Your client has got what he lusted after. I have my ten percent. And you will undoubtedly be well-paid for your successful effort."

"Yes," Soames said with a trace of bitterness, "so I shall." Exactly half what this American toad had made on the deal.

Ralph Briggs waited until Tony Soames' Town Car was a black speck in the distance before he spoke. "Well, fellows—that was the most fun I've had since me and sister Tabitha put the tadpole in Aunt Tillie's mint tea."

Dude scowled at the man called Cowboy. "Well, I'm glad it's done. I ain't slept two hours in the past two days. I had to ride out here on a horse," he rubbed his sore butt, "and I don't much like riding horses." He turned his frown on the antiquarian. "You sure played that one close to the edge, Briggs. Couple of times, I thought sure you'd blown it. Like when you turned your nose up at twenty-five thousand and told him to take a hike. But you sure had him figured right . . ."

"I am quite good at what I do," the antiquarian said with disarming candor.

"And when you called that other rich buyer and started the auction . . ."

"Oh that," Briggs said with a dismissive wave. "Merely a bluff."

Dude's eyes narrowed to thin blue slits. "Bluff? You mean there wasn't any other buyer . . ."

"Certainly not. I dialed the Time and Temperature number. Twelve twenty-nine P.M., fifty-two degrees Fahrenheit." Briggs lit a new cigar; the bachelor smiled his fatherly smile at the younger man. "If you are to succeed in your field of chosen endeavor, you must be prepared to take risks."

Cowboy decided that he admired the dapper little man. This one had a peck of gravel in his craw.

A stiff breeze whipped up dust and bits of other stuff.

Dude flicked away a green inchworm who was busily occupied with the task of measuring the length of his tuxedo sleeve. "Well, it turned out okay."

"Indeed. I'm forty thousand dollars richer than I was this

morning." The antiquarian danced a light-footed little jig. "Whoever said that crime doesn't pay?"

"I'd like to be a fly on the wall," Cowboy said slowly, "if the buyer ever wises up . . . That British fella's likely to be in deep trouble."

Ralph Briggs chuckled. "Yes . . . isn't it just *delicious*?" What a grand day it had been!

And then Briggs' worry-genes kicked in. What if—against all odds—Tony Soames *did* find out he'd been had . . . and came back to town with a whole gang of Square Heads—armed with Winchester carbines . . . Colt Peacemakers . . . Arkansas toothpicks? And what if Dude and Cowboy were not at hand to back him up? The townsfolk would be of no help. Leave now with your new bride, Marshal—it's best for you and best for the town. Nosir, we don't want no more killins 'round these parts. Bad for business.

Well, he knew damn well what he'd do. At ten minutes before high noon, he'd kiss Grace Kelly good-bye. Put her pretty self on the buckboard seat, slap the horse's sweaty rump with his hat. Watch her leave . . . maybe for the last time.

Then he'd roll the cylinder on his well-oiled Colt and check each cartridge. Stick the cold eight-inch barrel under his belt. And . . . all alone . . . walk down the dusty street.

Toward the train depot.

And *destiny.*

"Let 'em come," he said in a slow drawl.

Anne Foster sat in front of the fireplace, hugging her knees. Watching the flames lick at the split pine logs.

The journalist had given up staring at the photographs she'd taken of Ralph Briggs' clandestine meeting on the rocky summit of the Iron Kettle. She had wonderfully crisp black-and-whites of the antiquarian passing the stolen artifact to the man who'd arrived in the Town Car with the thug. She had, in fact, gotten more than she had dreamed of. Several of the shots she'd made through the excellent telephoto lens included the two armed men who were there with Briggs.

His partners in crime.

One was from out of town. The other was a respected citizen of Granite Creek. What to do with the photographs . . . Hide them away in some secret spot? No. She'd burn them. Anne had the incriminating prints in her hand . . . was reaching out toward the fire. The telephone jangled. She let it ring ten times, then relented.

"Hello."

"Hi, it's me."

Her heart raced. "Oh . . . Hi, Scotty."

Parris chuckled. "You sound kinda down."

Anne swallowed a lump in her throat. "It's been that kind of day."

"Well, I'm double-glad I called. I've got something to show you. Something that'll cheer you up."

She felt a sudden flood of exultant hope. He was going to tell her all about it. Explain why he and Charlie Moon had helped Ralph Briggs sell a stolen artifact. Somehow . . . it would all make sense. "Why don't you drop by?"

"I'll be there in ten minutes."

Scott Parris, who was concentrating on the task of steering the Volvo through wisps of fog along a narrow mountain road, glanced at the woman beside him. Anne had barely spoken. Well, she'd evidently had a rough day. Best just to leave her be.

He was mildly startled when she did speak. "Scotty?"

"Yeah?"

"Have you seen Charlie Moon recently?"

That was an odd question. "Sure. Matter of fact, Charlie was in town yesterday. Why do you ask?"

"Oh, just wondered." She darted a look at him. "You two do anything . . . interesting?"

He shrugged. "Oh, not much. This and that. You know Charlie."

"I wondered," she bit her lip, "whether you've learned anything about that flint blade."

He frowned, and squinted to see the splash of yellow headlights on the damp asphalt. "Flint blade?"

"The one that was stolen from Nathan McFain."

"Oh, that. Yeah, we talked about it some."

"Anything new on who might've stolen it?"

The chief of police grinned indulgently. "If there was, it'd be police business." He glanced at her profile, ivory in the dash lights. Her expression was thin-lipped and hard. Poor kid must've had an awful day. Well, he'd soon take care of that. He turned off abruptly into a winding gravel driveway. And pulled to a stop under a neatly trimmed willow that sat in front of the stone house like a fragile mushroom.

She blinked. "This is the Waring place."

He grinned, and cut the ignition. "All sixteen acres of it."

Anne turned to look at him. "Why are we stopping here?"

He threw his hands up in mock dismay. "Well, I'm outta gas." He attempted a leer. "So it's either snuggle up to keep warm—or you got a long walk back to town."

Despite herself, she smiled. "You're an idiot."

"Yes," he said earnestly, "but I'm *your* idiot."

He got out, slammed the Volvo door, and breathed deeply.

She was at his side. "You still haven't told me why we've stopped . . ."

"Did you know this place was for sale?"

"Of course. It's been on the market for months."

"And it once belonged to your uncle. You used to visit this place, when you were a kid. It's the place you've always wanted."

She gave him an odd look. "How did you know that?"

"It's my job. To know what you want."

"Well, it doesn't matter," she said glumly. "This property is way out of my price range."

He snapped off a stem of willow branch and put it between his teeth. "I've cut a deal with the owner," he said. "Soon as the paperwork's done, it's mine."

She gave him a dazed look. "Yours . . . ?"

He took her by the shoulders. "Or . . . if you'd like . . . it's *ours*."

Anne couldn't meet his eyes. "I don't see how . . ."

"How what?"

She forced the words past her lips. "I don't see how you could afford a place like this. I know what you make, Scotty. And what you have in the bank."

"Wow," he said with an amused expression, "sounds like you've been checking up on me."

She choked back a sob. "Oh, Scotty . . . how *could* you?"

He watched, openmouthed, as she turned and stalked away across the frost-killed lawn toward the road. "Hey, babe—where are you goin'?"

"Home," she called back shrilly.

"But it's almost three miles. You can't . . ." But she could. And would.

He fumbled around in the Volvo glove compartment and found the small Motorola transceiver. The dispatcher answered his summons almost immediately. "Hi, Clara. Who do we have on duty . . . in an unmarked car?"

"Officer Alicia Martin. She's at the intersection of Poplar and Fifteenth, speed control duty."

Perfect. "Send her up to Ayerst Road, on the double-quick. Tell Alicia to look for a woman walking downhill. About one hundred fifteen, five seven. Red hair."

"Sounds like Sweetums."

He had expected Clara Tavishuts' snide remark. "Yeah, Clara, it's Anne. And no, it's none of your business. Just have Officer Martin pick her up and take her home." The chief of police turned the transceiver off without the usual formalities and threw it on the seat beside him.

Scott Parris sat in the old Volvo, watching the slender figure retreating downhill. What had he done? Was it a crime to buy your sweetheart her dream house and practically propose? Within thirty seconds, he saw the familiar square profile of the unmarked Ford coming up the road. Anne hesitated, then got in. The Ford did a neat U-turn. So Anne would soon be safely home.

But what had gotten into her?

His mind was racing blindly along dark byways.

This wasn't the first time he'd asked Anne to marry him. But, he promised himself, it would be the last. True, she was drop-dead gorgeous. Smelled like honeysuckle blossoms. Brilliant conversationalist. Wonderful companion. She was almost perfect. Except for this one little thing . . .

She was completely nutso.

Might be in her genes.

Their offspring would be a brood of darling little red-headed lunatics.

Nope, this would never work.

He sat there for an hour, into the beginnings of twilight. The morbid thoughts ran around his mind like crippled grey-hounds on a ghostly racetrack. Chasing a phony rabbit that was always three strides ahead.

He barely noticed the headlights in the driveway.

Alicia Martin leaned on the Volvo. "Hi, Chief."

He got out, slamming the door. "Don't 'Chief' me, Officer Martin. I'm off duty."

"Me too," she said with a pixie grin. "I was about to head for home when the call from Dispatch came in."

He grunted and muttered something under his breath.

"So if I mustn't call you 'Chief,' what'd be the proper form of address?"

He shrugged. "Scott, I guess."

"Then you can call me Alicia."

He looked at her face, framed by shoulder-length blond hair. Alicia had pretty blue eyes that sort of twinkled when she was laughing at you. Nice smile, too. An uncomplicated young lady. Definitely not nutso like someone else he knew. She'd make some young man a fine wife. If a fellow bought her a nice house, she'd appreciate it.

"Is that okay with you . . . Scott?" *Scott.* Gee, that sounded funny. Like the chief was a regular person.

"Yeah, Alicia. That's okay." But it wasn't. He stomped across the well-trimmed lawn, toward the house.

She was at his side. "I delivered your package home. Safe and sound."

"Thanks."

Poor, sweet man. And he was so sad. "Sometimes," she said, "life stinks."

He sighed. "Yeah. Tell me about it."

She moved close enough to brush her arm against his. "Sometimes it gets awfully lonely."

"Indeed it does."

Should I? What'll he think? Oh, to hell with it! She took his large hand in hers.

He was startled, and embarrassed. On the other hand, it was very pleasant. Reassuring. Like a father-daughter thing. Except she wasn't his daughter. She was a rather attractive young lady.

"Officer Martin . . ."

He's on duty again. "Yes sir?"

Scott Parris cleared his throat. And stepped gingerly into the minefield. "I'm sure there must be a departmental rule against the chief of police holding hands with one of his officers."

She took a deep breath. "I checked the manual. There is no such rule."

He grinned weakly. "You're sure about that?"

"Yes sir."

Anne had meant to stay at home. Take a long, hot bath. Go to bed early. Not think about *him.* Or the house. Or the terrible trouble he'd gotten himself into. Sleep without dreams, that was the ticket.

Within fifteen minutes, she was dialing Scott Parris' home number.

No answer, except for his terse answering machine message. "Leave your name and number and . . ."

Of course he wouldn't be at home. Not for some time. Anne knew her man. Knew where he was. She threw a tweed coat over her shoulders, got into her Mercury and sped along Pine Ridge Avenue. Past the aging red-brick high school. Across the rusting iron bridge over the frigid river. Up Ayerst Road. Where their dream home waited.

Thank God! His old Volvo was still there, parked in the winding driveway.

But so was another automobile. It was the boxy-looking Ford the cute young blond girl had picked her up in. Alicia Somebody in the unmarked car who thought Anne didn't realize she was a plainclothes cop. Thoughtfully summoned, of course, by Chief of Police Scott Parris. To take his runaway girlfriend home.

Anne slowed the Mercury.

They were standing there on the lawn, the two of them. In the moonlight. Scott Parris and the cute little blond girl.

Holding hands.

It was fortunate for all concerned that Anne did not carry a pistol.

Scott Parris sat in Charlie Moon's office. The *matukach* stared out the window at a dismal world. "Women," Parris said.

The Ute, who had his boots propped on the battered desk, frowned thoughtfully at this philosophical remark, but did not offer any comment. On the wall facing Moon's desk, an inexpensive round clock hung precariously on a loose thumbtack. As if exhibiting some mechanistic acrophobia, the second hand moved in nervous little jerks.

Minutes passed.

"Don't be so damned taciturn," the white man said sullenly.

Moon scratched at his sideburn. "Amongst my own people, I talk arms and legs off. But those of the European persuasion expect us indigenous folk to lean toward taciturnity. So—not wanting to disappoint—I'm a man of few words when I'm in the company of you chatty *matukach*."

"I don't think 'taciturnity' is a real word," Parris grumped.

"Sure it is. Look it up."

He rubbed at bloodshot eyes. "Damn it, Charlie, Anne is driving me over the edge. I think I'll give up on women altogether."

"You could become a monk," Moon said earnestly. "Go live in an abbey. Practice the virtues of obedience. And chastity."

Parris groaned.

"And," the Ute added, ". . . taciturnity."

"Charlie, you ever have woman problems? I mean really *bad* woman problems."

"Not me, pardner. I don't mess with really bad women."

The white man pulled at a numb ear that had once been nearly severed from his head by a lunatic. "You know what I mean."

"Oh. You mean bad problems with women. Sure. Once in a while."

Parris, who felt his load lighten, looked up eagerly. "Gimme a f'r instance."

"You remember Myra Cornstone?"

"Sure. Kinda thin. But a nice-looking young lady."

Moon looked at a spiderweb of cracks in the plaster ceiling. "Well, for a while I thought she kinda liked me. Then, for no reason, Myra started treating me like I was the North Vietnamese."

"Women," Parris said.

"You know," the Ute said, "it's no wonder Anne don't want to marry you."

"What?"

"Well, face facts, pardner. She's a real good-looker. Smart, too. Makes good money. And you're about fifteen years older'n her."

"Twelve," Parris growled.

"Point is," Moon said, "she's too good for you. You need to set your sights a bit lower."

"Thanks. Now I feel lots better."

"Glad to help, pardner." Moon looked at the ceiling. "Of course, if someone would go talk to Anne on your behalf . . . someone who could convince her that you're a lot better'n you actually are . . ."

Parris aimed a finger at his friend. "Don't you even *think* about it."

"Okay. But later on, don't say I didn't offer to help."

"Whatta you mean, *later on?*"

Moon took his big feet off the desk. He got up, towering over his friend. "A good-looker like Anne—'specially young as she is—ain't gonna stay unattached for long."

Parris stared bullets at the Ute.

Moon shrugged the bullets off. "So what'll you do when you find some other guy's pickup parked in her driveway?"

The white man's blue eyes narrowed. "I'll pull the bastard's arms and legs off. And beat him to death with 'em."

Moon patted his friend on the shoulder. "That's the right attitude. So if you want me to drop by sometime and straighten things out between you two . . ."

"Forget it," Parris snapped.

"Okay. Just tryin' to be helpful."

There was a long silence.

Moon leaned on the window frame and took it all in. The autumn sky was cornflower-blue. The dead leaves on a Russian olive rustled in a light breeze. A hawk circled lazily. The day that was so dismal for his friend was bright and beautiful to the Ute. "They say the rainbows are biting anything up at Yellow Fork. George Blackhair swears he caught a three-pounder on a wad of bubble gum."

The white man snorted. "Bubble gum?" Sounded fishy.

"So you want to go wet a hook?"

Parris sighed, and shook his head.

Moon frowned thoughtfully at his friend. This was serious.

SOUTH OF MEDINA, SAUDI ARABIA

He was in his western home, which sat precisely astride the tropic of Cancer. It was a more convenient place to receive the British visitor than his eastern palace, being a mere two hours' drive south from the modern airport at *Al Madinah.*

The ardent collector of man's most ancient and precious artifacts was alone in a large, circular parlor that was a penthouse atop his mountain sanctuary. The room was elegant in its austerity. The wall was a rim of thick plate glass, interrupted at three-meter intervals by stainless steel supports. The uncarpeted floor was polished Canadian oak, the circular ceiling paneled with alternating triangular spokes of rosewood, mahogany, and maple. A chandelier of antique Belgian crystal was suspended from the precise center of this disk. Directly under this crystalline pendulum were the only pieces of furniture in the room. A simple round table of varnished maple. A straight-backed, uncushioned chair.

In the chair sat the Arab, his manicured hands flat on the table.

It was dusk. The thirty-six electric lamps in the chandelier were not energized. The vast circular room was lighted only by the blood-red disk that was already half-sunk in the Red

Sea—and a silvery full moon rising from behind the bone-dry heights of the *Harratt Rahat.*

He heard the droning hum of the elevator. The tapping sounds of hard-soled shoes in the hallway.

There was a light tap on the south door.

It would, of course, be Anthony Soames. The collector tolerated no surprises in his home. The Arab hesitated, then spoke in a voice that was surprisingly deep for such a thin man. "Enter."

The door opened smoothly; there was no squeak of hinge.

The Brit stood in the doorway, hat in his hand. A small parcel tucked under his arm.

His host smiled thinly. "Come in, Mr. Soames."

Tony Soames marched across the polished floor, the sharp clicks of his footsteps echoing off the plate-glass walls. He paused before the table. "Good evening, sir."

His host nodded indolently. The Arab did not bother to look at Soames' eager face. The collector's hawk-like eyes were focused on the parcel under the man's arm. "You have it." It was not a question. This Englishman had spent his money . . . not a fortune, but four hundred thousand American dollars was not a paltry sum. If Soames did not have the treasure, he would not have come.

"Yes sir." Soames placed the box in the center of the round table.

Unconsciously, the collector licked his lips. He removed a miniature remote-control device from his shirt pocket, pointed it at the ceiling, pressed a black button. The chandelier lit up, casting a dazzling light on the table. The Arab pulled the box to him with an eager, possessive gesture.

Soames managed not to smile. But he thought his thoughts. *Like a kid with a birthday present.*

The Arab looked up through narrowly slitted eyes as he spoke to the Brit. His tone was soft, amiable. His eyes, which spoke louder, were not. "Mr. Soames—you have spent a great deal of my money to acquire this item. Let us hope that I will not be disappointed."

Soames swallowed hard. He did hope. There was a rumor about an Austrian citizen who was merely suspected of cheating the Arab. He had been buried upside down in the dunes. While still alive . . .

The wealthy man opened the box. And removed the object, which was folded in silk. Very slowly, he unwrapped the treasure.

The visitor clenched his hands behind his back. And held his breath.

The Arab took the flint blade in his hands. He caressed it, feeling the sharp corrugated edges, the smooth, hard surface. It felt cold in his fingers. He held the thing up to light streaming from the chandelier. And drank in the colors, which were pink . . . blue-gray . . . with tiny veins of scarlet. Like arteries in a translucent fish. He looked up at his nervous guest. And smiled.

Tony Soames returned the smile. Unclenched his hands. And began to breath again.

GRANITE CREEK, COLORADO

The doorbell rang.

Anne, who had been sitting by the telephone, hurried to the door.

But the man standing on the porch—with a clump of wilted flowers in his hand—was not Scott Parris.

"Oh, tansy-asters," she said. And accepted the sad-looking blossoms.

"You like 'em?"

She nodded. And sniffed at the light purple petals. "The frost has already killed most of them. But I still have a little bunch out by the garage."

He grinned. "Not anymore you don't."

She shook her head. Worlds may collide, but Charlie Moon would always be the same.

The Ute policeman removed his black Stetson, and turned it in his hands. "You don't seem too pleased to see me. You was hoping it was somebody else?"

"If you mean your bosom buddy, no."

He looked over her head. "Can I come in?"

She turned away. "I suppose so."

Well. Not exactly a warm welcome. He followed her meekly into the parlor. Anne sat on an overstuffed stool, and stared at the fireplace. A few wisps of smoke curled around blackened logs. The fire had almost gone out. Almost.

Without waiting for an invitation, Moon plopped his massive frame onto a brightly flowered couch. "So how've you been?"

"Better," she said through clenched teeth.

"Me too. Gout's been kicking up lately." That should get at least a smile.

It did not.

She turned to give the dark man a closer look. Even sitting down, Charlie Moon looked tall. "You've never come to visit me before." Must be a reason.

"Well," he said, "I sorta heard you was . . . well . . ."

Her eyes narrowed. "You heard I was *what*?"

"Without a man," he said quickly.

"What?" she screamed.

"Well, Scott . . ."

"Don't you dare mention his *name* in my presence."

"Okay. I heard you and What's-His-Name had called it quits."

She paled. "Did *he* say that?"

"Who?"

She closed her eyes and clenched her fists. "Charlie Moon, you are the most infuriating man I ever—"

"Anyway, I thought about it. Such a waste. You're not all that bad-lookin', not for a woman your age."

Her back stiffened. "And just how old do you think I am?"

"Hey, not too old for me. Among the Utes, age is respected."

She rolled her eyes at the ceiling.

"And," he continued, "you're smart as a badger. Make good money, too. At least that's what What's-His-Name tells me."

"Please stop. I'm overwhelmed by your compliments."

"See, I'm kinda unattached too, since my last girlfriend sent me packin'. So I kinda thought maybe I'd come courtin'.

See if you wanted to go down to the corner drugstore and share a chocolate ice cream soda. Two straws."

She smiled, and threw a pillow at him.

He shrugged sadly. "So I'm not your type."

She got up from the stool and sat on the couch beside him. "So what're you *really* here for? As if I didn't know."

"Well, it's about that guy whose name I daren't mention in your house."

"Naturally."

"See, What's-His-Name's been hangin' around my office. Cryin' in his beer."

"Good. I'm glad to hear it."

"That's cold."

She turned on him, blue eyes blazing. "Look, Charlie Moon—don't you come around here with your soft soap, thinking you can smooth things over. I know what you and . . . and What's-His-Name have done." *There. I've finally said it.* "I was at the Iron Kettle."

Moon smiled easily. "Your pictures come out okay?"

Her eyes were big as blue saucers. "You *know*?"

He chuckled. "You think a pale-faced town-woman can sneak up on an honest-to-God Indian?"

"You actually saw me . . . ?"

"Sure. That red hair kinda stands out. I kept an eye on you for quite some time, while you was stumblin' along the ridge trail. Watched you set your camera up on that little tripod."

She blushed. "Then your friend . . . he knew I was there?"

Moon shook his head. "What's-His-Name had way too much on his mind. You coulda come ridin' over that ridge on a two-humped camel and he wouldn't have noticed."

"You didn't tell him?"

"Nope."

"But why?"

"Figured it was better to let you tell him."

"Well, I haven't. And that is not the point. The point is," she jabbed at his chest with her finger, "you and Scott . . ."

"I thought we wasn't s'posed to say his name out loud . . ."

". . . helped Ralph Briggs sell the flint blade from the mammoth site."

"That we did."

"You admit it—just like that?"

"Sure."

"But Charlie—it's unethical to sell other people's property. Not to mention against the law."

He gave her a wide smile. "Shoot, I know that. I'm a lawman—remember?"

She was dumbstruck.

"Understanding what the law's all about," he said earnestly, "takes a lot of interpretation."

She felt oddly like Alice. Stranded in Wonderland. Chatting with a tall, dark version of the Mad Hatter. "Interpretation?"

"Sure. Like you said, a fella can't just go around selling another guy's property."

"I sense that you are going somewhere with this."

"Ask yourself this question: who owns that flint blade those scientists found with the mammoth bones?"

"Why . . . Mr. McFain, I suppose."

"He's dead," the Ute said.

"His daughter Vanessa, then."

"I don't think so."

"The paleontologists?"

He shook his head.

"The Southern Ute tribe?"

"Wrong answer again."

"What's the right answer?"

"The person who owns the thing—is the person who made it."

"But Charlie, he's been dead for some thirty thousand—"

"Most everybody sees it like you do. The scientists find it, so for a while it kinda belongs to them. Then Nathan McFain decides it's really his, so he grabs it—and as long as he can hold onto it, it's his property. The Southern Ute tribe suspects Nathan has moved his fence onto tribal land, so maybe the elephant bones—and everything that's found with 'em—belongs to the People. Then Nathan reports the thing stolen. I find out that Ralph Briggs has it, and he's about to make a sale."

"How did you find out about Briggs?"

"Somebody told me. How about you?"

"There have been rumors for years that he peddled . . . let's say . . . questionable merchandise. And I thought it odd that he'd hung around the mammoth dig for so long. So I was keeping an eye on him. And then this British fellow shows up in town. I check on him with my contacts in London and find out he has a rep for dealing in stolen artifacts. When Briggs drove out to the Iron Kettle, I knew something was up. But it seems like you were a step ahead of me."

"Yeah. Guess I was. Anyway, because Briggs is a citizen of Granite Creek, I called on my buddy—can I say his name now?"

She sighed. "You may."

"I called GCPD and asked for my pardner, Scott Parris. The evening dispatcher up here is Clara Tavishuts—she's my third cousin—says the chief of police is best man at Piggy Slocum's wedding and has left strict orders that he is not to be disturbed till after the reception is over. I tell her this is important police business. Clara says the chief especially don't want to be bothered by no police business. Not unless somebody he is very fond of is stone cold dead or about to become that way. So I headed up here, got to Scott's place around midnight. Found him snoozing on his couch—still decked out in his fancy duds. I brewed him some strong coffee and told him what was up. See, Briggs was about to make his move early the next morning so we had to leave in a hurry over to his place . . ."

"Oh . . . that explains the tux."

". . . and play our hand before the antique dealer had time to close his deal." He grinned at the memory. "Me and Scott, we back Briggs into a corner and tell him the way things are. Scott lets him know that if he don't play ball with us, his future around Granite Creek ain't worth a pitcher of warm spit."

"That," she said with a grimace, "is a horribly mixed metaphor. And disgusting."

She evidently hadn't connected "pitcher" with "play ball." "Anyway," Moon continued, "we pull on Briggs' chain some, and finally he sees the light. He admits he has an appointment the very next day with his foreign contact—to sell the artifact.

We tell him how it is. He can go on with his sale—even keep his ten percent broker's fee. As long as we get the rest."

She shook her head with dismay. "But you're both police officers—sworn to uphold the law. You can't just go around making deals with crooks!"

"Ha," Moon said, "you shoulda seen us."

"I believe I did."

"Oh yeah. I forgot."

Curiosity was getting the best of her. "So how much did Briggs get for the flint blade?"

"Four hundred thousand dollars."

"Four hundred thou . . . but that's *incredible!*"

"So me and my pardner, we get to split three hundred and sixty thousand." Moon's countenance took on the serene appearance of one lost in rapture. "That's one hundred and eighty thousand dollars apiece."

"So it was Ralph Briggs who stole the flint blade from the McFain home."

She'd made a natural enough mistake. But there was no reason to tell the journalist more than she needed to know. "I can see why my pardner likes you so much. You're as smart as you are pretty."

"Save it, Charlie." But she smiled. Just barely.

"So," he said with a gesture of upheld hands, "that's what happened."

"But it just isn't *ethical* . . . taking money for something that isn't rightfully yours . . ."

"Maybe not, but we did it anyway."

She scowled at Moon. "I'd certainly like to hear an explanation."

Moon frowned, and thought about it. "I don't think I can explain it."

"That is not an acceptable answer."

"It's the best I can do."

"You think I'll keep mum about this, don't you?"

Moon grinned boyishly. "I sure hope so." He sure did.

"Give me one good reason why I should."

"Me and Scott would sure appreciate it."

She blushed with anger. "That is not a sufficient reason."

"Thing is—if it becomes public knowledge that me and Scott just raked in three hundred and sixty thousand bucks, it'll cause all sorts of problems for us. Like visits from land developers and condo salesmen. And all kinds of needy relatives we never knew we had, just crawlin' outta the woodwork." He paused to clear his throat. "Not to mention the IRS."

In a murky sort of way, it was gradually becoming clear to her. This pair of lawmen—though basically honest—had been tempted beyond their ability to resist. They were like hungry little boys in a watermelon patch. Children who needed an adult to look after them. Anne put her head in her hands. "I just don't believe this . . ."

"Oh," the Ute said, "you can believe it all right. See, the thing is, neither one of us has any money left for income taxes. I've put all of mine in no-load mutual funds. My pardner, he invested his share in real estate."

She stared at the fireplace. "I already know about the real estate, Charlie. Scott bought a very expensive piece of property. A lovely home. For me. I feel so . . . so awful. So *guilty.*"

Boy, was she mixed up. "There's no need for you to feel guilty."

"No?"

"Nope. Scott wouldn't have spent a dime of the money on *you.*"

She gave him a stony look. "He wouldn't?"

"Not a chance."

Her lovely blue eyes narrowed to reptilian slits. "Who *does* he intend to spend it on?"

The Ute—who was becoming distinctly uncomfortable—pretended to take an interest in an oil painting hanging over the fireplace. Aspen on Salt Mountain. Not bad.

"Charlie . . . I already know who she is."

He kept his gaze on the painted aspens. "You do?"

"Of course. The little blond."

"Little blond?" Was it just a lucky guess?

He sounded so innocent. Like he had no notion of who she was talking about. Anne Foster could still see them, standing on the moonlit lawn. She'd been holding Scott's hand. Alice

Something-Or-Other. Or was it Alicia? The brazen young policewoman certainly hadn't wasted any time filling the void. But it wouldn't work. She was too young for Scott. It was a silly infatuation. "I do understand, Charlie. She's just a child. Insecure . . . in need of a father figure."

His poker face slipped away. She *knew.* "Well," Moon said, "now that you mention it . . ."

"I can understand how Scott might take an interest in someone so . . . so . . ." She choked on the word "young," and swallowed hard. "But I can't understand why he'd spend all that money on her." It just didn't make sense. Scott had always been so *sensible.*

The Ute policeman shrugged. "I guess it just seemed like the best thing to do."

And then it dawned on her. What if the sly little policewoman had found out about the sale of the McFain blade . . . Was she was blackmailing the pair of them? She shot the Ute a threatening look. "I think you'd better tell me what's going on, Charlie Moon!"

"Oh, I don't think I ought to do that . . . it's my pardner's secret. I couldn't tell."

"Why not?"

"Code of the West."

She stared daggers at him. It was such a silly thing to say. "That's silly."

The Ute policeman shook his head stubbornly. "Not to me, it ain't."

"Charlie Moon—if you don't tell me, you'll be sorry."

He set his jaw defiantly. "No way you could make me go against my pardner."

She gave him an appraising look. Poor Charlie Moon. Almost seven feet tall. Over two hundred pounds of muscle and bone. But he was just a man. Didn't stand a chance.

Moon jammed his black Stetson down to his ears and got up to go.

Anne Foster was staring at him with those huge, luminous blue eyes. Like her heart would falter and stop, her soul turn to vapor and fade away. And then the dreaded thing happened . . .

A large tear appeared in the corner of her left eye.

"Hey . . ." he said.

The tear slipped onto her cheek. And began to make a moist track along her lovely face.

"Listen," he said, "there's no reason to . . ."

The elegant performance was repeated in her right eye.

Moon felt the very ground cut from under him. He thought about it. Rationalized about it. There was, of course, the Code to be considered. Come hell or high water, a man always stood up for his pardner. But shoot, it sounded like she already knew who the money was being spent on. And Anne was a stubborn woman. What she didn't know, she'd eventually find out. Better for Scott if she heard it from him.

So he told her what he and his pardner had done. And why.

Anne was astonished at what she heard.

But what neither of them knew was this: Charlie Moon knew only half the tale.

And not the better half.

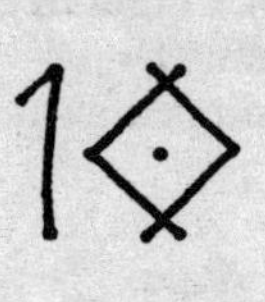

VISITING THE DWARF

ON THIS COLD night, Daisy Perika prayed for many things.

For an easy winter, so the rutted lane from the gravel road to her mailbox would not be a yard deep in ice-crusted snow or—when the thaws came—knee-deep in mud. For the Social Security checks to arrive in her mailbox on time. For the safety of her nephew; Southern Ute policeman Charlie Moon faced many hazards. As usual, she petitioned God to help Charlie to find himself a wife. A good Ute girl would be the best thing. Maybe someone from the Unintah reservation. Barring that, maybe a Cheyenne, an Arapaho, a Shoshone. A Pueblo woman would be acceptable. But not one of them uppity Navajos, God—thank you anyhow.

Daisy rolled over; she hugged a rumpled pillow to her ear.

Almost as an afterthought, she prayed that cousin Gorman Sweetwater would not drink himself to death. And that he would not come to visit unless she needed him for something . . . the porch was getting rickety again. Maybe he could hammer a few nails into it.

She yawned.

Though the old woman had eaten a bowl of posole which was liberally salted with tongue-searing green chili and fatty pork, she did not pray for a night free of troublesome dreams. Perhaps this was an oversight.

Within minutes, she slipped away from this world and its many cares.

Now, the old woman sleeps.
But it is the shaman who dreams.
And in her dream, she understands what she must do . . .
where she must go.

Daisy awakens suddenly. Yes. She has not visited the little man for a very long time. Father Raes Delfino—a worrier to his marrow—has warned her about communing with such creatures. But tomorrow, she will go into the canyon. Not that she intends to do anything that would offend the Catholic priest. Just visit the place where the dwarf lives . . . leave him a present or two. Maybe rest for a few minutes. What harm could come of that?

She'll have to take the children along, of course.

Fortified with a breakfast of scrambled eggs and pork sausage, the children were happy to be outside with the old woman. Sarah's black cat was also pleased to be released from the trailer for such a happy jaunt. Mr. Zig-Zag darted here and there, sniffing at dead flower-stalks, hollow grasshopper skeletons, and invisible tracks of a tiny deer-mouse who had come this way during the previous night.

Though the sun was well over the eastern peaks and warm on their necks, it was a crisp autumn morning. The girls—bundled warmly in coat and scarf—tagged along at Daisy's side, laughing, occasionally skipping away a few paces to examine wonderful things. A dead tree that looked like a ghastly monster with outstretched arms. A clump of wild mistletoe hanging from a sickly piñon. A speckled granite boulder shaped like a duck's head. But they did not stray far from the old woman, who carried a double-barreled shotgun under one arm and cast wary looks this way and that. It was Butter Flye who asked about the need for the weapon.

"Might see a fat cottontail," the old woman replied, aiming the long barrels at the imaginary rabbit. She had intended to shock the blue-eyed *matukach* child.

"You shoot 'im, I'll skin 'im," the Arkansas girl had responded promptly. "Then we can fry 'im up for lunch." She licked her chapped lips.

Daisy was surprised at the response, and pleased. This was a sensible child.

Sarah Frank deliberately ignored this foolish exchange. The very notion that someone would murder a little bunny rabbit. And then eat it! Disgusting.

Sarah's pet rubbed his ribs on the old woman's ankle.

Daisy made a face at the black cat, who returned the stare with a glare of yellow eye. She cut her eyes at the Ute-Papago child. "I'll have to be careful what I shoot at. Wouldn't want to mistake Mr. Rag-Bag for a rabbit."

Sarah also ignored this jibe. "He's Mr. *Zig-Zag*," she muttered under her breath.

"You know," Daisy continued to no one in particular, "if you skin a cat and cut off its tail, you can't hardly tell it from a skinned rabbit."

Now Sarah shot her a dark look. "*I'd* know the difference."

Daisy, pleased to have gotten the desired response, gave up the game. The weapon, of course, was not for slaying furry creatures for her iron kettle. No fool in her right mind would eat leather-tough old rabbit when she had tender store-bought chicken in the refrigerator. No, she'd brought along the twelve-gauge for quite another purpose. It was for the Magician. The mud-covered trickster had best not show his dirty hide around here unless he wanted to dance the high-step! But something about her enigmatic night visitor nagged at the shaman's mind. His sleight-of-hand conjuring of that white egg . . . it had seemed to have some special purpose. A sinister meaning that she could not fathom.

Daisy, being of a practical nature, dismissed the worrisome puzzle.

But if she crossed paths with the Magician, she'd learn one thing for sure. Whether he could run faster than buckshot.

Though the grade was slight, the trail into the canyon was uphill. By the time they reached the appointed place, the old woman was heaving with deep breaths. Despite the crisp air in the deep canyon, great beads of sweat stood out on her forehead like melted pearls.

The children, of course, were just warming up to this little walk.

Daisy Perika paused at the old piñon. Her *sleeping tree* . . . a place of visions. She leaned the rusty shotgun against the gnarled trunk, and eyed the hole in the ground. It was maybe a foot and a half wide. And very dark inside. It had once been home to a badger, but the masked varmint was long gone. Someone else had moved in. Someone much more interesting than a member of the weasel family. And considerably more dangerous.

Butter noticed that Sarah and the old woman were staring at the hole in the ground. The white child walked toward it, only to be frozen in her tracks by a sharp call from Daisy.

"No. Come back here."

Butter obeyed, though not happily. Grown-ups were always keeping you away from the most interesting stuff. Like late-night TV when naked men and women wrestled under rumpled sheets. The yellow-haired child muttered to the older girl: "What's wrong?"

Sarah answered in a whisper. "That's where the *pitukupf* lives."

"What's a pitookoof?" the *matukach* child asked. Sounded like a sneeze.

"A dwarf," the older child said.

"Like in Snow White and the Seven . . ."

"Sort of. But this one lives alone."

Butter sighed with heartfelt pity. "He must get all lonesome out here all by hisself."

Sarah shrugged. "I guess that's why Aunt Daisy comes out to talk to him sometimes. She brings him presents, too."

The little white girl nodded. It all made perfect sense. Except for one thing. Why would anyone want to live in a dirty hole in the ground? Probably because he was some kind of little bum. She hoped the old woman wouldn't hang around here too long. Butter wanted to go hunting. See Daisy shoot a rabbit!

The old shaman stood for a long time, oblivious to the whispered exchanges between the girls. She stared at the badger hole. Thought her roundabout thoughts. Wove her strands of twisted logic. She had half-promised the Catholic priest that she'd have no more to do with the *pitukupf.* Well, she'd actually half-promised not to *talk* to the dwarf.

She'd never said she wouldn't listen if the dwarf talked to her.

Daisy reached into the deep pocket of her dead husband's wool overcoat. Her fingers closed around the little treasures. Well, they weren't actually gifts she'd brought out here for the dwarf. Just . . . well, supplies. You never could know what you might need on a walk into *Cañon del Espiritu.* A little bag of smoking tobacco. Not that she smoked, but tobacco had certain medicinal properties. Useful if one of the children got stung by a yellow jacket. The yellow jackets had been gone since the first frost—but how can an old woman remember everything? She had also brought some pretty peppermints, wrapped in cellophane. Daisy didn't care much for candy, but the girls might want some. And there were more than enough peppermints to go around. She nodded at Sarah.

The Ute-Papago child came near. "Yes, Aunt Daisy?"

The old woman put out her hand. "There's some candy here. Two each for you and the white girl."

Sarah accepted the wrapped peppermints. And counted six pieces. She looked up at the old Ute woman.

The shaman said nothing. But she looked toward the badger hole.

Sarah—who had been here before—understood.

Good girl. Daisy reached into the overcoat pocket again. And put the plump little sack of tobacco into Sarah's hand. No words were necessary.

Sarah Frank immediately went to the badger hole. She squatted, carefully placing two peppermints and the sack of tobacco at the crumbling edge of the dark burrow. The little girl got up and backed away slowly, her eyes fixed on the offerings. Half expecting a tiny hand to emerge and snatch the gifts away.

Daisy watched with satisfaction. If it ever came up in a conversation with the Catholic priest, she had not left any gifts for the *pitukupf.* The child had done it, and without a single word of instruction from her. Father Raes was a clever fellow, but he'd have to get up very early in the morning if he wanted to stay a step ahead of her!

Butter Flye tugged at the old woman's coat sleeve. "Hey."

She glared down at the pale, chubby face. The accusing blue eyes.

"How come she can go to the hole and I cain't?"

"Hush," Daisy explained, pleased that she had such a way with words.

The little girl muttered something that sounded suspiciously like a very grown-up expletive. Something she'd picked up from her no-good father, Daisy thought—and wisely chose to ignore it. The suggestion was, in any case, anatomically absurd.

Sarah doled out two peppermints to the smaller child.

Butter pocketed one, unwrapped the other with grubby little hands, popped it into her mouth. And smiled up at the old woman. "Thanks, Daisy."

"Hmmmf," the old woman said. But she was becoming almost fond of this foulmouthed little blackguard. The tribal elder sat down under the dreaming tree. She leaned against the piñon trunk, and cradled the shotgun in her lap. Daisy gave the girls a stern look. "I got to rest some. Might close one eye, but the other one'll be open. So don't you two wander away."

Sarah nodded solemnly and took a firm grasp of Butter's tiny hand. "We won't, Aunt Daisy."

Like an old hen in a straw nest, Daisy settled her bottom to get comfortable. She closed her eyes.

They stood and stared at the odd old woman.

"She don't got one eye open," Butter observed.

Sarah did not respond.

Gradually Daisy's face relaxed. Her mouth fell open.

Butter wriggled free from the older girl's grip. She moved close to the sleeping figure. And peered into Daisy's mouth. The old woman was very still. Seemed not to breathe . . . Butter turned to frown at the older girl. "I think she's dead."

Sarah shook her head. "No she's not."

"She *looks* dead."

"That's just the way really old people look when they sleep."

"Oh."

Daisy did, of course, dream.

She dreamt perfectly ordinary dreams. Of absurd conversations with perfect strangers. Of a spotted horse who talked endlessly about tribal water rights. Of a fine meal of fried oysters at an Ignacio service station. Of a visit from Cousin Gorman Sweetwater, who announced his upcoming marriage to a Chinese woman who anchored the news on a Denver TV station. Such stuff as that.

But the Ute elder did not dream the shaman's dream.

The children invented games to pass the time. Kick the pebble at the prickly pear. Spit on the spiderweb. Toss the stick at the stump.

The old woman's nap dragged on. Ten minutes. Twenty. Half an hour.

The games became tedious.

Butter took a hard look at the reclining figure. "I still think she's dead."

Sarah expertly tossed a juniper twig at the stump. Hit it dead center. "I'm ahead three points."

The white girl had a tight-lipped, determined expression. "If she's dead, we'll have to pile rocks on her. To keep the buzzards from pecking her eyes out." Butter found a half-pound slab of sandstone and was about to drop it on the sleeping woman's abdomen.

Sarah quickly took the rock from the smaller child's hands.

Butter was not annoyed by this intervention. But she was terribly bored.

The older girl decided that a nap was the best way to keep the smaller child out of mischief. "Let's sit down and rest." She maneuvered Butter under the juniper tree, and sat down by Daisy. Sarah leaned her left shoulder against the sleeping woman, and hugged the white child with her right arm.

Within moments, Butter was yawning. Finally, her eyes closed.

Sarah knew that she must remain awake. And watchful. What if a mountain lion creeped up on them? Someone would have to wake Aunt Daisy, so she could scare it away with the shotgun. But the sun was high now, and quite warm on her face. The bed of juniper needles was so wonderfully fragrant . . . a mountain bluebird sang the sweetest song . . . and she was so snug in her heavy coat and long woolen stockings. Mr. Zig-Zag climbed onto her lap and licked her face with a sandpaper tongue. Within a few minutes, the Ute-Papago child was feeling deliciously comfortable. Quite against her will, Sarah Frank's dark eyes closed. Soon, she was fast asleep . . . under the shaman's sleeping-tree.

Sarah Frank sat cross-legged in the lair of the dwarf. It was a funny little room. The walls were dirt and rocks; long hairlike roots hung from the ceiling. The only light came from a small hearth, where embers of aged piñon burned cherry-red. Gray smoke curled upward into a sinuous tunnel. The badger hole, she assumed. Somewhere just above, Daisy and Butter were sleeping in the sunlight. The *pitukupf* sat on a stool by the hearth, staring oddly at his young visitor. He seemed ill at ease, but he was very gentle. As if concerned that he might frighten the child.

He was terribly old-looking. And had ugly yellow teeth. But she thought the little man in the green shirt somewhat comical, and almost cute.

He spoke to her.

Sarah could not understand a single word he uttered, though it did sound like the Ute tongue. But the most absurd things occur in dreams . . . she understood his thoughts.

This is what the little man was thinking:

He was displeased with Daisy Perika and had no intention of appearing to the aged Ute woman. But the dwarf knew that the child had left gifts for him. While Sarah watched, he cracked a peppermint between yellowed molars. Then he poured a dab of tobacco in a brown leaf and rolled a small, crude cigar. He touched the end of this assembly to the embers, then began to puff with evident appreciation. Sarah—who did not approve of this unhealthy habit—wrinkled her nose and tried not to inhale the pungent smoke.

When his homemade cigar was spent, the dwarf came close to the child, uttering unintelligible, though soothing words. She understood that—if she was willing—he would send her on a wonderful journey. To a strange place where she would witness a marvelous event.

She loved to travel.

"When would I go?" she asked.

And got her answer. She would take her leave *on that night when the moon did bleed.*

The child—who knew full well that the earth's satellite could not bleed—thought this a most peculiar thing to say. And wondered if this little fellow was on the up-and-up.

The dwarf was not a patient soul. He required an immediate decision. Would she go?

Sarah hesitated, then nodded her assent.

The *pitukupf* took a small blue feather from his shirt pocket, and touched her forehead.

So it was that she departed from the badger hole.

The Ute woman and the pudgy *matukach* child stood watch over the unconscious girl. The old shaman was astonished. She had never imagined that this might happen. For one thing, Sarah was only half Ute. But on the other hand, it was the child who had placed the gifts at the badger hole. Maybe the little man didn't care if you were half Papago as long as you brought him presents. The thought galled the Ute elder.

Sarah Frank groaned. Her eyes, half-closed, rolled upward. Only the whites showed.

Butter Flye, who was hungry for lunch, tugged at Daisy's coat. "Why don't we just wake her up?"

"Because," the shaman said, "she isn't sleeping."

Butter looked up quizzically. That didn't make any sense. Unless . . . "She ain't dead, is she?"

"No," the Ute woman said, "she's not dead." *Not exactly . . .*

Sarah's legs jerked spasmodically; she moaned. The child opened her eyes and looked around wildly. Who was this old woman . . . this fat little white girl? Mr. Zig-Zag came and leaned against her chest. And purred. And gave her a lick on the nose for good measure. And then it began to come back to her. She stood up stiffly.

Daisy patted her head. "You all right, child?"

Sarah, still somewhat dazed by her experience, nodded dumbly.

The old woman shouldered the twelve-gauge. Despite her intense curiosity, Daisy Perika would ask no further questions of the child. It would not be proper. So the trio headed down the long, sandy trail toward the mouth of the canyon. Toward a certain kind of reality.

Butter Flye had picked up a stick. She used it to knock dead flowers off reedy stems.

Mr. Zig-Zag made a useless leap at a small rodent, who disappeared into a tiny hole in the crotch of a scrub oak. When the cat gave up his futile pursuit, the gray mouse poked its head out to deliver an outraged diatribe to the feline.

Sarah Frank floated along, barely feeling her feet touch the ground. She was adrift in a current of most peculiar thoughts.

Thanksgiving Day

Daisy Perika paused near the entrance and shuddered. The towering excavation tent—with its three great peaks—suggested an enormous black owl. With dark brow, leathery wings spread in malign reception. Not sleeping. Waiting.

For a lunch of mice, perhaps.

The Ute elder looked down at these two of such tender

years, one clinging to each hand. She spoke to the chubby white child. "You sure you want to do this?"

Butter Flye—who was sucking at her thumb—nodded. She seemed not the least alarmed to return to this place. It was, of course, not in the belly of night as on her last visit. But the pale autumn sun cast long shadows of the old woman and her charges. The shades clung to their heels like hopeful tenants . . . ready to claim right of occupancy should the human souls depart.

Under the central peaked dome of the tent, the quartet of academics sat around the card table. The two elderly paleontologists, the pretty young archaeologist, the perpetually amused physician who played well at all the world's best games.

Moses Silver folded his hands like doubled fists on the flimsy table. He eyed each of his companions in turn. His daughter returned his weak smile. Robert Newton avoided eye contact. Cordell York was, as usual, quite at ease. Moses cleared his throat. "It seems, my esteemed colleagues, that we find ourselves on the horn of a dilemma."

"In light of the nature of Mr. McFain's most peculiar death," Newton muttered, "one finds the expression . . . somewhat unseemly."

"Robert, I do beg your pardon," Moses said. *Stuffy old goat.*

Cordell York—who was enjoying himself immensely—grinned wickedly. He winked at Delia, who pretended not to notice this small attention.

"Please," she said, "let Father have his say." To encourage him, she patted Moses' liver-spotted hand.

She was more like a sorrowful mother than a respectful daughter, Moses thought. He lowered his eyes to study his hands. Hands that had done so much work. For so many years. He stretched out his fingers, and studied these remarkable products of a billion years of tedious evolution. Soon the skin . . . the flesh . . . the tendons . . . all would be dust. Only the fragile bones would remain. And these only for a time. "There are certain issues that must be resolved."

Cordell York tapped a long pipe stem against his lower incisors.

Clic-clac.

Clic-clac.

Clic-clac.

Moses fixed his tormentor with a cold glare.

The physician, thus challenged, clamped the pipe stem between his teeth.

Moses continued. "The flint artifact removed from the premises by Mr. McFain is lost to us. Perhaps irretrievably. Even though we have several excellent photographs made by the journalist, we are not in possession of the one piece of unequivocal physical evidence that would verify the association of early humans with the mammoth remains. So," he attempted without success to make eye contact with the doleful Robert Newton, "our only remaining evidence is . . . the markings on the femur." His meaning was perfectly clear. It was time for a firm decision from the world's expert on butchering marks. Were these incisions on the mammoth's femur evidence that some ancient hunter had carved himself an extremely rare steak off the hind leg of the elephant? Or were they merely the marks of a predator's tooth? The answer, in light of the missing flint artifact, seemed all too obvious to Moses Silver. But Newton had been noncommittal.

Robert Newton had gotten the general drift of things. He sat there, staring at the table, rubbing his callused hands together.

Cordell York relighted the pipe, and made three quick puffs. "Robert, it's time to stand up and be counted. So tell us, old boy—is it or ain't it?"

Newton licked his lips. "As you all know, I have studied the markings on this femur with considerable care. I have taken high-resolution microphotographs. I have compared the shallow incisions to dozens of others from fossil bones known to be the result of stone-age human butchering practices. I have also compared the markings with modern carnivore tooth marks on bones of prey; these were made by a variety of predators, including African lion, Bengal tiger, Canadian wolf, and . . ."

York was chuckling, the expensive pipe rattling between his teeth. "For Pete's sake, Bob, shit or get off the pot!"

Newton paused, and blinked at the arrogant man. "Sir, if you wish to know my conclusions, you will hear me out. One does not appreciate interruptions." He sniffed.

This unexpected show of spirit amused the surgeon, who made a small, sarcastic bow. "Forgive me if I have offended in any way. Please continue. Toward your conclusion. No matter how long it may take." York glanced at his wristwatch, then at a calendar tacked on the tent pole.

Robert Newton, who had somewhat lost his place in the carefully prepared monologue, paused. "Oh, piffle," he murmured. One might as well go to the bottom line. "I conclude that . . ."

Three scientists leaned forward with great expectation.

". . . it is not possible to come to a firm conclusion. What one needs is further supporting evidence. It is a great pity that we no longer have the flint blade."

Delia bowed her head. She wanted to cry.

York was hugely enjoying the farce. "Well, thank you, Robert. You are a thoughtful and thorough scientist. You have not disappointed us—you have, indeed, fully met—nay, exceeded—all our expectations. I daresay this is your finest hour."

Robert Newton was quite relieved at what he perceived to be a compliment, and nodded gravely to indicate his appreciation. "One is always happy to serve . . . in the cause of science."

Though the hint of a sardonic smile played at his lips, Moses Silver was deadly silent. The paleontologist was lost in a marvelous fantasy. He would, despite his considerable age and stiffening joints, leap across the table like a gazelle. Grab the wishy-washy old bastard by the throat. Strangle him to death. He could see Newton's face turning parchment-white, his blue tongue protruding from his mouth. No protest from Delia or Doc would deter him from his sacred duty. Hordes of uniformed police could come to save Newton—but they would not pry him off. They could club him with baseball bats, he would not let go. Not even when they emptied their revolvers into his body. And when he was dead, ten strong men would not be able to unclench the death-grip in his fingers. No. If the survivors wished to bury them separately, they would have to cut off his hands at the wrists. Or—and this thought pleased him—they could cut off Newton's hollow head at the neck.

His morbid reverie was interrupted by a rude, raspy voice.

"Hey. You got company."

All heads turned. It was the old Indian woman. Daisy Something-or-other. With a little girl hanging on each hand. Delia went to greet the elderly woman. "It's so nice to see you."

Daisy did not respond.

"What brings you to this neck of the woods?" York asked.

"Well," the Ute woman said earnestly, "it's Thanksgiving Day."

"Indeed it is," the physician said.

"On Thanksgiving Day, Indians and whites get together. And eat venison. Corn on the cob. Lime Jell-O with grapes in it. First time, the Indians brought the grub. This time, I figured maybe you folks would whip something up."

They stared at the solemn-looking Ute woman for a long, painful moment. She was very old. Must be demented.

It was Cordell York who broke the silence. "I'm afraid all we can offer is tinned beef. And perhaps some tomatoes."

He pronounced the word to-mah-toes, and this annoyed Daisy Perika. She considered such variation from "normal" English to be an unseemly affectation. "I was hoping for turkey," she said. "And cranberry sauce."

The scientists decided that this must be some sort of jest.

"Heh heh," Moses said. His face was turning a dull red.

"Ha," Robert Newton added politely. "One is thoroughly amused."

Delia seemed embarrassed.

Daisy sighed. Boy, this was a typical bunch of educated white people. Slow as third-class mail.

Delia kneeled to speak to the children. "Do you want to see the bones we've uncovered since you were here last?"

The children nodded in unison, then headed toward the edge of the pit.

Daisy Perika shook her head wearily. "Butter's been pestering me for the last three days to bring her back here. Don't know what she sees in this place; it gives me the creepy-crawlies." The Ute elder glanced at the excavation. Looked like they'd patched up the big tusk Nathan broke off when he fell.

Delia watched the girls, who were standing a yard away from the edge of the excavation. Staring at the fossil bones. Whispering to one another. Pointing. "The children don't need a tour guide today."

All three men pretended to be quite pleased by the Ute woman's visit. Robert Newton was most solicitous. "Is Mr. Flye's little girl getting along well?"

Daisy shrugged. "I guess so. But it's been hard on Butter, what with her father takin' off an' leaving her all alone."

The scientists exchanged uneasy glances. All were aware that the big Ute policeman was this old woman's nephew. It was Moses Silver who asked the question on all their minds. "I don't suppose there has been any report of Mr. Flye's . . . whereabouts."

Daisy smiled. People always thought Charlie Moon told her everything. Wouldn't do to disappoint them. "My nephew's looking everywhere. I expect he'll turn 'im up sooner or later."

Engrossed in their thoughts, they did not notice that the children had lost interest in the excavation pit.

"I wonder," Cordell York mused, "where on earth he could be."

Butter Flye's small voice shattered the silence. "He's here."

The startled adults stared at the small child.

Delia, pale as freshly fallen snow, stared past the little girl. "What did you say?"

Butter let out a long sigh. "I said he's *here*."

Moses gave the child an odd look. "Here? Where?"

"Under the ground."

It was Robert Newton who took charge of the situation, and this bold initiative surprised his colleagues. "Excuse me, little miss. Would you like to tell me just what you mean?"

Butter led the old man to the edge of the excavation pit. And pointed to the animal's pelvis. "He's right under there."

He kneeled by the child. "Ah . . . and how do you come to know this?"

She looked at him with an expression of exasperation. "Because he told me."

Newton nodded. "Oh, well then . . . if he *told* you."

The Ute woman felt panic rising in her gut. Next thing you knew the mouthy child would tell them how she'd wandered away that night. How she'd been found in the tent, little better than dead. Charlie Moon would be sure to hear about it. And he'd come and take the children away from her. No, this thing had gone far enough. Daisy grabbed the little girl by the hand. "I think we'd better be going."

The scientists watched the old woman lead the children through the tent door. And then they were gone.

"Poor child," Newton said.

They exchanged wary looks.

Moses noticed that Delia was extremely pale; her hands were trembling. He remembered his daughter's breakdown after the miscarriage. "Dear . . . are you all right?"

She nodded. "That little girl—she seems so certain . . ."

"That's absurd," Moses said gruffly. "Horace Flye's ghost has *not* come back to tell his daughter where he is buried."

"Perhaps the child dreamed it," she mumbled. Dreams do tell the oddest tales . . .

"It is a fact that Mr. Flye is missing," York pointed out. "The Indian policeman suspects he has met with foul play—and that his body is hidden somewhere on the McFain property."

"It is impossible," Moses said flatly, "that Mr. Flye's body could be buried beneath the mammoth's pelvis."

York was frowning, like a student dealing with a difficult math problem. "Unlikely, perhaps. But certainly not impossible. The soil under the fossil bones, though undisturbed for millennia, is primarily sand. Not that difficult to remove and replace. Someone could have interred the body at night. Packed in the loose soil over it, added a little water to make it set. It would have been dried out by morning, looking quite natural."

"But it doesn't make any sense," Moses said. "Why hide a body where people are digging?"

York tapped his pipe against a tent pole, emptying a thimble-measure of gray ash. "It is my understanding that Mr. McFain planned to construct a museum on this site. Therefore, while it was necessary to expose the fossil bones for public view, it was essential that they remain in place. It would have been quite contrary to the property owner's express instructions to excavate *under* the pelvis. For that reason, it would be an excellent place to hide a corpse. A very secure location indeed." He scanned his audience. "Tell me . . . can any of you find fault with my logic?"

Moses opened his mouth to answer, but could think of nothing to say.

Again, it was Robert Newton who took the initiative. "Well, if one may offer an observation . . . there is only one thing to be done."

They all knew what he meant.

York nodded his agreement. "Your have hit the nail on the head, Bob. The child will certainly repeat her ghost story to other ears. And that big Indian cop is a friend of the family. We'll have to face up to it sooner or later—best take the initiative."

"When we don't find Flye's body," Moses said wearily, "we're all going to feel pretty silly about this little misadventure."

"Indeed," York replied. "But what if we should find it?"

Delia stared wildly at the physician. "What do you mean?"

"Well, we've been concentrating on the issue of *whether* Flye's body is buried in the excavation. If we should find his remains, the more interesting question would be—who put him there?"

"Who do you think?" she asked.

He flashed her a charming smile. "Someone who's very clever, I'd say."

SUPD, Ignacio

Daniel Bignight knocked lightly on Charlie Moon's office door, which was half-open.

The Ute policeman looked up from a clutter of papers, grateful for a respite from tedious work on the duty roster. "Come in, Daniel."

The Taos Pueblo man dropped an envelope on Moon's desk. "We're taking up a collection. It's for Officer Chavez. Tomorrow's her one-year anniversary with SUPD. Thought we'd get her some flowers. Maybe take her to lunch."

Moon pulled a fiver out of his wallet and put it in the envelope. "Good idea." He gave the officer a thoughtful look. Daniel Bignight had been in a glum mood since that night on the bluff overlooking Nathan McFain's pasture. Most likely, he was still upset over the "banshee" incident. Well, it had been pretty funny. But anyone can get spooked. Especially when it's dark and the wind moans. And every shadow has teeth and claws. And you've already been thinking about ghostly things. Moon reminded himself that he'd been the one who'd planted the banshee suggestion. He'd done it to keep Bignight awake. And maybe for just a little bit of fun. But now the junior officer was embarrassed about how he'd reacted to some imaginary spook. It'd gotten to be a morale problem. Putting Bignight's mind at ease would require just a touch of finesse.

"Daniel," he said slowly, "maybe you can help me with something."

"What's that?"

"It's about that night when Nathan McFain died."

A mask slipped over the Pueblo man's face.

This wasn't going to be easy. "I should've stayed awake. Been more help to you than I was." Moon drummed his fingers on the desk and assumed a thoughtful, worried expression. "Some peculiar things happened there that night. Nathan's death looks like an accident. But it could be somebody chased him into that tent. Then shoved him onto the mammoth tusk. So if you could try to remember exactly what happened . . . Anything you saw or heard might be important."

Bignight looked over Moon's head at the wall. "You wouldn't of wanted to hear what I heard, Charlie. Not if you lived to be a hunnerd and ten."

"Tell me about it."

Bignight looked the big Ute square in the eye. "Old Nathan McFain's dyin' wasn't no accident. It was that bant-shee that killed 'im."

Moon tried to keep a straight face. Wasn't easy. "Why do you think that, Daniel?"

"If I live to be a hunnerd and ten, I'll never forget it. That damn bant-shee . . . it called for *me*, Charlie."

"What exactly did it—"

Bignight, who was barely listening, continued to mutter. "Thought I was a goner for sure." He turned away from Moon. Stared out the window, into the cold gray twilight. "Some nights, I think maybe it'll come back for me."

"I need to get this straight. The . . . uh . . . banshee—it called your name?"

The roundheaded man nodded. "Sure. Just like you'd said, Charlie."

Moon—surprised at how suggestive this Pueblo man was—swallowed a smile. Best to keep talking, let him get it out of his system. "You mean your first name . . . *Daniel*?"

The Taos Pueblo man looked gloomily at the floor; he rubbed the toe of his scuffed boot over a knothole in a pine plank. "It was even worse'n that. It was like that bant-shee knew ever'thing about me. It called me just like my grand-momma used to holler for me when I was a little kid."

"And how was that?"

Daniel Bignight ducked his head shyly; he spoke barely above a whisper. "She called me . . . Danny."

Moon nodded thoughtfully, as if this was important information. "When the . . . uh . . . banshee called for you . . . what did it sound like?"

Daniel Bignight closed the door behind him. "It was a long scream . . . kinda like this." He took a deep breath. "Daannneeee . . . Daannneeee . . ." He looked hopefully at Moon. "Does that help any, Charlie?"

"It might." Poor, superstitious fellow.

"You need me for anything else?"

"No, Daniel. You can get back to your work." Whatever that was.

The Taos Pueblo man slipped through the office door and was gone.

Charlie Moon smiled and shook his head. Daniel Bignight was a good, reliable officer. But it was amazing what a man could hear on a dark night. When the north wind howled in the pines.

11

THE MOON DOES BLEED

Cambridge, Massachusetts
Three Days Before Christmas

Because of the sensational nature of the subject matter, the very existence of the gathering was a secret. Which, quite naturally, guaranteed that word of it would get out. And those notables who did not receive invitations, though highly displeased, were also intrigued. A few made discreet inquiries about attending. But attendance at the meeting was by invitation—very sorry, but no exceptions can be made.

Cordell York had taken great care in preparing the invitation list. The guests were a stellar array of world-class scholars, among the most glistening apples on the tree of knowledge. Handpicked not only because of their unquestioned expertise in various arcane specialties, but even more for their considerable influence in their respective communities of paleontology, archaeology, and anthropology. If they said a thing was so, few of their peers would dare voice a doubt. But there was risk involved. If these giants so much as smiled at a fellow scientist's claim, the pygmies would laugh out loud.

Every bit as important as the scientists were a pair of writers representing the journals *Science* and *Nature*. These sober scribes would interpret this evening's drama for those who funded grants, reviewed scholarly articles for publication, and made decisions on issues of promotion and tenure. These observers were loved and courted, feared and shunned. An unknown drudge's reputation could be established by gracious praise—an established luminary's light forever dimmed by malignant twist of phrase.

Rich Colombian coffee and delicate French pastries had been served. The guests muttered among themselves about why such an unprecedented meeting had been called. And why Moses Silver and his daughter Delia were present. Though they had been largely forgiven for the lurid stories in the popular press about their supposed mammoth kill site, the Silvers were the cause of much whispering. And some thoughtful speculation. It seemed unlikely that folk of such modest accomplishment would be among the invited guests. So the Silvers must be a part of the mystery. Perhaps it had something to do with their infamous mammoth dig. Had the missing flint implement been recovered? Without that notorious artifact, there was no shred of indisputable evidence that the Silvers had an absurdly old human kill site. Even with the flint blade, the claim of a thirty-thousand-year-old human kill site in the Americas would remain highly suspect in some quarters. It just didn't fit all the other evidence . . . or the conservative mind-set. There was, the orthodox camp would point out, always the possibility of some sort of accidental association between fossilized bones and more recent human artifacts. For example: some hundreds of years ago, a burrowing animal may have disturbed the site—moving a more recent artifact near a much older fossil bone. It had happened before. At best, such speculations could delay general acceptance of findings for decades. At worst, Moses Silver's hopeful view would simply be dismissed as insupportable—and forgotten.

But, someone suggested, perhaps the Silvers had found another flint implement among the fossil bones. When buttonholed and probed with sly questions, father and daughter were equally tight-lipped, offering only smug shrugs.

Robert Newton was cornered by a paunchy anthropologist from Southern Methodist University. What gives, Bob—are you in on this? Newton had been characteristically terse. One must wait and see.

And so there were incessant murmurings, knowing looks exchanged. There had been a series of perfectly absurd (but delectable) rumors. These were the favorites:

(*a*) *One of Moses Silver's graduate students had found a perfectly preserved woolly mammoth under the Alaskan permafrost.*

(*b*) *Delia Silver had discovered a huge cliff dwelling in southeast Utah; skeletal remains abounded . . . and there were hundreds and hundreds of black-on-white Anasazi pots.*

(*c*) *Indisputable skeletal remains of a Clovis big-game hunter had been unearthed by a back-hoe operator who was making trenches for irrigation pipe in a Delaware cherry orchard owned by Robert Newton.*

And the list went on.

But on one issue, there was no doubt. Whatever the reason, Cordell would not have summoned them here without good cause. Something was up. Something *big.*

Cordell York was quite at ease; and well he should be. The surgeon-turned-paleontologist was in firm control of the agenda. It was not by chance that the gathering was in the spacious library of his lovely home.

Moses and Delia Silver were pleased to have Cordell take the lead. It would not do for either of them to trumpet their findings before a covey of such skeptical competitors. Robert Newton—who was easily intimidated by pizza delivery boys, wiseacre freshman students, and elderly nuns—was certainly not equipped to stand before this suspicious crowd of self-important academics and do what must be done. He'd never carry it off.

Delia whispered in her father's ear. "Are you all right?"

The old man nodded, but his hands trembled with a nervous palsy. All of his professional life, Moses Silver had dreamed of such a sweet rendezvous. Now that the hour was upon him, his flesh fairly crawled. What if something went sour? But the encounter could not be put off any longer. The preliminaries were over.

It was time to do or die.

At precisely 8 P.M., Cordell York went to the head of the long oak table, and gently tapped a wooden pointing stick on its surface. A half dozen conversations were immediately hushed. Those among the distinguished company who were still standing promptly found their seats. He was that sort of man.

Now, the game was about to begin.

York—an ardent devotee of baseball—saw himself standing alone on the mound. His pitching arm long and limber. Nerves cold as a well-chain. Nonchalantly, he rolled the leathered sphere in his hands. Cast a cold, insolent stare at these so-called heavy hitters. He sneered, wound up for the first pitch . . .

York's deep voice was like velvet, his toothy smile brilliant. He beamed at his audience. "Welcome, ladies and gentlemen. It was very kind of you to come on such short notice, particularly with the holidays virtually upon us." York nodded to indicate the man seated at his left hand. "I'm sure you all know Professor Robert Newton."

There were smiles. Everyone did. Bob Newton—the leading expert on butchering of ice-age animals—was extremely competent. But so very hesitant to take a stand. In fact, he was known widely as a WWOF. Wishy-washy old fart.

Now York looked to the father-daughter pair on his right. "And you all know Professor Moses Silver, a very distinguished member of our community."

There were nods and mumblings. Distinguished? Well, hardly. True, Moses was competent enough. But he'd spent his career digging up rather mediocre stuff. Such an unlucky fellow. Pity . . . but you made your own luck.

"And his daughter Dr. Delia Silver, an archaeologist whose knowledge of lithic artifacts is second to none."

There were more perfunctory nods and polite smiles. Except from a scowling elder who considered himself clearly this young woman's superior in the understanding of stone implements.

"Now," York continued, "we'll get directly to the business at hand. You are all well aware that the Silvers have recently begun work on a new mammoth find in southern Colorado."

"We've already read all about it in *Time* magazine," a Smithsonian paleontologist muttered. This brought guffaws of laughter.

York chose to ignore the jibe. "What they have is a fine specimen of *mammuthus columbi*. Adult male. Aside from the fact that the skeletal material is well-articulated, the find initially appeared to be nothing out of the ordinary. Not until some rather provocative incisions were discovered on the left femur."

Everyone knew about the so-called butchering marks. They also knew that the mammoth fossil was definitely over thirty thousand years old—two millennia before humans had arrived on the continent. So the marks must have been made by nonhuman predators. The missing flint blade was probably placed under the mandible by a prairie dog. What was Cordell York getting at?

York smiled sharkishly at Robert Newton. "Bob, would you care to comment upon the marks?"

Newton, who had been munching a sugary French pastry, stood up. He wiped at his chin with a linen napkin, looked up and down the table at faces turned expectantly toward him. "I have made a thorough study. There can be not the least doubt—these are indisputably butchering marks. Made by a flint implement. Probably a bifacial." He sat down. And proceeded to finish his pastry.

This announcement produced raised eyebrows, sidelong glances at other colleagues, and other expressions of disbelief. Had poor old Newton finally lost his senses?

York clapped his hands lightly and smiled affectionately at his elder colleague. "Bravo. A brilliant, decisive report, Bob."

Robert Newton, who was more at home with fossilized bones than with live humans, did not perceive the gentle sarcasm. The old gnome smiled appreciatively. He had traces of powdered sugar on his mouth.

There was a titter of laughter.

A fat old professor from Cornell was not amused. He grunted to get York's attention.

The surgeon acknowledged him with a slight nod.

"It's almost Christmas, and I've got six grandchildren waiting for me at home," the archaeologist grumbled. "I think most of us have already heard about these *supposed* butchering marks on a thirty-thousand-year-old mammoth thigh bone. We've also heard about this mysterious flint implement you found under the jawbone. I, for one, am quite eager to examine this . . . this *artifact.* But it seems to have disappeared." He smiled coldly at Moses Silver, who was about to rise from his seat.

York held Moses back with a warning glance, then addressed the surly professor from Cornell. "We all share your dismay at the disappearance of this remarkable artifact. But events have overtaken us. The existence of the flint blade . . . is no longer of any very great importance."

The gathering's attention was galvanized by this last statement.

On the table at York's hand was a black plastic box; it had the appearance of a television remote-control unit. He used this to switch on a transparency projector. He pressed another button; a white screen unrolled behind him. A third electronic command gradually lowered the ceiling lights.

Cordell York stood in the glare from the projector, his face a ghostly white. It was a full ten seconds before he spoke, and his voice was barely audible. "Late last month at the McFain mammoth site a most remarkable discovery was made. While my status there is little more than that of an interested observer, I have been singularly honored. Moses Silver has asked me to present a brief report for your benefit."

All along the great oak table, the tension increased.

The journalists from *Nature* and *Science* struggled to scribble notes in the dim light.

Now York's voice rose a few decibels. "You are all aware of the dating on this specimen of *mammuthus columbi.* Thirty-one thousand years before the present, give or take a few decades. The original dating has now been replicated at three first-rate institutions. There can be no question of its accuracy." He turned to show his fine profile. "Ladies and gentlemen . . . under the pelvis of the mammoth, we have found the fossilized skeleton of a human being."

Most were stunned into utter silence by this pronouncement. But not all.

"Bullshit," someone whispered hoarsely.

"An intrusive burial," another doubter snorted.

Then others found their voices. The buzz rapidly grew to an outraged roar.

Cordell York held up his hands to still the tumult. "Please. One at a time."

They were silenced. But a dozen hands shot up.

York nodded at the representative from *Nature.* "Yes, Delbert?"

"This is such an astonishing revelation . . . I hardly know what to say. But I'm sure we'd all like to know more about the human skeletal remains. Is there any chance that the burial was intrusive? Could the human bones have been put in place thousands of years after the mammoth died?" Like at least twenty thousand years later.

York smiled. "You will recall that I said the human was *under* the mammoth pelvis." It was more satisfying to feed it to them nibble by nibble.

The writer from *Science* asked the obvious question. "Have the human skeletal remains been dated?"

York assumed a look of innocent surprise that fooled no one. "Oh . . . did I forget to mention the dating? Do forgive me." As if he did not trust his memory, York referred to a flimsy sheet of paper. "The human remains are, statistically speaking, no different from those of the *mammuthus columbi.* Approximately thirty-one thousand years."

There was an audible gasp from the assembly.

For almost a century, the 11,500-year-old spear points found near Clovis, New Mexico, had been accepted as the earliest date for human presence in the Americas. It had taken years of painstaking work at the Monte Verde site in Chile to push that date back just another thousand years. There were those, of course, who believed the Monte Verde complex contained human cultural materials that were much older. But such interpretations did not meet with the approval of the orthodox community.

The curmudgeonly old man from Cornell found his voice. "If spring wasn't months away, I'd suspect you were pulling an April fool prank on us. Are you seriously proposing that this mammoth site has produced evidence of human remains in the Americas—firmly dated at thirty thousand years ago?"

"Thirty-*one* thousand," York said with a wry smile. "Would you care to see photographs?"

They responded with nervous laughter. Would a starving man salivate at the offer of a sirloin steak?

With a carefully rehearsed casualness, York placed a transparency on the projector. A crisp black-and-white image filled the screen. The great slab of mammoth pelvis was a slightly tilted ceiling over a small, narrow vault. In the tomb was a partially excavated human skeleton. A yellowed skull lay on its side. The jawbone was disarticulated, so the face grinned mockingly at the gathering of scientists. A few other fossilized human bones were in evidence. A scattering of shattered ribs. A well-defined scapula. A long, slightly curved humerus was in two pieces, the lower segment projecting toward an elbow joint that was still unearthed.

"The skull indicates a male," York said. "Young adult. Seventeen to twenty years old at time of death. Note that the upper arm and several of the ribs are fractured."

They all spoke at once.

"This is amazing."

"Simply astonishing."

"Unbelievable."

"There is more," York murmured modestly. He placed another transparency on the projector.

And they saw that there was something more. Something quite wonderful.

"This was found within a meter of the human remains."

The Cornell archaeologist got up from his seat. Ignoring all protocol, he brushed by York, and leaned to squint at the screen. "Good heavens," he muttered.

York nodded. "Yes. It is quite a beautiful artifact. As you can see, it is manufactured from a white, glossy flint whose origins are not yet known to us. The implement is just over twenty-one centimeters long. Though it has a concave base, it is not fluted. Of course, at such a great age, one would not expect a correspondence to the much more recent Clovis culture."

The archaeologist shook his head in awe at such a find.

"Considering its length and mass—and the very close proximity of the hunter to his prey—Delia Silver has concluded that this device was not used to tip a dart such as would have been launched with a throwing stick. Therefore, we conclude that our hunter was carrying a spear. Probably intending to drive it between the mammoth's ribs. Such a venture would have required that other members of his troop—who would have been placed on the east bank to block the mammoth's escape—were busy keeping the animal's attention away from the spear-carrier. He may have come either through the marshes to the south or north—or, more likely, he approached the animal from the base of the small bluff which is situated on the western boundary of the pond. In either case, he was playing a very dangerous game. And lost his life for it."

A noted physical anthropologist—eager to have his say—found his voice. And made the expected observation. "From the condition of the human bones and their position immediately under the mammoth's pelvis, it appears that this unfortunate hunter met his death when the mammoth fell upon him."

There were several nods of agreement around the table.

"It certainly appears that way," York said slowly. "But the mammoth was not entirely responsible for this death."

This anthropologist raised an eyebrow. "Indeed?"

The surgeon placed another transparency on the projector. The audience saw a close-up of the rear portion of the skull. There was a circular hole in the bone. "This is the wound that caused the death of our hunter," York said.

"But," the anthropologist countered, "could not such a wound have been caused by the mammoth's tusk?"

"It could have." York pulled a pipe from his pocket. "But it was not. We have made casts of the tips of each tusk. They do not match the shape of the injury. But we have unearthed something that does." The surgeon nodded at Delia Silver.

She laid a rather pretty object on the table. It was glistening white. And very hard.

"This object," York said, "was found within six centimeters of the victim's skull. It fits perfectly into the circular wound."

Those near their host's end of the table leaned forward to see; others stood up and craned their necks.

"What's this?" The anthropologist laughed. "Looks like a damned hen's egg."

York struck a small match, and touched it to his pipe. "It is a quartz nodule."

The anthropologist allowed himself a mild smirk. "The fact that the stone fits the hole in the poor fellow's head doesn't necessarily mean it's the thing that made it. There are probably a hundred rocks laying about the site that are just as good a fit."

The surgeon smiled indulgently. These old curmudgeons were so amusingly predictable. "There are, in fact, very few stones of any sort in the pond sediment. Several geologists have assured us that this particular stone did not find itself in the pond site by natural processes. It was probably removed from a riverbed. And it was certainly carried to the site where the mammoth hunter died."

The anthropologist, outmaneuvered at every turn, snorted to indicate that he was reserving judgment.

York continued. "Note that the injury is in the upper posterior section of the skull. In the left parietal bone, to be more precise. Since the necessary velocity to penetrate the skull could not have been obtained in a parabolic arc, the missile must have been launched from well above the victim's position. The only location where the murderer could have stood is on a small bluff immediately above the site of the pond."

The word brought a gasp from the staid audience. Several repeated his word.

"Murderer?"

But surely it could have been an accident.

The surgeon clamped his teeth on the pipe stem. "We take the position that the ice-age hunter was a deliberate target. After all, there would have been no good reason to strike the *mammoth* with a stone—it would have only served to alarm the animal. Hardly a prudent thing to do with your comrade so close to the beast. Unless, of course, you wanted to arouse the animal. Either way, it appears that the motive was the death of our young spear-carrier."

An aged paleontologist picked up the white stone; he held it between thumb and forefinger and studied it thoughtfully. "Could one produce such severe damage to the human skull by merely throwing a stone?"

York nodded. "A very astute question. To penetrate the parietal bone to the extent observed in the victim, this quartz nodule must have been launched with a very considerable force. We believe it likely that some sort of sling was used. Unless," he added with a sly wink, "the fellow who heaved the thing was . . . hmmm . . . a stone-age version of Satchel Paige." York glanced at his expensive wristwatch. "I realize that many of you must be tired. Anxious to get back to your hotels. I don't want to bore you, but I have a stack of transparencies for those of you who have nothing better to do."

There was nervous laughter at the joke. A strong man could not have dragged the frailest of their company from the room.

"Oh, very well then. Let me see if I have anything more you'd like to see." York riffled through the stack, then placed a transparency on the projector. It was a composite, comprised of four black-and-white photographs. Three views of the skull. A close-up of the lower jawbone. The resolution of the photographs was stunning. The surgeon stood silent. Letting them take it in. He knew what would happen next . . . precisely who would respond.

Almost unnoticed by his peers, an elderly Princeton anthropologist got to his feet. This old fellow—a specialist in forensic science—was one of the world's foremost authorities on human skeletal characteristics. Over a long career, he had assisted the authorities in identifying dozens of skeletal remains. At the peak of his morbid avocation, he had examined a San Francisco murder victim's bones. The unfortunate man, he informed the detectives, was a laborer who had carried heavy loads on his left shoulder. Unfortunate fellow had suffered from a number of debilitating ailments. Including arthritis in his knee joints. And syphilis.

The detectives were duly impressed. But could the professor offer any clues to the man's origins?

Well, he was most likely a tourist.

Could he make an educated guess as to where the traveler came from?

He could. The victim was definitely from the Western Highlands province of New Guinea. Almost certainly a member of the Tungei tribe, which had six original clans and one more recent addition (the *Menjpi*). The dead man was most likely of the *Kenjpi-emb* clan. Based upon his deductions, investigations were made further afield. The professor was proven correct on almost every count. The one exception: the Tungei tribesman belonged to the *Kupaka* clan. He'd shrugged it off. Nobody's perfect.

Now, leaning on a varnished maple cane, the forensic scientist limped his way toward the projector. And removed the transparency. There was an immediate outcry from several outraged colleagues. He did not notice, nor would he have cared. The old man held the transparency in the light from the projector. He turned the film this way and that . . . and stared without blinking. And muttered to himself. "Hmmm . . . young male . . . certainly no facial flatness . . . unremarkable cheekbones . . . relatively small teeth . . . aha—Carabelli's cusp . . . yes . . . Y-grooved lower second molar . . . lack of shoveled incisors . . . hmmm . . . no lingual cusps . . ."

Gradually, voices were hushed. The room grew quiet as the dark grave under the mammoth pelvis. The physical anthropologist squinted at the transparency. He nodded. "Yes. Quite remarkable."

Cordell York leaned close to him. And gave him a rhetorical nudge. "What, precisely, do you find remarkable, Professor Weiss?" Like a competent trial lawyer, the surgeon knew the answer before he posed the question. As did Robert Newton. And the Silvers.

The elderly man—who had almost forgotten where he was—turned to stare uncertainly at the gathering of scientists. "Why, this fellow under the mammoth. There is absolutely no question about it."

"About what?"

"Why, he is . . . was . . . quite definitely a *Caucasian.*"

The Cornell archaeologist was immediately on his feet. "Let's not make any hasty judgments. It's well known that such features pop up in Native American populations from time to time. For example, one only has to recall that Kennewick Man has Caucasian *features* . . ."

The expert looked down his nose at this simpleton. "You are correct in pointing out that the so-called Kennewick Man has Caucasian features. But such features do not *pop up* like dandelions following a rain. They occur," he added with cutting sarcasm, "in those of Caucasian heritage. Kennewick Man was a Caucasian." He tapped his finger on the transparency. "This is the skull of a Caucasian. Do I make myself clear?"

The archaeologist started to reply, then thought better of it. He sat down.

The forensic scientist—who had already forgotten this unworthy foe—was muttering to himself. "I'd need to make a careful examination of the fossil materials, but you can bank on it—this skull is indistinguishable from early European stock. There is not the least trace of Mongoloid features."

The academics were absolutely stunned.

The journalists were enthralled.

A prominent paleontologist from Berkeley—one of the few who had remained silent—stood up. "Well, that about puts the icing on the cake." She smiled at the Silvers. "Moses—though I am not entirely pleased to say so—you and your charming daughter have turned our world on its head. I'm sure I speak for all of my colleagues when I thank Cordell for inviting us." She glared pointedly at the grumpy archaeologist from Cornell. "It has been a most singular honor to have been present."

There were murmurs of assent from the distinguished gathering.

The Cornell archaeologist—who could feel which way the wind was blowing—decided to lean just a bit. He smiled beatifically upon Moses and Delia Silver. And shook their hands.

The distinguished journalists from *Nature* and *Science* were writing furiously.

Far to the west—a dreamtime away from the bustling city where the scholars are gathered—is an eternally quiet country. In this timeless place, brooding, broad-shouldered mountains are draped with fresh white shawls . . . chill night winds flow like black rivers through deep sandstone cervasses.

Near the mouth of one such canyon is the Ute shaman's trailer-home. Inside this warm sanctuary, a child prepares for bed. First, the innocent says her nightly prayer. *Now I lay me down to sleep. I pray the Lord my soul to keep. If I should die before I wake . . .*

When her brief petition is completed, Sarah Frank takes a final look out the window. And sees an almost full moon . . . A thin slice has been severed from the shining disk. The moon is wounded . . . and seems to drip with blood.

So this will be the night. She feels the cold presence of fear.

If I should die before I wake . . . I pray the Lord my soul to take . . .

Daisy Perika—had she known of Sarah's vision—could have told the girl this: the *pitukupf*—like many of his ilk—has an obscure manner of speaking that leans toward the poetic. The Ute shaman would have laughed at the notion that the moon could bleed. This is how the illusion came to be:

When the moon rose over the San Juans, it had the dull metallic glow of an old silver dollar. It would have remained this way until the first glimmering of dawn except for a low-pressure system moving out of Four Corners country. Bone-dry desert winds were spawned at the edge of the storm. They waltzed gaily across the desert and kicked up their heels at solemn Navajo wallflowers who dwelt in Beklabito and Redrock and Greasewood Springs. As the dust particles rose miles high, they absorbed or reflected the shorter wavelengths of light. The residue that filtered through was of reddish hue.

It may be that what followed was merely the result of suggestion influencing an imaginative young mind. Had the winds not raised the swirling sands to the upper edge of the atmosphere—and the moon retained its silver sheen—perhaps Sarah would have dreamed a child's dream. Of dancing pinto ponies . . . fragrant blue flowers . . . pink cotton candy . . .

But what Sarah Frank saw from the small window of the bedroom was . . . *a moon that bled.* And so she knew that the journey promised by the *pitukupf* would begin on this very night. The little girl did not pack her tattered suitcase or make plans to purchase a bus ticket; she knew it was not to be that sort of journey. She got into bed, and pulled the covers to her chin. And trembled with anxious anticipation of her departure.

She did not have so long to wait.

The child's consciousness floats like a golden maple leaf on the surface of a crystalline lake. The surface of the earth lies far beneath the still waters.

As she drifts over the world, the child is aware of *everything.* The single aspen leaf that shudders in the cold breeze . . . the pungent aroma of a broken blade of grass. She experiences the perceptions of all the creatures. Fear. Hunger. The thrill of being alive.

And the dreamer is aware of an unseen companion . . . a guardian . . . a guide.

Sarah knows that she must not stray too far. She might not find her way back to Daisy Perika's home. She speaks to her companion. "Are we almost there?"

There is no answer. And the whole world is covered with darkness. She wonders when morning will come. "What time is it?" She hears the response.

It is early . . . and late.

This practical child, who has little interest in riddles, is annoyed by the answer.

But it is early. It is far before the time of pottery, or woven basket. Of all the world's animals, only the wolf has been domesticated. The brilliant mind that will invent the bow and arrow will not be born for many centuries. It is also late. In the Age of Man, already the eleventh hour approaches.

The dreamer drifts below a rolling sea of clouds. Her peculiar perspective is both above and before. She perceives a world at once familiar and alien.

Attached to the mountain's shoulders are long, muscular arms that bristle with pine and spruce. These limbs terminate in weather-worn hands that reach out to caress the lush, rolling grasslands. Between the fingerlike mesas are deep gorges gouged by rushing streams carrying snowmelt. The water-stained walls—fractured with a multitude of narrow, shadowy crevasses—echo with the lonely call of the great white owl. The sandy canyon bottoms are carpeted with great clusters of yucca spears and thick patches of prickly cactus.

Well beyond the snowcapped mountains and stark sandstone mesas, a rolling prairie spreads toward a distant horizon. There are endless meadows of hardy grasses and communal gatherings of tall cedars where yellow-beaked ravens gather in noisy community. Small camels graze peacefully here . . . nervous herds of three-toed horses clatter across stony ridges. In low places there are lush cattail bogs and brackish ponds crowned with jittery halos of black mosquitoes. The cruel grit-laden wind snaps its lash fiercely here—whipping up undulating waves on the seas of blue dune grasses.

Nearer to the canyons, the wind is a gifted craftsman of infinite patience. The artful breeze sings a solemn hymn . . . and slowly sculpts sandstone into fantastic shapes. The most impressive is the great tower that stands alone and aloof. Over the ages, it will be known by many names. First Man. Old Woman's Thumb. Apache Sentinel. The Devil's Hitching Post. Chimney Rock.

This is—on the whole—a harsh, arid land. But hidden among the folds of the mesas' pleated skirts . . . under the overhangs of jutting ledges . . . nestled in spruce-shaded bogs . . . there are damp emerald glens. In such places, delicate blue frogs croak raspy love-songs. Among pulpy ferns, ruby-eyed spiders weave intricate webs. Like pearls embroidered on a delicate veil, glistening drops of amber nectar are suspended from these silken fibers. Perhaps to attract the thirsty moth who flutters by in search of yucca-bloom.

Sarah would tarry in such an enchanted place . . . She yearns to touch the poisonous frog's glistening cerulean skin . . . to rescue poor moth from the eight-legged monster's snare. It is a lovely, frightening place. But is this her final destination? It is not. This is but a way-station; a stopping-place on a long journey just around the corner of time.

The old ones know that such shadowy places do not exist to serve as comely boudoir for lovesick frogs. Or for the culinary benefit of spiders who sit and watch with a multitude of unblinking red eyes for the unwary six-legged creature. No. Their purpose is of a more cosmic nature. Though the whole of darkness seems to approach from the east and retire to the west, the elders know that this is merely a shadowy illusion meant to deceive mortals. Here is what the old sages have perceived: With the coming of dawn, the monster of night is shattered like a broken pot . . . into many shards. The dark fragments immediately seek out a multitude of cool sanctuaries where they may hide during the sunlit hours . . . and they will tarry there till day's end. As twilight approaches, there are gleeful stirrings in countless dark retreats. At the appointed hour, these shreds of night come forth to form a population of shadows . . . darklings . . . inky ghosts.

Does the sleeping child doubt this report?

The spirits had expected as much. Look closely—do you not see them?

Yonder, a mossy smudge slips from under a cleft of granite. Over there . . . a parasitic shadow attaches itself to the trunk of a knobby tree—its fellow rests behind a pockmarked boulder. One darkling rides on the limbs of a muscular feline who has teeth like curved daggers. Another wisp embraces a tuft-eared rodent, who stands frozen in fear of the yellow-eyed cat. As the far horizon bleeds crimson across the bed of the sun, these anxious graylings whisper sweet gossip . . . touch cool fingertip . . . lightly kiss lip to lip . . . sigh . . . and finally merge into the cold embrace of twilight. When this entwining is duly done, the whole of darkness has truly come. The multitude have become one.

A night of such singular character cannot be filled with rest and peace for those who move within it. This is, by its nature, an anxious time devoted to searching. Fleeing. Devouring. Being devoured. This strange congregation of creatures slithers, shuffles, sniffs, scuttles . . . snarls. Elfin rodents blink from dark burrows with enormous, bulging night eyes. Huge bats emit shrill echo-screams and fasten needle-teeth to dragonfly. Three-horned pygmy deer dart among thick shadows. Slow, cumbersome ungulates browse on sweet grasses or clip moist green leaves off low-hanging branches. Fleet-footed, hooked-tooth carnivores stalk the slower creatures. These predators—madly excited by the lust of pursuit—are eager to stain tooth and claw with warm crimson.

But it is all quite innocent. And necessary. A nightly quest for food; merely this and nothing more.

The dreamer understands, and quickly departs for a more suitable place.

Sarah's spirit sits alone on a towering pinnacle of stone. Beneath the little girl's perch is a small encampment. The dreamer sees round elk-hide tents with south-facing entrances . . . a scattering of weary women . . . thin children too weak to cry. A aged, crippled man sits by a dying campfire; he chants a guttural prayer-song . . . imploring Spirit Who Thunders for his blessing on the hunt. The urgent howl of a starving dog echoes off a sandstone wall, then trails off into a pitiful whimper.

The darkening world extends beyond far horizons. The child's vision is not limited by physical eyes—a half-day's walk away from the camp, Sarah sees a weary beast that has drawn blood—and bleeds as well. The unfortunate creature is hunted by a determined pack of hungry carnivores. His day is almost done.

The pursuers—who number about a dozen—are wiry, muscular men. They wear long coats of finely stitched deerskin, their feet are shod in fur-lined boots. Each carries a fine birch throwing stick and a dozen flint-tipped darts. Most keep a bone-hafted knife of obsidian in their simple tool kit. The leader carries a stout spear tipped with a magnificent white point that is called moonstone among their clan. These are—it may be truly said—men of few words. They do not speak as they trot along the rolling prairie highlands like a pack of gray wolves, following a trail of crushed grass and broken reed. But if they are without words, they are not lacking in purpose. These are determined men. And dangerous. Because, like the hooked-tooth cat and the tuft-eared mouse, they are ravenously hungry.

The leader of the pack pauses; he raises his hand. The others gather near him. He points. By his feet is a bloody flint-tipped dart. The animal has shaken it loose.

The trail leads around a low ridge, into a reedy marsh. Now they can hear their victim. There are deep guttural grunts, a shifting of heavy joints . . . long rasping gasps for air. The wary hunters—who have lost several comrades in such places—approach the bog cautiously. Crawling over the crest of the ridge, they spot their quarry below. Almost within a stone's throw. The great beast is standing on the reedy bank of a small pond, filling his gut with muddy water. The water hole, surrounded by tall reeds, is encompassed on two sides by a thick stand of willow and cottonwood. On the far side of the pond from the mammoth is a bluff. It is not high, but the bank is far too steep for even a healthy animal of this size to climb. And this one bleeds from a wound in his leathery neck.

The leader calls a meeting; the men squat in a small circle, and listen. The chief of the hunt explains his plan with a few words and many expressive gestures. They will make a small fire and light pine-knot torches. Then form a wide arc and close in slowly on the beast, making plenty of noise. This should drive him farther into the water. While their prey is distracted, one of their number—a privileged hunter—will circle around to the bluff on the opposite side of the pond. That man will make his way down the steep embankment, and into the pond. He will approach the beast through the water, while the others hoot and wave their torches. When he is close enough, this courageous man will drive a long spear between the ribs of the beast. And penetrate the heart. The wooden shaft of the lance was cut only ten moons ago not a day's walk from where they stand. But the gleaming tip—it is crafted from the sacred moonstone—is very old. And has magical powers. No beast who feels the prick of it in his flesh can live.

The leader stands now, and raises the spear above his head. Who will accept this challenge?

There is a noticeable hesitation. Men stare dumbly at the ground. They think of their women . . . their children. It is dangerous enough to attempt to frighten the animal into the pond with fire and noise. These huge beasts are both intelligent and unpredictable. The prey may charge. It is sufficiently risky to wave the torch and block the path of the wounded animal—only a man who places small value on his life will dare to come close enough to drive a spear into the heart of the beast. No, it would be better to wait until the animal grows weaker—and be ready to run if the prey charges. Even if the beast escapes from the pond, the men can follow his trail until he finally bleeds to death. But no one will question the leader, who is determined to have a glorious kill. And the chief of the hunt will not withdraw the challenge.

Someone must volunteer . . .

A young man among them is visited by a most singular apparition.

Wispy as evening mist, she floats above them. It is a girl-child, though certainly not of his tribe. Her hair and eyes are black as night . . . and she is dressed in strange garb. She watches him.

The young man, though startled, is not unduly alarmed. He is of a people who oft see visions. But what does this mean—is the girl-child a witch come to curse the hunt? Or is she one of those Wandering Spirits—those who come and go as they please—and sometimes bless the affairs of mortals? He cannot decide whether this is a good omen or ill. The vision above him gradually fades. But the young hunter will remember the dark eyes of this child yet unborn. And he will see her again . . . after many ages have passed away.

His reverie is interrupted by a harsh call from the leader, who persists with his challenge. Who will take on the noble task that must be accomplished if the people are to eat meat during the long months of chill winds? Who among them is worthy of this high honor?

An older, wiser man smiles and mutters under his breath; the leader should accept this great honor all for himself. Unless some other fool is willing . . .

The youth steps forward and accepts the flint-tipped spear. He will go.

He is congratulated by other hunters, who slap him on the shoulders with both hands and offer hearty words of encouragement. They are, in truth, grateful to be relieved of such a hazardous task. One of their number has already been disemboweled by a sweep of the great curved tusks. Another lays in his dome-shaped hut with both legs broken . . . the same as dead. It is a common price to pay for a kill that will feed the tribe through those six moons when snow covers the earth.

The hunters find a sheltered spot behind the windswept ridge, well out of the sight of their prey. A lean man strikes a thumb-sized chunk of flint against a piece of precious blue-black pebble. Sparks fly onto a handful of fuzzy gray moss. He feeds the first hint of flame with bits of red-willow shavings, then with resinous spruce twigs. One by one, the pine-knots are lighted.

It is time.

The hunted creature looks up from the reed bank and sees this relentless pack of predators . . . his hateful tormentors. He throws back his great head and bellows out a challenge that can be heard for miles. The earth fairly trembles. It is a magnificent gesture.

And a wasted effort.

The hunters respect their prey, but are not impressed by mere noise. They are filled with enthusiasm and tell themselves this: by the time the greater disc has lightened the sky, there will be slices of fresh liver roasting over their campfire. Then they will send a messenger to their winter camp at the foot of the great rock pillar called First Man—to bring the good news to their families. So that their women and children may come to help butcher the kill. And feast upon the flesh of this great beast.

These half-starved human beings survive with a simple culture of hewn wood, chipped stone, and polished bone that has remained almost unchanged through a thousand generations of their kind. They are ignorant of such things as do not feed their bellies or satisfy other urgent needs. Not even the wisest among them realizes that their ancestors—adrift in long rafts of sealskin stretched over ribs of whale—had been cast ashore upon a continent where the earth had never felt the trod of human foot. Being continually occupied with thoughts of fresh meat, neither has it occurred to them that they are the fathers and mothers of great nations yet to be born. These are, by harsh necessity, a practical folk. Being realists, they consider themselves among the weakest of all the animals, and so they are. But someday . . . within a few ticks of the cosmic clock . . . their seed will build glistening cities . . . split atoms . . . and travel to worlds far from this one.

The men, spreading apart, wave their torches. They call out loud taunts.

The beast, as expected, backs uncertainly into the waters of the pond. He considers the steep bluff and pauses. There is no escape in that direction. He turns, lowers his great head, and makes sweeping gestures with the curved ivory tusks. The meaning of these invitations are not lost on the hunters.

Come near and I will disembowel you.

It is—at least temporarily—an impasse.

The beast has two choices and the hunters know from long experience that he will make his choice immediately. To charge amongst the dancing eyes of fire, or to wait.

The flames are terrifying, like the eyes of many ravenous beasts.

He waits.

If he is to live through this ordeal, the beast must not catch his scent. The volunteer has removed his clothing and smeared his body with slimy mud from a foul-smelling cattail marsh. All he wears now is the polished wooden pendant around his neck. It is a carving with the shape and spirit of the bear-tooth. Because it has been made and blessed by his crippled uncle—who is a powerful wizard—this facsimile is far more potent than the real thing. The youth hopes that the talisman has sufficient magic to protect him. He grips the heavy wooden spear; his hands tremble with anticipation of the final kill, the ultimate glory of the hunt. And the potential rewards of that victory. He smiles in remembrance of a dark-eyed beauty who has been looking his way of late. She will be greatly impressed by the tale of this hunt, and his valiant role in it. It may be that she will come and sleep where he sleeps . . .

Another stands not far away, and glares at the youth. This one also lusts after the young woman. The older man fondles a leather implement hidden in the folds of his garment. It is a sling. With it are three smooth stones selected from a dry riverbed. Two are brown spheroids. The third is somewhat oblong . . . and it is formed of white quartz. It resembles an eagle's egg; surely this will give it special powers.

As the bone-yellow moon rises through misty clouds, the great beast still faces the screaming pack of human carnivores. The huge creature sways back and forth. He flings his trunk over his flattened head, and bellows. He lifts heavy legs from the muck, and puts them down again. All the time, he bleeds from the wound in his neck. And his massive feet are sticking in the mud; each effort to lift them drains his waning reservoir of strength.

It has been a long struggle. The band of hunters is ravenously hungry for fresh meat. They form up to flank their leader and approach the prey. They must hold his attention, so the young hunter can make his approach without alerting the beast. This encounter will be far more dangerous than they imagine. Especially for the eager youth who anticipates the tales he will tell of his boldness in the hunt—the admiration and pride in the eyes of the young woman.

Unexpectedly, the great beast falls silent. Weary unto death of his futile struggles in the muck, he falls to his knees and lowers his head. As if bowing down before them . . . these relentless carnivores who are destined to eradicate his kind.

And rule the world.

The leader of the small company, sensing an easy victory, slaps his thigh and laughs. This successful hunt will establish him as one to be reckoned with. Yes . . . after this, even more men will follow him.

The oldest man among them, faint with hunger, imagines a thick chunk of roasted flesh. Dripping savory grease into the fire. He licks his cracked lips. With enough fresh meat, maybe he will live through one more winter.

But it is not yet finished . . .

While the other hunters (all but one!) have kept the attention of the wary beast with waving torches and loud taunts, the spear-carrier has made a wide circle to the rear of the pond. And slipped silently down the stony bluff toward the water's edge. Everything, he believes, is going according to the leader's plan.

But not quite.

Someone has followed.

The naked youth takes the first tentative steps into the dark pond. The black water is ice-cold on his legs; he shivers. His fear is mixed with an odd sensation . . . a buzzing, tingling hum that prickles the skin on his neck. It is a warning. And then, like a flash of lightning on a dark landscape, comes the revelation. In an instant, the hunter *remembers* what shall come next. He has experienced this terrifying encounter far more times than a man of his tribe can count.

A thousand thousand times . . . and more.

He knows that it is time to die.

Though burdened with this heavy truth, he approaches the great beast with legs that cannot but go forward. What must happen is, so it seems, ordained. Once that darkness falls, he will persist in his relentless hunt . . . pursue the guilty soul of his murderer into eternity itself.

But *to every thing there is a season, and a time to every purpose under the heaven.*

Men's greatest triumphs, sweetest songs, foulest lies, bloodiest wars, most dismal follies . . . all must finally have an ending.

On occasion, someone will intervene and say: "Enough."

On this night . . . *a little child shall lead them.*

And so once more the grim-faced hunter wades deeper into the moonlit ripple of frigid waters to approach his destiny. Once again, the unseen figure waits behind him in the shadows at the top of the low bluff. As the youth comes near to the heaving, hairy side of the great animal, ready to drive the long spear into the throbbing heart of the beast, the man in the darkness looses a brown river-stone from the sling. It smacks the mammoth on the rump . . . the startled beast raises from its kneeling position . . . turns its massive head.

The hunter knows full well what must come, as surely as night follows light.

He has seen it all before. A thousand thousand times . . . and more.

It happens so quickly—within a few beats of his heart.

The stricken mammoth sees the terrified young man with the spear . . . bellows its outrage . . . sweeps long tusks toward this small adversary. There is

a thunderous roar; a yellow arc flashes by his face.

The youthful hunter attempts a step backward. But he has sunk almost knee-deep into the thick ooze . . .

His feet are rooted in place.

A second missile is launched from the bluff above the pond . . . a white, egg-shaped stone.

There is a thin whistling sound . . .

It strikes the spear-carrier's skull.

. . . a sudden, mind-numbing pain.

The young hunter grabs his head, feels something hard protruding from his skull. He stumbles like a drunken man.

The mammoth takes another half-hearted swipe at the stricken man with its long tusks; the hunters rush into the pond—hoping to distract the animal with loud cries and the sting of flint-tipped darts.

It is all over so quickly. A hail of ineffective missiles are launched. The dying animal, oblivious to this assault, has simply lost too many gallons of blood. The mammoth stumbles, reels . . . and falls onto the injured spear-carrier. The great beast struggles only for a moment . . . and sighs like a weary soul ready for that final sleep. Then, ever so slowly, the huge creature sinks into the dark grave where he will lay for a thousand thousand days and more. But not alone.

Then . . .

Filthy water fills his mouth . . . he struggles . . . gags.
Bones snap like dry twigs.
He sees the yawning mouth of the pit . . .
is swallowed up in darkness.

Then . . .

Someone comes . . . someone merciful.
It is Death. She whispers to him . . . caresses his face.
Pain slips away like melting wax.
It is over.

Indeed, it is finally, truly finished. His weary soul is released and now may find its rest.

The murderer pauses on the brow of the bluff; he must have his moment to gloat. His rival has been eliminated, and he is greatly pleased. But he must return to the pack before he is missed, so the shadowy figure leaves the bluff. Like a stealthy rodent, he scurries unseen through the hillside brush . . . slips furtively along the reedy bank of the black marsh. He is secure in the knowledge that his young rival is no more. The woman will be his alone. But two things bother him. First, there is the nagging sense that he has done this all before. Many times. And he is filled with the superstitious fear that someone . . . a stranger . . . has witnessed his crime.

The child has seen it all.

The leader pauses as he wades toward the still form of the fallen beast. He pulls his foot from the sucking muck, and recalls the mammoth's vain struggle. The seasoned hunter scoops up a handful of ooze from the bottom. He rubs a sample between thumb and finger. Sniffs at it. Grunts his displeasure. He holds up his hand to halt those who follow and mutters a guttural command.

They understand. It is the dreadful black sand that will swallow a man alive.

Except for one soul whose overwhelming hunger overcomes his fear, they retreat to the reedy bank. He wades through the black waters, barely able to pull his feet from the clutching muck. The desperate carnivore climbs upon the beast's quivering leg and begins to hack away great chucks of bloody flesh. While his comrades watch, he gorges himself on this raw meat. On orders from the leader, the hunters break up dry reeds and tie them together in bundles. They will produce a makeshift raft to rescue the enthusiastic butcher . . . and as much precious flesh as can be salvaged.

Later, in the depths of winter, tales will be told of the youthful hunter's bravery. Songs will be sung about his great heart, how he carried the long spear, how he crept up behind the animal with sweeping tusks—only to be crushed when the beast fell. So the hero will not sleep with the young woman. He will have neither son nor daughter to remember his name. Alas, his remains will not be carried back to the camp for the ritual burning. His body has vanished under the dark waters.

Though most are sorrowful at the loss of the young man, these are not a sentimental people. There will be time later for such mourning as hard-pressed nomads can afford. Thoughts quickly turn to filling one's stomach. There was little enough meat to be salvaged before the beast was swallowed into the belly of the black sands, but it will feed a few mouths for a few days. At the edge of the pond, the surviving hunters make a circle of heavy stones. A surviving pine-knot torch is used to ignite birch twigs. Soon, a small fire snaps and pops. More fuel is added. Dry branch of pine and cedar. Stringy flesh roasts over the flames.

The child who dreams moves away.

At the camp near the base of the great rock pillar, there are those who anxiously await the return of the hunters. It is especially the women who watch the forest for any sign of their men. The few aged souls who have survived many cruel winters wait patiently for either food or starvation. A small floppy-eared canine who is more wolf than dog lays his muzzle between his paws and whines.

One keeps himself apart from the others. He is old now, terribly crippled from an encounter with a great bison. Under the moon—now sailing high across a choppy sea of iceberg clouds—the wizard sits cross-legged before a fire. He tosses a handful of gray moss onto the embers. And bits of precious dried herbs.

The fire-spirit accepts the offering; bluish-yellow flames dance before the wizard.

He pulls up a pinch of loose skin on his thin neck and pierces it with a cactus spine. He repeats this ritual with seven spines, leaving all in place. Blood trickles onto his chest. The throbbing pain quickens his perception of things unseen. The wind suddenly whips the flames, sending smoke into his face. The gaunt man closes his eyes, breathes the acrid fumes deep into his lungs, as he whispers the powerful words passed down from shaman to shaman over many centuries. He waits.

Presently, he perceives the hunters . . . and the hunted. His closed eyes see torches waving in short arcs, his old ears hear—though faintly—the hoarse call of hunters to the cornered animal. The men are afraid of their prey, and rightly so. He can feel their racing heartbeats thudding under his own ribs. Gradually, the whole scene unfolds before him. The wizard watches the beast back slowly into the brackish waters of a reed-lined water hole. He feels the fear and desperation of the wounded prey. And senses its elemental urge . . . escape . . . escape . . . escape.

But the weary creature does not charge.

The wizard sees the brave youth—his nephew—with spear in hand. Approaching the great beast from behind. The vision fades. The old man opens his eyes.

Thinking his vision finished, he is greatly astonished.

In the smoke above the fire, the old man sees the face and form of a child.

* * *

It is a girl, with dark skin and oddly slanted eyes. She is not of his people, nor does she speak his tongue. And yet she is of a kind with him. Closer to the wizard than his wife, his sister . . . even his mother.

Now, her lips move. The child's words are alien, but in his soul the old man understands.

He inquires politely: from what far world does she come . . . Does she have a name?

And so she tells him her name—and of her world and herself. Her mother and father are dead—now she lives with an old woman whose home is . . . or will be . . . by the mouth of a nearby canyon. She describes another child with pale skin . . . whose hair is like fine gold. And she reveals many great wonders that are yet to be. The girl also tells her tale of a great beast whose bones will lie undisturbed for ages and then be uncovered . . . The bones of a young man will also be found. And then she falls silent.

The wizard is also silent for some time, and heavy with sorrow. Then he tells her of many secret things . . . and much of what has been.

As they commune, the flames flicker.

The earth turns.

Young stars are born quietly in wombs of glowing dust.

Old stars expand like crimson cosmic balloons . . . and perish in terrible fury.

Their very cinders are swallowed up in the ultimate darkness of infinite gravity.

And forgotten.

Vagabond comets swing past earth's star in lonely, elliptic orbits.

And fall into the outer darkness from whence they emerged.

And forgotten.

Immense herds of great beasts are slaughtered without thought of economy.

And perish to the last living creature.

And forgotten.

Great empires are born, and flourish. Grand cities are built on glistening seashores.

The nations rot from inner corruption and topple like aged trees. The cities crumble into rubble and are covered by the sands of time.

And forgotten.

Through all of these things, the flames of the distant campfires flicker.

The people are born. They hunger and lust and strive. And die.

Their whitened bones are scattered like fragments of chalk under the dust of ages.

And are . . . so it seems . . . lost to all memory.

But forevermore, nothing in creation . . . that was . . . or is . . . or is yet to be . . . shall be forgotten.

Not one strand of gray hair on the old woman's head.

Not the least sparrow that falls.

Not the most feeble cry of despair.

Because . . . amidst the churning chaos . . . an eternal flame flickers.

It is . . . so it may seem . . . a small light.

But the fullness of night cannot comprehend this radiance.

Nor can all the powers of darkness extinguish it.

Sarah felt herself being pulled back.

Butter Flye was tugging at her arm. "Wake up."

Her limbs felt so very heavy.

"You're snoring again. I cain't sleep when you're makin' all that racket."

But Sarah is barely aware of her surroundings. The Ute-Papago girl had seen the ages unrolled like a scroll before her eyes. She has seen it all. Now, she knows many things. Secret things. It was quite a long time before she found her voice.

She looked sideways at the smaller child. "Butter?"

"Yeah?"

"The man who took you away that night—was he like you? I mean . . . did he have blue eyes . . . and yellow hair?"

The white child hesitated, then nodded. "And he was really dirty."

Sarah sat up on the edge of the bed. And considered all the

strange things that had happened. The mud-caked man who had taken Butter to the excavation tent—he was that young hunter who had waded into the water behind the elephant. The same night visitor who'd showed Aunt Daisy the "egg" which had struck him in the head. The little girl thought she understood why—after such a very long time—he had come back. It was not only because he was awfully tired of being scrunched up there in the dark . . . under the elephant. There was another, more important reason. The Magician wanted his bones dug up. He wanted someone to know he had been murdered.

She knows. And because time is a great sea for spirits to swim in, she has told his uncle.

So now the fallen hunter can rest.

But Sarah is puzzled by one remaining mystery. Why did the Magician take Butter Flye to the excavation—and show her where his bones were hidden? *He could have taken me.* Perhaps it was because of Butter's blue eyes and golden hair. Yes . . . that was it. The hunter and the little white child—they were of the same tribe.

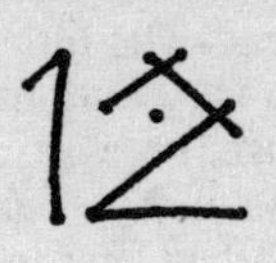

THE HOLIDAYS

On the Eve of Christmas

In the hubbub of animated conversation, happy squeals and squawks from the children, bubbling coffeepot, KSUT's Christmas music program blaring over the small FM radio—it was difficult for those gathered in Daisy Perika's small kitchen to hear the approaching automobile. Only one among them—and he was expecting this particular visitor—heard the rhythmic throb of internal combustion engine, the protesting creak of springs and chassis. But Charlie Moon gave no sign that he noticed the arrival.

There were squeaks as the porch steps were climbed, then a light knock.

Daisy turned the radio down. The elderly Ute woman hobbled across the cracked linoleum and opened the trailer door.

Anne Foster was standing on the rickety porch, her arms filled with wrapped gifts. She flashed the dazzling smile. "Merry Christmas."

Well, this was a nice surprise. Daisy stepped aside. "C'mon in, if you can find room. This place is crowded as a herd o' goats in a phone booth."

The lovely woman didn't look directly at Scott Parris, who had got up from his straight-backed chair. Anne kneeled by the girls. And gave them each a box wrapped in iridescent blue paper decorated with floating angels.

The Ute-Papago child—fascinated by this woman's waves of strawberry-red hair—was very shy. "Thank you," Sarah whispered. She immediately decided to save hers for Christmas morning. That was when Daddy and Mommy had always opened the presents.

Butter Flye was a product of more aggressive genes. She shook her box. It rattled. "What's in it?"

Anne laughed. "Open it and see."

Butter began to tear at the wrapping. Under the angel-paper, she uncovered a pretty red box. Inside was a doll dressed in red silk pajamas. Fantastically chubby cheeks. Impossibly golden hair and periwinkle-blue eyes. The little girl looked up at the red-haired woman. "It's a nice box."

"Nice *box*?"

The child nodded earnestly. "Toe Jam'll like it. He's gettin' tired of livin' in that ugly old shoe box."

Anne didn't dare ask what a Toe Jam was.

Daisy opened her present. It was—though the old woman did not realize it—a very expensive gift. A marvelous reproduction of a black-and-white Anasazi bowl. "Thanks," she said. "It's nice." *Just what every Indian needs. Another clay pot.*

Moon nodded politely at the newcomer. Anne gave him the hint of a conspirator's smile, then flashed a sly look at Scott Parris. "How have you been?"

Parris shrugged. "Oh, okay, I guess." He wondered whether she had a gift for him. And how come—on this particular evening when he happened to be here—she'd driven all the way from Granite Creek to Daisy Perika's home. Must be a coincidence.

Moon found a week-old newspaper that needed reading. Daisy, at a nod from her nephew, also found urgent things to occupy herself with. Like sparkling clean dishes in the sink that—for some obscure reason—needed another rinse and wipe.

Anne took Scott Parris' arm. She whispered in his ear. "I want to apologize. For how I behaved the last time we met."

He frowned thoughtfully. "When was that?"

So he's still miffed. But she played along. "When you showed me our . . . your new house. It's really lovely. And it was very sweet of you to send that young policewoman to pick me up."

"Alicia—Officer Martin . . . *told* you I sent her?"

"She didn't have to. I was expecting someone from the department. I knew you wouldn't let me walk all the way home. Later, I felt just terrible. Thinking of how I left you standing there . . . so alone."

Well, not quite alone. His ears turned a dull red. "I'm glad you got home okay."

Poor thing. She wouldn't tell him how she'd gone back to the Waring place and caught him holding hands with the pretty young policewoman. Not tonight, she wouldn't. "And I have a confession to make."

He allowed himself a thin smile. "Policemen and priests hear lots of confessions."

"I know that you and Charlie helped Ralph Briggs sell the stolen artifact."

This revelation fairly knocked the wind out of him. When Parris found his voice, he asked: "But how did you . . . ?"

"I was there, of course. Doing my job. Being an investigative journalist."

Snooping. "Well, you shouldn't have been," he grumped. "That was . . . ahh . . . police business."

"Business, yes. Police business . . . I'm not so sure. Later, I found out you and Charlie kept most of the money. Poor Ralph Briggs only got ten percent."

The Granite Creek chief of police frowned at the red-headed woman. "Where'd you hear that?"

Anne avoided the least glance toward Charlie Moon. "I have my ways. And my contacts."

"Sounds like you twisted Briggs' arm," he growled. *Little*

twerp must've talked. Or maybe it was some big twerp. He shot a mildly suspicious look toward Moon.

The Ute policeman kept his face behind the newspaper.

Anne did have contacts. A cousin who worked at Granite Creek's oldest bank had—for the price of lunch—revealed the fact that Scott Parris had cashed in his life insurance to make a down payment on the Waring property.

"So," Parris said wearily, "I guess you want to know why we took the money. And what we did with it. Well," he added with a stubborn jut of his chin, "I can't tell you."

"No need," she said innocently. "Whatever you and Charlie did, you must have had your reasons."

He was staggered by this generous expression of trust. And felt somewhat guilty . . . of several misdemeanors he could not quite recall.

Moon who was looking at the want ads, had heard just enough of the whispered conversation. Boy, this was some kinda slick woman. He had already told Anne Foster that all the money they'd raised from Briggs' sale of the artifact was for a blue-eyed blond girl—the survivor of Horace Flye, who was rightful owner of the "artifact" her father had made with his own hands. Charlie Moon had used "his" half of the proceeds to set up a trust fund for the child, funded by no-load mutuals. Scott Parris had located the little girl's paternal grandmother in Arkansas. He'd bought them a nice farmhouse on twenty acres near Pine Bluff. It had green shutters. And a huge yard shaded with maples. After the holidays, the Granite Creek chief of police would take Butter back to Arkansas for a reunion with Grandma Flye. And a housewarming. Parris did not yet know it, but he would invite his sweetheart to go along with him. Anne would drop a hint when the time was right.

As the evening wore on, Charlie Moon noticed that his elderly aunt seemed somewhat distracted. Daisy was glancing this way and that—like she suspected somebody was hiding in a dark corner. About to leap out and grab her. Probably she was just overtired.

Daisy Perika was weary. For two nights, she had suffered an annoying experience. As she drifted off to sleep, the shaman would feel the presence of a troubled spirit. It muttered unintelligible things in her ear, tugged at her covers, haunted her dreams. Losing sleep was bad enough—but now it had gotten worse.

Today the haunt was present while she was wide awake.

She could not see his form clearly—it was but an indistinct shadow that flitted at the corner of her eye. But the Ute elder could smell the distinctive odor of tobacco as he passed by. And sometimes, she could feel his breath on her neck. What was this ghost doing in her home—did it intend to speak to her?

As if discerning her thoughts, the presence whispered into her ear: *Hello, old woman. Merry Christmas!*

This unexpected greeting naturally startled the Ute elder, who dropped a saucer in the sink. Daisy thought of a tart reply but Charlie Moon was giving her one of those funny looks. Like maybe she was feeble-minded. So she held her tongue.

It did not matter. The disembodied voice was quite willing to carry on a monologue. *Well, it looks like my daughter did get her house for Christmas. So I guess somewheres a bullfrog has learned to play the five-string banjo and sing 'Yeller Rosa Texas.' I could sure go for a cuppa that coffee but I don't know where I'd put it. Heh heh.*

What meaningless nonsense—this must be the spirit of a lunatic! Or worse still, maybe it was one of them awful demons Father Raes had warned her about. The shaman decided that the best course of action would be to ignore the ghost—maybe it would go away. And so she did. The voice was silenced, but the pungent odor of tobacco hung in the kitchen like an invisible fog. She wondered if any of her visitors had noticed the almost overpowering smell. They had not.

Moon left the newspaper in his chair. He put his arm around his aunt's shoulder. "You want some help with the dishes?"

She shrugged off the hug. "Get outta my way, you big jughead."

Well, she seemed normal enough. Poor old thing was probably just jittery because of all the company. And the holidays had a way of unsettling some people.

Anne had seated herself at the kitchen table; Daisy poured her visitor a cup of black coffee. Anne took a sip. Tasted it. Tried not to swallow.

Daisy slapped her on the back; Anne gulped and swallowed.

The old woman grinned. "You like it?"

Anne tried to find appropriate words. "It certainly . . . has character."

"It'll grow hair on your chest," the Ute woman said with an evil cackle.

The lovely woman hoped that this lavish promise was a great exaggeration.

The evening droned on sweetly. Gaily wrapped presents were opened. Stories of Christmases past were recalled and told with heartfelt nostalgia. These tales were much improved by the passing of years and the imperfections of memory.

Two pots of coffee were consumed by Daisy and the men.

The little girls ate shelled walnuts and peppermint candy. And drank sickeningly sweet store-bought eggnog. Finally, Daisy Perika tucked them into bed at the far end of the trailer. And closed two doors between their bedroom and the kitchen.

Scott Parris had gone to the Volvo on some small errand. Anne found her opportunity to corner Moon.

"Charlie?"

Last time he was alone with this woman she'd snookered him good. That's what she thought, anyway. It'd be best if she kept on thinking it. "Yeah?"

"I've been watching all the local papers. There hasn't been a word about Mr. Flye. Do you suppose . . . he'll turn up somewhere?"

He thought about it. "I doubt we'll be seeing anything of Horace Flye again." The Ute policeman prayed he was right.

Butter Flye got out of bed. She opened the beautiful red box and whispered, "Mr. Toe Jam . . . do you like your new home?"

He looked up at her with black, beady eyes.

"I knew you would," she said. "Well, good night." She picked the homely creature up and kissed him on the lips. If a horned toad can actually be said to have lips.

Anne glanced at her wristwatch. It was almost eleven. The elderly Ute woman was looking bone-weary. Soon it would be time for all to say good night. Then they would part and go their separate ways. She tugged at Parris' sleeve. "Could we go outside for a moment?"

He'd been dreading this. She'd been so nice all evening. So proper. Like his younger sister. "Outside?"

"We have to talk."

Uh-oh. He followed her numbly through the trailer door. Onto the creaking wooden porch. Down the squeaky pine steps. Into the dismal embrace of a chill night.

"Scott . . ."

"Yeah?"

"I have something I'd like to say. Something important."

He shrugged. "Okay." Here it came. The big kiss-off.

"Lately, things have been pretty rough for me. For you too, I guess. I don't see any point in prolonging the mutual suffering. So I have a . . . a suggestion to make. About us."

There was a plum-sized lump in his throat. This would be the Let's Always Be Friends routine.

Anne looked over his shoulder at the long mesa . . . the stark silhouettes of the Three Sisters. The squatting pueblo women leaned forward to listen.

"My thought is . . . I wondered if . . ."

Parris closed his eyes. "Yeah," he croaked, "you want to be friends, right?"

"Oh yes. The very *best* of friends."

He swallowed the lump. Well, that damn well tore it.

Anne took his arm. "Did I ever tell you about my father?"

He shook his head.

There was a sly smile in her voice. "Daddy was my mother's best friend. And she was his."

His heart did a one-two punch on his ribs. Scott Parris turned toward her upturned face, a pale oval mask lit by starlight. He chose his words carefully. "I want to make sure

I understand this . . . uhh . . . what you're saying. Your parents . . . they *were* married to each other, right?"

"Of course," she said softly. "*You're* the bastard."

Daisy, who was peering out the kitchen window, had turned the kitchen light off. *The better to see you with, my dears.*

Moon was leaning, looking over his aunt's shoulder.

"My goodness," the Ute woman muttered, "would you look at all that carryin' on? I never seen so much hugging and kissing."

Moon nodded. "They do seem to be on friendly terms."

Daisy pressed her nose against the fogged glass pane. "Wonder what brought this on?"

"Careful planning." He patted her shoulder. "Looks like I'll be best man."

The old woman snorted. "And how'd you come to know so much about other people's business?"

" 'Cause I'm the man who made it happen," he said smugly.

Daisy Perika turned; she looked up at her nephew with a mixture of disbelief and amusement. "You?"

The tall, dark Cupid looked down his nose at her, and winked. "You bet. I did it. I did it all."

Christmas day at the mouth of *Cañon del Espiritu* was clear, and cold . . . and altogether too quiet. The north winds sprayed a peppering of sleet against the trailer's aluminum walls.

Daisy Perika was quite alone with the children. Scott Parris and the pretty redheaded woman were up in Granite Creek. Probably making plans for a spring wedding. Charlie Moon was likely over at the McFain ranch, comforting Nathan's daughter. That skinny young woman didn't have a drop of Ute blood—and she was one-eighth Navajo to boot. But Vanessa would make Charlie a good enough wife—if and when he was of a mind to have a woman in his house. Which the way he was goin' might not be for quite some time.

The old woman was not in a Christmas mood. Daisy knew that Butter Flye would be going away to Arkansas in a few days—to live with her grandmother in a nice house. On a little farm with a barn and dogs and hogs and goats and such. The chubby white child was rude and brazen. And full of mischief. Daisy refused to admit that she would miss the freckled imp. After all, she did have Sarah Frank for company.

Of course, with Sarah there was that annoying black cat. Mr. Dirt Bag was shedding black hair all over the trailer. But even this problem had a positive side. She could always get a rise out of Sarah when she insulted the animal by not remembering his right name.

Daisy was preparing a lunch of cold chicken and black bean soup when she heard the hum of Father Raes' aging Buick. He pulled up close to the trailer-home, slammed the sedan door, and made his way quickly to the porch, holding his black hat tightly on his head. The wind whipped at his woolen scarf and the skirts of his dark overcoat. She opened the door before he had a chance to knock; he hurried gratefully into the warm kitchen, rubbing his hands together.

The priest shared their modest lunch. He chatted with the children. Learned that Butter was going to live with her paternal grandmother. Exacted promises from Sarah Frank to come to Mass every Sunday that transportation was available. The girls took the gentle man back to their end-bedroom and showed him Butter's box of pretties. And the horned toad, of course. Toe Jam, who had finally sensed that it was winter, was becoming lethargic. He was sleeping under the sand, with only his homely face showing. He did not even open his beady eyes to acknowledge the priest's presence.

While Father Raes Delfino visited with the children, Daisy used the opportunity to wash a sink full of dishes. Finally, he returned to the kitchen.

"The girls are napping," he said, and sat down at the table.

Daisy turned up the burner under the percolator. "You want some coffee?"

"No thank you." The old woman's coffee was absolutely abominable.

"I could heat some water." She opened a cabinet door and pushed sundry boxes and jars aside. "I think I got a tea bag here somewheres."

"Tea would be nice."

"So how've you been?"

"Very well."

Daisy sensed something ominous in the tone of his voice. She made the tea without further comment.

He drank it gratefully, in little sips.

It was hard to like a man who drank tea when there was good coffee to be had. But she had always had a special place in her heart for this kindly little priest. The Ute elder sat down, and enjoyed a cup of extraordinarily strong coffee.

He cleared his throat.

Uh-oh. Here it comes.

"Odd," he said.

"What's odd?"

"Your home is filled with the aroma of tobacco. It is particularly strong back in the children's bedroom."

Well. Father Raes Delfino could smell it too. "You don't need to worry. Them little girls don't smoke."

He took a sip of the bitter tea. "I never imagined they did." But there was another possibility that troubled the priest. Tobacco was—so the Utes believed—a gift prized by the *pitukupf.* Daisy didn't smoke, but this old woman probably kept a supply on hand for the dwarf. And so he pressed the issue. "As no one in this home uses tobacco, does it not strike you odd that the aroma should be so overpowering?"

Daisy frowned and seemed to consider the possibilities. "It may be that horned toad the white girl keeps in a box. From time to time, he likes to smoke a cigarette."

The priest closed his eyes and bowed his head. *God preserve me from this woman.*

Daisy chuckled merrily. And she was. It was the season to be so.

The good man made himself this promise: *When I return to Ignacio, I will renew my request to the bishop for a transfer to a seminary teaching position.*

The Ute elder felt a sudden surge of sympathy for this innocent little man. "I was just teasin'." She leaned close and whispered to the priest. "You want me to tell you the honest-to-God truth?"

He smiled wanly. "Why not?" *It would be a novel experience.*

"That tobacco smell is from a ghost."

Of course. Haunts could be blamed for all mischief. "Whose ghost?"

"I been doin' some thinkin'—it's most likely the little *matukach* girl's father come back to watch over her. When the child goes back to Arkansas, that smell'll go with her."

"I see," he said wearily. "A spirit who smells of tobacco." The sly old woman had a thousand excuses. "You know, I've had a most interesting conversation with the girls."

Damn! Should have known better than to leave 'em alone together. He could get that black cat to talkin' if you gave him enough time.

He turned the warm teacup thoughtfully in his hands, dreading a confrontation with Daisy Perika. *She is a very recalcitrant old woman. But these are important issues, and as her priest, I must not shirk my duty.* "Our little Miss Flye tells me that you took her and Sarah Frank . . . for a walk. Into *Cañon del Espiritu.*"

So that was what it was all about. She nodded innocently. "It's good for children to get out and get some exercise. They'd been cooped up in here for days."

"Furthermore, Butter Flye recalls you stopped at . . . at that badger hole."

She shrugged as if this were tedious small talk. "There's lots of them badgers up in the canyon."

The priest took a deep breath. "I have been under the impression that you and I . . . that we had come to a certain understanding regarding . . . the dwarf."

"You mean about how I wouldn't be havin' any business with him?"

He nodded at his teacup.

"Well," she said firmly, "I've kept my word." One hand was behind her back. The fingers crossed.

The priest did not look up. "You did not leave the dwarf . . . an *offering*?" He found the very word repugnant.

Daisy shook her head. "You mean a present for the little man? No I didn't."

"Butter Flye mentioned some candy."

She pretended to think hard, as if attempting to draw up a memory of some inconsequential event. "Well, I did give the girls some peppermints."

"Butter tells me that Sarah left some by the badger hole. For the *pitukupf*."

Daisy's eyes widened. "She did?" *Please, God . . . I hope little big-mouth didn't say nothing about the sack of tobacco.*

Father Raes Delfino nodded gravely. "Indeed she did."

The old woman shook her head. "Well, I guess Sarah must've heard some of them old stories. You know, how if you leave a present for the little man, maybe he'll do you a favor." She shook her head and sighed. "Children," she said. "You can't watch 'em every minute. You want some more hot water on that tea bag?"

Now he gave her a penetrating look that would have flummoxed a more timid soul. "Daisy," the priest said in a tone that could fracture granite, "I would not like to think that this innocent child is beginning an unhealthy relationship with some . . . some supposedly benign spirit entity. It would displease me greatly to think that Sarah is taking up where you've left off. Replacing you, as it were."

"No," the Ute elder said after a thoughtful pause. "I wouldn't like that very much myself." And she meant it.

"Good," he said. "Then we do understand each other—we're together on this issue?"

"Sure we are," the shaman said. "You and me, we're like two old dogs pullin' at the same leash."

He smiled, but weakly. The priest was troubled by something obscure . . . a tiny barb in his flesh. It was not that Daisy's metaphor made no sense. Little that this old woman said was totally intelligible. No.

It was that sly glint in her eye.

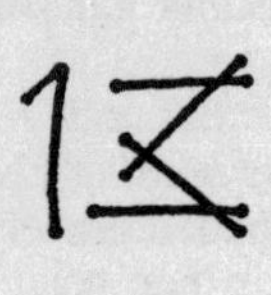

A PACK OF LIES

IT WAS THE first day of the new year.

The north winds that had howled through the night were now reduced to an occasional sigh. It was a bright morning, full of promise. Moon pulled the SUPD Blazer beside Vanessa McFain's van, and left the engine running. He stared at the ranch house. A thin wisp of smoke was curling upward from the massive stone chimney.

In only a few weeks, so much had happened.

A prominent local rancher had died in a bizarre accident. An Arkansas man was—as far as official police records were concerned—missing after abandoning his vehicle at Capote Lake. But Horace Flye had not driven his pickup to Capote Lake. Whoever had parked the old truck on the sloping bank of the lake had—like any sensible driver—set the parking brake. But Flye had told Moon that the parking brake should never be used. It stuck. So somebody—under cover of night—had driven Flye's truck away from the RV park at the McFain ranch. At first, Moon had assumed that the same person had hauled Flye's body away in the old pickup and buried it somewhere near Capote Lake. But who would have a motive to kill the drifter from Arkansas?

When Butter Flye had shown him her box of "pretties" the Ute policeman had not understood the significance of the few chips of flint among the bits of colored glass. The possibility that Horace Flye had pulled a fast one had not occurred to him until that long, sleepless night when he sat staring dumbly at the cover of *Time*—and realized that the color of the blade was quite similar to the chips of flint Flye's child had given him. So Moon had carefully moved each sample over the color photograph of the flint implement on the magazine cover. Attempting to determine whether one of the chips had come from the "ancient" artifact. And finally, one had matched. So if his daughter had some of the leavings from the manufacture of the blade, Horace Flye must've made the thing—and planted it under the mammoth's jawbone. But why—for a prank?

Someone, it seemed, had not been amused.

There had been no proof that the Arkansas man was dead. Maybe he had ran off and left his daughter. But Moon had had his doubts.

So the Ute policeman had gathered a sample of Horace Flye's unwashed clothing from the little trailer. And called up the woman with the body-sniffing dog. But the animal hadn't found the least scent of Flye at Capote Lake. So Moon had sent her to the McFain ranch. She'd rented a cabin and taken her remarkable little pooch for a long, meandering walk. The dog had accomplished his grim purpose within the first hour; the woman had called Moon at home to tell him precisely where to find Flye's body. He could have turned the information over to the sheriff's office. And if the county cops were extremely fortunate, they might have found enough physical evidence to identify the murderer. But it didn't usually turn out that way.

So Moon had gone fishing.

He'd let the people on the ranch believe that someone might just show up *later* with a body-sniffing pooch. Then he had camped out on the bluff overlooking the pasture and waited to see who would come out after dark to move the body. After several hours of watching on that first night—after it seemed that his ruse had failed—he had turned the vigil over to Daniel Bignight. Moon had been asleep when Nathan McFain came outside. Unexpected clouds had made the night dark as pitch. If something hadn't startled the old rancher, Bignight might never have noticed what was going on. And Nathan would have hauled Flye's unearthed body away, practically under their noses. But something had frightened the rancher. Probably, Moon thought, it was a guilty conscience. And the cold fear of being discovered.

On the way to Nathan's funeral, he had prodded Delia Silver with suggestions about the authenticity of the artifact Cordell York found under the mammoth's jawbone. Delia—who had shared her terrible secret with no one—had been almost grateful to talk to the lawman. The archaeologist was suspicious from the first moment she'd inspected the thing under a magnifying lens. The first hint was a subtle feature. When a flint blade is manufactured, most flakes break off completely. A few come only partway off, leaving behind a thin sliver that's much like a loose shingle on a roof. When the flint artifact lies around in the dirt for a few hundred years, groundwater gradually seeps in these little fractures. And takes in tiny grains of soil with it. But in the case of the "thirty-thousand-year-old" flint blade, there hadn't been any dirt at all under the fractures. The thing looked quite new.

But such evidence was merely suggestive . . . not conclusive.

So the archaeologist had inspected the flint implement more closely. And found tiny, silvery traces where chips had been forced off the edge of the blade. Traces, she realized, of metal. Steel, probably. Someone had used a modern tool to manufacture this "artifact." And planted it in the mammoth's grave.

Her father—who would benefit most from this "proof" that he'd found an incredibly old human kill site—would be the prime suspect behind this fraud. So Delia had found herself in a very tough spot when Cordell York had suggested that an "independent" expert should examine the flint blade. This was not unreasonable—independent verification of important scientific data was a common practice. But Delia was desperate to avoid such an examination. The first expert who examined the "relic" would spot it as a three-dollar bill in thirty seconds flat. Her father's reputation would be forever tarnished.

There seemed to be only one solution. The "artifact" had to disappear forever. So Delia had immediately volunteered to personally deliver it to the independent expert. On the way, she would manage to destroy the offensive piece of stone—grind it to dust if necessary. If Nathan McFain hadn't grabbed the fake, she would have disposed of the damning evidence that suggested either she or her father—or perhaps both of them—were the worst sort of frauds.

Her father, of course, would never have considered such an unethical scheme.

But who had made the thing and planted it—and why? She had immediately suspected Nathan McFain. The entrepreneur's plans for a museum would have been considerably enhanced by the discovery of such a remarkable artifact. And Nathan had managed to snatch it away as soon as mention was made of a careful examination by outside experts. Maybe he had panicked.

But somehow, Nathan McFain quite didn't fit the profile. For one thing, he wasn't all that stupid. And not the sort of man to take such a ridiculous risk. But who would be stupid enough to plant such an obvious phony? Who would be such an idiot . . .

Of course.

Delia had invited Horace Flye to her cabin. He'd shown up very late that night. She made him a cup of tea. And, almost casually, asked him what he knew about the flint blade. The Arkansas man—who was rather proud of himself—readily admitted he'd made the thing with long-nosed pliers. And planted it among the fossil bones.

Why?

Why, to help her and her father, of course. After several hours of trial-and-error flint-knapping, Flye had manufactured the evidence the Silvers needed to "prove" that this huge beast had been killed by humans. And he'd planted it under the fossil jawbone. As a favor, because he liked the both of them. Her especially.

She appreciated his good intentions, but where did he get such a ludicrous notion?

Horace—who was not a man to hog all the credit for himself—admitted that Delia and her father were largely responsible for his idea.

What on earth did he mean?

He had explained. She'd manufactured a projectile point, her daddy had planted it for their suspect employee to find in the excavation. And she'd told Flye all about their plan to test his honesty. Yep, he observed, her old man was a smart cookie. And, he added, she was slick as boiled okra. Knowing that women appreciate such compliments.

Patiently, Delia explained the awful fix he'd put them in. As soon as Nathan McFain turned the fake loose long enough for an expert on lithic artifacts to examine it, the game was up. Her father's reputation and career would be ruined. Not to mention her own. Unless she could get her hands on the phony blade and destroy it.

Horace Flye—who had no idea how easy it was to spot such an amateurish fake—was mortified by what he'd done. After promising to "make things right," he wandered off into the night. Delia had no idea of what he had in mind. But when he didn't show up for work the next morning, it appeared that the silly man—shamed by his actions—had simply fled. She wasn't surprised. Not until she learned that he'd left his trailer-home behind—and a six-year-old daughter. Then the young archaeologist began to worry. But Delia didn't know that Horace Flye had attempted to steal the artifact from Nathan McFain's home. Nathan hadn't reported the "theft" until several days after Flye's disappearance. When it was convenient not to have possession of a valuable artifact that would be claimed by the Southern Ute tribe if the court-ordered land survey went against him.

After the funeral, Vanessa McFain had told Moon about being awakened late at night by the sound of a loud argument downstairs. Men's voices. Her father was yelling at someone—Horace Flye, she now supposed—calling him a damned thief. The other man was yelling back, protesting that he couldn't rightly be called a thief—how could a man steal what was his in the first place? By the time she got out of bed and went to see what it was all about, the parlor was empty. She looked outside and saw no one. But arguments between her father and his ranch hands, even loud ones, were not uncommon. So she went back to bed, and slept in that morning. Her father had shown up for breakfast, looking exhausted. She'd asked him about the ruckus the night before. He'd shrugged it off as nothing important. When they learned that Flye had left without his daughter, her father had a ready explanation for such behavior. That lying hillbilly from Arkansas was a no-good bastard who didn't even take care of his own child. And Nathan was glad to be rid of him. It was no great loss; Jimson Beugmann would do the chores for those eggheads who were digging up the mammoth bones.

Vanessa claimed that she hadn't mentioned her father's late-night argument with Flye again because it didn't seem all that important. She'd had no idea the police suspected foul play until Moon dropped the hint about body-sniffing dogs. But Vanessa had remembered something that was important. One afternoon when she was upstairs, the telephone had rung a half dozen times. Thinking her father was at the barn, Vanessa had picked up the phone in her bedroom. And heard the beginning of a tense conversation between her father and someone with a familiar voice. It was a conversation about business. She had intended to place the phone back on the hook when she heard the antiquarian say he "had a hot prospect." And so she listened.

This valuable piece of information had led Moon and Scott Parris to Ralph Briggs. The Ute policeman and Parris had laid their cards on the table for the antiquarian. The flint blade was a fake. If this fact came to light, the Silvers' reputations could be ruined. And, worst of all from Briggs' perspective, the thing wouldn't be worth a nickel to anyone.

There was, of course, the matter of ownership. The "artifact" had never belonged to Nathan McFain. No, like Moon had told Anne Foster, the flint blade belonged to the man who'd *made* it. Not some stone-age mammoth hunter. Just a foolish man from Arkansas who was trying to do a favor for Delia Silver and her father. And, of course, have a little fun to boot.

So where did that leave Briggs? The antiquarian had a well-heeled client who was eager to buy the worthless chunk of rock. A wealthy Arab who'd made a habit of smuggling national treasures out of a dozen nations.

Moon—with backup from Scott Parris—had explained the facts of life to Ralph Briggs: with Horace Flye missing, whatever the Arab was willing to pay—minus Briggs' fee—rightly belonged to Horace's little daughter.

Briggs, a romantic at heart, had been eager to play the game.

That part had worked out pretty well. Butter Flye was now better fixed financially than anyone who worked for the Southern Ute Police Department.

But Moon wondered. If Horace Flye hadn't had any heirs—what would he and Scott Parris have done with an opportunity to snag all that cash? He thought about competing options. But there was no real contest. With his share, he'd have bought a small Hereford ranch up on the Gunnison. And retired from police work. The thought of this missed opportunity threatened to put him in a melancholy mood.

He cut the ignition and got out of the SUPD Blazer.

Vanessa McFain was pleased to hear the heavy knock on her door, to see Charlie Moon's face. Aunt Celeste had not yet ended her visit; the elderly relative took quite an interest in Vanessa's caller.

Vanessa brought Moon's breakfast on a lacquered tray.

The women exchanged anxious glances.

He stared woodenly at a large bowl of oatmeal; shriveled raisins floated on the gray gruel like unsuspecting flies who'd died of food poisoning. There was unbuttered whole-wheat toast on a china saucer. A green-tipped banana. Maybe this was a tasteless joke.

Vanessa seemed hurt by his lack of enthusiasm. "Charlie, I know how you like fried meat. And fried eggs. And fried potatoes. And butter. But all that cholesterol will kill you."

"Red meat," Aunt Celeste added darkly, "is the enemy of good health."

Vanessa nodded her agreement with this sage observation. "But this," she made a hopeful gesture toward the oatmeal, "is wholesome, nourishing food. Lots of fiber. *Good* for you."

Moon had one word for this stuff. *Goop.* He frowned at two dozen raisin eyes. They stared boldly back. "Uh . . . well, I sorta already had some breakfast at home this morning."

Sorta? Aunt Celeste gave this unrepentant carnivore an accusing glare.

But it wasn't a bald-faced lie. He had, in fact, found three stale glazed donuts in a brown paper bag by the coffee can. The cupboard needing a good cleaning-out, so he ate them. He'd been saving himself for one of Vanessa's special he-man breakfasts to jump-start his day. Moon had hoped for crispy chicken-fried steak. Scrambled eggs soaked in real butter. Big heap of home fries. Gobs of ketchup. Biscuits made from scratch. Orange marmalade. Black coffee strong enough to give the spoon a rash. Or almost anything a sensible young woman might put on the table.

But not *oatmeal.*

Vanessa looked dolefully at the unwanted breakfast. And sighed pitifully.

Didn't move him.

Moon—who was made of good stuff—held his ground. He patted his belt buckle. "Too bad I'm already full up."

Now Vanessa's eyes looked like they were about to cry.

Oh boy. Moon peeled the half-ripe banana. Ate it with gusto while the women watched. This sacrifice should be enough to satisfy them.

It was not.

Aunt Celeste stared at the oatmeal bowl.

Vanessa gave him an imploring look.

Well, to keep the peace, a fellow must sometimes do downright repellent things. He picked up the spoon. Hesitated. Then manfully attacked the enemy. It seemed a bottomless bowl. He finally swallowed the last spoonful. Felt a mild surge of nausea. *Got to get this taste outta my mouth.* "Well, that coffee'll sure hit the spot." He reached for a steaming cup.

"It's good for you," Aunt Celeste said.

Well, that's a sure-enough tip-off.

Vanessa touched his arm in a consoling fashion. "It's made from bran, wheat, and molasses."

"Caffeine-free," the older woman added brutally.

He steeled himself. Took a sip. "Real tasty." *Why me, Lord?*

When the bland meal was finished, Aunt Celeste insisted on doing the dishes. Moon and Vanessa took a walk. Across the yard, soft from recently melted snow. Under the bare, outstretched arms of the great cottonwoods. Past the horse corral, around the barn. She paused at the half-finished pond. The big yellow Caterpillar, its rusty blade pushed against the pillow of earthen dam, was dozing like a hibernating beast. Vanessa looked across the pasture, toward the excavation tent. Except for frequent checks by Jimson Beugmann, all was quiet now. The Silvers were at home for the holidays. The excavation trenches had been refilled and would not be disturbed until the father-daughter team returned with a crew of graduate students and a substantial National Science Foundation grant. Then there would be visiting professors from a dozen universities. The rental cabins were already reserved from April through the next autumn. Yes, for the foreseeable future, the McFain Dude Ranch would prosper. The ancient Caucasian hunter, already dubbed "McFain Man," would make her father's name immortal. Daddy would have been so pleased. She brushed away a tear from her eye.

"You know, Charlie, I still wonder if my father's death was really an accident. Maybe somebody pushed him onto that elephant's tusk. Maybe he was . . ." She couldn't say the terrible word. But she thought it. Murdered.

"I'm sure it was an accident." Moon put his arm around her thin shoulders.

"I guess you're right." Vanessa put one boot on the earthen dam. Most of the clay surface was smooth.

But not all of it.

Charlie Moon held his breath. Under this innocent young

woman's boot heel was the remains of a small excavation. It had been made within a few hours after the murderer learned that body-sniffing dogs would be used to find Horace Flye's corpse. Moon had no doubt about what had happened on that night. Vanessa's father had come outside under cover of darkness for a single, guilty purpose. Nathan McFain had intended to remove the corpse he'd buried in the stock pond dam before the trained dogs could find it. But for some reason not to be known on this side of that deep river, the rancher had stopped digging before the task was completed. He had only exposed Horace Flye's left arm . . . and then he'd run away like a crazy man. Bignight, who'd been startled by all the commotion, had thought he heard the "bant-shee" calling his name. After Charlie Moon had found Nathan's impaled corpse in the tent, he had headed across the pasture . . . on his way to break the news to Vanessa. At the pond dam, Moon had been hailed to a halt by the exposed arm, an outstretched left hand that was missing a middle finger. The mutilated hand had seemed to be desperately grasping for something. Justice, maybe. But justice—if that's what Nathan's peculiar death really was—had come too late to do Horace Flye any good. The Ute policeman had stood there for several minutes, thinking hard about several weighty matters. Proper legal procedure. His duty as a sworn officer of the law. Right and wrong. But most of all, he had thoughts about the living. About what was good for them.

And what wasn't.

Moon had used a shovel he'd found in the barn to push Flye's outstretched arm back into the earthen grave. Then he'd tamped the soil down. Some dark secrets, like moldering corpses, best lie quietly. If the remains were found, Vanessa would eventually have to face the fact that her father had killed the man. Maybe it was cold-blooded murder. Or maybe Nathan had never meant for Horace Flye to die. With both men dead, it was a legal issue that hardly mattered.

Vanessa moved bits of the loose dirt with the toe of her boot. "I've been so tired lately."

Moon stiffened. It would be better if this particular corpse was buried a bit deeper. "What you need is rest. A good night's sleep'll do wonders."

"Daddy could snore his way through a thunderstorm." She leaned against Moon. "But I've always been a light sleeper. Lately, I've been laying awake at night. And thinking over everything that's happened the past few weeks. And wondering what I should do."

Moon managed to tear his gaze away from the scarred earth at their feet. "Well," he said slowly, "there's always plenty to do around a ranch. Before the ground freezes hard, you oughta get Jimson Beugmann to start up that old Cat's diesel. Tell him to push some more dirt onto this dam." *Over Horace Flye's grave.* "I'd make it about a yard thicker, maybe two feet higher." He looked toward a gathering of low clouds rolling in from the west. "We're gonna have lots of snow, once it gets started. And when the spring runoff starts, you'll want to catch all the water you can in your new pond."

She squeezed his arm. "I could stock it with some rainbows. You might want to stop by and do some fishing."

Grilled rainbow trout and scrambled eggs made a mighty good breakfast. But Charlie Moon didn't think he'd have any appetite for fish caught from this particular pond. He looked at her upturned face. It was, though strained with worry, a pretty face.

She looked back.

This silent communication was interrupted by a shrill bellow from Aunt Celeste, who was somewhere on the opposite side of the barn.

"Vaannneeee . . . Vaannneeee . . . you out here?"

"Excuse me, Charlie." Vanessa went to meet her elderly aunt at the corner of the barn. They exchanged a few words. The older woman nodded, then headed back to the house. The young woman returned to Moon with an explanation for the interruption. "I have a phone call from one of my mother's relatives in Michigan. Sorry they couldn't get to the funeral, want to know if they can be of any help, and all that. Aunt Celeste will make excuses for me; I'll call them back tonight."

Moon, who had little interest in her Michigan relatives, nodded absentmindedly. It was such a small matter—but Aunt

Celeste, like Nathan, called her niece "Vannie." In the depths of the policeman's consciousness, a small disturbance began to trouble the waters. It was nothing more than a whispering eddy on the dark shores . . . and the succession of waves conveyed no useful intelligence. Such annoyances were best relegated to the deep.

And so Moon dismissed this peculiar feeling of unease.

But when unperturbed by interference from logic and analysis, such deep currents gain in strength. A vortex eventually began to whirl. And bubble. And without the least warning—like an unwatched pot on a low flame—it boiled over.

In an instant, Moon understood what had actually happened on the night Nathan McFain had died. She'd reminded him of what he already knew from her sleepwalking experience years ago. Simple things. Like the fact that her father was a sound sleeper. And she wasn't. So it would have been Vanessa—not Nathan—who would have been awakened by Horace Flye's bungled burglary attempt.

And then all the pieces fell neatly into place.

The rancher had *not* come outside that night to dig up Horace Flye's corpse. Sometime long after midnight, Nathan had awakened. And realized his daughter was out of the house. Might have figured Vanessa was sleepwalking again. He'd hurried outside to find her. And called her name. But Nathan had not called for Vanessa. Like her Aunt Celeste, her father had called for *Vannie*. That's when Danny Bignight had thought the banshee called his name. The Taos Pueblo man had made an understandable error. *But my mistakes can't be excused quite so easily.*

"Vanessa . . . I need to ask you something."

"About what?"

"About the night Horace Flye disappeared. You told me you woke up. Heard your father arguing with someone downstairs."

She gave him a wary look.

"Everything you told me—it was a pack of lies."

She tried to look away, but his gaze was magnetic. She swallowed hard. "That's not true."

His voice was a low growl. "You know better."

"When you questioned me after Daddy's funeral, I told you the complete truth." But she wilted under his disarming gaze. "Well . . . except for one teensy-weensy little thing."

"Which was . . . ?"

Now she looked at his boots. *My, he has big feet.* "Well, there *was* an argument downstairs that night. I only changed one little detail. See, it wasn't my father who argued with Mr. Flye. Daddy was asleep and snoring like thunder when that awful man broke into our home. And tried to steal the artifact off the mantelpiece. I went downstairs . . ."

As she proceeded to tell her tale, the lurid scene played slow-motion in Moon's mind, like a series of old black-and-white film clips running at one-quarter speed. Horace Flye creeps into the McFain home. Vanessa is startled from her half-sleep by an unusual sound. She pulls on a robe and slips downstairs. Surprises Horace Flye in the parlor. The Arkansas man, who has the artifact in his hand, protests that he is not a thief—because the flint blade *don't belong to Mr. McFain.* And he ain't leaving without it. She'd best get out of his way.

Vanessa orders him to put it down.

Flye blusters. He is a man who has fought bears and wildcats and whipped 'em all. He is for damn sure not afeared of no beanpole-skinny woman. With the flint blade gripped in his mitt, he turns his back on Vanessa and heads for the door. In his frantic life, Horace Flye has made many errors. Sometimes a dozen or more in a single day. But showing the back of his head to this particular young woman is his final blunder.

Vanessa, cool as a Quaker farmer at an October hog-killing, lays the man's skull open with a heavy iron poker. She is gratified when he falls like a sack of ripe turnips. But the troublesome varmint is bleeding on the floor she waxed just hours ago. More than a little vexed and somewhat in a hurry, she wraps him in a rug—it is a nice little piece of yarn from Costa Rica—and drags his limp body outside onto the porch. Thinking it will be inconvenient if another insomniac should pass by and ask what she is doing with this warm corpse wrapped up like a burrito, she decides it would be prudent to stash the body someplace until she can think of something better to do. She drags Flye's corpse to the pond dam and starts to cover him in the loose clay. The work gives her some time to think. People will wonder what happened to Flye. It'll have to look like her daddy's ranch hand got tired of working and left in the middle of the night. Vanessa has him half-buried when she remembers his pickup. And the little camp-trailer. A man with wheels wouldn't just walk away. It will take no great brain to realize he must still be nearby. Vanessa finds the truck keys in his pocket. After she completes the burial, she hikes up to the RV park and has a look. It'd be too hard to connect the truck to the camper in the pitch darkness and this wouldn't be a good time to use a flashlight. So Vanessa leaves the trailer behind when she drives Flye's pickup over to Lake Capote. When the man turns up missing, it'll look like he drove off and got himself lost or something. But not on the McFain ranch. Being in good shape and having long legs, she walks back to the ranch well before first light. And spends an hour cleaning up the coagulated blood off the parlor floor. It is the very dickens of a job, but she gets it done before Daddy is awake and hollering for his breakfast.

And that was that, except that she has regrets about two things.

First, if she had to do it over, she'd make a better job of it.

Secondly, she didn't know Flye had a little girl in the trailer. She feels just terrible to have made an orphan of Butter Flye. She weeps bitterly for several minutes.

While she drips saltwater into her handkerchief, Moon is dealing with his own thoughts. Like how maybe he isn't quite so smart a policeman as he thought he was. Or ought to be.

Vanessa, who had put away her hankie, tugged at his jacket sleeve. "I didn't mean to kill him, Charlie—you've got to believe that."

"Hmmmf," he said. Being short of things to say.

"Anyway, no jury would convict me. He was a burglar who broke into our home in the middle of the night. And I'm only a . . . a defenseless woman."

In spite of his inner fury—primarily directed at himself—

Moon smiled bitterly. Poor old Horace Flye hadn't had a prayer when he met up with all six feet of this poor defenseless woman. But she was right about one thing. No Colorado jury would put a woman behind the Walls for braining a burglar in her own house. Sure, she'd buried the body. Then had the presence of mind to drive Flye's truck to Capote Lake. But a C-average defense attorney freshly graduated from Podunk University Mail-Order Law School would need about a minute to convince a jury that she'd done all this in a state of understandable and forgivable panic.

Vanessa took a deep breath. "Charlie, I hope you're not upset . . ."

"Why should I be? All you did was tell me a pack of lies."

She pouted. "That's an exaggeration . . . It was only one little fib, Charlie. Whether me or Daddy did it doesn't matter all that much. Either way," she added brightly, "it's really all in the family."

"On the night your father died, he must've come out here looking for you."

She nodded sadly. "I was terrified that those body-sniffing dogs you'd mentioned would find Mr. Flye's body. So I slipped out of the house late that night. I had already uncovered one arm . . . in another five minutes I'd have had the body in my van. I was going to dump it somewhere on Indian land . . ."

"On behalf of the Southern Ute Nation, I thank you for thinking of us . . ."

". . . when my father came outside to look for me. I ran inside the barn. Daddy stood right here and called for me. Vaaannneee . . . Vaaannneee . . ."

Sure. Nathan was the "banshee" Danny Bignight heard calling his name.

She went on, breathless. "I was just terrified that he'd see Mr. Flye's arm sticking out of the dirt. It was so awful . . . I just couldn't bear it. I ran back to the house and . . . and waited to see what would happen. Daddy was out here awfully long. I thought he must've found the body. The suspense was just unbearable. I'd made up my mind to go out to see what he was doing—when you showed up with that woman . . . Delia Silver. And told me Daddy was dead. I thought he must've found Mr. Flye's body and had a heart attack. And I thought you must surely know about the body. But when I came outside the next morning . . . the arm was buried again. I realized Daddy must've found it and covered it up."

Moon shook his head glumly. "It was me. I thought your father had dug up the corpse. Which meant he'd put it here. But Nathan was dead by then. So I pushed the dirt over Flye's arm. To keep you from finding out . . ." The Ute policeman was beginning to feel outrageously stupid.

Such a sweet man. "Imagine that . . . You believed my father had killed one of his employees—and you covered up the evidence. All to protect me from a scandal." Vanessa stood on tiptoes and kissed him on the cheek.

It was like rubbing salt in the wound. "Thanks," he said gruffly.

Her lips made a pretty, though teasing smile. "But it does sort of make you my accomplice."

It wasn't funny. He kicked at a heavy stone—scuffing the shiny toe of his brand-new bull-hide boot.

His feelings are hurt, poor dear. Best leave him be for a while. She did.

Finally . . . "A penny for your thoughts, Charlie."

"A penny don't buy much these days."

"An apple pie, then. Hot from the oven."

He growled. Like an old bear, she thought.

"You're *very* upset with me, aren't you?"

"One thing I still can't figure out."

"What's that?"

"You must've been the one who worked out the deal with Ralph Briggs to sell the flint blade. So why'd you tell me what he was up to?"

"I told you the honest truth about that. After that awful woman brought Daddy the legal papers, he knew he'd have to turn the artifact over to the Silvers. It would have hurt his pride to do that. And he could've lost it for good if the Utes won the boundary dispute. So I think Daddy decided to pretend it'd been stolen—and arrange the sale through Mr. Briggs." She gave Moon an accusing glance. "If the Utes hadn't started that nasty fight about the land boundaries, Daddy wouldn't have been put in such a terrible spot."

The Ute policeman sighed. "What can I say? Us Indians are always causing trouble."

She pouted. "And *shame on you* for not trusting me, Charlie Moon!"

"I hope you'll forgive me," he said with exaggerated politeness. "I can't imagine what I was thinking. It's not like you'd ever tell me a lie."

Well. He was still in a snit. She gave him a moment to cool off, then changed the subject. "Why do you think Mr. Flye said the artifact didn't belong to Daddy?"

He shrugged. It was best she didn't know that Flye had made the thing. The more people who knew the flint blade was a phony, the harder it would be to keep the secret.

She was giving him a searching look. "You must've talked to Ralph Briggs—did you manage to prevent the sale?"

Charlie Moon was suddenly on the defensive. There'd be sure-enough hell to pay if Vanessa McFain ever found out that "Daddy's artifact" had been sold to a wealthy foreign collector for a bushel of greenbacks—and she didn't get a red cent of the take. What he needed was a deceptive answer that was not a bald-faced lie. "I talked to Briggs. But he claimed he had no idea where the artifact was. He said he'd never got it from your father." That had been the antiquarian's first story—before Scott Parris threatened to get a search warrant and have a bunch of ham-fisted cops turn his antique store upside down. Then he'd prudently decided to make a deal.

Vanessa looked doubtful. "Do you believe him?"

The policeman nodded. "I'm satisfied he doesn't have it." Quite true.

She gave him an odd look. "So where is it?"

It was Moon's turn to swallow hard. "Well . . . gone for good, I guess." *I hope.*

Then maybe it really had been stolen. "I'm sure you did your best." Poor Charlie. What he needed was an ego boost. "You're a very clever policeman."

Sure. Clever enough to get everything upside down and backward.

There was a long silence between them. And much soul-searching.

She touched his hand. "Charlie?"

"Yeah?"

"You'll get over being upset with me . . . won't you?"

Knowing that he would—but not caring to admit it—he grunted.

Knowing her man, Vanessa understood this to be "yes." And felt much better. She looked up at him with enormous, come-hither eyes. *It gets terribly lonesome out here when the snows come. The winter nights are awfully long. And cold.* "Maybe you could . . . drop by for a visit. From time to time."

He was silent as a stone.

She squeezed his arm. "Charlie . . . ?"

"I'll think about it."

He thought about it. It was about time he found a woman to settle down with. Vanessa was easy on the eyes. Smart. Resourceful. He'd always liked her. Now that she'd inherited a fine ranch, he liked her a little more. A man could run a hundred head of Hereford stock here. And raise some fine quarterhorses. Not that it was all about the ranch. This young woman needed someone to keep an eye on her. See that she stayed out of trouble.

But there was a but.

Deep down, he'd known for weeks that something was wrong. For weeks, there had been small, sinister indications that he'd chosen to ignore. But during the course of this morning he'd come eyeball-to-eyeball with the dark side of Vanessa's nature.

The Sugar Bowl Restaurant, Granite Creek

Charlie Moon—who was to be best man at the wedding—had driven his pickup to Granite Creek to confer with the hopeful groom. Anne was doing all the really important planning, so there was little for them to do but talk about this and that. Like how Moon would keep the ring in his pocket until just the right moment. And how peculiar it would be for Parris to be married again. Jokes about how Anne would make him walk the line. Parris silently wondered whether there was a rental tux in Colorado big enough for the Ute. And . . . whether it would be needed . . . whether this marriage is to be.

For the last three nights, he's awakened in a cold, clammy sweat. After dreaming the same bizarre dream:

The church is filled to overflowing with strangers. There are heaps and mounds of flowers everywhere—all white lilies. He stands before the altar, practicing his lines. I will . . . Forever. I do. I do. Charlie Moon is at his side, with the gold wedding band in his pocket. And a heavy revolver strapped to his side. The Ute is outfitted in an absurd lime-green tux . . . and he wears something on his arm.

"Charlie," he whispers, "you shouldn't pack a gun in church."

"It is necessary," the Ute policeman replies in an ominous monotone.

"But why the black armband?"

Moon crosses himself. "It is customary."

The priest looks up from his prayer book, toward the rear of the chruch. The organist immediately begins to grind out "Here Comes the Bride." All dressed in . . .

Parris turns. Anne is coming up the aisle, on the arm of a solemn-faced, cadaverous man. She is all dressed in . . . black.

Parris tells himself that his troubled sleep is a symptom of pre-wedding jitters. Yes. Only that and nothing more . . .

It was mid-afternoon, and quiet in the Sugar Bowl Restaurant. Aside from the two lawmen, there was only an elderly waitress who'd already taken their orders. She was out of earshot, reading a *Glamour* magazine article entitled "Ten Ways to Drive Men Mad." Sad to say, she would have to settle for being a mild annoyance.

"Well," Moon said, "I guess I ought to bring you up to date on the Horace Flye business." His pardner was up to his armpits in this mess already, and deserved to know the truth.

Scott Parris listened without comment as the Ute summarized the essential facts. How Vanessa McFain had confronted Flye during the late-night break-in of her home, how he wouldn't give up the flint blade he'd pinched off the mantelpiece. Moon described how she'd cracked the Arkansas man's skull with the poker, buried his body in the pond dam, then drove his truck over to Capote Lake. And, when Moon had hinted that body-sniffing dogs might be brought to sniff around the McFain ranch, she'd slipped out that night and proceeded to dig up Flye's body for reburial in a less conspicuous location. Only Vanessa was interrupted by her father, who'd come outside looking for her. Poor old Nathan, he must've thought she was sleepwalking again. Vanessa had hightailed it back to the house. What happened to the old man after that was a little fuzzy. But something must've spooked Nathan . . . maybe he saw Flye's hand sticking out of the dirt. Whatever the cause, he'd taken off in a dead run. And ended up in the excavation tent. Too bad the old man had fallen on the mammoth's tusk, but accidents do happen.

Parris thought about it. "She can't risk leaving Flye's body buried on her property. She's bound to move the corpse someplace where it won't be found."

"I'm sure she already has," Moon said. And that was best for everyone involved. Like him and his pardner. If Flye's body turned up, you couldn't tell what might happen. If push came to shove, folks might start talking. Delia Silver, who already felt terribly guilty about Flye's disappearance, might reveal the secret about how he planted a fake artifact in the mammoth excavation. If the rich Arab heard about this, he'd want his money back. Probably send someone to collect it from the antiquarian. And Ralph Briggs might decide to tell his tale. About how a couple of sworn officers of the law had helped him sell a fake artifact for a tub of money. And spent ninety percent of the untaxed income on Flye's orphan. It could get awfully complicated. Yes, it was best for everyone that Vanessa hauled Flye's remains away. Far away.

"Miss McFain," Parris said, "is a rather enterprising young woman." His eyes twinkled. "I kind of thought you and her might . . . well . . ."

"I kinda like Vanessa," the Ute admitted glumly, "but after what I've learned about her, I don't think it'd work out."

"See what you mean," Parris said soberly. "Lying and killing aren't the best traits in a woman."

"Oh, that's not the half of it."

"There's more you haven't told me?"

"Well, you know how women can be . . . they're never quite satisfied with a fellow the way he is. Always want to *change* him."

Scott Parris wondered what Anne might have in mind for him. "Change isn't necessarily a bad thing." Not for the other guy.

"Easy for you to say," Moon muttered darkly. "You don't know what Vanessa's got in mind."

"Something drastic?"

"She wants to . . . sort of convert me into something I'm not cut out for."

Parris chuckled. "What exactly does Sweet Thing have planned for you?" The other fellow's troubles were always amusing.

The Ute looked somewhat green around the gills. "It's hard to come right out and say it."

"Give me a hint."

"Rhymes with librarian."

"Hmmm. Let me see. I got it . . . she's a Libertarian."

The Ute shook his head.

"Unitarian?"

"Nope."

"Rastafarian?"

"What's that?"

"I'm not sure. Something to do with funny hair and steel drums. Anyway, I give up."

Moon sighed. He rolled all five syllables of the foreign word over his tongue; it left a bad taste in his mouth. So he spat it out. "Vegetarian."

"Great day," Parris said with a straight face, "the woman is heartless."

Moon nodded his earnest agreement, and shuddered as he imagined Life With Vanessa. Oatmeal for breakfast. Raw carrots for lunch. He could not imagine what sort of horror would be served up for supper. But she was a clever woman; probably knew thirteen ways to disguise tofu so it looked like actual food. At best, a man would be driven to a lot of in-between-meals feeding on the sly.

Parris realized that his buddy was taking this hard. A diplomatic approach was called for. "Maybe you could work out a compromise."

The Ute looked more than a little suspicious, and then some. "What kinda compromise?"

"Oh, I dunno. But if you could manage to chomp a few stalks of celery once in a while, I bet she'd fry you a chicken now and again."

"You really think so?"

"Sure. But you'd have to be willing to be . . . well . . . a little more flexible in the way you look at food."

Moon thought about it. That wasn't an altogether bad notion. If a man started gradually enough, he could eventually do really detestable things he'd never thought himself capable of. And Vanessa was a pretty special woman. Who owned a nice little ranch. Not that the ranch had all that much to do with it. Well, maybe forty-nine percent. Or fifty-one.

The waitress—who had arrived with a heavy tray—put a turkey sandwich and iced tea in front of Parris, then winked a thickly mascaraed eyelash at Moon. "Hiya, cowboy." She unburdened herself of the massive load of calories. "If I remember right, you get the chicken-fried steak, double serving. With mashed potatoes and brown gravy and biscuits."

"Right," Moon said. "But I'd like to order a side dish."

She put pencil to pad. "And what'd that be?"

Moon took a deep breath. "A . . . vegetable."

Scott Parris was astonished; the man must be in love.

The waitress blinked at the Ute. "So whadda you want, big fella? I got your black-eyed peas. I got your boiled baby carrots. I got your creamed corn." She deduced from his wistful expression that her customer was not greatly enthused by these offerings. "How about some nice pickled beets?"

The Ute thanked her, and politely declined. "I was thinking of something more . . . healthy."

Frustration animated her wrinkled face. "Tell you what—I could open you a can of spinach."

Moon grimaced. "Spinach?" She must be joking.

"Sure," the old crone cackled, "same kind that makes What's-his-name . . . Sockeye strong enough to whip ol' . . . uhhh . . . you know . . . Pluto."

"I don't hold with whipping dogs," Moon said.

"I think she means Popeye and Bluto," Parris offered.

The waitress shot the chief of police a withering look.

"Or maybe not," Parris added hastily. "Sockeye and Pluto, now there was a bad pair to draw to."

Moon was perplexed about what to order. Black-eyed peas were fine fodder for Texans. Beets were . . . well, beets. Carrots were for cottontails. Creamed corn wasn't all that bad if a man had some pork chops to go with it. He'd never actually tried to get spinach past his lips, mainly because it had the unappetizing appearance of something regurgitated by a pitifully sick cow. But he was determined to consume a serious vegetable. Something *good* for him. But what? As sweet rains come when they are most needed, inspiration visited the Ute policeman. He recalled a snippet of tribal lore . . . Chief Ouray had fed his sleek horses bushels of a particularly pungent bulb to keep them in good condition. It was "powerful medicine for their hearts," the wise Ute leader had told his doubtful wife, who was annoyed with such extravagance. In a flash of inspiration, Charlie Moon put his finger on a grease-stained menu. "This'll do nicely."

The waitress' voice cracked. "Onion rings?"

"Yes ma'am." Chief Ouray had fed his horses *raw* onions, but that was a trifling technicality.

"Honey, them things is deep-fried in pure lard . . ."

"Then make it a double order." *If a man sets out to eat more healthy, he might as well go whole-hog.*

TURN THE PAGE FOR A LOOK AT JAMES D. DOSS'S NEXT EXCITING CHARLIE MOON MYSTERY . . .

GRANDMOTHER SPIDER

When Sarah Frank, the nine-year-old orphan who is living with Ute Shaman Daisy Perika, kills a small spider on the old woman's kitchen floor and neglects to perform an ancient Ute ritual for it, Daisy cautions her that Grandmother Spider herself may come forth from her cabin under Navajo Lake. And when two men mysteriously disappear from the shores of the lake that same evening, caused by something policemen called to the scene describe as "big as a house, with lots of long legs," Charlie Moon must take Daisy's warning seriously. Mystery, mysticism, and dark humor join forces in a case that leads Charlie Moon and Police Chief Scott Parris into a tangled web of curses, lies . . . and murder.

INSIDE THE MINING City Cafe, the lunch crowd had thinned. A scattering of long-haul truckers sat around munching extremely greasy cheeseburgers, which they washed down with scalding coffee. The lawmen retreated to a booth in a shadowed corner, where they spoke in low, unhurried tones. The main topic was Scott Parris' engagement. The date was not yet set, but Charlie Moon was to be best man. There were details to discuss. Jokes about whether there was a tux west of the Mississippi big enough to outfit the Ute. There were also serious questions. Why hadn't Anne set a date for the wedding? How would Scott deal with her being out of town chasing stories half the time? What'd he do if the pretty journalist felt compelled to accept a job somewhere far away from Granite Creek?

When Scott's mood turned mildly blue, Moon sensed that it was time to plow some new ground. "So what's the police business that brings you down here?"

Parris rotated the heavy coffee mug in his hands. "Nothing

important. A friend of the mayors—some big-shot lawyer from Denver—he's got himself a cabin up on First Finger Ridge. Came down here last week to open it up for the summer. His wife has called several times, but he don't answer."

It was common, especially after heavy snows, for trees to fall on the lines. The phone had probably been dead for months. Electric power was probably out, too. "Must be a line down," the Ute said.

"Not according to U.S. West," Parris said. "Phone line checks out okay. Maybe he never got to the cabin."

"Or maybe he don't want to talk to his wife." Moon grinned. "I've heard that married life can get tedious."

"Tedious is a helluva lot better than lonesome, Charlie."

His tone was so earnest that the Ute did not respond. And then something bubbled up from the depths of Moon's subconscious. "When did this lawyer get to his cabin?"

Parris consulted a neatly kept notebook. "April first, assuming he got there at all. He was supposed to call his wife that night. He didn't. She started calling the next morning. No answer."

A cold something touched the back of Moon's neck. First day of April. That was when the men had disappeared from the shore of Navajo Lake. The same night, just minutes later, Daisy had taken a shot at something . . . and Sarah Frank had seen a "big spider." And now this lawyer wasn't answering his phone. There probably wasn't any connection. "Pardner . . . maybe I should go up to that cabin with you."

Parris laid his greenbacks on the table. "You think I'm gonna need some help?"

The rocky lane followed a wriggling line of utility poles up First Finger Ridge. There were no fallen trees to interrupt the flow of electricity or conversations.

There had been an uncommonly early thaw; several small streams were splashing their way down the slope. The sun was pleasantly warm, the temperature balmy. At higher altitudes there would still be thick white patches hiding under the blue spruce, but the winter's snow on this sunlit slope was completely melted. The insects knew this and were pleased; energetic deerflies buzzed through the rolled-down windows and hummed about the men's faces.

Parris pulled to a stop in a level clearing. The cabin was nestled among a picturesque grove of spruce and pine. In front of the structure, several naked aspen were showing tender buds.

The log structure looked quite normal in every respect save one.

The front door was open; a light breeze moved it back and forth on well-oiled hinges.

Moon remarked that on such a warm day a man might well leave his door open to air out a place that had been shut up for the long winter.

Scott Parris added hopefully that telephones fail for all sorts of reasons.

But experienced lawmen develop a keen sense about such things. The policemen were filled with a feeling of unease—even dread. This had the empty, abandoned look of a dead man's house.

They climbed three pine steps to a sturdy redwood deck.

"Hello," Parris shouted.

He was answered by a heavy, almost palpable silence.

Moon held the door steady and banged his knuckles on the varnished pine.

Still no answer.

Parris called out again. "Mr. Armitage?" A pause. "Anybody home?"

The place was quiet as a tomb.

The lawmen entered the cabin, still announcing themselves. There were cold ashes in the fireplace but no sign of an occupant. Muddy footprints led through the front parlor, down a short hallway toward the kitchen.

Parris paused to study an array of papers on a desk by the front window. "Looks like he was doing some legal work."

Moon followed the footprints into the kitchen, which was uncommonly neat and tidy. The back door was not latched. The breeze that had opened it was about to close it. The same breath of air brought a familiar, unpleasant odor. The Ute policeman pushed the door wide open and looked outside. The muscles in his jaw tensed. "Scott."

"What've you got?"

"Better come and see."

Parris appeared behind the Ute. "You find him?"

Moon, standing in the open doorway, nodded.

Charlie Moon was blessed and burdened with a formal education. He could trace the flow of electricity through a simple circuit, appreciate the lilting song of a Shakespearean sonnet, discuss the rise and fall of the Roman Empire. If hard pressed he was able (should an urgent need arise in the course of his law enforcement duties) to find the solutions to a quadratic equation and plot the results in the complex-number plane. The concept that negative numbers had imaginary square roots did not lock the gears of his mind into neutral. But for all this Moon was Ute to his very marrow. It would not have occurred to him to touch a dead man's body unless there was a very compelling reason to do so. There was no such necessity.

Scott Parris was also keeping a respectful distance between himself and the corpse. It was the medical examiner's job to poke around the lawyer's mortal remains. Doc Simpson would probe and sample and sniff around like a bloodhound. Photographs would be made from a dozen angles. The Granite Creek chief of police was already planning his department's work. A thorough search would be made of house and grounds for any physical evidence that might remain. Neighbors—such as there might be—would be questioned.

"I've never seen anything quite like this," Moon said.

Parris tried to respond; the words hung in his throat.

The corpse's yellowed face was a reflection of horror. Shrunken eyes stared blindly from gray sockets. White teeth and bluish gums were bared of lip. The mouth yawned open in an endless scream. And this was not the worst part.

The head was separated from the body.

The torso was unremarkable except for one feature. On each side of the breastbone a pair of gaping wounds penetrated deep into the chest cavity.

Scott Parris broke the silence. "God almighty."

Despite the stench, Moon was compelled to take a deep breath. "Looks like somebody took an axe to his neck." Within a foot of the man's pale, shriveled hand there was a small camera. "Maybe he took a picture of whoever did it."

"We should be so lucky." Parris kneeled by the corpse. He pressed a handkerchief over his nose and mouth and frowned at the chest. "These are way too big to be bullet wounds," he said in a muffled voice. "And there's hardly any blood on his shirt."

Moon's thoughts were running in dark channels. Evidently, the lawyer had seen something outside, something so interesting that he wanted a picture. If he was working at the desk when he saw it, he would've grabbed his camera and headed out the front door. So whatever he'd noticed had been somewhere to the south of the cabin. *From whence cometh the unknown thing that snatches men off the earth.* And then he headed back through the cabin, making muddy tracks all the way to the back door. So whatever he wanted to photograph had been heading more or less to the north . . . passing by the cabin. After he'd gotten outside the back door, he'd dropped the camera. And besides losing his head, the victim had suffered two mortal wounds in his chest. Overkill. The Ute stared up the steeply-pitched roof of corrugated steel at a perfectly blue sky. Whoever . . . or *whatever* . . . it was didn't even bother to take the camera. Why? Didn't notice it? Didn't care about leaving evidence behind? Moon wondered whether there would be any images on the negatives. And if there were, whether he'd want to see them. "What'll you do with the camera?"

Parris considered his options. The F.B.I. Forensic Laboratory came immediately to mind. And the state police had a first-class photoanalysis team. But it would be nice to keep this investigation in the family. "I've got a friend at the university who's served as an expert witness in a half dozen crimes where photographic evidence was submitted. Guess I'll ask him to have a look at the film."

Moon frowned at the flies buzzing around the corpse. "We better throw a sheet over the body."

Parris stared at the gruesome scene. "You know, I keep thinking something . . . really crazy."

Moon nodded. Whatever had happened here was crazy.

"These big holes in his chest," Parris pointed, "they're about the same size. It's just that . . . it looks like a damn snakebite." He was immediately embarrassed at having blurted out such an asinine remark. *Even in the tropics, reptiles just didn't grow big enough to . . . and monstrously large snakes don't bite big holes in your chest. They crush you to death.*

The Ute policeman was more circumspect and economical with his words. Besides, a sensible man wouldn't care to mention the absurdly superstitious thought that had been tickling at the dark side of his mind. *Spider bite.*

Three hours later, the remote cabin site was crawling with state police and officers from Granite Creek P.D. The elderly medical examiner had arrived with his two young assistants. Dr. Simpson was, as was his custom, grumbling: about having to work in this black mud, how those damn deerflies were "biting my ass off," and "why couldn't these slow-witted donut eaters manage to find bodies before decay had set in?" He, of course, was having the time of his life. Within an hour, Simpson had completed a preliminary examination of the corpse and declared that sufficient photographs had been made. The M.E. barked instructions to his assistants, who eased the greater bulk of the attorney's remains into a black plastic body bag and pulled the zipper. The head, lifted indelicately by the ears, was packaged separately in a scaled container that resembled a hatbox.

The lawyer's camera was tagged and placed in an evidence bag. On the morrow, Scott Parris would deliver it to Rocky Mountain Polytechnic and ask Professor Ezra Budd to examine the instrument and develop the film.

Moon, disinclined to witness the gory proceedings, stood well away from the commotion. He seemed so detatched that a casual observer might have assumed the policeman was daydreaming. But the Ute was staring intently at a profile on the far ridge: a single spruce standing among a great company of its fellows. Near the crest of this particular tree was a slight interruption of natural symmetry. This distortion alone was not sufficient to attract his attention. There were many ordinary causes for a disruption of branches. It was what Moon saw above the tree that most concerned him. A half dozen large birds circling patiently. They were neither hawks nor eagles.

He thought about it. Climbing a thick spruce would be quite a troublesome task. And this was Scott Parris' jurisdiction, his investigation. Moon eased his way over to his friend's side. "Scott?"

Parris turned. "Yeah, Charlie?"

"I think you'd best call in a Medivac 'copter."

The *matukach* squinted, following the Ute's gaze to the far congregation of spruce. "You spotted something?"

"Maybe." *Or somebody.* The buzzards circled high over Second Finger Ridge, so it might not be too late.

Corporal Rodriguez spoke through the microphone built into his orange Kevlar helmet. "Sarge, it's a body. You copy me?"

The helicopter pilot had seen more than his share of corpses; his response was a professional monotone. "Roger that, Corporal. We'll descend to seven meters over the target. Prepare the sling."

The ungainly craft hovered low, flaying the spruce branches with a noisy whirlwind. Rodriguez buckled himself into an array of heavy canvas straps. On signal from the pilot, he lowered himself toward the body, alternately cursing in English and praying in Spanish as he swung to and fro, a living weight on a perilous pendulum.

The pilot was pleased to hear the VHF radio report over the roar of the engine. "Sarge, it looks like . . . he's alive!"